acts of mutiny

Derek Beaven lives in Maidenhead, Berkshire. His first novel, *Newton's Niece* (1994), was shortlisted for the Writers' Guild Best Novel Prize and won a Commonwealth Prize. *Acts of Mutiny* is his second novel.

Praise for *Acts of Mutiny*:

'The symphony of voices is beautifully harmonic, and although there's a knowing, gently satirical edge to the portrayals, they ring very true.' Tobias Jones, *Observer*

'Derek Beaven's second novel seems likely to confirm his status as a first-rate novelist . . . An extraordinary novel.' David Nokes, *Sunday Times*

'His is a prodigal talent.' Lorna Sage, *London Review of Books*

Also by Derek Beaven
Newton's Niece

acts of mutiny

DEREK BEAVEN

FOURTH ESTATE • *London*

For David

Acts of Mutiny is a work of fiction. Any resemblance of its characters to real people, living or dead, is coincidental. The vessels upon which the action takes place are similarly imaginary.

This paperback edition published in 1999

First published in Great Britain in 1998 by
Fourth Estate Limited
6 Salem Road, London W2 4BU

A catalogue record for this book is available from the British Library.

ISBN 1–85702–662–4

Typeset in Plantin by Avon Dataset Ltd, Bidford on Avon B50 4JH
Printed and bound in Great Britain by
Clays Ltd, St Ives plc, Bungay, Suffolk

Contents

PART ONE

Motion

1

I HAVE A knot in my tongue. Left over right, tuck under. Right over left, tuck under. The rabbit comes up through the hole. Or does the dog go round the tree for his bone? My child-knots forgot their creatures. I produced only poor knobs of string, for all my father's detailed instruction. His prim exemplars shone from my bedroom wall, white cord on a mahogany panel: bowline, reef, clove hitch, carrick bend, sheepshank, figure of eight, Turk's head, eye splice . . .

This morning we buried him over at Sidcup. There was a reception at his sister's, a gathering of family, and of family ghosts. I choked on sandwiches, lacked conversation. Then I drove alone from Bostall Heath down towards the river edge, past Lesnes Abbey Woods, past Bostall Lane Infants – which still stands. To my roots, downstream of the City, downriver of the new Thames Barrier. Water folk, Navy folk, my family have been here for generations. I was the one who broke away. Since quitting the Navy I have worked at the airport, on the other side of the capital, in Immigration.

The street is unchanged. These are turn-of-the-century terraces, smoke grey, built by the Royal Arsenal Co-op. Nothing can shift or clean them. On our side the row heaves into a small rise, about twelve feet proud of the pavement – as if on the lift of a frozen wave. The house itself looks as it used to, the gate jammed not quite open, always to be dodged around. There is the same crumbling pebble-wound at eye level in the flight of sixteen concrete steps up to our front door. My father called them 'the ladders'.

I see myself with my albatross eye. Just this afternoon. I am

3

poised to go in, but turn towards the weather, snow clouds heaping up over the Isle of Dogs. Because I have not been a dutiful son; for years I never visited, and all the differences are reproaches. To the right is the vast Thamesmead estate, where once the road petered out. There was a green foot-bridge over the railway line. I would watch my father bicycling away to his plot, a vegetable sack slung across his brawny shoulder, growing smaller against the duns and sedges. In the distance, the Plumstead marshes rotted off level towards Barking Reach.

Over the opposite roofs, Canary Wharf tower: a designer biro stabbed up through the earth's crust, scribbling on those sagging grey-bellies. The first snowflakes are already coming dark on the flurry.

From here we would have smelt London's soot fallout, or, according to the swirl of the wind, the West India Docks, the arsenal's chemicals, the mud at Galleons Point. Here in the dark of each new moon my father had us turn over our silver money for luck. Now it is too late. Delaying at the door, I find excuses. If I drove straight back across the City I could avoid the blizzard – even pick up the tail end of my shift at the airport. Or I could wait for Carla at her flat and try to talk things through. After all we had only just begun, she and I.

But I ought really to go in.

Entering the hallway is like being swallowed. As if through the second door along Pinocchio might actually find his old man, the naval artificer, still working by his lamp at some Marconi chassis, waiting, with the smoke wisping up from the solder. I do half expect that special smell, of burning dust and Fluxite, mingled with the leftover flavour of kippers. But it is empty, of course, and icy cold.

The house has been modernised and remodernised. The back room no longer swims in its browns and greens. He is not, of course, at the table, his repair gutted on the spread newspaper, his sweet-tin of resistors and condensers tipped out all of a wire jumble.

We once squeezed in. We were pressed by furniture: lac-quered, oak-stained, brown-draped. Even when I was a child it was out of date, like a workman's Edwardiana, pickled. The two bucket chairs in leather, shiny with use; the heavy oak table and five mock-Chippendale chairs; the gloomy bureau; the rust-

4

coloured dresser; the wireless table in the corner; the china cupboard – there was scarcely room for the fireplace. There was scarcely room even for the tea kettle on its hinged iron platform beside the grate. My grandfather the gunner, who lived with us, would swing it round into the flames, and then force his huge khaki-shirted frame slowly along the last side of the table and into his carver, beating upwind, braces strung tight and heaving at his waistband like the main-sheets of a square-rig.

The place is quite empty, and brims with its own incommunicable loss.

On the tight margin of floor in front of the hearth I can imagine my small self – stretched out by the french windows' gloam. I lie reading my *London's River at Work and at War*, lost in its illustrations, a romance of barges. The sails are tan, the river mud-green, the lines of the vessels wood on wood. And there are tramp steamers, painted iron with a fuss of tugs: grimed hulls, the ochres and rusts of their superstructure. Dark outpourings of smoke blot cranes and whole expanses of page. That was the river I knew; an oilscape of docks. Even the sun – I lived in sepia, my growing up here was an unbroken stream, brown as varnish, leading inevitably to the sea.

I swear the boy looks up. Is it me he is afraid of?

My scalp tingles. I remember another time back there on the doorstep with Erica my mother. We too are hesitating to go in, having hauled our suitcases to the top of 'the ladders'. She grips my arm. We are coming home. I remember it well. Clear, in fact, as daylight. It is from my first voyage in a voyaging life. But – this is the astonishing thing – in forty years I swear that particular scene and that childhood sea-passage have never once entered my head. Of course, it is coming to me now, there was a whole year I did not live here at all. Had gone to the ends of the earth with ... Mr Chaunteyman was his unusual name. And I am caught up suddenly in a romance of names: Penny Kendrick, Robert Kettle; and the Indian Ocean. Clear as you like.

2

It was January 1959. They met on the journey out. Before Port Said they pretended there was nothing between them. After Aden it was undeniable. Yet 'nothing' of it had been spoken. Penny was joining her husband in Adelaide. Robert was going up-country.

'I'm starting with a team at the observatory, the tracking station,' he had said. Every sentence in each other's hearing took on an extra meaning, like a jewelled, coded gift.

Now they and the Madeleys stood together near the aft end of the boat deck, past the run of white lifeboats. The sun dropped without ceremony into the Indian Ocean just to the left of the ship's wake, scorching it for a moment or two with orange flares. On cue, there rose a warm, slightly scented breeze from the sea.

'I suppose we really ought to be getting ready for dinner, if you'll excuse us, Penny, Mr Kettle,' Mrs Madeley said. 'Come along, Douglas, I think.' She picked up two of the empty glasses with their fruited cocktail sticks, as if to include the pair of them in her command.

'Calm as you like.' Douglas addressed the sea but was following his wife with cautious, elderly steps.

Penny seemed to comply. 'Yes. I must decide what to wear. So uncomplicated for the men, isn't it. They can just rush down at the last minute and hurl themselves into a dress suit.'

Robert felt desperate with her; then hated himself for it. They strolled back as a foursome, past the housing for the smoke-stack, towards the stairs in the white steel wall of the bridge. To their right the shapes of five lifeboats were slow white moments running out.

Penny stopped to rummage in her bag. He waited beside her.

'We'll see you shortly, then? Perhaps a drink before?' Mrs Madeley raised her voice from the companion-way door, which she held open. Strains of some light string trio crept up from below. Douglas, his long tropical shorts unflattering above brown knees and scout socks, had reached it now and was edging inside.

'Probably see you in a minute,' Robert called. He dreaded

the next ritual Pimm's. 'Isn't there a film tonight, Douglas?' Penny's words 'so uncomplicated for the men' mocked him. His feelings were jangled.

Yet Penny had managed to contrive them a moment; effortlessly, daringly – unless she *was* only checking her bag for her compact, or whatever, and actually did intend to follow the Madeleys away.

'Not our sort of show, Mr Kettle,' Douglas answered. 'We like musical comedies. Can take any amount of them, can't we, dear?' They disappeared downwards. Penny straightened, and allowed her straw bag to hang from her shoulder again.

So at last Robert was alone with her; really alone for only the third time on the voyage.

'In Adelaide?' She continued the conversation several days old. He read her tone, as if the intervening time with its meals and games and the ship's daily run had collapsed. 'Did you mean an observatory in Adelaide? There would be one?' she asked.

'Oh no.' His nerve wavered. They had missed each other. She had not known where he would be going. She had not allowed for it. 'Well, yes, there is one in Adelaide. But I meant up in the salt lakes. Beyond the hills . . . North. The desert. The Flinders Range.' Some anxiety made him forbear to trot out the government name of the town-cum-missile-base, although there was no real reason why he should not. There was no secret. Nothing to feel ashamed of. For a moment his sunburn from the Red Sea began to itch again, and to ache.

They waited for a moment in the deck tennis markings. Then she moved under the boats to lean on the rail; and he stood next to her.

'When I mentioned the tracking station, I thought you'd know.'

'I don't. Tracking what? And what lakes would they be? I don't know anything . . . about the lie of the land.' She shifted her hands on the rail, through which as always the churn and drive of the engines could be felt, a constant background.

'I thought *he* might have told you. Your husband. You said he'd gone out to Adelaide "in the weapons interest".'

'To the research establishment at Salisbury, yes. But he doesn't write to *me* about that sort of thing – they're not quite supposed to, are they? Anyway, it isn't really an interest we've managed to have in common.'

Robert laughed and caught her smile, the lipstick now star-glazed. How unfamiliar it was still, that here, close to the Equator, day just switched off, and then it was dark; without lingering or pause for reflection. What *did* he write to her, then, was what he wanted to ask. But dared not.

He looked up at the swinging, coruscating lightfield itself, and tried to make himself consider it professionally. But it had such a personal quality – as if the huge stars were curving down to meet them and the dusted blackness was only something rushing the other way.

Besides, more intense even than the visual drama above was the knowledge that her hand on the rail was a mere inch from his own. But he would not look at that. Achernar, the southern tip of Eridanus, River of Heaven. Follow the jab down: Reticulum, the Net, just rising. If they could stay out here all night, they would see the Southern Cross. He had waited to see it last night. It reminded him that a difficult and salty continent lay somewhere down there, under the dark line of the horizon. Keeping still, they could hear the subdued crash of the bow wave, and feel the ship's eastward movement. It was dodging sideways in order to call at Colombo, and then Singapore. It gave them some time.

Her voice: 'I didn't have the courage to ask you before, exactly what on earth we're going to do when we get there. Because it makes a difference to what we do now, doesn't it.' She stated it flatly, not as a question.

So they were a fact. She had just given it form and lodged it in between sunset and dressing for dinner. He was amazed, full of joy; that people could do that, and it was them. And he was also afraid. Shouts and laughter reached them from just below. Late for their high tea, a party of children, myself the last amongst them, could be heard along the promenade deck. They funnelled inside somewhere, chattering. Robert felt for her hand, and held it, touching his fingertips cautiously round to her palm.

She returned the pressure. 'You can change your mind. If you're not sure.'

'I never imagined. I'm sure, but I never imagined.' He noticed how snatches of illumination leaked out from the decks below or crept between cracks in the fittings.

'Liar, darling.' She smiled again.

Ventilator cowlings, pipes, davits, and a spice wind from behind them: their astonishment continued, as the ship slipped on into the tropic dark. He felt they were bathed in a wordless beauty that did not belong in the world. Yet it was palpable; it was all around them.

For the first time in his life he felt at home. 'You are braver than I am.'

From that moment the whole ship also acknowledged them as a fact. And although people said nothing quite directly – although they continued furious and put out – they no longer attempted, in the shape of Mrs Madeley, or Mary Garnery, or Paul Finch-Clark, or a general conspiracy that operated out of the *Armorica*'s paintwork, the furniture, or the tannoy, to keep them apart.

3

Flashes of memory are glittering, dangerous things. Lifted from the Falklands War, I was too ashamed to show my face. For some weeks I believed myself one of those poor souls who cracked on the way south and had to be flown home before hostilities even began. No shame in that – it happens. But to me it felt as though I had let everyone down, the family member at last who shirked when England expected.

It was only gradually my nightmares started to cohere. Subtly my coward's badge was streaked through with fire. I had been there after all, trapped in the inferno of my burning destroyer; yet still unshakeably convinced I had ducked my duty.

Even as the true events bore themselves in, I could not relate to them. I watched news footage of my stricken vessel and remained disconnected. A carapace had shaped itself so closely around the horror that as it split open I was both naïve and knowing at once. But that was a military disaster, and the eerie phenomena of battle stress are now well documented.

Memories have their species, though. Mine of Penny

Kendrick and Robert Kettle is like a swarm of finches, if such could accompany so large a ship so far from land, roosting suddenly on the wires above the boat deck in order to catch their words, or sense their thoughts. Their love is birdlike, full of vibration and scribbled chattering. Or like the schools of flying fish that would skim and dart on the bow wave. Or like a current and its accompanying breath that presses imperceptibly now this way, now that upon the vessel's direction, enveloping them both. This is a memory of what must have been. It is the most beautiful of all the memories, one of ornament, how it was between them.

And I would spend my time telling you of them only, bringing them to their consummation, had not voices of an altogether different nature begun to attend the passage. Consider the steely-eyed albatross, riding empty air above the mainmast head, looking down. This *was* – I saw it happen.

And there is the memory that comes back like a spit in the face, like a gob of poison. It was Hugh Kendrick's visit long after we had arrived in Adelaide, with his terrible story of the lovers in the desert, and what I had done. That strikes at me with its own coil, clear, and of a piece – with detail like scales. How I felt like a salamander in the fire that night after the scare at the township dump. That memory refuses to leave me, yet I cannot make it fit.

You are cast adrift with me now, and must trust in my navigation.

Creatures of air see nothing beneath the surface. The ocean has layers. Deep down there are lanterns, great-swallowers, dragonfish, star-eaters who rise up near the surface only for the night sky, and then sink back nearly a mile at dawn. Beneath them in turn it is perpetually sunless. There the blanched light-emitters blitz and glow. Angler fish, gulper eels, black bristle-mouths, oarfish. No living mariner knows of these depths; though thirty thousand corpses reach them a year, and scarcely a news column of concern.

Consider the scars across the forehead of an old sperm whale. These tell of the giant squid. Consider the tentacles. Consider the hideous beak. This is a species that eludes us, lying in wait, unfathomably huge, maybe. It is rumoured to rise up once in a century to take a ship or two. It throws us into confusion.

But memory can play us false. No record of the *Armorica* exists. Not with the shipping company itself, nor with Lloyd's, nor with the Maritime Museum at Greenwich; not even at the Admiralty. I have rung everywhere and anywhere that passenger liners might be registered or listed. It is the same polite response: that I must be mistaken. We have nothing here on file in that name, sir.

I have pulled rank, requested double-checks, paid for searches. I have been told to 'hold the line' and have patiently held. I have insisted: 'But I was there. I once sailed in her.' To no avail. And my family also deny knowledge. My aunt claims she is too upset to think about such things. Anyway, she has no recollection of all that. Why had I never bothered asking when my father was alive? It is almost as though I had killed him myself. Erica, my mother . . . is too ill. Moon-faced, full of drugs, she attended the hospital rather than the funeral. They may give her electro-shock. Under general anaesthetic, of course: what only the body undergoes, the nurse said, the mind need never know.

Memory is a dangerous subject. Let me warn you once more. Quite apart from this bereavement, I have been under pressure. There was a woman the other day – she was brought to an interview room. I found her badly disfigured, burnt, presumably. The eyes brown, the silver hair still showing traces of a youthful black, the skin a pale tan – what original was left of it. She was scarred massively at one time or another, but who knows by what. Perhaps an unfortunate household accident. And she might have been anything, Kashmiri, Kurdish, Algerian, Vietnamese. She was screaming in a quiet, tired way that was horrible. She could have been white, even. I lost my temper – I suffer from dark moods. I almost lost my job. The department has to be careful; we pride ourselves. She was referred and will be deported, of course.

She claimed . . . but how can you determine a torture victim? The doctor examined her. What are its precise badges? Terror? Depression? Incoherence, yes. Apathy, very often. She could give no precise account of what she had experienced. She was crazy, certainly; and articulately incoherent in her own version of English. There was an accent, but not a definitive one. She had seen God up there on the way. Courtesy of Qantas. She was the Holy Ghost and I was the recording angel.

Then she demanded asylum, claiming Commonwealth citizenship – for what that is worth – but could give no country of origin. I have seen a lot of claimants, fished out of passport queues, flushed out of cargo holds. I have seen forged documents exposed, and various scars upon the body, some genuine. The airport becomes its own island beach, where the world's wretched are washed up. She could, as I say, have been anything. She called me 'frozen-faced *douanier*', and she is right, it is my official persona – policeman of boundaries. Perhaps it was Carla's presence that made this particular encounter stay in my mind, just after the night of our intimacy. A woman's body, that *Terra Australis Incognita*. Carla is a member of my department. We sometimes work together.

Could I have mistaken the name? *Armorica*? It is some slip, perhaps, where an idea loops back on itself and we find ourselves positive about an erroneous fragment. That is a commonplace of the witness-box, after all. No two people ever see quite the same incident. Details get confused. Could I have crossed one ship's name with another? A burnt woman . . .

While I should have been writing reports, I have been researching passenger lists: for the relevant years from the relevant companies. No Ralph and Erica Lightfoot appear. No David Lafayette Chaunteyman. There are two Kendricks and one Kettle, but they are not Penny or Robert.

4

If you asked me to describe the night of my return to Abbey Wood with Erica, I could not. There may have been scenes, recriminations, blows. What I do know is that afterwards the name *Armorica* never crossed our lips. Not once. The voyage's memorabilia were trashed from our luggage: the menus with their little seabed illustrations, the brochures of ports, the bus tickets, waiter's bills and so on. Our Australian effects, my school notebooks – even Erica's snaps were handed over to be destroyed. When we returned and my grandfather was 'gone', the house was brought ruthlessly up to date. A proper television went in, fitted carpet, a three-piece suite, all hire purchase. It was fumigated of its past. And the television stayed on all the time, sealing them into their marital capsule.

And this is my utter frustration now, of course: that for my father's honour, my original voyage was so rubbed out. Within those walls it had absolutely never happened, though I can hardly think our self-censorship had the power to extinguish a whole ship from public record.

My father hated memory. He never spoke of his war. Out of the Navy for good by VJ, he went to work in the arsenal – like everyone else. It remained for some years a large employer. All the while some kind of suffering was palpable in him, but unarticulated. You could see it in his arrogance, his ironic grin, as if he were perpetually biting back the pain of an inventive old-world punishment. Hating religion by the same token, he shrugged off any approach of emotion with grim clowning. He used that peculiar baby-talk larded with back slang, which tends to lurk in the Navy. By these means he cemented what must have been our conspiracy, for it was always to him that I took my troubles, right from a toddler. I regarded him as my special protector; like a joking Jesus.

I try hard to imagine him in his own youth, cycling up to the grammar school at Shooter's Hill; I rode there myself in my teens, on the same bike. Though he left at fourteen and was sent soon enough to HMS *Ganges* at Ipswich, the 'stone frigate' hell-hole, where his own dad had once been an instructor.

I went through sixth form and qualified for my commission because the war had changed everything. There was technology and free education. And he told me in a gruff voice how I had 'bloody gone aft', how he 'wouldn't know how to speak to me no more' – *Ganges* being to Dartmouth what the beast is to beauty. Gone aft! Dad, no one 'goes aft'. It was wilful and jealous, this adherence to Jack Tar, who never slings his mental hammock but in a wooden man-o'-war.

Once I was commissioned, the eddies of career kept me in the northern hemisphere. Not so unusual. It is not all 'See the world'. So it was perhaps not until seventy-nine that I first found myself south of the Line. That would have been with *Zebra*, the best destroyer I served in. I was in my late twenties, keen, good at my job, making progress.

13

We waved our flag at Cape Town and sailed east for Sydney on a goodwill visit, bound for Hong Kong. Oceans are all different. To trace the famous old trade routes of the roaring forties holds an excitement, a freshness. I enjoyed my baptism in those last-discovered waters, the southern seas. We hurried along to Australia at a steep clipper-fast run, and made landfall.

But just as we approached Sydney harbour a flotilla of small craft blocked our route. We had to hold off: yachts, cabin cruisers – even a few old steamers. They were making their way out past the Heads which mark the harbour's entrance. It seemed as though the whole population had taken to the water, skittering and skimming about like a vast shoal haunting a reef.

The few Sydney folk who had not got themselves afloat were up there waving right on the bluff, or drawn up to the very edges in their cars – we could just make them out and just hear, dimly on the breeze, the noise of their horns mingled with the hoots and blarings from the little fleet.

In the midst of them stood a great white passenger ship dressed over all, proceeding out to sea. Every few minutes a blast of sound would come from her funnel across the swell, and the small fry would reply at once hooting back; and then tack or dart all the more.

We lined the wires; it was a sight. I turned to speak to the man next to me, and found Tommy Hall-Patterson, our Principal Warfare Officer. He said it was the send-off for the liner *Avalon* on her last voyage. He was a distant, rather isolated man; but a hard-nosed sailor, one of the old school. Hated to see a damn good ship go to waste, he said. 'She's the last of the three white sisters, the *Avalon*, the *Armorica*, and the *Hispania*. There goes what it's all been about, Ralphie. You see that glorious thing, beside which this old tub, though I love her dearly, is no more than a rocket-launching sardine can sharpened at one end . . .' He paused. 'Look at those bloody lines. Isn't she a vision?'

'Absolutely,' I said.

'And what are we having to do with her?' he continued. 'Sell her to the damn Chinks. She's off to Taiwan to be broken up. With all her bloody glad rags on. Makes me livid.' He nodded towards her. '*Great steamers, white and gold*, you know that? When you see the like of her, what do you think?' His angry eyes turned from the *Avalon* and seemed to bore into

14

me. I hesitated, not knowing what sort of reply he was after.

But he carried on: 'For three hundred years, the Royal Navy has kept the seas so that a creature like that could slip off Clydebank and go anywhere she wanted without fear of bloody molestation. But there's no more cash, boy. We're all washed up. Men have given their lives for a cause and what does it amount to. The Jap, the Yank, the Russian, the damn German and the heathen bloody Chinee; these shall inherit the earth, and there's not a thing we can do about it.

'And if anyone has the balls to say nay,' I can hear his cultured, old-fashioned voice even now, 'if anyone questions the damn carve-up, Ralphie, why then it's all hell and four-minute warnings. Short and curlies, eh? No one can move a damn muscle, for the awful poise of the balance. If poor old Britannia dares draw the line again what a bloody flap there'd be. Before you know it an unstoppable escalation, some idiot politician presses the button, and the lot of us gone up for good. You and I, Ralph, will never see active service. Have you grasped that? Lucky, are we? By God, I'd give anything for a crack at someone about this.' He indicated the *Avalon*. 'But the bastard politicians will cut us, and cut us, and cut everything down to the bloody bone. No merchant fleet left and nothing to defend.'

His fist tightened on the wire before him. 'But we never lost a war, did we? Battle or two maybe, but we never lost a war. Eh? No Vietnam. D'you see? No bloody Vietnam. Well, I'll soon be hanging up my hat, boy. But what about you?'

I had no answer. After eyeing me meaningfully once again, he went about his business. He was a good man; the sort you would want next to you in a crisis. Though of course he did not see active service; while I, of course, did.

But later that day, when we were all in a bar in Sydney somewhere, he made a point of buttonholing me and buying me a Scotch. He insisted he had confused the names. Two sisters only: *Avalon* and *Hispania*. Why he should have made a mix-up like that he had no idea. Two sisters only.

'What?' I said.

'That's all right then. That's all right.' And I cudgelled my brain then for the other name he had let slip.

But now glimpses of the *Armorica* burst softly around me

like the artillery of butterflies. The barrage of memory takes its own time, its own slow motion of opening.

5

It had not been calm all the way. In fact, the *Armorica* was late because of the Bay of Biscay. Only a few days out from Tilbury and the English Channel, a huge winter storm had forced her to turn head on to the waves, and stand far out into the Atlantic.

'It claimed in the brochure this ship had stabilisers,' Barry Parsons said to the steward that lunch-time, when the motion first went beyond a joke. Penny overheard him trying to help his green-faced wife out of the dining-room. All morning there had been wry smiles and comments about sea-legs. An ominous pewter sky bottomed wider and lower, beaten out by a dinting wind. The lounges were suddenly deserted; the clamorous gloom penetrated the cabins themselves. But Penny had always reckoned herself the kind of person who would, when put to the test, make a good sailor.

In her neat blouse, her light jacket cinched at the waist, her long skirt of brown serge, and her court shoes which turned out slightly when she walked, she presented herself for lunch; though at the back of her mind she did worry that a ship made entirely of steel – it was, wasn't it? – should be able to creak and grind so.

The dining-room was large, brightly lit and expensively panelled. But, lying between the outermost cabins each side of D deck, it had no windows or portholes – and therefore no reassuring horizon. She shared a table with the Finch-Clarks, and now their little girl. Children were permitted at lunch. It was a table at the edge of the dining area, where carpet gave way to wood. About her, the slightly built Goan waiters coped with chops, game, fish, soup, and deployed their twin spoons to serve level vegetables on a treacherously sloping plate. The air was full, too, of the usual cuisine smells, made sharper and a touch greasier, she felt, by the worsening sea. Yet she began her meal in a spirit of bravery: with a portion of asparagus in butter, excellent as always. And then the lamb.

But now a tray full of upturned coffee-cups slid off its side-table and avalanched pieces of crockery past them. A bad wave. From around the dining-room there were shrieks and remarks from folk caught up in similar local calamities. Hardly a moment to recoup before there came another. Tests of character. Penny gripped on to her own table with one hand while maintaining her plate with the other. Gravy trickled over her fingers. She could see the Parsons couple. They had been unable to move. Half slumping, half standing a few yards away, they clutched at the door-frame, the handrail and each other. She could see white knuckles. Then all the debris came cruising along the floor as the ship tipped back through what now seemed an enormous angle.

And slowly – but not so slowly that it became acceptable – up again.

'I'm afraid we can't have the stabilisers out in this sort of a sea, sir. They'd break off.'

'What!' Barry Parsons's fleshy presence boomed. 'You're joking, I take it.' But its sound was as unconvincing as an echo.

'Absolutely not, sir. They said yesterday we were likely to run into some heavy stuff. Just have to head up and ride it out. Besides, they only affect the roll, not the pitch, stabilisers.' The steward gestured with his flattened hand. 'The captain won't want to get stuck in the Bay, see. I'm sure you'll understand.' He grinned. He was enjoying it, Penny thought. 'I'm afraid it's likely to get a touch worse than this, even. Which is a little unusual even for this time of year, sir, I admit.' Definite relish.

Queenie Parsons just managed, 'Worse?' Then, 'But this is a liner' died to a whisper as she fought with incredulity, terror and her stomach. Hanging on, the Parsons couple appeared to Penny as ham dramatics conversing from across an unkind wooden stage. But she was hanging on to the table herself, surprised, yes, genuinely surprised that the captain could allow roughness to get to the point of breakages.

'You'd think they'd know what to expect, wouldn't you? And have special racks or whatever – for the things. You'd think they would.' She made the remark to no one in particular, voicing her disquiet.

Paul Finch-Clark leaned in to the table and managed to make a quip about Battersea fairground. Something else smashed.

17

Penny caught the words '. . . You realise it isn't quite what it looked like from dry-ground level.'

Little Rosalind Finch-Clark gripped her chair at both sides, watching with wide eyes as her plate of half-eaten poached egg on toast moved now towards her father, now towards Penny.

'When does it stop?' Penny called out.

It was the steward who replied. 'Not for a few days, I'm afraid, madam.'

'A few days! Like this!' She found her voice joined by several from the neighbouring tables. Then she glanced to where the Parsons couple had been standing. They were now nowhere to be seen. They had been slid out of the ship and sluiced away, so she could fancy.

A general lurching exodus from the dining-room was in progess, however, for the big sea continued. Every wave was a bad wave. Penny regarded her fellow travellers, trying herself to decide what to do. The ship's creaks and groaning had increased, quite alarmingly. Surely that was not right. A noise overhead. She looked up in case signs of fracture should appear in the ceiling. She expected the lights to flicker. There was indeed an air of consternation. Sparks or water would burst through the walls.

Only the hardiest old birds of passage were still eating, managing their plates with a degree of superiority. One or two were still calling out to waiters as if a regime of bouncing, splintering glassware and cascading cutlery were just what their specialist, when reminding them to go south again this year for the winter, had ordered. An old woman in pearls summoned assistance from her seat two tables away. 'Cabin, I think, steward.'

And of course the steward was propelled into action, partly by sycophancy – probably; but Penny would have liked to think, compassion – and partly by the momentary angle of the ship. 'Directly, your ladyship.' And, proud it seemed of his white uniform, and the braid in colours-of-the-line looped at his left shoulder, he rescued her theatrically past them all, one arm for the dowager and one for the ship.

The dowager nodded politely to Penny. 'I went through the Suez Canal for the first time in thirty-seven, and since then I've done it eighteen times, this way and that, regular as clockwork. Not counting the war, you see – and the Arabs. Isn't that so, steward?'

'Certainly, your ladyship.'

And certainly she was remarkably good at the alternate steep climb and drop which they had settled into: 'Just take it carefully, and keep your cabin. That's my advice, if anyone wants it. Keep your cabin, keep your head, and thank God you won't be stuck in Kensington all winter.'

Yes, the extremity of the movement could begin, Penny supposed, to be something they might at least accept, if not adjust to. If there were really no alternative, and if the ladyship, whoever she was, could do it. Think of England indeed. Indeed she tried.

Most of what was loose and fragile had now broken; most of what could be spilled, had spilled. Most of those diners who were still making up their minds about how to leave and where to go had found regular fixtures to help them – in the reciprocating cling and brace that was necessary. So when no one else mentioned that it sounded more and more as though the vessel were on the point of ripping in two, Penny clenched her teeth. Nevertheless, in that very act her thoughts turned first to the boys, at her mother's school in Essex, and next to Hugh, already on the other side of the world. If she were to drown she would be of no use to any of them.

And the next thing after the thought of imminent death was the awareness of fear. Close upon that, nausea. And between the first consciousness of sickness and the worst feeling imaginable were about three suffocating minutes amid the smells of pheasant, liver, mayonnaise and chocolate.

D was one of the lower decks. Its floor and walls staggered by; its door heaved open. She managed to find a closet on that level; though, regrettably, she was not the first. Monstrous, her mouth like a burst porthole. Like an act of recall; but so painful, all the confused past springing through, still fully formed. And with that over she felt drained, but just about in command – and in the greatest need of air.

6

A good open-air walk ran along the whole length of both sides of A deck. It was the kind of broad, sideless corridor Penny was familiar with from popular ocean films in which five days of love culminated in New York. It ran along the whole length, that is, except for the steerage class – that old label for poorer travellers. On this level, she noted, the steerage was sealed off from the main part of the vessel, to port and starboard, behind impenetrable steel dividers in the bulkhead.

Coated and belted now, wind-whipped, with hands outstretched, she made her way towards the bow – along the scrubbed planking where in undreamable fair weather deckchairs might be set. It was to press uphill for several seconds, march deceptively level for a moment, and then loom dangerously giant-strided. Wiser to stop and hang on to a frame or to the rail when the ship's nose went down. Queenie Parsons's last words kept running through her head, 'But this is a liner!'

Truly, Penny had not imagined the white floating city which had so taken her breath against the drabness of Tilbury dock could be subject to anything like this. If they were not exactly storm-*tossed* – the ship *was* too grand and provident for that – yet it was obvious their assurance was being very seriously examined. Astride the huge ridges of complex and crazing black, the *Armorica* was undergoing, yes, something of an inquisition. The groaning and creaking, so audible in the dining-room and now mingled with the debate of sea and wind, were proof enough of that, if proof were wanted.

There, up ahead, the part of the bow she could see had gone in, and a wash of foam came over all the great steel winches and fittings, flushing and draining away as she watched. She would never have thought so high a point as that strong, curved prow could be at risk. Surely this could not go on. Surely. The grown-up in her told the child not to be silly. But she remained unconvinced.

She passed a Lascar with a mop, a small figure, of brown imagined bones inside his maroon jacket. Dealing, presumably, with some mess, some distressed passenger's sick, he seemed hardly to be holding on to anything. He stared at her with opaque eyes, then looked away. These outdoor folk, diminutive, cropping up like sad, solitary djinns, she had already found them unsettling. Should she speak? Technically they fell outside the ship's account of itself, they did not exist. Yet everyone knew the terminology: Lascars. How was that? She found herself several yards past him in only two steps. And she worried about the life-jacket instructions. Would she get the ties the right way round? The diagram was confusing.

At the forward reach of A deck she came with surprise on the Sinhalese couple tucked away in a protected nook. She had seen them about, of course. But, like everyone else, had not yet found it possible to speak. They were standing with their backs to the steel, the woman wearing a coat over her blue sari. He, smiling, smaller than his wife, was neat in his Burberry jacket and fawn slacks. Penny stopped about a yard from them. She leaned on the rail and looked out at the same prospect, comforted a little that they seemed in no immediate hurry as regards lifeboats. Indeed, the man was about to raise a pair of binoculars to his eyes. On seeing her he stopped, took the strap off and volunteered them. She shook her head and smiled queasily. Now she had ceased her struggle along the deck, it might be that the nausea was about to return.

'No, please. Have a look.' He insisted, holding the glasses out.

She looked. The horizon, looming nonsense for half the time, did her stomach good; though to tell the truth there was little to focus on that was not frenzied water, or ragged grey cloud. She stood, resting her elbows on the rail, in those moments when she had not physically to cling to it. She surveyed the waves, broke off. It was quite dismal. She looked again, held on, and then again. Momentarily she caught sight of something far off in the whelm; which promptly disappeared. Maybe flotsam, the corner of a box, waterlogged, she thought. A tea-chest, possibly, like the ones her own belongings were packed in. A piece of wreckage, or something thrown overboard from a tanker. Nothing worth looking at, really, but even rubbish gave the eye a mark. Like a gravestone. She suspected no life-form could live in all that desolation; they were utterly abandoned.

'My name is Piyadasa. Is it your first trip?'

'Yes.' She managed a weak smile.

'It is very rough.'

'Yes.'

'Please carry on looking.'

Magnified, each wave was colder and more intimate. She found herself noticing the skid of water over water, the detachment and reattachment of drops and strings, the innumerable facets of unnameable colours – unnameable because they were all the same colour, and yet clearly not. She thought less about the depth.

She handed the glasses back. 'Thanks very much. Not feeling too good.'

'You should drink tea.' The lady smiled.

'I don't think I could drink anything, just at the moment.'

'Perhaps without milk or sugar. Perhaps even gunpowder tea.'

'Gunpowder tea?' Penny felt her eyebrows rise.

'Any kind of tea you like.'

'Oh. Do you think so?'

'Ask my husband. Even beef tea.' Mrs Piyadasa laughed. 'Why don't you come along with us. We're just going inside. They will bring you something. Come with us. My husband knows everything there is to know about tea. He grows it, and then he sells it.'

Her husband acknowledged his expertise with a wry expression.

Penny was on the point of demurring, as if she ought to be seen to deal with her fear and nausea alone.

'This way.'

Thus she found herself back inside, kidnapped, as it were, by kindness. Yet the gunpowder tea, brought by a steward to where they sat in the main lounge, helped. As did the polite conversation. She took to the plump, smiling lady. 'Yes, we live in Colombo. You must visit us there.' Mrs Piyadasa seemed in no doubt that they would make it safely home. Penny was impressed.

'She misses her children,' said the husband.

'Yes, I do.' Mrs Piyadasa mimicked a sigh of grief and turned up her eyes. 'Not seasick, but homesick. I have three boys, one girl.'

'I miss mine,' Penny said.

'You have children?'

'Two boys.'

22

Mrs Piyadasa took a small book of photographs from her handbag. They sat for some minutes, comparing ages and characteristics. Then there was a pause.

'So you have never travelled abroad?' Mrs Piyadasa adjusted her sari under her large cream cardigan.

'I went to France with my parents before the war. Several times. We took the boat train; but it was nothing like this.' Penny smiled.

'Ah, before the war,' Mr Piyadasa said. 'The war changed everything.'

Penny nodded and found herself smiling again. Then she felt disconcerted. It was an obvious remark, the sort heard in all sorts of small talk. It was a conversation filler; and yet it struck her peculiarly now. She was an educated, articulate woman, but it had never quite occurred to her as it did now, the effect of the war. She had come to womanhood through the conflict, and at home the scars had always been patent, everywhere. Even now, more than a decade on – could it be so long? – London still had enough gaps in its blackened fabric, still had bomb-sites, was gritting its teeth, flexing its sooty muscles and struggling on. And out of town there was the accelerating attempt to put all that in the past, rebuild standards, families; she and Hugh and the boys growing up with a new town on their doorstep. And there was the rhetoric of course; of starting again, an end to poverty, the promise of the Commonwealth.

But now she felt the words shake her. If the ship did not sink she might be the guest of oriental strangers in a city she could not begin to imagine. What would their house be like? Would she be expected to take off her shoes? She would make some religious *faux pas*. But no, it was not that. It was that everything really was different, absolutely and completely different – because of the war. She had thought it was over and done with. She had not realised. No one had realised. She looked around at the few uncomfortable-looking occupants of the main lounge, the chairs heaving to ludicrous angles, the low tables that would now shed whatever was placed on them. No one had realised. And herself: she had never actually spoken before to anyone who was not white.

Mrs Piyadasa was saying something about shopping in

Oxford Street. Penny pulled herself back from her reverie. The nausea returned, distinctly flavoured now with intellectual disorientation. She found herself craving air again. She got up and made her excuses, pulling a grim face and holding her midriff by way of explanation. The Piyadasas smiled and nodded as she struggled towards the exit. There was a need to be close to the terrible water, to see it and know its extent – in order to be ready for it, perhaps.

7

The young man came and stood a yard or so along from her. She had wedged herself in a half-plated nook which ended A deck's forward reach, in order to look over the spray-tormented bow. It was the starboard reflection of the place she had met the Piyadasas; where now in fact rode opposite her, clutching the steel section of rail, a boy. She could not see me, of course, because her view was blocked by the stair housing dropping from above to the lower foredeck. And in any case we had not met, so I should have meant nothing to her. Nor had I learned yet to play with the young girl who cultivated her attention. I was convinced I should never get to know the other children on the ship. My imagination was stirred, too. I was afraid of the cold, the anonymity, of drowning.

Penny regarded the man briefly before nodding and turning her gaze back to the sea. They had spoken once or twice – at coffee – at least she thought so. He was young, younger than herself, still in his twenties, maybe. Tallish, with bones regular enough, a nice smile and ample dark curly hair, now made somewhat nonsensical by the wind. His eyes were kind.

The eyes, yes. Maybe he was the man she had encountered at the purser's office, when she was spending the first few mornings going here and there about the ship, getting her bearings, discovering all its mahogany-panelled passages, its labyrinthine secrets; before this extraordinary movement had exerted prior claim over everything else. She could not be certain. For, in the days of the voyage so far, faces had only just begun to assemble themselves, names to enter her reckoning.

One could easily get appearances confused. And she could certainly not remember his name.

So Penny endured a few more minutes. The seasickness receded a little.

'I knew it wasn't going to be easy to get away. Are you scared?'

'Of course.' She swallowed. 'Is it obvious?'

'No. I was just trying to find someone else in the same boat.' He pulled up the collar of his coat with his free hand and held the lapels closed under his chin. 'So to speak.'

She laughed in spite of the joke and her stomach. The wind snatched a shower of fine icy spray from the summit of one of the ridges and hurled it into their faces, before the next inexorable heave of the decking could lift them. Her companion gripped the end of the mahogany rail. Penny noticed how tightly she herself had hold of an upright steel stanchion that appeared to support the deck above. It must in fact run down like a rib through the whole ship. Her knuckles were quite locked. The stanchion itself was freezing wet but the flange offered a good purchase, and because of its security she could sometimes, daringly, provoking the storm almost, lean out to learn better what was coming.

'I never imagined . . .' she began. 'That it would be like this, I mean. And the noise. Listen. All that . . . grinding and groaning. It's solid metal. How can it do that? I hate it. At least out here in the wind you can't notice it so much.'

The great structure started its drop away again from under their feet. For a moment they were weightless.

'I wouldn't pretend to have the answer. At all. Oh God.' Then: 'It's just very, very . . . I don't know what. In there,' he gestured to the cabins, 'it's like a ship in one of those films.' He shouted over the weather. 'Too swashbuckling for me, I'm afraid! That's why I'm staying out here as long as I can. The sight of what's actually doing it to you makes you feel slightly less ill.' His looks belied the assertion. 'But I do agree. It is the noise that's maybe the worst of it. It's the absolute cream on the custard. Sorry!'

They shared a tight smile: another attempted joke and the tasteless mention of food.

'Sorry. But if it *were* just the movement . . . Well, that's what every sailor sings about, isn't it? It's as British as . . . I don't know, Trafalgar Square. And being British we *ought* to be able to cope. That's what they keep telling us. And if this were a little old battler – with the salt-caked smokestack, et cetera – you'd expect it. But this is huge, and up to date. The latest thing. And cinema liners don't lurch, otherwise Fred and Ginger could never have danced a step; kissing would have been right out.' A plunge. 'You need a level base for that sort of carry-on. I believe.' He hurried on. 'It actually sounds as though the damn thing's going to break, doesn't it; and nobody warned you, or sang about that.'

Penny nodded cautiously and turned her head. Another sting of spray. She noted with surprise that in all his chatter he had actually caught her own earlier thoughts – about the sound – and voiced them.

He took out his cigarettes, looked at them, met her eye, grinned ruefully, and then put them away again. 'Ugh. Funny thing. No comfort there.' They stood, volunteering nothing further for a while, riding it out, watching the intricate variations with which the sea and sky were confronting them. Then she remembered his opening remark.

'I'm afraid I didn't quite understand what you said at first. Something about it being difficult to get away?' Shouting again as the wind tried to snatch the words from her mouth.

'Oh yes. Difficult to get away from England. Won't take you to her heart but won't let you go. Horrible old spider, in fact. She wants the blood out of a man. Sorry.' He apologised again. 'I've probably said something unforgivable. Perhaps you're incredibly patriotic and terribly sad to be leaving. I don't know. It's just the way I feel.'

'I am sad. To be leaving one's home. For good. Don't you think?'

'I've no regrets. Honestly. A grasping, petty and superstitious land infested with churches. But then I consider myself a scientist – for whom God can't strictly be said to exist.'

'I see. And not a very poetical description, either.'

'I probably shouldn't be saying this. Probably socially quite beyond the pale; I can never tell. They pull everything out of shape.'

'What?'

'Churches. I mean the map, even. Wherever you go. That's

the one good thing about the view here; not a steeple in sight.'

'My. You do have a chip.' She felt herself put about. His words provoked a longing for railway lines, green fields, and, indeed, the needle spire of Chelmsford cathedral which had always been visible from her bedroom window at Galleywood.

'I'm sorry,' once more excusing himself, 'I'll shut up. Bad taste to call religion into disrepute, I know. Digging myself deeper. I shouldn't have forced my opinions on you. You're probably a devout something or other and I've offended you for ever. Probably the weather.'

Just after the lowest point of the downward plunge, one could sense the very moment when gravity came back through the soles of the shoes.

'Yes,' he said. 'Let's talk about the weather. I wonder if people can ever get used to this.'

Then she laughed again. 'I don't mind hearing someone's opinions.'

Peering past her, he considered the swell ahead. He pointed. 'Here comes something!'

An irregularity in the pattern: ridges too close together; big ones, brimming, high and innocent. The ship went down in front of them as usual, and then rose significantly higher; higher, and poised. An exceptional wave began its course almost casually along the length of the water line under them. It passed where they stood and became a huge fulcrum somewhere about the neighbourhood of the dining-room. Then the dive. The bows went right under. A rush of tide and foam sluiced off the fore-deck and drained around the tubes, bollards and hatches not so very far beyond them.

'God,' she muttered audibly in the moment of slack that followed – as sometimes they did when the ship seemed not to know what it would do next.

'The seventh wave. Isn't there something about the seventh wave? You see, I had a hunch England wouldn't make it easy to get out. At least this much of a fight convinces me I've taken the right route!'

Yes, it was nice to talk to someone. She had not talked to someone, a personable young man, in fact, in her own right since . . . 'I'm going out to Adelaide,' she said firmly.

'Oh, really? Me too.'

He was nice to talk to . . . Since her marriage. She had no idea. How nice it was to be spoken to as herself. Then, helplessly, from her clutch on the stanchion: 'I'm joining my husband, you see.'

'Ah, yes. And leaving your mother.'

'I suppose I should be getting back to my cabin.' She touched the place on her cheek where the wind felt almost like a bruise. The cold. And not just her cheek. Really, it got through coats and layers. It limited the time you could stay out. Or perhaps the main lounge again, Mrs Piyadasa.

'Must you? There's a man in mine.'

'A what?'

'A man. The man I share with.'

'You have to share?'

'Yes. Don't you?'

'There is another bunk. But it's empty.'

'You must have more clout than me. My other bunk is full of a seasick man. It's pretty disgusting.'

'I didn't realise people *had* to share. I mean except families. Heavens, I should hate that.'

'Yes,' he said.

'For four or five weeks, cooped up with someone you've never met.'

'Yes. I keep wondering who I should have tipped, or rung up beforehand. That's the trouble, not having the right connections or the absolute know-how. I'm sure if I did offer someone money he'd just look at me – it would be the wrong bloke.'

'Yes,' said Penny. 'But he'd just look at you and then take the money.'

'Exactly.' He laughed. 'I'm sorry, sir. The ship's full. There's nothing I can do. But thank you very much all the same.'

This laughter in the face of the sea – Penny felt slightly uncomfortable, though – over and above the discomfort of the storm, which in all truth she had briefly forgotten. But she could put no name to the feeling. She waited. She thought the man was virtually bound to ask her about Hugh next. A man would. For all sorts of reasons.

So she pre-empted him. 'We haven't been introduced. Penny Kendrick.' She held on and stretched out her free hand.

'Robert Kettle.' He clasped hers during the transition from

28

suspension to effort, and then drew back to his place at the rail. 'Both "K".' He smiled.

She smiled back. But the 'K' was Hugh's name, of course. 'My mother owns a preparatory school in Essex. That's where I grew up – among lots of little boys away from home.'

'I went to one of those once,' he said. 'Always marching and doing drill. Present arms with miniature hockey sticks. But not for long. My parents couldn't afford to keep me there. We weren't really in the right league, financially. I suppose they were making a desperate bid for social—' He failed to finish as once more the spray surprised him.

'Oh, I see.' Then she realised why she had felt uncomfortable. It was the way they had linked themselves through the character of an inevitably corrupt purser, or accommodation officer. It reminded her of the little boys at the school; how they sought to cope with life away from home by such creations. Everyone outside their world was an articulately structured joke. Poor little devils. One thing her mother's school had taught her was that she did not want her boys to go away like that. And yet that was where they were now, her boys, and she was here in the midst of these unlooked-for waves talking to an unlooked-for Robert Kettle, who would probably see the point and then apologise. But I didn't mean it like that, she found herself protesting. I didn't want it to happen like this. This is just temporary.

And she thought of all her furniture down there in the hold, their bed and their books, and her poor violin, and the Finch-Clarks' enormous cat in its cage.

8

'Hey, be careful with that, kid!' Mr Chaunteyman had given me half a crown and told me to keep his service revolver dry on deck. He was an American, Navy too – though he never wore uniform. We were going to Australia with him, Erica and I. That much was clear. I had the gun strapped to my waist. It weighed me down on my left. I had pinned on my sheriff's star and wore my cowboy hat, which the wind now thrummed at somewhere behind my head. The cord threatened a strangle, but I would not take it off.

I had turned one side of the brim up to the crown with a safety pin, Australian style. Failing anything to serve as an authentic tin visor I was Ned Kelly in mufti, on his boat. I had stalked the heaving promenade deck for twenty minutes looking for people to shoot: possibly one or two of the Commies I had heard about from Mr Chaunteyman's lips. Luckily the other children were not in evidence. Then I had fetched my raincoat and come forward here.

I too thought the ship would soon shake to pieces. Images of my life ran appropriately before my eyes. Scenes of home – containing unfortunate further images of death. Such scenes, for example, as had welled once from the open experiment on top of our wireless when I was little. My father placed a stout board to support the metal frame; the cathode-ray tube perched in its own scaffold. We drew the drapes across the french windows and clicked the knob. And were transfixed by scintillation.

The television was the great metal granny of all knots. But I was warned off. My father tended it jealously, as a household god. Through its face our English future brightly spilled; with its back parts he had sole communion. The private glows and buzzes, the electron lens, the HT circuit – 'twenty thousand volts, boy, all right?' – the decoders, oscillators, transformers and valves remained a mystery to me.

It was unhealthy, and suffered intermittent snowstorms. In the midst of them I watched cowboy fantasies: *The Mystery Riders*, *Roy Rogers*, or *Renfrew of the Mounties*. North American corpses were two a penny. During weekends he set up a mirror and stood behind it, twiddling, tuning, testing, to attain that fullness, unstable as the grasshoppers on Bostall Heath, of which the contraption was capable. And then one Sunday he unclipped his Avo meter. He put down his insulated screwdriver with a grunt of satisfaction. Now the confusion was of real sea, and genuine weather. A poor, monochrome vessel was beam-ended on the Goodwin Sands; it rolled back and forth inside the screen, endlessly, helplessly.

The horror rose to my lips. 'They'll be all right?'

'Two of them were saved. But the captain always goes down

with his ship.' My mother's look assumed a glassiness as she said it. I had not seen her face so before.

Thus I realised early that there might occasionally flood in a loss which was unendurable. The skipper of the *Enterprise* had given his body to the waves; he breathed in lethal sea water as surely as I drank my National Health orange juice.

My mother's cousin 'went down with the *Hood*', but to that bare phrase my small imagination could attach no picture at all. I put death in a far-off quarter, snow-bound, snow-blinded, epitomised solely by that other terrible captain: Scott of the Antarctic, whose recovered boat–coffin clung to the Embankment by Tower Bridge, and whose bereaved son painted snow-tormented birds in the screen of our television.

Then one evening Erica took me to a slide-show talk given by Sir John Hunt. It was at my school in Bostall Lane. The conqueror of Everest was some years happily returned. But Edmund Hillary and Sherpa Tensing stood on the snowcap screen against a glare of magenta-blue, still planting the Union Jack. And after that I was reassured; for there was no undiscovered place upon the globe, no unexpected continent, able to surge in, disaster-filled, cannibal-fretted, sacrifice-plagued, species by man-eating species. Death was a thing of the past, and I learned to sleep by blocking it out. Until this ocean, and this storm. My beliefs heaved and bucked under me.

Regarding the Atlantic, though, I knew my father and grandfather had led charmed lives. It was Erica who had told me. Both career seamen, they were survivors of the two world wars. My grandad missed Jutland, being fortunately on weekend leave when his ship rushed hooting out of Chatham. He had already retired, and was only hooked back out of honourable discharge because there was a crisis. The worst shock he got in the war to end all wars was from a streak in the phosphorescence. Too paralysed to sing out – a potentially capital omission – he stood watch in his trance as the tell-tale slice closed and closed, aimed dead at the engine-room below him. Against the intimate torpedo there is no defence. Desperate small-arms fire would be as useless as prayer. Only at the last minute did the streak turn miraculously away, and he caught a glimpse of its dorsal fin in the moonlight; though not of its hammerhead sneer.

One of the few sailors ever to be saved by a shark, then, my grandfather Frank Lightfoot began in sail, abided in steam, and ended on shore; a charmed life indeed, if tedious. When he fell from the old *Impregnable*'s rigging, he was preserved by a Scotsman, who caught the youthful seat of his pants as they passed the lower yard-arm. After that he was unsinkable, undrownable, unexplodable. His recollections covered a vast red world of experience.

Such had always been the integrity of the family story. The males at sea, or foremen at the arsenal, the women at home – except in times of national emergency. We were the kind of folk who could put together a down payment, tough but reliable souls, salts of the earth. The kind who never had calamity or Zeppelins predicted for them.

Therefore my grandmother Lightfoot, not long married, with an infant, was surprised to find herself out at work and hardly in her new Co-op home at all. She was frightened too, making ammunition for the Somme. It was to keep up the payments, and do her bit while big Frank was escorting his convoys.

She had to leave my toddling aunt with a neighbour each morning and take the workers' train from Abbey Wood. And once within the great black curtain wall of the arsenal she must give herself over dutifully to production. Extending her pretty finger ends, she picked up on each of them, including the thumbs, a cartridge-paper hat from the bench to her left. Then held them up – like a raw crown roast. She plunged them into the fish-glue in front of her on the stove. Judging the clutch to avoid a progressive cooking of her skin, she drew them out again, dripping, steaming, stinking. At last with a pianistic flourish which was entirely her own, she pressed her whole batch firmly into the empty cases, waiting at her right and newly machined – like brass lipstick holders. So each of her innocent digits made a neat bullet hole, time and again.

Erica, while powdering her nose once, had spoken of the Blitz and hiding under the stairs. But no one had actually died. They were stairs I should never see again. Nor should I ever set eyes upon the family I had been born into: immortals, familiar with weapons, innocent of death. Now we had left England, in circumstances I bluffed myself I had the hang of, and everything was new. We were wilful outlaws, pirates. The huge waves queued up in front of me. The wind tore at my hair. I stared back at the immense grey sea.

<h1 align="center">9</h1>

To put out to sea from Spain in a square-rigged ship was to swing past Africa to the Caribbean. The winds and the currents insisted. But for the English there was first the problem of our own dangerous coast, followed by the Bay. That was the trickiest part. Once an overloaded merchantman from Bristol or London got safely clear of Biscay's lee suction, and past Cape Finisterre, the rest of the Atlantic could seem plain sailing. Barring the usual accidents and hurricanes, of course. And from the eastern seaboard of America there was one route home: on the Gulf Stream with the westerlies that bring the English weather. As far as we were concerned the Atlantic was for centuries a clock-wise swirl of goods, criminals, slaves and starvelings policed by the Navy, one vast market of forces. It was a slow-motion whirlpool.

The great age of piracy lasted little more than ten years. That was in the early eighteenth century. Violent, torturing wretches, the pirates were products of the trade routes. They were its children, ex-Navy, ex-merchantman, bent on revenge. They rejected privilege, Church, State, marriage, property – they espoused instead whoredom, social equality, a kind of welfare and rough justice. They were radical mutineers, leftovers from the old days of the Levellers. Their communism foundered, as it had to, on its ultimate powerlessness.

Now, on that blasted nook of the *Armorica*, for all my romance of swashbuckling and daredevilry, I sensed at last the seriousness of what Erica and I had done in running away. Women and children cannot afford to split. Their mutiny comes home to roost. It began to dawn on me: Erica and I were actually mutineers to the bones, and must take whatever came to us. Yet even if that were drowning in this great swell, I knew I did not wish to return to Abbey Wood.

There was a custom in those days to keep one room 'for best', on the off chance of company. People were wary of

33

trusting any show of their arrangements. This dusted sepulchre is what we are really like. Judge us by these fixtures and fittings, not the grubby cram we actually live in.

Had we been religious, we should have come back from church in our Sunday clothes, guests to ourselves almost, to eat the roast off that fine dark table in the front parlour. We were not. Our Sunday meals were, like all others, served in the cramped back room. We never went to church. We had not God but Tradition: King's Regulations and the Articles of War.

So it was only on very special occasions we might use it. And we kept ourselves dutifully ready.

Our particular 'best' room functioned, then, like nothing so much as the Great Aft Cabin, waiting, ever waiting, for its true Admiral to come aboard. I was not officially allowed in, except for formal punishments: the cane was kept in a drawer. The door was always closed with the key in the lock – because the latch had gone some time during my father's childhood, and had never been seen to. So it was bypassed, unmentionable; it became almost sacred, perhaps. There was no fire kept up in that elaborate fireplace. No point.

That room rose through the storm to my mind's eye, cold, prim, bleaching in the wan sun which crept through the large projecting window. Raised up to the height of 'the ladders', our view was that same panorama of distant cranes and the Isle of Dogs. You might gaze out as if across the waters of a dull home port. In the evening a last light could sometimes strike right through to the wallpaper opposite, where above the useless piano *The Fighting Temeraire* hung amid the pattern of small buff flowers.

Mirrored and picture-railed, it was all a waste of space. And time. The hanging-bowl lampshade in marbled glass was two decades pre-war – the kind that marked out aged people. On the mantelshelf either side of the clock stood two lacquered bronzes of horse and tamer. Around the table in the bay window, the slim, japanned dining chairs. The chesterfield suite, antimacassar-draped. The bookcase-escritoire. The carved ivory trophies from Shanghai. The model junk, the brass gong, the shells, the Benares coffee-pot for the coffee we never drank. Against this Atlantic gale that room shimmered insistently.

Six months before, a gleaming Buick had drawn up outside

in the street. And Mr Chaunteyman, US Navy, came up the ladders and was ushered straight in.

He suddenly fulfilled us. He was the expected officer, a junior Lieutenant-Commander. That must have been how he slipped so unchallenged, even fêted, past my father's defences – who thought it was himself the American visited, the American with the matinee idol's line moustache, like Errol Flynn's. And Mr Chaunteyman did not have the brash crew cut of so many ordinary American servicemen of that decade. He kept a dignified shine to his thick, dark wave. Mr Chaunteyman was a true gent.

They met at a do in Greenwich Naval College, to which my father and some of his associates, as local 'other ranks', were invited. It was a gala occasion; my mother bought a new dress. It was a success. And they struck up a familiarity; Dave Chaunteyman impressed them with his informal style. He was in England, he said, to teach an anti-submarine course. Hey, he moved around the world a heck of a lot. He had visited before, during the war. Couldn't get over the place. It was so staid and quaint. So small and kind of cute. And our house: smoky, homey.

My parents bathed in his attention. In the new world, said my father, social divisions were out. There was no more rationing; the war years were over. He was a civilian citizen and the view ahead would be chromium-plated, televised. Who cared for old-fashioned niceties? This was what *he* had fought for. Soon, in the nuclear age, there would be no need even for the dirty fabrications of Woolwich Arsenal. He might get a job over the river at Dagenham, making Fords. Own a new car. Drive to work across the free ferry. Who could tell? They were on first-name terms at once, Dave, Harry and Erica. My parents were ripe for the dazzling.

Of course my grandfather, his mind going, would first hold court when Mr Chaunteyman called in for English tea. In the heyday of empire he had been at the Spithead Review. On a later inspection he had exchanged a few words with Queen Alexandra and been brushed by the King's overcoat. He might even sing; before he subsided into his nap. And then my father started to talk, there in the front parlour, about the real below-decks and the bloody hard world it had been. Mr Chaunteyman

brought gifts and opened him up. Week by week I would hear
something shocking: my dad's own mutinous anger leaking for
the first time into words.

But the change in my mother I felt through my skin. Erica
began to dress as young as she was, and to wear her blonde
hair in the latest film styles. She hummed about the house and
bought flowers instead of winkles from Woolwich market. Her
make-up was on all the time: while she vacuumed, or while she
hung the washing on the haul-up clothes-horse over the bath.
She nagged my father for a gramophone. Two or three times a
week she escaped by trolleybus to the pictures.

Mr Chaunteyman stirred his tea and rolled his eye. Erica
was very pretty. Therefore, even when I thought of our sooty
house and examined the likelihood of the officer and the
shorthand typist, I saw nothing preposterous in the courtship –
that he should have gone to these lengths. The risks, the
adventure, the distance. Love had been sanctioned by the
movies, by television. I was, in a curious way, thrilled. Besides,
she had engaged my complicity.

And it was only one week before this storm that I had
deliberately packed a selection of items into a miniature blue
suitcase – stealthily in my bedroom by nightlight, right under
the knot board. Ready for the flit, and its consequences. I too
was infatuated with him.

10

A dry blow. I learned to tighten my stomach against the fear,
gritting it out.

And of the blue suitcase? 'God gave the frog legs to swim
with. And hop,' said Mrs Trevor. I would gaze out of the dull
schoolroom to where the dirty clouds rolled by, until her Welsh
tones reclaimed me. 'Now by the way, you children, I hope you
all say your prayers every night. Have you finished listing your
amphibians, you, that boy at the back? Is there anybody here
who doesn't say their prayers?'

'God get me out of this' were the words that came to mind.
Childhood, we had been told, was magical.

'Chairs on desks, hands together, eyes closed. Vespers, ready!'

Now the day is over
Night is drawing nigh;
Shadows of the evening
Steal across the sky.

My benighted personal devotions were a mishmash: ritual, obscure, a touch orgiastic – I was ashamed of the scenes in which Mr Chaunteyman's image became entangled. They were in a way taboo, involving the *I-Spy Book of the Wild West*, the things in the blue suitcase, and a picture torn from a magazine.

The blue suitcase was not an article of ordinary luggage. When the time came to up-anchor, my proper things were carried in proper containers. The blue suitcase was almost, but not quite, a toy. I could think of no adult use for it: just too small for overnight, just too deep for documents. So it had ended up in my bedroom, where its contents worked my worship. All the more intently since his coming.

And in this climate of mutiny what of my father? On a Saturday he might take me on the free ferry. Around Woolwich Market Square every building was the colour of soot. Then there was a widening, a vista, a dropping-away towards the ferry ramp road. Our bike wheels hammered on the cobbles and shocked across the old tramlines. We rode past the queuing cars and lorries. One of the three ferry boats was always mid-stream, paddling its flat dollop of a hull through the toxic gap between us and the opposite bank. Below the water-line, black; above it, a shade of bright nautical tan, soot-smirched, grease-stained. And the tub had two bridges, was double-ended. Her best features were her two thin smokestacks. They gave her a hint of Mississippi, which must have struck my father particularly.

'Dave Chaunteyman, Ralphie. You get on all right with him, don't you?' We were wheeling our bikes on to the pedestrian section.

'All right.' I thought of my torn-out picture.

'Like one of those smart gamblers, in't he, boy? Like you see on the films.'

'Yeah.' It showed two painted lovers, kissing.

'What they call a handsome sailor, eh?'

'Do they?'

'Now don't give me any of that, you little bugger.'

There must have been something in my face. I had no idea why he was suddenly so protective of the man. We waited for the ferry boat to swing out against the rip, then went below.

'Look at that lot, mate. D'you see?' He always showed me the engines at work turning the paddle wheels. 'Chunky, eh?' Two huge steel rods shoved sideways out of the lower regions. Shaped like the cranks of my bike, though infinitely magnified, oiled and engineered, they looked like silver sea monsters who would at turns rise up and gnaw the drive. The assembly roared and clanked and hissed, and smelt of power.

'Nothing to the big ones, though.'

I looked up at him. 'You're going to be all right, aren't you?'

'All right? I should think so. What d'you mean?'

'Oh, nothing. Just wondering. You wouldn't understand. Come on. We're nearly at the other side.'

Some instruction had been rung down from the bridge. You could see the bells that clanged and the two men stoking in the dark bowels. Sometimes he was like putty in my hands. I knew who Erica was with. I pulled him away from the engines to see the docking procedure and to watch the wooden paddles mill the water into a tainted foam. The smell came up with each blade like a mouthful of salty petrol.

'What do you mean, wouldn't understand?'

'Nothing.'

'Come 'ere, you cheeky little sod. You'll get a clip round the ear.'

I pretended to dodge.

'You and me, Ralphie, eh?' he said. He caught me hard and clutched me to him so that it hurt. 'You and me against the world.'

We rode off to explore the ships in North Woolwich: Victoria Dock, Royal Albert Dock, King George's. Not many in. We were like two seamen prowling the wharves, looking for a berth, ready to sign on for some adventure. 'It's in the blood, Ralph. Handed down. A man can't fight against his own nature.' The rusty hulls towered over us, the rusty cranes towered above them. Hardly anyone was about. I would peer up the gangways to where the silent sailors lived. They gave nothing away.

So my father led me from tanker to tramp along the cobbled

concrete, across the rusty crane tracks. Where we could not cycle, we lifted our bikes over heaped-up anchor chains and the great twists of steel hawser. The water beside us was green–black and scummed at the corners. The artificial terrain of this north shore stretched away to a hinterland of waste called Custom House. And westward now I knew the swinging road bridges were the connection to the East End and up towards the City. It was enemy territory for us over here, deprived, bombed out, desperately poor – my father called it 'cannibal country'.

'Come on then, Ralphie. We'd better go back now before they get wind of us. They'll be after you, all right. They'd fancy getting their teeth into you.'

11

The forms of mutiny are legion. They are a gamut of crimes. After muteness, slowness to respond, and questioning an order, there is insolence. Say, swearing at an officer. But think also of whispering, spreading dissension.

Disputing the navigation is mutinous, so is complaining about treatment and conditions, combination, or circulating written material. Soon we come to the more fundamental notes: conspiracy, violence to superiors, striking sail – in other words, refusing to work. Insurrection, taking up arms, disclosure of secrets, communication with the enemy, incendiarism, murder, rebellion, seizure of the ship – the sequence swells to a crescendo – piracy, egalitarianism, the construction of an alternative and licentious marine economic under iron hand. And the ship is a famous microcosm, naturally; something of a well-tried metaphor. By this token, all crimes by another name are simply mutinies against the nation, which is doing its best for heaven's sake, steering its lawful course.

So let all who sail in her bear in mind mutiny's traditional punishments. They swell in sympathy – beating with a knotted rope's end, caning with a rattan, the cat-o'-nine-tails, confine-ment, irons, gagging, the grampus, the gauntlet, death by flogging, death by hanging, death by drowning, death, death . . .

Like an insistent drumming in the brain. Mutiny and Punishment are the systole and diastole, the Navy's heart-throb.

Before we did the deed Mr Chaunteyman went away for two months. He flew places: he was *off to California in the mo-o-orning*, as they sang on the wireless. 'What d'you want me to bring you, kid?'

I told him I wanted an Indian head-dress – and waited in an ecstasy of yearning. When he came back he brought instead a shrunken head and a three-stage plastic rocket that ran on tap water and compressed air. It was from Disneyland. You pumped it with its own plastic pump, and it would go up three hundred feet. But we had nowhere wide, open or spacious enough to try it out. Whereas in Australia . . . That word was now being breathed secretly between Erica and myself.

He also brought a rubber toad, and a model dinosaur. The hollow shrunken head was female, charcoal black, with long raven hair and a string to hang it up by. 'Hey, Disneyland's just wonderful. One day I'll take you.' And if I had been disappointed at all about the head-dress then my heart leaped up again: after Australia, the world.

My father still said nothing, seemed to suspect nothing. His electrical repairs, however, veered into chaos. As the season closed in he would sit at night as usual with someone's television eviscerated on the back-room table. But in the blaze from the hearth, under the intense glare of his clip-on lamp, he sweated with frustration, and swore wickedly under his breath – because the picture would not hold still, the resonances would not be tuned, there was sound-on-vision, inexplicable ghosts, fireworking valves; even, one torrid winter evening, a cathode-ray tube catastrophe. Not the grand implosion, but a vicious glass scar cracking right down the screen's face as the vacuum gave. And the radios fared no better. Hisses and untraceable dry joints bedevilled them. His storm was micro-electrical.

Though I understood nothing about his circuit diagrams, with their arcane signs and calculations, I felt their significances almost dance in my stomach. The power that ruled the world moved enigmatically – and I had begun to be convinced that by virtue of our enchanting visitor I, like my suitcase, possessed a core of magic deep inside me. The feeling persisted on the *Armorica*, under my seasickness.

Perhaps I had not made myself clear to Mr Chaunteyman. An Indian head-dress – an Indian head. He might have misheard. The head was extraordinary, in its own right. With a a fine nose and shrivelled ears, it had a grisly beauty. I would run my finger down its cheek, then turn it over and peer inside. Its smeared and gluey-brown interior looked quite convincing as skin. It had pride of place in the suitcase. I had read of the Amazon jungles, the South Seas, the Coral Islands, the Typee.

Our leaving had been a sudden stroke, while Dad was at work. I wondered now, to the throbbing wind, why I could recall no agonising, no regret, no attachment. Beyond Mr Chaunteyman I had no emotions. In fact, the more I examined the mental snapshots of home, the more I saw nothing but the dirty tidescapes of the river whose approaches I haunted. Once I had gone with another boy to look at the three-masted schooner that had come in to Greenwich all the way from Norway. Masts and wharves and the masts again of the *Cutty Sark*. We went under the foot tunnel, scared out of our wits that the Teds we had seen on the other bank would come down to meet us half-way. But we emerged unscathed. 'Run away to sea?' my friend said, jokingly. I had blushed. Then we rode back through Charlton along the riverside. What they call Mudlarks. Now my impressions remained of shadow along the wharves, and the astonishing mud laid bare by the tide. Of a filth hanging on to the timber baulks, fascinating, weed-dressed, under a fitful sunset.

We poor sailors have always been good with the needle. We can seam and pocket like invisible menders. Like flatfishes who flounce on to the seabed and take up its imprint, even the shingle's detailed patchwork; we are good at matching appearances, and hiding them.

We sailors have always been the slaves Britons should never be. We sewed up our lips – you would never have known us complain, authentically, officially, of our conditions of service. Murmuring, after all, was mutiny; and punishable. Inarticulate as children, we cried only over food – or grog. And now I, overnight it seemed and with hardly a look back, was glad to be away. My Atlantic was a tantalising enigma, the gateway to

41

something, hiding everything. My father's betrayer, I made myself one with that great ocean – I had become that rarest and most serious of beings: a full-blown mutineer. And with my rebellious magic might yet regulate the forty-foot waves.

12

Joe Dearborn, the man with whom he shared his cabin, called Robert the mad scientist. Joe himself was one of those necessary phenomena who turn up uncannily on cue. If there had been any doubt as to *his* existence, Robert concluded ironically that he would have had to invent him. It was just his luck. Several days into the severe weather Joe was still laid low, but the word about curative teas with strange-sounding names had got about. In his case it was a preparation of the African Zizyphus tree – the original lotus. So the cabin steward claimed, winking at Robert the only hoodwink that was to get past his companion in the duration of the voyage.

'Could you be a mate, Bob, and get them to send me another cup of this stuff? It does wonders. I wish I'd known about it before.'

Their cabin was very small. Robert, as lucky first comer, had secured the top bunk. Viewed from this vantage point it was nothing more, under a low white ceiling, than an assembly of cupboards and drawers faced with hardwood, a mirror, a sink, a porthole, and an angled, rattling door.

'Ah well,' Joe had said. 'Maybe we'll swap half-way.'

The only disadvantage to the arrangement was that whenever he wanted to go to bed to sleep or study, he had to climb a ladder past the wiry, living presence. In his top bunk there was a personal light, and a personal ventilator, and a curtain. But they could not insulate him.

'I can't see how you can do it. Take me, now. I don't mind a good book; in fact, I've been quite a reader in my day. But it really does beat me how you can swot that stuff all the time, Bob. Do you honestly find it interesting, or do you have to force yourself? You do, don't you?'

The trouble was that Joe was nobody's fool, and so his

comments were neither idle, nor ignorant. Effortlessly, good humouredly, they pinned Robert squirming. He had to take his room-mate very seriously, precisely for being so sharp – and such a pervasive force in the cabin, even when he was supine with seasickness. In fact, he *grew* by confinement – because he was always there. Many of Robert's most basic functions had now to be experienced entirely within, so it felt, a Dearborn universe. He radiated outward from his bedclothes in innocent shafts of neighbourliness, bounced from the wooden surfaces, reverberated from the ceiling, mingled with the soft pulse and rattle of the engines, and reeked from certain drawers. It was a complex, wonderful thing. Robert hated it.

Joe had an ivory chess set wedged, open, on the locker top beside his bunk. It was very beautiful, oriental, with one army of combatants stained a bright, Chinese red, as if they were exotic food. It was designed for travelling: the little board contained within the box, and each square walled off with a delicate, carved, and partly padded barrier. So every piece sat always in silk-upholstered luxury. He had got it in Singapore on the way out.

Joe worked for a Kalgoorlie mining concern, and was going home via Perth. He was not Australian, but had been out there so long that he might just as well have been. And he had made good – enough to travel in a degree of style these days, and take his time. 'Need a little bit of a holiday from Mrs Dearborn, Bob. Every couple of years. Not that I don't . . . Ah, but you know how it gets. She's an Aussie, herself, so she doesn't miss the old country. But I do. And catch up with the old folks before they pass away. Little bit of business for the company. I reckon I owe it to myself by now.'

But he was the first person Robert had come across who glossed – or unglossed – the authorised version of emigration. It was a short time after their first meeting, while Joe was still standing. 'Hoping to make a new life for yourself, are you?'

'Yes I am, Joe.'

'Poor sods!' He jerked his thumb backwards to indicate the rear of the ship.

'Who do you mean?' Robert asked.

'The folk in the stern. Packed in like sardines. Have you seen what it's like?'

'No. Are they?'

'You wait till we get into the sunshine. Then you'll see 'em. You can look over the end of the boat deck and see the whole steerage full of broiling Pommy skin, like chicken under a grill. Christ, it hurts your eyes to look at them. They think they're at bloody Blackpool.'

'That's all right, isn't it?'

'Surely. Like our two gentlemanly governments struck a knock-down deal on Leeds and Manchester for a tenner a head. Two would-be lairds over a dram, Bob, what do you reckon: Menzies and Macmillan. "I'll take any number of your Northern Whites, Harold. Any number." "Good show. On the hoof, or carcass?" Or those folk who got bombed out of London and live in those little concrete sheds, what d'you call 'em?'

'Prefabs,' said Robert.

'Yes, those things. Macmillan says, "Take 'em away. At last the invisible solution again." '

'What to?'

'Poverty. Crime. Housing. The whole bloody class. Transportation, Bob. Only you cut out the cost of the irons. What do you think of that?' He chuckled. 'Men, women and children, done to a turn. You'd think they'd know better by now.'

'By now?'

'The poor never learn when they're being done over.'

Robert found himself riled. 'Why are they being done over? It's a good deal, isn't it? They're not stupid.' His own trip was company paid. 'Just because people are working class doesn't mean they're any different from anyone else. I'm working class myself, Joe' – whatever that meant – 'I'm just lucky enough to . . . People think about it, talk about it. They know it's bound to be a bit of a sweat that cheap. No one would expect a luxury cruise for ten quid, would they? Come on. But they're prepared to put up with it for a month or so. Why not? For the chance. For the sake of a new . . . crack of the whip.'

'That's a good one. A new crack of the whip. Do you know anything about Australia, Bob?'

'I've read what I can.'

'Glad to hear it.'

Robert had tried to set himself a schedule of study, intending to put enforced idleness to good use, and to allay his anxieties about the job he was going to. When the voyage was new, before the storm swell began to develop, he divided up his day. He was full of good resolutions. For him, leaving England was supposed to be a cleansing. England felt soiled, fake, and Gothic. He did not know why.

He came clean at coffee one evening. People getting to know each other – sitting casually in little chance groupings under the frosted shell lamps, amid a strange, sea-borne, luxurious smell of coffee and fruit and wood dipped in spice dipped in salt dipped in alcohol. He spoke nervously about himself, possibly a little too loud: of the fake Gothic of the London grammar school he had gone to. Of the genuine Gothic of the Oxford college he had won an exhibition to and eventually joined. Then industry. 'Gothic and square,' he said. 'Like an order at a transport café.' They laughed politely. He did not know how angry he was.

'What's the square?' she wanted to know. Then whispering: 'Do you mean you're a Freemason?' The young woman whose name he now had, Penny Kendrick.

'Oh, God, no. Square and functional. I call it laboratory architecture. And then I'm not sure whether it shouldn't be lavatory architecture.' He blurted the phrase.

A look of disapproval crossed her face. Other heads turned, and then turned away.

'Science has to strip away the decorative, doesn't it? The ornamental. Where I've been working it was all corners and wiring. Can you imagine? Metal chassis – what's the plural? Chassises? Well, those; things with valves in. Wirelesses without the cabinet.' He was relieved to see her smile again. 'And instruments oddly piped together. Half neat and precise; half shambles. Strange, really. I suppose I'm not used to . . . all this.' He indicated the fineness of the ship, was it? Or the sea? Or the ragged, low-bellied clouds brewing out of sight in the dark beyond the windows of the main lounge.

Anyway, as far as he was concerned a pall of post-war vileness had settled over England; much like the pre-war variety, though that was no more than the vague drift of a half-forgotten London childhood now. No, after the war, he had done his national service. 'Barracks? I try not to remember that. Square *in excelsis*. Square even without the wires. Square bash!' And had then gone to university together with older men, some still the returned servicemen, stragglers, showing up out of their experiences.

He had qualified quickly, working hard and barely noticing; and found himself 'in industry', helping to develop, eventually, the new field of radio-telescopy. It was in an enormous, and poisonously drab, factory complex near Hounslow. From the window of his shared laboratory a sad, soaked, unrelieved vista of sub-industrial housing stretched as far as the eye could see. It still looked battle weary. But he did not say this out loud. Nor did he quite acknowledge, even privately, that while the company he worked for ostensibly made radio receivers and recorded the latest pop singers, the project he was involved in was funded by the War Office.

But his feelings on England were untypical among his fellow scientists – who seemed rarely, if ever, to have opinions about anything – and his feelings were now especially untypical on board the *Armorica*. He knew that, at least. And why could he not be generous, or at least patient? He was not willingly subversive.

Later, in his top bunk, Robert found himself plagued by the notion that in his new life he had already made a social gaffe and offended her, them all, by his reference to the lavatory. It was exactly the sort of line that brought screeches of laughter on *Workers' Playtime* or *Midday Music-hall*. It was exactly the smoky, faded smuttiness he wanted to put behind him.

Robert entered the voyage as if it were a novitiate. It was the last thing he would have admitted.

And for the last thing at night his self-imposed rigour required him, from the beginning of the trip, to digest a technical manual they had sent him from Australia relating to the circuitry of the equipment he would be using. It was also designed to protect him from Joe, who seemed by magic in those first days to appear, ready to turn in, just at the same moment as Robert.

From the lower bunk would come: 'OK, I've moved. Your go. Can you make an atom bomb, yet?'

Despite the technical manual, Robert had from the very first found himself engaged in a series of chess games which he

46

began to fear would continue even beyond the journey's end. Maybe even at the tracking station, under the night sky, there would come in, mixed with the abstract hiss and jargon of the stars, Joe's voice from the crackly transmitter of some sheep-run to which he would insist on driving, late and often, 'Pawn to queen's bishop five, Bob.' He had constantly to break off from his reading, or even from composing himself for sleep, peer down from his bunk on to the exquisite board, and bluff out a convincing move.

He must fight back: but that was to enter a kind of strategic meta-chess. And even as Robert began to plot tactics, Joe went down with seasickness.

'I really appreciate this, Bob. It really helps take my mind off feeling so rough. Jeez, I envy blokes who can call themselves good sailors. I'll be all right in the Med, mind. It was the same in that bloody troop-ship when I was in the Army. Anyway, Nelson was always crook when he first put to sea, so I hear. Are you sure you want to move there; you're just walking into big trouble? The big trouble with you, Bob, is your mind's not on the job. Come on. Three more moves and we'll call it lights out. Fair goes?'

13

The ship's struggle with the Atlantic grew into a fact of life, and Robert's studious good intentions gave way to the effort of keeping his stomach and his spirit from exchanging acids.

There are different kinds of seasickness, and different ways of dealing with them. Only one is to lie down. As he had already explained to Penny, Robert saw the enormous seas as England's long reach of spite. His contest with Joe, laid out on his bunk, felt pointless and irritating; but his battle with England was full of purpose. And so he would haunt the decks as long as the cold permitted. He had only the faintest notion that the possibility of happening upon Penny again was an underlying motive. They found themselves in no new friendly exchanges, though when they did meet they would smile, and nod, and briefly remark.

Perhaps it was fortunate, then, that he did not see her come out of one of the bathrooms on B deck on the second night of the storm. It was about nine-thirty. I was waiting outside in pyjamas and revolver. She almost crashed into me as the ship swung. She was unsteady on her feet, and unsteady in herself. I could see that. I had no idea who she was. She looked dreadful, pale, red-eyed, lank-haired. I stared at her. She passed me and then stalled as the floor rose.

'Sorry,' she muttered, her hand against her back, moving on down the corridor as soon as the angle allowed. Then she disappeared into a cabin I presumed her own.

Robert was on the deck above, in the small starboard bar quaintly called the Verandah – one they were keeping open. He was talking to a good-looking man who was always there. Or rather the man was talking to him, or to anyone. Dinner-suited, he had an accent and appearance that seemed BBC with a dash of receding fighter pilot. He was very drunk.

'So when all's said and done, what d'you think of the field?' He swilled the brandy round in his glass.

'Sorry?'

'Totty. Seen anything you fancy? Quite a line-up from what I can make out. Members' enclosure. Should be a good trip.'

'Oh, I see.'

'Starched petticoats. Now there's a thought, eh? Starched petticoats. Your turn.'

Robert made his way across the drunken floor and clung soberly to the bar.

'God,' he said.

Protectively the barman handed him two brandies.

When he returned, his table-mate grunted confidentially. 'Time and place, old chap. Not yet. Too rough. But just wait for the Tropics. They go mad. Can't get enough of it. Got to build ourselves up, eh? They go mad. English women, eh? Eh?' His eyes closed. He slumped back in the chair. Robert watched the glass he had just signed for slip from the man's hand, empty itself over his trousers and fall on to the carpet. The ship rolled it casually against the far partition, where it smashed.

'Don't worry, sir,' the bar steward called. 'Everything under control. It's when the chairs go you've got to start worrying.

Notorious this ship, but don't let on I said so. Jumps about like a porpoise as soon as the wind blows. Mind you, this is a blow and a half and no mistake. But we learned our lesson a couple of years ago coming home.'

'How was that?' Robert struggled back to the bar rail and took hold of it again.

'Shouldn't really tell you this. It was here in the Bay, but all the other way round, if you see what I mean. We were caught by a following sea and had to lay ourselves across it.'

'To miss Brittany?'

'Exactly, sir. To miss Brittany. Armorica, so I'm told. The olden name.'

'Really? I didn't know.'

'The company's old route, sir. Started last century, running grain and guns to our various southern allies. Long tradition at sea. Trading nation.' He winked at Robert and touched his nose. 'We'll carry anything. Every ship's got a memory.'

'You were going to tell me . . . ?'

'Oh, yes. Following sea; we got across it. Wallowing about like a whale, she was. The water came over the stern – the cabins in tourist class go right down under the water-line. They have an F deck, you know, and the stern's like open balconies anyway. To give a bit of light and space. Did you know that? Very nice. But not funny when half the herring pond jumps in on you. And up here in the first class main lounge,' he gestured in that direction, 'the piano broke loose and went for a run. Caught a passenger against one of the pillars.'

'Was he killed?'

'Not quite. We dug him out from under a pile of tables and chairs.'

'They were there with the piano?'

'Exactly. Arrived simultaneously. But we learned our lesson. Four hundred items of furniture smashed, to say nothing of the glass and crockery. Passengers screaming and panicking. So we don't think too much about it now. Plenty more where that came from.'

'Furniture?'

'Exactly. Or whatever you like. We keep calm, they keep calm. She may have the lines of a goddess, but she can be a hysterical cow sometimes, the *Armorica*. Don't tell anyone I told you.' He touched the side of his nose again. 'There was one time as well when she developed a list to starboard. It wasn't heavy weather or anything. Up goes the captain. "Those stabilisers got out of line? Let's have 'em in. Switch off the gyros, please, Number One." They're all ex-RN, see. So off goes the gyros and in come the fins, and slowly, very slowly,' he matched his gesture to the inclination of the ship, 'the bloody thing starts to list a bit more. Then a bit more. Then a bit more.' He chuckled and eyed Robert's dormant drinking companion.

'And then?'

'He stuck the fins back out pretty sharpish.' He polished a glass. 'Heavy on fuel. She's a seven-day ship. Her sisters are nine. It's the liquid ballast. The more she uses up the lighter she gets. And the sillier. Now, I have it on good authority from someone who was there . . .'

'On the bridge?'

'. . . On the bridge; that the old man said it was only the fins keeping her from rolling right over.'

'Turning turtle?'

'Exactly.'

'They're not out at the moment.'

'No. Can't have them out at the moment. Too rough. They'd break off. Can I help you, sir?' He moved away to attend to someone else who was fortifying himself against the night, leaving Robert to ponder further the differences between a ship at sea and a brochure on dry land.

But everyone has to sleep sometime. The trouble was, Robert only needed to enter the cabin to switch Joe on, no matter how ill he was claiming to be. It was as though there were a transistor in the door handle.

'Ah, there you are, Bob. I think I've got an interesting little dilemma for your knight here.' And: 'There are heaps of folks about, Bob, who think the Japanese will never be able to make a really good camera. See this?' He held up a twin-lens reflex he was cradling in his bedclothes. 'Singapore. Fifteen quid. Professional goods, would you believe. Hold still, I'll take your picture.'

'How can I hold still?' Robert demanded, petulantly.

'Bloke I knew said it would fall to pieces. Watch the birdie, say I, Bob. Tell me mate, were you ever married?'

'No, Joe. I'm afraid I haven't had that good fortune yet.' It was Joe's sheer accuracy that Robert found so difficult. Joe was concerned about him. He was a fellow traveller, and wanted to be.

'There's one or two interesting women on board, that's for sure.'

How did he know? Robert wondered. He had hardly been out of his bunk.

'You know they test the bomb in Australia, don't you, Bob? They'll test anything there.'

Robert said, 'Do you think we'll see sharks?'

'You won't see any sharks on this cruise, mate. Take my word. Not unless someone lets blood. Takes a good old-fashioned naval action to get the sharks interested. Now in the Pacific . . .' Joe gave a grim laugh. 'Nah,' he said. 'It's all right. I was never in the Pacific.'

Robert believed in the deterrent.

He said the next morning, 'It's not that I don't admire the Bertrand Russells, the Canon Collinses of this world.'

'What? *The* Bertrand Russell? The philosopher? What's he been doing?'

'The Ban the Bomb marches. They march to Aldermaston and so on. Where they make the . . . well, I don't know which part of the bombs or what exactly they do make there, because it's so secret . . .' He felt it was his business to know but not to disclose – but then he really had been told nothing. The industry was compartmentalised, its units sealed, the best form of secrecy. The left hand never knew what all the other left hands were doing.

'Aldermaston! I was brought up in Tadley. What's all this about Aldermaston?'

'I don't even know where it is, to tell the truth. I only know they march there, the Aldermaston marchers.' And suddenly, at the newspaper picture in his mind of the young people of his own generation with their duffle-coats and courage, becoming friends, lovers even, he was moved and sad. 'Those are the headlines; and the newsreel pictures. Nobody mentions where it is, as such. They assume it's common knowledge – which of course it is. Even signposted; though not in big lettering: "This way to the nuclear . . ." Well, of course not. Reading way, isn't it?'

'Course it bloody is! Bloody Reading way. Here's me down under for the best part of my life, Bob, having to tell *you* where Aldermaston is. But now you're telling me that's where they make them. How long's that been going on? I thought it was Cumberland or somewhere safely in the wilds. Just turn your back and they're at it. That was down the road from us when I was a nipper, Alder-bloody-maston.'

Robert wanted to justify himself; to show that he was not just another white-coated yes-man who rattled along doing very nicely on government research, while washing his hands of the ethics. He did question. He did feel enormous reservations about, yes, England again. England at the root of it all, almost. Bloody-handed, clever England. He wanted to shout, 'I've read Spengler and Marx! I play the piano!' But he would merely have made himself ridiculous.

'The Russians are stockpiling nuclear weapons. What's the alternative? Human nature, I suppose; that's at the root of it all. No one can afford to back down. Nobody likes it, but nobody wants the world to be incinerated. Blown to smithereens. I don't. What's the alternative, Joe, once two sides have got the damn things?'

Joe churned in the lower bunk and asked him to fetch the basin again. Robert got down and did so.

'Don't ask me, mate. I'm just one of the poor bloody infantry.' He retched uselessly and painfully over the bowl. 'In Australia it's a different matter, anyway. How would you like fall-out clouds drifting over your back yard? My bloody back yard. They do, you know. Or did. Drift. Maybe your papers don't run those headlines. Don't want to know. They wouldn't care, would they? Of course they wouldn't. Whack! The black cloud. Whack! That island up the coast from Perth, Monty-something. Whack! Maralinga. No risk at all. No risk to Westminster, more like. It just happens to be right where we live. And quite a lot of us don't like it, no matter for Bob bloody Menzies.'

So Robert was left tarred as an apologist for the arms-race lunacy; even by this voyage going out to further it.

The steward knocked and came in with Joe's tea.

'Thanks, old sport.' Joe fished for a coin on the locker top beside him and handed it over. 'Out of hours, mate. Appreciate it.'

'Thank you very much, sir.' The steward left.

'Good bloke, that.'

Joe's forearm appeared to be tattooed, so that the finish of something mostly covered by pyjama sleeve and dressing-gown cuff could be seen on his wrist. Robert wondered idly what it was of.

'Sailors!' Joe gave a laugh. 'Trouser pirates. Couple of pulls of merchant seaman we used to ask for at the bar, just to wind the poor joker up.'

'Oh,' said Robert.

'It's your move.'

14

At last there came a time when the *Armorica* turned her back to the wind, and Robert could anticipate the Med. Now, on the way in, the acute flexing of seascape seemed so mundane as to be beyond comment. Everyone had grown used to the bad weather. They had all worked out ways of shortening sail, as it were. It had become routine to cross even the smallest interior spaces as if at one minute you were scaling Everest, and the next leaping off.

The wind eased. On the unabated swell they were running eastwards now, level with Gibraltar. The creaking and groaning sounds lessened slightly, and the following motion was different: longer, less aggressive. He had begun to find exhilarating the sudden compression of the ship's lifts, and the remarkable weight loss next, by which he could cross the assembly area in only four or five strides. As the children did. Indeed, he felt like a boy again, and looked gingerly around to check that no one had seen the excitement on his face, and, once, when the space was momentarily empty one morning, the wheeling of his arms.

A link with Penny had forged. Imperceptibly, out of nothing, amid all these fantastical comings and goings it had taken shape. He knew it. She must know it. They had flashed signals in each other's eyes. Surely they had. She kept appearing in his thoughts, would not be displaced. He imagined the entwining of her legs. She was a mermaid.

'We'll be docking at Gibraltar only to refuel, I'm afraid, ladies and gentlemen.' The Chief Officer made the announcement. 'And that'll be tonight. As you'll all be aware, the conditions have been somewhat exceptional, we don't mind saying so, even us toughened old salts.' He laughed. 'We don't often find ourselves in forty- or fifty-foot seas on this run. More like Cape Horn, to be honest.' He grinned again at the few people gathered round the board marking the mileage of the ship's daily run.

So at least they were admitting it, Robert thought. Once he grasped that they had weathered a storm which the crew also had struggled to cope with, then the large number of breakages, the several days of slips and spills and sliding became indexes of their courage, rather than of their own mere landlubberliness. He recalled his conversation with the steward of the Verandah bar. And felt better about it. In all probability the *Armorica* would not turn over now, for all the extra demands that had been made on her tanks. They would make it.

The Chief Officer continued. 'To be perfectly frank I don't recommend Gib in both the middle of winter and the middle of the night.' The small group, which included Penny, responded with a polite chuckle, while the deck moved under them as usual. 'We've lost several days, you see, and shall have to make up for lost time. As to disembarking procedure . . .'

But Robert's attention became diverted because Penny spoke separately in an undertone to her neighbour. 'Not so long ago I'd have given almost anything to set foot on dry land, but if it's just during the small hours, I don't see the point either. Do you? It would just be nothing at all.'

'We shan't be going,' the neighbour replied, a woman called Mrs Burns who had once, with her husband, shared Robert's table for dinner. Since the storm, she had been absent. He suspected she had been able to eat nothing at all.

'It would be like, I don't know, Eastbourne in the blackout springs to mind,' Penny said. 'I think I'll concentrate on a good night's sleep. Picking up the pieces almost. I just hope my violin's safe; hasn't broken loose, or been crushed by some huge thing that has. I wish there was some way I could look.'

'Oh? Do you play?'

'Less than I'd like to, what with my young family. It was possibly going to be a career, but I've had to give up all that. Probably wouldn't have come off. Still . . .'

Robert made himself turn away. He went off through the double doors to get a Scotch, and resolved to resume his schedule of work, swell or no swell, Joe or no Joe. And anyway, Joe was up now, and going about his business.

In the main lounge there was a large decorative mural showing what had been explained as an Armorican scene. A party of lords and ladies in medieval costume looked at the sea from the rocky coast of Brittany. A sailing cog ploughed the distance. The painted waves, with their tender, painted crests, looked all too easy. It was a naïve offering.

Allowing himself to be swept towards the other end, he braced himself against a pillar, and then sat down on the piano stool. He opened the keyboard, rested his fingers idly on the keys, but did not press them down. From a nearby table, three older ladies, heavy with pearls and in severe grey perms almost identically decayed, dared him to play. Duly annoyed, he moved off again.

She was a mermaid, of course, and he would probably make a fool of himself, as he had done some years before. The signs were the same. It was the close, tempting fit of mutual attraction within a cluster of people all getting to know one another. And surely, surely there *was* some indefinable link between them, in the air. But it went together with the absolute *impossibility* of their clashing circumstances. The more he discovered about her, the more he was drawn to think of her. The more he learned about her world, the less it offered any firm ground where they could meet.

Yet here they were, in the same bewitched boat. Why should it be that when there were plenty of ordinary, nice, pretty women about the towns and cities of England, he must eschew them? He supposed there must be some cause; but did not wish to discover in detail what grubby quirk it might turn out to be. Probably to do with a nasty-minded God, and better left untouched. He would study. He must just take care not to ruin everything, the whole future. Four weeks or so of the high seas, then Adelaide and up to Woomera, a corner of untillable soil

named after the aboriginal word for a spear-thrower, because
the military used it to launch guided missiles into the very
centre. To see how well they worked; how well the tactical armaments of the deterrent might deter. There he would attend the
tracking station, looking up at the stars with radio equipment,
tracking . . . who knew what exactly? And on this basis he would
build a new life for himself, a better life than the grubby, rainy,
pompous, clapped-out little island of his birth could offer.

Scotch in hand, he stood outdoors from the bar on the
promenade deck with his back to its cold steel wall, looking out
as he had grown so accustomed to. The interminable ridges
stretched off into the north, grown oily, now, under a darkening
afternoon sky. Penny Kendrick swam in them, holding her
beautiful violin in front of her breasts and slinking her hips to
the deep like a wild sonata. Sharks swam with her, nuzzling her
side, rasping her lovely belly with their sandpaper skin. 'Damn!'
he said aloud. 'Damn!'

15

The Med had an altogether different feel to the Atlantic; it
flattened as it warmed. One day, morning was open like a dish,
a glazed Greek wine bowl, and as shallow. Though this was
midwinter, Penny had the strong sense that not so very far away
– maybe just out of view on either side – coastal people were
sitting out, drinking coffee, eating olives.

Past Crete the light hardened and clarified. The sun became
an active agent. It was as if the cord in a slatted blind above
them had been pulled. She found herself unprepared, having
cast her predictions of the voyage according to the south coast
of England – not her own childhood, but seaside holidays in
Devon with Hugh after the war, and with the boys, when they
came along. She had expected blue: the air was white, the sea
very dark, and reflective as broken glass.

Clutching her straw bag, in which she had placed, on top of
a thin layer of odds and ends already there, her compact, her
great aunt's pince-nez, a French edition of de Beauvoir's
Memoirs of a Dutiful Daughter, her journal, her cigarettes, and

her pen, she made her way to the forward saloon, the observation lounge.

High nautical windows set tightly together in a continuous strip wrapped right round from port to starboard. Sitting close to them, where the chairs were laid out together, Penny could look down over the nursery and the enclosed play-deck area for little ones, on to the whole of the bright foredeck beneath her.

Once the storm had passed its height two or three days before, and she had learned that they might not all die but could endure sitting down to consider the next hour as well as the next wave, she had found the prospect far brighter here. More recently she had come to read, or write, or simply to watch the nose dipping and rising, gently enough now, as it stitched through sky to horizon, and back, and back again. It was quite hypnotic. Pure light poured in from the sky, and whelmed up from the water surfaces. It was like being inside the faceted eye of some fabulous ocean-going insect, homing to Arabia.

There was an Australian couple who had decided to take her under their wing: Clodagh and Russell Coote. 'Penny. How *are* you this morning?' Standing at the bar, drinks in hand, they were looking for where they should place themselves. 'Let me get you something,' Russell asked.

'Coffee would be lovely,' said Penny. 'Russell, thank you. Are you sure it's not my turn?'

'Nonsense.' Russell nodded to the barman. The Cootes were both tall and fine-featured. Clodagh tended to fragility. She wore a belted dress, white, with a print of large flowers – the sort of casual success which cheap fashions tried to imitate, achieving only cheapness. Penny was slightly in awe of them both, and wished to resist the feeling, but was unable to find any means of doing so. She was intrigued by them. The power of other people: her reading of de Beauvoir had amazed her, stirring up forbidden political emotions. She had not yet quite perceived herself as a dutiful daughter. With the assured couples around her, she thought constantly of everything she was leaving behind.

There had been a ballroom evening the previous night. Russell Coote had offered to dance with her. It was the first time the sea had settled down enough for social functions even to be thought of. Russell's immediate gesture, and the execution, were displays of an old-world gallantry she had never come across. He danced out of duty; his wife expected of him that he should ask a woman travelling alone to partner him and to join them at their table. He expected it of himself.

The two wives had shared him all evening. It was utterly chaste, the sort of manners one always thought of as English but, to be strictly honest, never found in England. At any rate not these days, she could hear her mother saying. Not since the war. Only in older men, Penny, for all one tries.

Her mother always romanticised the past. Here were manners from the new world. One would have said simply 'public school', except that was virtually synonymous with first class anyway, and not everyone had offered to dance with her. Besides, that phrase in a man meant all sorts of English things, like mud and dogs and father and teas and tears, and the smell of certain rooms and days, special words rooting back into a coterie that was home. There could be nothing like that anywhere else. Russell certainly lacked any such connection. He was perhaps in his late thirties. His family owned a grain-exporting concern in Victoria, he had said; they lived in the suburbs of Melbourne.

'Let's go and sit down.' Clodagh steered Penny towards the view. 'Russell can bring your coffee over.'

The accent was detectable, the intonation somewhat languid and cultured. Never having met any Australians, never having heard Australian speech – beyond a few newsreel fragments and one or two well-known radio voices – Penny still found herself perplexed by these faintly altered vowels. Penny almost 'Pinny', though not quite.

Her mother, owning the little prep school, had always laid great stress on the maintenance of vowels. She was a righteous, bitter woman. Nevertheless, Penny found it hard to believe that her future life would be among these people. She realised that this subject of accent, though it should have been appropriately trivial, was quite out of the question for polite small talk. She wanted to ask Clodagh Coote how she could make those sounds; but it would have been as unthinkable as commenting upon her name.

Yes, it seemed a very trivial matter – she knew it was – but it preoccupied her, and distanced her both from her own folk and from the Cootes. As if they belonged, Russell and Clodagh, in an unexpected and partly botanical oil painting.

She placed her bag and other materials beside the lounger-chair, and hoisted herself in via the sloping footstool.

'Well, we shan't see any more of that, thank goodness.' Clodagh waved dismissively at the sea as if it still contained the imprint of forty-foot waves. 'Penny, I can't tell you how bad I am at motion. I was completely wretched, wasn't I, Russell?'

'Oh, absolutely wretched, Penny.' Russell placed her coffee on the small, fixed table in front of them and slid into a chair himself. 'Clodagh wasn't cut out to be a sailor, I'm afraid. She'll be very glad to get it all over. She's longing to find herself back at home and on dry land.'

And churches, Penny thought. Until the young man had mentioned them, she had been unable to put her finger on what precisely it was she would miss. Home, England, was churches; quiet, grey guardians of the past, set like kindly and unalterable waymarks in a network of villages and towns. Why, you could virtually navigate in some parts of England by the spires and church towers. It was almost magical.

A girl of about ten came into the lounge and stood beside Clodagh's chair. She was neat and perhaps a touch overdressed for the warm morning, in a check woollen dress with a collar. Her hair was dark, unlike Clodagh's, and secured in two careful plaits.

'Mummy, I told Mitchell he had to take me with him, but he just went off with the others.'

Clodagh put her glass down and turned to her daughter. 'Which other children, dear?'

'It's those two boys from the deck beneath ours and another one. They're all going to play ping-pong and they said they didn't need me.'

'I'm sure there's something else you could do?' She adjusted the girl's collar.

Russell said, 'Go and tell him, Finlay, that he's got to let you play and that's all there is to it. Go along, now.'

'But they don't want me around. They say I don't know how to hit the ball.'

'Tell Mitchell he's supposed to be looking after you. He knows that.'

Finlay left uncertainly. Clodagh leaned back in her chair with a faint gesture of exhaustion. 'It's really wonderful for children, a voyage. There's so much for them to do, and see. It's very educational.'

Penny, still mildly disoriented by the names she had just heard, replied, 'Oh, yes,' and thought of Peter and Christopher.

An older man, another Australian – some sort of businessman, she believed – sat down beside Russell and drew his attention. She found herself watching, for a moment, the slight tip and fall of her coffee in the cup on the table.

Clodagh said, 'They are a constant anxiety. One just doesn't realise how much, until they come along. I quite envy someone in your position. But then of course they do have their compensations, I suppose.'

'In my position?' Penny said. Then she realised. 'But I do have children. Two boys.'

'Oh, I'm so sorry, Penny. I had no idea. You didn't seem . . . Oh, that's lovely. Are they already in Adelaide . . . with your husband, then?'

'No. They're in England. Peter's the older one, he's about Finlay's age; and Christopher is six. They're with my mother.' Penny felt exposed, though she had no reason to be. 'Hugh, my husband, wanted me to join him out there as soon as I could, after it was settled that the move was for good. At least for the foreseeable . . . The boys can come out later, when the school term's finished, probably. When everything's settled and there's a home for them to go to. They'll fly out. They'll like that. I'm with the furniture, you see.' She smiled. 'That's why I'm going by sea. Apart from the experience itself, of course. Hugh thought I'd enjoy it. It would relax me . . . And the firm were paying. So why not, we thought?'

'Oh, yes,' said Clodagh. There was a pause. 'Why not, indeed, Penny. So pleasant last night, wasn't it? We were so pleased to have your company. Russell's quite a good dancer, isn't he; though I shouldn't say so.'

'Certainly. Yes, he is.'

'I do like to dance.' Clodagh sipped her drink and gazed out through the panoramic glass at the drench of Mediterranean light. 'But I find it tires me.'

Seasickness, homesickness – are they not just labels for what no two people experience in quite the same way, as the stomach rises to the heart? What to do about tears? Looking firmly ahead at the view through the window, she felt in her bag beside the chair for a handkerchief, then pretended to be dabbing her brow and cheeks. And then she swallowed nearly everything back down again behind her coffee cup. Why had she been so uncharacteristically weepy the last two days? It seemed more than the situation called for. And, of course, she was relieved, actually, to be getting away from her mother at last.

'Excuse me one moment.' She pretended she needed to check their position.

In this saloon, in a special glass-topped desk, set in the exact centre of the windows' curve, a new white chart was clipped each morning. Penny allowed her eye to roam over it. Yes, she would not cry now. Coloured pins recorded their progress. She could recognise, in large type, Greece, and the thin, eaten slab of Crete. Jerusalem surprised her. She had never taken much notice of geography. The Holy Land, for example, had not been represented to her at school as a country in relation to others, but as a place in itself, a sort of first draft for the Home Counties.

She leaned forward to get a better view. She was surprised to see their route pointed at a corner of it. But there next to it of course was the Suez Canal, and that would imply Egypt. And of course in the Bible they were always swerving down into Egypt, for one reason or another – famine, the sword, tax, or tax avoidance, that sort of thing. The thought was in bad taste, she knew; but it had come to mind. Like the moment at which Robert Kettle had said 'lavatory', and people had changed the subject.

Repressing a smile: 'I'm so ignorant about where countries are.' Then another thought struck her. 'I suppose you really only find out by going there, don't you?' She said it out loud, now quite composed as she resumed her seat.

'I suppose you do,' said Clodagh. 'The Canal is vile. Take my word for it. Russell and I shan't be going ashore at Port Said.' She looked across at her husband, and then turned back. 'I wonder have you seen that extraordinary woman? My dear, so frail she can hardly walk. I mean the woman who appeared in the dining-room the other evening. I've seen her on one or two other occasions as well. I mean the woman who's excessively thin.'

'No. I'm afraid I haven't,' Penny said.

'I couldn't quite believe it at first when I saw her. Really no more than a skeleton in a dress. I didn't know what to imagine. She looked . . . I don't know . . . like someone who'd just come out of a POW camp.'

The conversation lapsed. Penny worked at her coffee, adding a little more sugar, and sipping, with the saucer under the cup in case the gentle swell should catch her out and ruin her skirt. She sensed from the corner of her eye Clodagh tucking the stray wisps of her ash-toned hair back behind her ears. Penny said, 'I'd like to know what to expect.'

She turned round involuntarily to look behind her, and found herself staring at Robert Kettle who was standing at the bar. They both looked away immediately. Penny realised with a start that she had completely forgotten having danced once with him last night.

16

Much later the same morning, Penny was sitting in a different chair, reading – with her book in the lap of her slick, grey worsted skirt and her pince-nez on her nose – when Finlay Coote came in.

'Have you seen either my mummy or my daddy?'

'They left to do some shopping, Finlay. I think they've gone to buy a film for their camera, and maybe Mummy would look for some new sunglasses. Or have you tried the cabin?'

'There's a giant squid. We've seen a giant squid. I want them to come and see. Over the side. What have you got on your nose?'

'They're my glasses, Finlay. They belonged to my great-aunt.' It suddenly occurred to Penny that the Cootes' declaration of a little desultory shopping might have been merely a cover. They had exchanged looks. A form of words to screen the fact that they were taking advantage of the children's daylight absence from their four-berth cabin. She pictured with horror little

Finlay opening her parents' cabin door to find Russell's half-clothed body working at Clodagh's flare of floral print across one of the bunks. Incomprehensible. The girl would be terrified. And it would all be Penny's fault.

Shocked at the violence of her own imagination, she spoke stupidly to the child. 'I wear them to scare people away and make me look like an old woman. My boys say I look like a granny. Do you want to try them?'

'You don't scare me,' said the girl, trying the glasses on her nose, torn between the fascination of looking through them, and the urgency of her story. 'Which deck's the shop on again, please, Penny?' She tried out the familiarity of a name.

Penny put the pince-nez on the arm of her chair. She could not but tell her. So Finlay slipped off after her parents. In any case they would be very foolish not to lock the cabin door; and, when she came to think of it, Clodagh was so ethereal and Russell so proper that the couple's relations had probably been suspended entirely for the duration – that film and sunglasses were devices in no way rhetorical. If indeed their children had not been immaculately conceived in the first place.

The news of the squid had stirred the occupants of the observation lounge. They were hastily finishing their coffee and tea, their Scotch, their old crosswords, and were fading off towards the decks in hope of viewing the monster. Penny found herself on the starboard part of A deck, where she had first encountered Robert. Nothing out of the ordinary. Except the sea had completely changed colour. It was a rich, nearly opaque green, tinged with pink, underslung with sienna. She looked towards the stern. The pink could be seen tapering to a bright streak behind them in the blue-black – where the wake severed it.

There was no question, now, but that the ship was moving past a cable of coloured water thicker than any creature's limb. Yet she could reconstruct how the children, standing on the white bars and looking down over the rail as they liked to do at the sheer of the bow wave, might have caught sight of the change and mistaken it for a long tentacle. And then from their desire of miracles created the squid. After all, they had already seen dolphins, and come in yesterday with a shark alert.

But what was happening? How *should* the sea acquire this

strange submerged patina? It was nothing to her; and yet she was frightened for a moment. She adjusted the straw bag over her shoulder on its long strap. The sun glittered off the water into her face. Further aft along the rail she saw Mrs Madeley, and moved to join her.

'Apparently, so Douglas says, we're entering the outfall of the Nile,' Mrs Madeley explained. Penny stared out ahead, but could see no land yet.

'This far out?' she said.

'Apparently. So Douglas tells me. He knows about these things.'

Now the colour below them had all but faded out, and they were reassured; until, yes, after a minute or two another seeming rope of rich underwater mud writhed past.

'It's rather wonderful, isn't it?' said Penny. 'We're miles out and the river still hasn't got mixed up with the sea.'

'I suppose so,' Mrs Madeley said.

Poor soul, Penny thought. She sensed Mrs Madeley's imprisonment in her pleated frock. She wanted to bring her out of herself.

'It's wonderful, really. If you told people the oddness of the sea they wouldn't believe you. It's like nothing one's known. Hard for us to believe, don't you think? We're quite lucky, to see such things.'

Mrs Madeley nodded.

Penny continued, 'It's like a holiday. Suspended time. We're floating. Well, of course we are.' She laughed, childish and light-headed.

Mrs Madeley looked at her uncertainly, and then back at the lovely, indescribable surface of the water. They stood side by side, seeing at last beyond England. And when she thought that she might have meant a holiday from Hugh, and that the journey's end would involve a resumption of their intimacy, and the restriction of her relaxing vision, with all its newness of colour and space, the deliciousness, the complexity, the ambiguity of a Tropic zone which heralded itself with streamers of pink, brown, incredible, confusing, frightening mud, she shut and locked the door on that too, and thought: This is merely the passageway to Australia, and Australia has colours and newness of her own.

And so the squid proved not to be itself at all. Still, who was to say positively there was no real squid, unthinkably giant, fathoms beneath the keel. It might have swum there, keeping pace, keeping an eye. On the impressionable deep it writes its absence with an ink jet. It prints and is gone – thankfully – *Architeuthis*, the ship-biter of legend. The sea, that is most of the planet, is unexplored. Only its fools have been dredged up. Who then but the very rash would expect no awkward surprises?

Off Alexandria the sea was really quite thick with mud. Robert watched it from the boat deck. He had Penny's crazy spectacles in his pocket and no idea where she was. She had thrown her book into her shoulder-bag and gone off to look for the squid. But from which deck? Now he had not seen her for some hours. She had not been at lunch – maybe had not felt like the formal thing but opted for a buffet, or a sandwich.

How much less complicated it would be if Penny Kendrick were not on board, were not married, older than he was, experienced, and the mother of two boys. It would be much less complicated if he did not have her pince-nez in his pocket, and the need to explain why he had kept it for so long, now, rather than handing it in to the Chief Officer, or the cheery quartermaster, to give to her in her cabin. But then there was no reason why he should not wish to give it to her himself. People could simply deal with these matters, without having to go through minor officialdom. People could make a friendly gesture.

It was, of course, no more than that.

Now they were off Alexandria and he had Penny's spectacles in his pocket. Narrowly avoiding Joe, he had come to the boats to see if by any chance she might be there. He paused under the towering yellow smokestack. It was deceptive up here. You climbed to gain a high station as if for an overview. But the vision was limited, completely blocked forward by the super-structure of the bridge, and interrupted to the side by the lines of boats.

He stood between two of them and surveyed as much as he could of the promenade decking below, hoping foolishly he might catch a glimpse of her. Behind him there were little shrieks, snatches of laughter, and shouts as two Air Force couples finished a mixed doubles of deck tennis. There were a number of relocating service families on board, officers with their capable wives, confident sons and daughters, acting as though America and Russia, poised to boil each other's oceans, did not actually exist.

Further away still, in the far corner, a group of five young men, all about the same age, and all wearing jumpers and exercise slops, were sprawled on the deck space amid a collection of bottles and glasses, mostly empty. He knew their nickname, but not its reason: they were 'Barnwell's aircrew'. It was some phrase that had been passed about, relating somehow to a grey-haired gentleman who went by that name.

But Robert had no knowledge as to whether or not there really was any connection. It seemed unlikely. They were a joke; or an annoyance. Since coming aboard at Gibraltar they appeared always in training, or horseplay. Their loud comments were usually at variance with the general tone of the first class. And just now while they were moderately subdued he was careful not to attract their attentions. He found someone at his elbow.

'Hullo, Bobby, sweetheart.' It was Mrs Torboys.

17

The family were new arrivals: 'Just call me Cheryl. I do so hate the stuffy English thing they have on these liners. We came up to Lisbon from Durban on a Portuguese boat and it was so relaxed and informal. They just adored the children.' Cheryl Torboys had a drink in her hand, the kind she liked best. 'It's called a pussyfoot. Can't think why, can you? I get them to spike it with vodka.' She stood beside him, generous and corseted, in her pleated sailor-suit frock, wide hat, and heeled espadrilles.

The Torboys family fitted in very well. Lucas, the husband, was jovial and outgoing, a slightly bald, rugged-faced man of about forty-five. Their girl and two boys injected the games of the ship's children with new and noisier possibilities. And

Cheryl, too, enjoyed getting things going. It was like a postcard, bright, glossy, cheeky sometimes; they broke down barriers.

'Cheryl. How are you feeling?'

Cheryl patted her abdomen just below the belt. 'How are you down there in the engine-room, darling? You can tell Uncle Bobby. We're not feeling too bad today, actually, dear.' The fade of the final 'g' on some of her words was a colonial marker. Robert had noticed it in one or two other people before. It set her apart from the received speech of England without denoting her precisely as South African, or Australian, or Rhodesian, or anything, really.

And perhaps that was it, Robert thought, working it out. They were joining the route at Gibraltar, and leaving – yes, how curiously apt – at Singapore; as if Cheryl's world were English but permanently uprooted, and she must wander the intemperate climes.

'What a relief to be warm in the sunshine at last.' She swigged back her thick, blackberry-coloured drink, and held the swizzle stick for Robert to eat the cherry and orange pieces. 'Naughty boy,' she said, laughing and licking her lips.

Robert liked her unconventional talk. He liked to be called sweetheart to his face. Her breath of alcohol, lipstick, and sexual candour was like his first hint of escape.

'We're quite the wild colonials, Lucas and I. You people at home don't know half the story. But he always forgives me. I think it's the sun. I love the sun. We had such parties in Pietsdorp – that was the name of our country house. We used to go up weekends from Jo'burg. It was so beautiful, lying out under the stars. I love it in the open air, nothing between you and the veldt, if you know what I mean. You do, don't you? Rogue.'

Robert lit a cigarette and exhaled through his nose.

'I shall have to take you in hand, Bobby. I can see that.' She raised her eyebrows extravagantly. 'Now don't get any ideas. Too much going on for that. Too bloody much going on. How are you?' She caught his eye knowingly.

Knowing what? Robert wondered. Knowing men looked at the top of the cleft between her breasts? It almost winked at him from inside the loose white lapels with their navy stripe, and was set off by a string of round, jet beads. He had Penny's spectacles in his top pocket.

'Oh, I'm fine.'

'Come on. Let's see where we've been.' She led him towards the back of the boat deck.

'Why?' said Robert.

'Safer to live in the past, darling.' They strolled slowly on the scrubbed deckwork across the markings, avoiding the two or three rope quoits lying about. A pair of children were collecting them and stacking them up in preparation for a game of bull's-eye near where the Air Force people had been.

Their feet moved through pools of shadow from the long line of tarpaulined lifeboats. Cheryl bumped into him and clutched his arm. He reached to guard the pocket. Then she inclined her head on to his shoulder. After a moment or so she pulled herself upright. 'Stability problems!' She giggled. 'The *Armorica* has stability problems!'

'What?'

'Chappie at Gib said we were lucky to have missed the Atlantic on this boat. He said in a really bad sea the *Armorica* stands up like a performing seal.' She laughed again, cheekily. 'That's why you had such a hard time. Wait a minute. Hold this for me a moment, will you?' She stopped and placed her handbag into his upturned palms. Then she opened it to take out a tube of sun cream, unscrewed the cap and, managing the glass from hand to hand, smoothed it on to her arms. 'Sorry about this.' She finished and saved him from his awkwardness with the bag. They continued.

'I think I've already spotted most of the potential romances on board. I can always tell, you know; who's blowing smoke-rings at whom, darling. I'm infallible, like the Pope. I've got the absolute eye for it. Always have had. It's a gift, a sixth sense.'

They reached the far rail and looked over. The sun was to the side of their wake, flashing now and then in its far turbulence. 'There are some dried-up old women on board who actually think I should be in my cabin, knitting.'

Immediately below them was the first-class swimming-pool with the covers still on, although two of Barnwell's aircrew were pretending to climb on them. Beyond the high rear wall of its square amphitheatre they could see the aft hatches and accumulation of venting shafts, like cowled gnomes in a mechanical garden. And beyond that, the euphemistically named tourist class, where seven hundred and twenty-two migrants occupied the final quarter of the ship. They were playing their part in a mass transit to be relieved, at least on the *Armorica*, by the square of their own little pool, for the moment also still covered.

The rest of the steerage deck was filled with adults sitting out, standing out, children playing out, families looking out. Many of the men wore dark trousers and had rolled up the sleeves of their shirts; many of the women wore sleeveless frocks. Some had shorts with turn-ups. There was no difference; but to a practised eye there was every difference.

Cheryl said, 'We're not really supposed to see them, are we? Ten pounds gets them to the promised land. Is it true they have to sleep segregated?'

'I don't know,' said Robert. 'Do they? Husbands and wives?'

'Men to port, women to starboard. Heavens, Bobby. I could never endure it.'

'I'm sure it isn't like that. The man who shares my cabin says these folk are the lucky ones.'

'But they have to give all their furniture away.'

'Apparently Mr Menzies is still desperate for English blood . . .'

'Like a vamp, Bobby.' Cheryl bared her teeth and looked him in the eye.

Robert laughed, enjoying her. 'I mean English stock. He's terrified of turning yellow. Or even black.' He took out his cigarettes, offered her one, then lit them both.

'Aren't we all, darling. Aren't we bloody all.' She drew in her smoke.

'So they'll take almost anyone these days, he implies. Menzies. Doesn't make any of us feel so good, does it. But on the assisted-passage scheme if they haven't got a boss out there to propose them, to speak for them to come out, then they go crammed in on something much more basic than this.'

'White niggers, you mean? Oh dear.' Looking at Robert's face. 'I've said something, haven't I? Something I shouldn't. Now you're going to get all stuffy and holy poly.'

'It's all right.' He did not want to lose her. 'We'll just agree to differ, shall we?'

'Let's. I want you to like me. I do really, Bobby. I know I'm

69

. . . I say the things no one's supposed to say. Any more. And I'm a frightful . . .' She giggled into the glass. 'Oh God. What am I saying? Too many of these, darling. A couple and I'm anybody's.' Then she grew cool. 'That's what they think, the old mems down there.' She jerked her head to indicate the main lounge on the deck beneath them.

Robert reflected on the set of retired home-and-colonials, who had colonised the area of the Armorican painting and were never seen to move. He had hardly thought of them before, apart from registering them as the financial lions of the trip. The stewards, of course, buzzed around their every whim, like flies. Robert thought them irrelevant – on the verge of extinction – but their valuations weighed heavily on Cheryl's mind, it seemed.

'Look, Bobby. Maybe I have been around a bit. Enjoyed myself. Life's too short. But that doesn't make me a bad person, Bobby. Does it?'

'Of course it doesn't.'

'You like me, don't you? Even if I'm . . . sometimes. I make myself . . . They hate me. The looks!'

'Don't be silly. Nobody hates you.'

'I'm a perfect tart – in their eyes. And I need a friend, darling. Be my friend, Bobby. Will you?'

'Of course I will, Cheryl.'

'Will you?' She put her free hand round Robert's neck and hugged him, nuzzling her face into his cheek. He felt the boning of her brassiere pressed against him. Then she broke off. 'Thanks, darling. You're a love.'

Why, in Cheryl's boat everyone was at it. Secretly. Below the water-line, as it were. Then there was nothing out of the ordinary in his feeling for Penny. And she would maybe even expect him to . . . The done thing when out of sight of land. The done thing; it would not surprise anyone. It would not change the world – it was almost *de rigueur*, helped oil the wheels, keep the ship on course, calm the waters, give the old buffers down there something to grumble about.

'You're not cross with me, Bobby?'

'I'm not cross with you, Cheryl.'

'Do you like me?'

'Yes. Of course I like you.' Now he felt just a little irritated.

'You don't think I make myself cheap?'

'No.'

'I suppose it's being a woman.' She stood away from the aft rail and, looking down, placed her two hands intimately on her belly as if to anticipate the baby's growth. The stem of the wineglass stuck out through the fingers of one hand, the handbag was looped over the other wrist. 'It makes us go a bit doolally; I suppose you know all about women. Shakes us up a bit, darling. Out of control. You see?'

'It's all right,' he said quietly. Acutely embarrassed, steadying her as much as he dared, he rescued the glass from her loosening hand. He felt for a moment as if he were holding a stethoscope, able to listen to things he should not hear through the glass's heel.

'Maybe.' She allowed her hands back on the rail. 'No. It isn't that. It isn't only being a woman. It would help to be able just to say to people, Bobby. Just to say what's going on.'

To Robert's amazement she started to cry. 'Where's Penny? I must go and find Penny.' She looked about her. 'Sorry. Have you got a clean hanky, darling?'

He had one in the side pocket of his blazer. Penny's lenses were wrapped in it. He managed to contrive its release. She dabbed her eyes and laughed suddenly with a disarming, almost childish, candour. 'Our ship's got a little parcel in its pouch.' She pointed down at the emigrants. 'But we have to pretend it's not there.' Then she handed the handkerchief back. 'Thanks. I'm sorry. I'm all right now. No, really I am. I'll go and find Penny. She's the only girl on this bloody boat who's not part of the rigging.'

18

Behind the Nile Delta, there was a cut in the water. The thick, almost rancid fertility, the mud mixed with sun-water to the colour of a crocodile's belly, gave way in favour of cloudy blue-green. We sighted at the same time the flat shore of northern Egypt, from which a pilot launch skipped out of the light to greet us.

By late afternoon the *Armorica* had rounded the sea walls of a land that sought to make vast square enclosures from its meeting with the Med. It looked like the board of an empty game. Finding ourselves within minutes harboured by a slick lagoon, we drifted gently in to drop anchor only a stone's throw from a city waterfront.

Backlit, the city was genuinely non-European, unreadable at first glance. There were white low-rise blocks everywhere. Closer up, an avenue of date palms, and the hedge of shaped evergreens between them, set off the facade. There was no other hint of vegetation.

A causeway of rusty pontoons was connected to the ship; preparations were put in hand to run out the disembarkation gangways. Amid all this a froth of small boats came around the *Armorica*'s hull. Their oarsmen lost no time in hooking up lines to the deck rails high above them, and opening negotiations.

'Bum-boatmen,' Mrs Burns announced to anyone who was listening. 'Don't whatever you do pay them the prices they ask.'

Having shifted decks again, Robert saw Penny at last. He recognised her arm and the back of her head below him. She was on A deck calling out to one of the boats. He heard her voice: 'For the wooden box and the little camel!'

The man shouted back up, 'These two? Box? And this camel?'

'No. The one with the red on it.' She pointed. Then: 'And the brass box as well!'

'Brass box!' The man held up a brass box from the array of bright things all about him. He wore a fez, and had mustachios. There was an excitement.

'Yes,' Penny said. 'How much all three?'

'Ten pounds!'

'Ten shillings!'

Indicating his merchandise, the man threw wide his hands so that his boat rocked. 'Special. Five pounds no less.'

They haggled. Penny would go no higher than a pound.

Finally the man raised his eyes to the heavens. 'OK. Yes. OK.'

They came up in a basket into which she had first placed her pound note, weighted with the stone. When Robert got down and made his way along the deck to her, she was standing, clutching them. She wore a blue dress he had not seen before.

Down on the dappled water, part shadowed by the waterfront buildings behind him, the man in the bum-boat smiled at them both, and waved. They smiled back.

'I don't know what I bought them for, really. I thought my children would like them; but now I have them,' she embraced the camel and the two curiously worked boxes, 'I don't quite know which to give to which.' She smiled at him again, helplessly. 'Why did I buy three, I wonder? It's the thrill. You get carried along. Would you like one of them? That would solve my problem.'

'I've got your glasses.' Robert took the pince-nez out of his top pocket. 'You left it . . . them . . . in the observation lounge.' He held them out.

'Oh! That's kind. I hadn't even missed them. Where did you say? Thank you so much. I must have . . . It must have been when I got up and . . . The little girl said there was something in the water, and I went down to have a look. I must have left them then. But I can't take them; I haven't enough hands. Now you'll have to help me out.' She gave him the brass box in return for her property.

He had to take it. And once he had he could not give it back; because her hands were full.

'Do please keep it. You'll be helping me out.'

'I couldn't dream of it.'

'No. I mean it. It's for you. That must be why I bought it.' She smiled. 'You must have it.'

'If you're sure . . .'

'Of course. Why not? Are you going ashore? Come with us. They say it's safer to go in a group.'

The pontoons wobbled beneath them and clanked softly to the tread. At the end a man in a dark suit but without a tie stood on the waterfront to look at their documents. Behind him a couple of Egyptian soldiers fingered their rifles. Once on solid and unyielding land the body continued to rise and fall with the pattern of waves.

The emptiness, the absence of people was striking. Robert looked back. The bum-boats still clustered around the white walls of the ship. They had their boat-house under a very long, low cover to his right, exactly along the edge. Behind that was the made-up road with more soldiers on it. Then came the line of palms, from which the official buildings were just set back.

That frontage gave on to an urban region so lacking in known visual clues the other senses became heightened. The air, overwhelming the sense of smell, was laden with what could only be sewage, food, and a sort of tobacco spice – all arid, or drying. And they were aware of the quietness; through which the sound of their footfalls mingled with the tambour of voices behind walls, the occasional unseen vehicle, and even, faintly, the calls of the bum-boatmen round the ship, now some distance behind them.

There were no shops with glass windows, no billboards, signs, no kiosks, traffic, bus-stops; few kerbstones to tell you where to walk. There was, if anything, an extraordinary freedom, set off against the guns of the soldiers. They walked cautiously inwards by a likely route, making desultory conversation – it was not a big place at all. There were buildings whose function was unapparent. There were some people. A few came out to offer goods for sale. A few children appeared and then disappeared. There were smiles, or scowls. Some street-level rooms had open doors. An old van passed them. The smell became sharper, more acrid.

'Pooh! It's so stinky!' Finlay Coote held her nose.

'You were the one who wanted to come, stinky.' Mitchell, her brother.

'Keep with us, you two. And don't do that, Finlay. It's offensive.' Russell Coote shepherded them back from the middle of the street. Clodagh, he explained, was lying down in her cabin.

All Robert's impressions of Port Said were modulated by his elation at the gift of the brass box, and by the nearness of Penny. At the corner of a sand-coloured building she turned to smile at him, and her body was wrapped in bright meaning. He returned the smile, amazed. And then they passed between them, these smiles, like proffered sherbet. They hardly knew each other.

Next he was walking just behind her. Mr and Mrs Madeley guarded her on either side. He heard them speculating about what the local currency actually was. Douglas was checking in the ship's folded guide sheet.

Russell Coote said, 'Given the choice, Clodagh and I would have preferred the Cape route, when all's said and done. But it does depend on the weather you get.'

They passed through several broader streets and then a narrower one, at the end of which, in a small debouch, shouting began. About twenty yards away, two men came rushing out of a doorway. The one had dark trousers and a white shirt. He stopped, squared up. The other, in pursuit, wielded a carving knife. He was heavily built, paunchy, and wore a cloth round his head. With what looked like a night-shirt flapping at his ankles, he advanced, stamped a sandalled foot, and lunged with the knife. There were more shouts as men clustered, forming a ring. The still-hot sky from which the sun had almost dropped made silhouettes of the low buildings; the white shirts were like agitated spirits suddenly let out of a bottle. They whirled around. Within the circle now the first man could just be seen. Someone had given him a smaller knife. More lunges came in. He parried, and then crouched again at the ready. The tails of his shirt hung loosely.

'Are you all right, Stella?' Douglas Madeley enquired of his wife, once they were safely away.

Robert found himself next to Penny. For some distance neither of them spoke. They had ventured inward and encountered something – which had not touched them. It was like a dream that marks its mood on the waking state. And so they were put to flight, but would hardly admit it. Now he searched for casual conversation. He felt any words that slipped between them would shine and remain in the air like the memory of blades. 'I ran into Cheryl Torboys earlier this afternoon; while we were still at sea. She was a bit upset. I wondered if she'd found you?'

They could see the dock again now. Perhaps not so many people after them had come ashore. Penny paused to light a cigarette. 'That's better.' She blew the smoke out. 'I hope it's not a terrible sin to smoke in public. Just have to risk it. No. I've been in my cabin, doing this and that. Writing up my journal.' She looked up at him. 'I don't want to let it all just go.' She pointed about her. 'Do you? But I haven't seen Cheryl. What was the matter with her?'

'She'd had quite a bit to drink. We were looking over the stern

75

and she suddenly started crying.'

Penny flicked the ash off her cigarette. Ahead of them, as they came out on to the waterfront avenue again, the *Armorica* stood painted by the setting sun. Like a castle, he thought; like a flag; like a coat of arms. The white, illuminated walls rose up sheer; light caught a sequence of portholes and embroidered them.

'It is real, I suppose. We can go there?'

'It is real. How beautiful, extraordinary. It's ours. Of course we can go there. Although it seems too . . . impossible. The high seas. A new life. Being offered to us.' She held his gaze, and then drew on her cigarette. He watched the print of lipstick on the tan paper of the filter.

The gully-gully man came out of nowhere. Dressed in a blue suit, without a tie, he looked the commercial traveller at ease. But he was all electricity and movement. He held an egg under Finlay's nose, took it behind his back; hey presto it was a chick. 'See! Look! Chick. Chicky.' He crammed the chick into his flies. He turned and produced an egg from his bottom. 'Cheekee!'

Finlay giggled.

'Come along, Mitchell, Finlay.' Russell marshalled his brood towards the ship.

'If we give him some money he might go away,' said Mrs Madeley.

The gully-gully man shadowed them a good deal of the way back, scurrying and twisting in front of them, developing chicks and eggs from surprising places, holding them out to the children. 'Look,' he said. 'See!' And laughed.

At the pontoons they were aware of the soldiers' hatred. A few of their fellow first-class passengers were gathered. Barry and Queenie Parsons were stepping along the dipping causeway. And some of the emigrants from the tourist class, those who had passports, were also collecting at their separate pontoons to filter back.

Robert heard a genial, blazered man wearing a silver moustache turn and say to his companion, 'Glad to see our precious cargo getting safely back on board.' The man turned, beamed at Penny. 'Hullo there. Had enough?'

They stepped on to the pontoon. Robert heard him continue behind him, as they eyed the other gangway. 'The Aussies call it "Populate or Perish". Entirely strategic. It's the only intelligent option. Slit eyes don't sleep for long, that we do know.'

My mother and I went ashore separately with Mr Chaunteyman.

19

At the captain's table by invitation, Penny was placed at a corner, marking her status without a visible husband as ornamental but awkward. Across from her sat Mary Garnery, that woman whom Clodagh had described as 'excessively thin'. Penny found her attractive and compellingly painful at the same time. Under discussion, while we lay still at anchor, was the situation in Aden, the next port of call. She said, 'I don't understand anything about it. Do they like us?'

She did not know the name of the man who answered. 'Not very much, I'm afraid. Rather the same as here.'

She nodded acknowledgement as she drew off her evening gloves. What for Robert and me is an adventure . . . And then she felt wretched, for she realised she had coupled her name with his in thought, as if they were a *fait accompli*. She could not eat. She took one mouthful of the soup and nibbled a piece of bread roll. She tried not to think of him again, not to turn round. It was absolutely intolerable. What was Robert Kettle in his dinner-jacket and black tie? No different from all the other men in the room, personable or otherwise. She did not know what he actually did, nor why he was travelling. Only that he was a scientist, like her husband. They had not had long enough together even to exchange such simple information. Their contact had been social and disrupted by cross-currents; they had passed secrets with their eyes only, caught in the swirl of other people's eddies. And yet in that delicious conspiracy had lain the prospect of something quite new, quite . . . emancipating. And then she told herself sharply not to be so ridiculous.

Michael Canning, the old ICS hand next to her, was talking. She suspected he would be interesting to listen to, if one were allowed to ask what one wanted to know. And that would easily explain why it was that she was interested in Robert Kettle.

Because, quite simply, he talked about things just that bit more openly than the rest of the crowd. That was it – and he paid the price for it, being a touch problematic sometimes, socially. So then of course there was no mystery. She was relieved. And Elsie Canning spoke of the wrench of leaving her husband when she had taken the children back to England for schooling, before the war. Fortitude was what it demanded. 'It's harder for the men, of course. Running the place. The heat . . .'

Without Penny seeing, a main course had arrived in front of her. She took a mouthful. She was just missing Hugh; or good conversation going that bit deeper and further. She looked around. They were surrounded by a blur of chatter from the other tables. These people were most of them so superficial. Robert Kettle was less so. Naturally he stood out somewhat, but that was all. She would be all right when she got back within her family.

On the other side of the captain, Mr and Mrs Piyadasa were guests as well. Their usual mild curry had arrived. Penny waved her fingertips beside her cheek. They smiled back. She thought of the invitation to spend the day with them in Colombo. But they were probably just being polite. The woman missing her family. Her boys.

All her life Penny had been in the company of boys: first living at the boarding-school, and then after her marriage to Hugh, with her own two, in the village between Hatfield and Stevenage on the Great North Road. There had hardly been a break. Not really. Not in terms of what home might mean. There had occurred, before all that of course, other young men; brief holidays.

'If you lose their respect, you lose the whole show.' There was a small silence; as if by a gap in the general conversation Michael Canning's last words had earned a wider audience than he intended. Penny looked down at the cutlet in front of her, the parsley sauce, the neat vegetables. Shakily she cut it about with her knife, rearranged it with her fork, as if to display good intentions. She prayed that in a minute or so her appetite would return and the world would be normal again. She pictured Hugh, in his glasses and sports jacket, sitting at work in an office in Adelaide. No, a lab. In his shirt-sleeves. Electronics and filing cabinets. The hum of fluorescent strip lighting, the buzz of high-voltage instrumentation. Gothic and square – Robert's phrase. No, not Adelaide, but Salisbury, some miles outside – the place he had roughly described in one of his letters.

Michael Canning was saying, 'You bomb a country to bits, demand total war for six years, and then ask her to maintain her territories all over the place. Bit of a tall order in anyone's book.'

For a moment Penny wondered where he was talking about.

'Quite,' said the captain. 'I was torpedoed myself. In the Atlantic. But the less said about that, frankly . . .'

She forced another morsel of food between her lips, but her throat resisted. She thought she heard Robert's voice seeking her out through the noise and chatter of the tables. Not what it said, but the tone, a haunting, tender note in the lower clef that her ear was attuned to and waited for.

She looked back behind her at last, but could not see him. And she dared not continue so, craning her neck, staring.

'How did you manage during the storm?' Mary enquired of her. 'It was maddening, wasn't it? There was nothing anyone could do.'

'I'm afraid the fresh air was the only thing keeping me afloat. That, and the horizon. As long as I could see what was going on I was all right.'

'Didn't trouble me at all.' The young man at the end of the table spoke between them again. 'I must be a naturally good sailor. By the way, I see from the papers the Italians have been up in the Himalayas looking for the abominable snowman. Once you start something, everyone wants to get in on the act, don't they?'

At coffee, Penny wanted to ask Michael Canning, as of a father, about the endurance of love and the power of abstinence. Why, how it binds us together here, she suddenly thought: abstinence. Michael liked her, found her attractive. He flirted easily. He was boyish, charming, just out of range of his wife. It meant nothing. It meant nothing that he admired her bare neck and her bosom, set off by her best evening dress. She thought not of the snowman nonsense, but about an abstinent yogi, called into being by some earlier chance remark of Michael's. She imagined him naked amid the Tibetan snows, eyes crossed and crazed, intent on melting the ice. On his forehead, in rare coloured earths, the design of the Union Jack.

Magic was what worked. She wanted the voyage to go on for ever, like a dream of the Sleeping Beauty. She wanted to go on to the deck and meet Robert, to talk under the stars, luxuriating in the savour of the strange Islamic town they had visited together only a few hours ago, as it rose off the flat, salt land. She had heard for the first time the muezzin.

I am a dangerous woman, she thought, on the instant. In future I shall cover myself up. She felt herself confused and for a moment floating.

Later, in her cabin, she tried the de Beauvoir, and put it aside. She spent some time staring at herself in the mirror, taking off her make-up. Then she opened her journal, designed, originally, as a surprise present for Hugh at the end of her journey. She was amazed to find herself write: *I do not regard myself as the spoils of war.*

She closed the book in a hurry and placed it under the mattress of the lower bunk as if to smother it; but it lay beneath her in the dark like a piece of pitchblende, refusing to keep shut up its dangerous emanations.

PART TWO

Cargo

20

AND NOW I have another memory that haunts me. It insists, and will not be put off – though it feels like an ending. Maybe under the skin of my whole account lies an invisible tattoo, done in hatred. Hatred is very dense, much heavier than gold, denser by far than lead. Where it lies compacted, the world's story is altered. Its emissions are lethal.

And the memory I have is like a radiographer's plate. It opens a flood of sorrow, a storm, shifting what we were carrying. The child I was seems to whisper directly in my ear. I begin to recognise myself as prime material, for Penny's thoughts smack of my own world: armaments and men.

One year on then, my mother pulled back the thin curtains behind the settee. She would draw them across every afternoon. Otherwise the late sun through our wide veranda window made the room such an oven we could hardly breathe. Hugh Kendrick sat down. Over his shoulder I watched the big heatball beginning to redden above the crossing at the end of our street, where a freight train was trundling at walking pace. The street was made of hard mud, broad for a street, though beyond the railway lines it narrowed to a mere track. Our house occupied its own corner; the window looked straight down at the crossing's alternating lights. Today the warning bell seemed loud and insistent enough to make almost no distance of the intervening two hundred yards. Neither did the train show any sign of coming to an end.

For hours the sky had plugged light into ground hard as rock. Now it was nearly evening. The street's surfaces were turning to rouge and umber, and the low white fence strips made stark perspective lines. Set well back on plots to either side, the bungalows, cheaply built, crouched under tin overhangs. Their shadows had just now opened to the angled glare. But the straw-coloured yards seemed all the more scorched. Cleared only lately from the wild, the settlement looked flat and discouraged, like the vegetation, as if day were a fist.

On the T-shape of dirt roads outside our own front patch stood Hugh Kendrick's borrowed car. It was a new Holden. Just over its saloon top the red lights on the crossing posts flashed side by side, backwards and forwards, reflecting in the shine. Meanwhile the bell clanged and the freight train's wheels still rumbled their undernote. These endless hauls picked their way down from Alice Springs like iron caterpillars, and bang, banged each segment painfully over the joints. A couple of neighbouring dogs were barking incessantly, set off by the continuing alarm.

Hugh Kendrick was fingering the brim of his hat. His news was frightful. Their regular family car was destroyed; and with it their life. Backlit, his face was darkened. He had been in some hotel, drinking more than a little. I smelt it in the air he breathed out. Erica served tea from her jazzy red cane table, making little half-phrases. The din from outside sounded like my heart.

'They were lovers, do you see. Can you believe that? Penny and this Robert Kettle. They met on the ship it seems, on the way out. They were lovers. Well. Perhaps you knew all along. Perhaps everyone on that damned . . . All the time I was waiting for her in Adelaide. All that time.'

Erica said nothing to engage him, placed the teapot and sat, fussily arranging her skirt.

For a moment Hugh's horn-rimmed eyes rested on me. Then he continued: 'I knew there was something wrong, of course, at first. The whole move would be a change, a shock. One makes allowances. Some readjustment was to have been expected. And then the . . . ' The vacancy filled the room. 'But I thought we'd coped with all that. To be honest I believed the whole business was behind us. As far as I could see we were jogging along comfortably. Nice home. The two boys. New country. Time the great healer, eh? Out of the blue last week, she takes the car. Goes off with him, just like that. After all these months. It was a plan. They'd worked it out secretly, against me, against the boys. That's what I can't understand, you see. It's not just for my own sake – a woman like that can bring the whole family down, can't she?' He looked up. 'She left a note. They must have been meeting all along, of course. Behind my back. Keeping secrets, betraying me, acting the whole time as though she . . . It was found burnt out . . . ' And then he broke down, in the tone of a child about to cry: 'It was found burnt out at Kingoonya. I bought that car before she came out. For my wife. For the family.'

'Kingoonya?' Erica repeated blankly.

Not far from our house ran the so-called Great North Road. Hugh's gesture indicated through the wall that strip of fraying tar. 'It's three hundred miles up. Half-way to Alice. Where the Stuart turns you can go straight on. There's a small town, no more than a way-station, really. Just past that. They must have driven her car – ours – off the road, splashed petrol from a can and set light to it. They didn't mean to be found. They didn't want to be traced.' He took his hand off the hat to adjust his thick glasses.

'Goodness. More tea? It must have been terrible for you.' Erica had no idea, about anything it seemed.

He found his pipe. 'D'you mind . . . ?'

'I don't mind, of course. Mr Ch . . . My husband may be coming a little later.' A hand to her curls. 'I'm expecting a telegram any moment. He's been away on business. On duty. The Pacific, you know. South Seas.'

She had no idea. She was stupid deliberately, obsessed with her looks and her pretty blonde hair. It was her strategy. She still thought Chaunteyman would come good – that he adored her after all and meant what he said.

Hugh Kendrick licked dry lips, made a noise in his throat, and pressed his face with both hands, still holding the pipe. 'It took a while for the military to notify . . . One burnt-out Holden looks very much like another.'

I had guessed we were to be abandoned here. We received money, and promises, with diminishing frequency. Surely Mr Chaunteyman had left the country for good. And us in it. I knew his heart – it was to be expected. In my view he stood smooth and revealed for the fork-tailed villain he was. I had conjured him up with my damned blue suitcase and look

85

where it had landed us. We had been betrayed.

'Do you see?' Hugh Kendrick leaned and sipped again at his tea. The audible creak of iron brakes from the freight train. The heavy frenzy of the bell.

He lit up the pipe and puffed between bared teeth. 'Penny, my wife, together with her lover . . . ' He spat the words. 'They went on. They burnt the one car and went on in Kettle's old station-wagon. With intent, do you see? An army transport driver came forward, once I raised the alarm. He reported seeing them. Passed them on the edge of the Prohibited Area. The testing grounds. It's signposted quite clearly. The direction he gave could only mean they'd entered the contaminated zone. And that, I'm afraid, was the last . . . ' And he broke down again, quietly this time, into his hands. Clenched in his grip the pipe's new-lit bowl smouldered close to his cheek.

It was not the first I had heard of my friends since the voyage. Erica and I had met the Kendricks once in the winter – when the nights might frost but the days were oddly warm. It was at some function at the Weapons Research, inside the wire. Mr Chaunteyman took us. Penny's eyes had lit up with the sudden gleam of recognition: 'Why, hallo! Surely you're . . . ? Didn't we . . . ? Good Lord! This is Hugh – my husband.' But I was allowed hardly any time with her, and Robert was far away. I had to play outside with the children where the concrete backed up against the perimeter.

Now in the silence that followed Hugh Kendrick's words, the image came to me of my two shipmates, sprawled at some dreadful noon in the Great Victoria Desert. I knew about the contamination. I had kept my ears open – at school, in the street, in delicatessens, those Australian milk bars. The testing grounds to the north were common knowledge. But with so many new lives and livelihoods dependent on the one industry there were no questions. We slept in a strange land far from home. Every now and then the desert visited us a little with a dust storm. Penny and Robert had gone up there – where the train had come from. They had exposed themselves to whatever had been done to the ground. And they had not come back.

And so for reasons of his own Hugh had traced our address and driven the half-hour from the Kendricks' Adelaide home to this nowhere township. He wanted something from Erica.

His eyes craved information, or absolution. Because we were all linked by the *Armorica,* the subject that was always dropped. We would tell him nothing.

Erica declared she was horrified. 'We heard an item on the radio. I'd no idea it was someone we knew. If there's anything I can do. Surely the authorities . . .'

Only yesterday Hugh had received a phone call at work. A spotter plane had sighted a likely vehicle. 'Some of the military are going in. Soon. Protective clothing . . . But after all this time, I . . . Oh, God. I couldn't stay in the house. And Robert Kettle would have known the country, been there once or twice. Some miles after Kingoonya there's the army track that takes you all the way. Fall-out levels; he'd have known about it. People are kept away. Do you understand? They seem to have deliberately . . . He . . . But of course that wouldn't kill them.'

'No?' Erica enquired. 'Then they might be all right?'

'We don't know the effects. It isn't the . . . radiation as such. That could even take years. We don't know how it operates. We've no data, except Japan. What they've done, it's a gesture. It's just a stupid gesture. They've gone up there to . . . it's so irresponsible!' His anger burst through again. 'Without water, the heat. There's no settlement, no shelter, nothing. This isn't England, you know. If they're not found, the heat . . .'

'We do know, Mr Kendrick,' she said. 'We know the outback is a killer. How long is it altogether?'

'I'm sorry. I didn't mean . . . It's been a week since that driver saw them. A week without water. I want to know why. I want to know what went on. The police said after so long there was very little likelihood, even if they'd had the sense to stay in the car . . .'

I am running out of my mother's house. The fly-screen slaps shut behind me.

21

On the veranda I pause, gulping air, relieved to escape from the two of them. But I have come out unarmed, except for the sheath-knife at the back of my belt. Something substantial would

87

be better. I possess my own rifle, nearly. Point two-two. 'A guy at the base heard you were keen. I'll bring it for you. Knock over a few rabbits, son, shall we? Soon?' – Chaunteyman. But Erica is yelling for me. If I go back she will keep me there.

So I am out of the gate and running towards the tracks. Along past the unbuilt plot on the near corner. I could reach out and spike my hand on its thistles five foot high. They are thick, baked razor sharp, hard as wire. In my head clangs Hugh Kendrick's phrase: 'One burnt-out Holden is very much like another'.

A woman pushes a pram along the hard dirt at the other side of the road. Another stands in her yard taking down clothes from a drier. It is nearly six. Soon the hotel bars will close and the men arrive back in cars, an hour and a half's cold beer on board. Beyond these fences lie lonely fields of scrub, a sea dried to zero. We are in a God-forsaken place, a ghetto for Pommie trash, I heard one Australian say. Hugh Kendrick traced us and has forced himself out here to find us. We feel awkward about his coming; we have been told not to talk about the ship. Erica hopes he will not notice the giant cracks already in our walls. The place is no place at all. I have a knot in my tongue.

I pass Garrity's house as the last of the freight train hammers so desperately slowly at the crossing. Chaunteyman is upper-most in my mind. 'It's the new frontier, kid. Hey, Erica, the northern hemisphere's played out. I feel out of sorts there, y'know. I'm a rover; what you call a free spirit. Even in the States a man like me can barely draw his breath any more. Take my word for it. A guy with a horizon in his eyes still. I want us to make a really new start. And a woman as beautiful as you has no business cooped up in that smoky little slum they call England.' Trash.

Perhaps Mr Chaunteyman had hopes, believed what he told us. It does not matter. From this minute none of that matters. Penny and Robert are dead among the crows. That is why I am heading towards the exchanging red lights, the bang-clanging of the bell. I have no father. My mother's face is cracking. There is no way home. It must be my fault. And at the hub of it all is the night of the ship. My heart foams with hatred.

I arrive breathless just as the conductor's van has passed. It dwindles into the distance as I cross. Then I scamper to the garbage dump on the other side. At last the ringing leaves off.

The sun is very low, partially obscured. It leaks brilliant cloud-strips. The westward landscape is the colour of resin, and runs away quite flat. Trees are black outlines, here and there, and a solitary wind pump stands, dark-etched in the middle ground. Bits of sombre hedge mark off the distance.

It is the dump I have been seeking. Snakes live in the wrecked cars and Kelvinator fridges. There are rugs, oil drums, and rolls of grown-over chicken wire. Defunct furniture is heaped in mounds of ash and soil. 'Snakes?' people say. 'It's quite a habitation for them down there.' I draw my knife. I am searching for the smashed car I and Garrity set up here just before Christmas – our crib.

Garrity has never seen television. I have educated him – the dump is our Colorado and I know intimately its infested ranges, mesas and canyons. But some days a truckman comes down to shift rubbish about, and bulldoze. So the bad lands might well have changed. The light is fading; quite soon it will be dark. All the familiar landmarks have disappeared. Walls of earth loom in unexpected scarps; there are ups, and drops, squeezed like volcanic folds. And wisps of dust blow in my eyes from the tops, for just now a breeze quickens. It is a strange pilgrimage, miniature and gritty, my trek across these stinking dunes.

Then, while I am in the central valley under a hang of car fronts, a cloud before the sun splits. The Rockies of chromium and rust on my left blaze up as if on fire. The dump is beautiful and terrible. It is the playground of children I am not supposed to mix with – and Erica has forbidden it me. Under blinding skies I have already searched it for treasures: imported American goods – prime among them a ripped wireless, half buried in earth and smelling of rot, which lies in my bedroom.

Up one of the steepest mounds there is the hint of a path. And, having gained enough height to command my private desert, I can rest a moment to see our township itself the other side of the tracks. Beyond that the eastern hills are genuine purple; they take the colour each evening, and stretch off towards Mount Lofty and Adelaide. But so beautiful, Erica says, the hills. And they are truly hard to believe, even after my whole year here, glowing like a tinted photograph. There, on the level plain before them, the freight train crawls south. It glints in the distance, running between the township and the Weapons

Research Establishment, where the men go to work.

But with time and light failing, I can only resume my quest and search over the next ridge, sheath-knife in hand. I find at last the wreck my friend Garrity and I used for a ritual. Down in the dump's trough it is directly in front of me, beyond an overturned utility van. It is a hulk: a fire-damaged Holden saloon with a bashed-in roof. There is nothing so special about that. In this country every car is a Holden of some kind; by and large, there is only one make. I think of identical shapes and configurations. Miles away to the north, Robert and Penny set fire to Hugh's car. Further on still they are even now lying in Robert's.

In a pool of shadow between a crazy bed frame with rusted springs and a galvanised storage tank, the car's window yawns a toothless mouth. I must go down, and step into the stiff dried weeds grown up so quickly since the last rainstorm. Even in broad daylight I would fight shy of treading here.

I try to thump each footfall of earth as I touch it. Downward, the underbrush grows darker by the second, but eventually I have done enough and am able to crouch by the car door at the slope's foot. With my face scrunched up, I make myself peer in. A knife is paltry defence – against a king brown, say. I expect an attack any moment.

But yes, the scarecrow figure we stole from the field beyond the Great North Road, the *guy*, lies, yes, exactly as we placed him on the back seat, fake face down, one barbeque skewer through his back, two through his backside, pinned to the upholstery. To be burnt. When they light the dump. Which they do periodically. We have seen them, Garrity and I. But not burnt yet. The man in the truck might come down and do it tonight, even. The paper trilby and the labels stuck to the guy's midriff still bear the inscription *Chaunteyman*, waiting for it.

Something gives under my shoe. I feel myself jolt and snatch my foot away. Then freeze. I have just enough sense not to go running. I can just make out, tangled under some stalks, a spread of old clothes and toys, spilled from that sack in the weeds higher up. I have stepped on the body of a child's doll, in a white-spotted dress, quite hidden in the grass. A stupid impulse makes me pick it up. I have broken its body.

It has the exact likeness of Penny, of course: a mocking

chubby likeness. When I turn it, the eyes blink open in the gloom. Then, heedless of fangs or anything, my body decides for me – scoots me to the ridge's crest before I know it. Because a six-inch stinging centipede drops out of the doll's crack and falls right next to me. In the air it leaves a kicking, twisting trace – the same shape as my scream.

Penny and Robert: it is as I feared. The cause is in my own heart and I myself am the instrument. Not Chaunteyman, but my own thoughts and deeds. My Holden crib staged some history I was supposed to suppress. It destroyed those I loved and who loved one another. There is something in the blood – my father was right. The wind shames me; but the sun stands full on the horizon, the pit is too dark and I shall lose my escape. No cloud flares now, the sky has turned smoky and there are a few faint stars.

Yet I still could go down again, quickly reach in and remove the stakes that hold the image there. Even if Penny and Robert are already dead and the act could make no difference yet it might just be done – a gesture of atonement and good faith. 'It takes guts, Ralphie. It's a man's world.' – Dad. Below me, the shadows of the dump's valleys are pools of murk. Hard to make out even the Holden's shape, now, the car, the bed frame and the doll are lapped by a tide of incoming night. Down in the long grass a rustle sounds like a slither, and I lose my nerve. 'I can't! I can't! That's enough!'

That night as I lie in bed I wish only to be as Penny and Robert, at one with their desert, whose colours are of rage, black-edged. My heart is a shrine to their bleached, anhydrous bodies, slumped out of a car's open door. I see the glare on their windscreen, the coachwork. And the two of them: inverted, borne on a life-raft of shadow. All around scorched air coats the pink dust, the bright scatter of flint. I have them die together, a heat death, in the instant; her forearm blistered, next to his. The contamination hints like an intimate opal under her wrist, where it touches the ground; and under his cheek – like the paint on the hands of my luminous watch. It glows in the dark.

Perhaps I am already dead and turned to nickel, gold, plutonium inside. Yes, surely I have died; that is Australia and thus are my very thoughts turned fatal.

22

We weighed anchor. Dawn steam rose from the Port Said lagoon. The early chill in the air was a brief concession to winter. 'That over there's the Nile, kid.' Mr Chaunteyman was staring into the distance. 'You see it?'

I believed him unquestioningly, in a kind of manly rapture. To compensate for the too-brief loan of his service revolver, he had already bought me a Winchester repeater popgun from the shop on D deck, and a real-looking six-shooter of my own, which he was teaching me how to twirl. In Australia we should have a fridge for ice lollies and a record-player for the latest pop records. With him I felt safe.

'Do you ever have a bad dream, Mr Chaunteyman?'

'Call me Dave, OK. How many times do I have to tell you.'

'OK . . . Dave. But do you?'

'The hell. I surely don't. Well, everyone has them sometime.'

'We had to . . . My dad taught me how to stop yourself dreaming.'

'Oh? Isn't that great!'

'He taught me mind control. For my tests. For the Navy. He said the mind's like an electrical circuit. He said it was a hard, cruel world and you had to be got ready. He wanted to harden me up. When he'd be there and there was a bad dream he'd teach me how to control it. But now he's not here.'

'Christ!'

'What tortures do the American Navy use?'

'Whoa there! Hey, son, we're the good guys, remember. Bad dreams, tortures. You want a drink already, candy bar? Is that it? Why can't you just ask for one. American Navy. Someone has been neglecting your political education, Mr Lightfoot. It isn't agreeable to a gentleman, kid, to find himself comparisoned with Japs. Or Commies. A decent man doesn't likes it, understand?'

'Sorry.'

'Good. Now those nasty little bamboo boys'll torture you in any number of ways before they take a second glance. They're inventive.'

'I was just . . . I just wanted to . . . I don't know if I've got enough grit. To take it . . . like a man, I mean, if it comes . . .

The Japs aren't ever going to get to Australia, are they?'

'Jesus, no. Don't you worry any on that score. They won't try any damn thing again if they know what's good for them. Not after the licking they got last time. Know how to get a Jap out of a cave? Flame-thrower. Know how to get a Jap out of a war?' He chuckled.

'Yeah.' I made myself chuckle too. 'But in the US Navy. Do they have punishments, then. Tests . . . ? I was going to tell you . . .'

'What the hell d'you want to go on about things like that for? Torture. Punishments. D'you want me to tell you about the cat? You've done something you shouldn't? Now listen. A nice guy like me does not order up my shipmate for a flogging. Hell knows there've been some I'd have liked to. But nobody gets the damn cat. It doesn't happen any more. What's with you this morning? Think ol' Dave's going to come after you, do you?'

'I thought if I told it to you. He said not to tell anyone, my dad. But . . . He said we have to preserve the British . . .'

'Yeah. England expects. But that's all over now, for Christ's sake.' He looked at his wrist-watch, an enviable knobbed and knurled creation he called a chronometer. 'The lime-juice legacy. Post colonial frenzy. Know something? It's only three years ago your guys ripped up this harbour entrance and blocked the waterway. But that's all over too. And your Marines only killed six hundred or so Egyptians. Right over there.' He pointed. 'How about that? Not good guys, eh? Stupid guys. Who uses the Canal? Yeah. Stupid guys. England's all over. It's blown; just forget it.'

He adjusted his jacket and touched his moustache. 'But I believe I have an appointment with your mother in just one minute, kid. Do me a favour and keep an eye on that Arab down there. I've been watching him. I think he's up to something. Wait right here and don't come down. This is the mysterious East, son. Your mother and I'll be busy.'

For twenty minutes, as conscientiously as I could, I watched the Arab who sat on the foredeck, surrounded by his wares. Seemingly he had woken with the ship. Next to one of the winches, he was motionless under a large head-blanket. It made a tent against the sun. Hardly any other passengers were about.

Bored and beginning to sweat, I turned to look at the receding city.

Within moments, however, there came a sound of thumping plimsolls from behind me. I knew what they announced and prepared myself, hunching over the rail and affecting to take no notice. But it was to no avail: Barnwell's aircrew, jogging their circuit of the deck as a squad, broke off and slung themselves either side of me, panting.

'Been to a party then have you, mate?' said the one closest to me.

'No.'

'Oh. Thought you'd gone and got lit up somewhere.' They guffawed.

'Nice pyjamas, then,' from the one on the other side. 'Friend or foe?'

'Friend.'

'That's a relief, mate. Bet you'd go down a treat in Cairo.'

Their laughter burst open raucously.

One who had not yet spoken intervened. 'He's not a Gippo, Tosher. He's just been down in the hold all night. Getting toasted. And that's how you'll end up, Michael, my lad!'

'Shut it, Maclean.'

'Yes, corporal.'

'Rest over. Come on, you lot.'

'Oi, oi,' said the first. 'Just socialising with one of our young nobs. Nice weather we're having, don't you know. Warming up, in't it, for the time of year? Know how we used to kill flies in the desert? I'm talking to you, sunshine.'

'No,' I said.

'That's enough, Tosher. Get moving.'

'Treacle-belly flap cock. You take the treacle, see . . .'

Once more the others roared their amusement.

'Bet yours bloody glows in the dark by now, Len.'

'Yeah. Get Barnwell to run his ticker over it for you. He likes you, Lennie. You're always up his arse, aren't you? Get him to check your prospects.'

'Shag yourself, mate.'

'You're going on a fucking charge, Maclean. Now get formed up.' To me: 'Sorry, mate. No shore leave. Can't be too hard on 'em.' But the corporal was smiling too. They trotted off.

Because it was a Sunday, services of various denominations would be held. And Robert would take care to avoid them. He walked slowly to the head of the promenade deck, and then down where the stairs dropped into a region of no man's land, until he stood before the short run of steps up again to the cluttered foredeck.

The *Armorica* eased her way across a glass-green surface to join a queue of three other ships waiting to enter the Canal. In the brief delay we held water, effortlessly, between Ports Fuad on the left, and Said on the right. It was indeed a gateway. Eastward, in the huge lagoon from which the Canal was constructed, Fuad lay, a low, commercial reef. Various smaller ships were moored up against its sand-coloured wharves. Set back from its waterfront, drawn sharply dark by the sun's morning angle, and interspersed with the odd miraculous cypress, modern housing ran in a pattern of flattened cubes. Rebuilt, Robert supposed: though there was actually no sign of bomb damage. One might believe it had never happened. Further down, in the direction the bows pointed, there were small cranes and the spoil of dredging; and the smoke smudge from a cargo vessel. But of what he knew had actually taken place there were no certain traces at all.

23

He turned from the further shore's haze. A bum-boatman far below had kept pace with his progress and now hoped to catch his attention. Robert ignored him, and hung instead over the starboard gunwale. From here he could stare back on to the former British government building, just slipping astern. Russell had helpfully pointed it out last night. Drenched in brilliant morning, with its flag-pole, its two storeys of sugar-white arches supporting the central domes, it seemed to have risen from the water. And beyond the place floated the odd little city itself, where he and Penny had walked. That was bright, too, and rendered romantically simple by only a slight distance.

Robert had dreamed badly. It had been a fretful night.

'Sleep all right?' Joe had said, returning from the toilet. With his mouth still full of toothpaste, Robert gave a lying, thumbs-up sign.

'I'll give you a few pointers. You ought to know one or two things about how to conduct yourself in Australia, Bob. Gestures with the thumb, for example. Slightly different connotation down there, don't ask me why. It's not just a matter of hitching a lift, or all the best and a jolly good show. All right?'

Robert grunted and returned to the sink.

But Joe warmed to his subject. 'One other thing. The root.'

'The what?' Robert mopped his mouth, and, having rinsed his toothbrush and shaving equipment, straightened up.

'The root. See, Bob, the Aussies are easy-going blokes, friendly and so on. Really friendly. They like their beer and they stick by their mates. But they don't like the English. I mean they don't like the recent English.' He jerked his thumb very significantly in the direction of the ship's stern. 'And do you know why?'

'No.' Robert groped: 'Convicts? Being shipped out in irons?' But of course that was a century ago. He wondered, looking at Joe's expression, if he had blundered into an unforgivable. 'The root of it all?'

Joe relaxed into a grin. 'You mean the stain? Of course, you're right, Bob. Someone should have told you, though. Glad you brought it up here, with me. Never mention the stain, whatever you do. Never, never, never. By buggery. But the root, that's something quite different . . . The sheilas.'

'Sheilas are women, yes?'

'Exactly. You know what sheilas are. You don't know what the root is.'

'For Christ's sake, Joe.'

'Root is what sheilas are for. Root is what you'd call fuck.' There was a pause. 'I see.'

'It's called that—'

'Root?'

'Yes. It's called that, in my opinion, Bob, for a peculiarly Australian reason. Shall I go on?'

'I suppose you'd better.'

'It's completely underground and in very short supply.' Joe roared suddenly with laughter. Robert found himself laughing too. 'But here's the catch, Bob. This lot in the stern.' He gestured again. '*You* lot, I should say. You make-a-new-life-for-yourself folk – because although you're getting this all paid for, mate, you'll find you're in the same back end of a boat when you get there – *you* lot have views on the root which don't fit in with that oddly beautiful and arid thing, the landscape down under. Do I make myself clear?'

'No.'

'The Pommies breed, Bob. Understand? The Pommies come and they all live together, and they breed. They have women, and they're always pregnant. There's always kids and mess and women's stuff. You can see it. You can almost see it happening. It's all too visible. And you can hear it, if you walk too close. If you go to where the bloody Pommies cluster together. Bloody shrieking out. It's the root too blatant, not in the spirit of the root, Bob. At least the Eyeties and the Greeks and Hungarians and whatever can be kept out of sight; and whatever they do, they don't do it in English. Get it?'

'OK.'

'Good.' He laughed.

Robert laughed, astonished that somewhere in the world the English were seen as sexual.

'Oh, and one other thing.'

'Yes?'

'Australians don't have wet dreams . . . or anything in that kind of line. They don't need them, you see!' He hooted with laughter again.

Robert allowed himself to chuckle. 'Well, I suppose I'd better get down to my studying again.' He picked up a book. Any book.

'Aah, let it go, mate. I'm only giving you the drum.'

'Well, I think I'll go and look at the papers.'

'Come back after brekker. We'll take my chessboard to the library. Say, six moves each and I promise I won't say another word.'

Mortified, Robert escaped.

Now, looking directly astern, he saw a stub-shaped mark, past the city, furthest away of all. It poked up like a blurred matchbox from the waste of brown grit right back near the Med – they had passed it on their way in. It was the plinth of the de Lesseps statue, set up to greet ships from Europe. The portrait itself had been smashed off after the Anglo-French invasion. Robert had discovered the fact for himself. Russell had not mentioned it; nor had the ship's guide sheet. So it was the one sign of a moment of Whitehall panic. A disgraceful incident, not really admitted as such – more generally referred to as a fiasco. Everything all right now. Everything back to normal. Everything except Berlin cooled off – and that never cooled off. I should be enjoying myself, Robert thought.

But what would she expect of him, physically, if they should ever . . . He muttered out loud, 'Don't be bloody stupid.' He tried to fix his mind on the post-breakfast entrapment Joe had contrived. Despite his loathing for chess, and his lack of expertise, Robert had grown intensely irritable at the thought of another losing position. He found himself preoccupied – with what, he did not quite know. The board's ivory problems nagged at his attention. He liked her hair especially; it was shortish, like a soft, fresh cap, framing her face.

Could he only summon up the courage, he would like to explain to someone – about Penny, of course; to Cheryl, possibly, if he could get her early enough in the day. Or to some man on board, maybe, who did not have 'Made in England' stamped on his heart. Curiously, it might have been Joe, if he had not snared him into this ridiculous duelling.

Robert sighed. He felt something of the movement under him at last, a tremor of the lagoon. The propellers were biting harder. He wondered if he would have to defeat Joe to stand any chance with her. Superstitious thought, locking horns, getting nowhere. That was wearying. He was crazy to think of it. Crazy.

It was not long before the ship slipped quietly between the low piers just proud of the water, and into the entrance to the Canal proper.

She had two children, for God's sake. If he had only found an honest chum on board of the same age and in the same condition, as lovers in plays and stories always did. But he had not; and was debarred from contracting one by the illicit nature of his passion. If he were a rogue, or an American, to be meddling with other people's wives. Even a lathered cad, like that awful man in the bar. But he was not. With his class and background, there were no models, except love itself – whatever that was. In the night it had been his whole body, trying to get his attention, to shout to him: Penny Kendrick! Her! Nobody else! And he was shouting back: Impossible!

And what did *she* feel? What on earth was the meaning of the beautiful regard she bathed him in? For looking and seeing had done it – and that delicious soft smell she had about her. Not words – they had said very little to one another. It was what they had left out and given over to the subliminal nuances of the body, surely. Or he would not be feeling like this. Did she know she was doing it? Did she do it to everyone? Who could forget the gesture of the brass box? Or the moment when she turned to him without fear at the shock of that sudden knife fight? Or the indescribable elevation in his heart and the constriction in his throat when they walked back together past the gully-gully man?

Joe came down the steps and joined him. 'Nice day. A penny for 'em.'

While Robert's back was turned, an Arab had silently taken up a place on the foredeck, between the winches and the parked lading booms. Either that or he had been there all the time, unnoticed. He had spread out an array of dark, intricately tooled leatherwork – two whole saddles, assorted knives, swords, boots and whips. In the midst of his wares he was sitting down, waiting, swaddled in a blanket against the sun, or the early cold; and arched over by an immense pale sky. The lagoon and the flat land beyond him had begun to give light back, now that the last of the morning mist was lifting.

'What's on your mind, Bob?'

'Nothing.'

A few flies gathered, and would settle on the skin where the perspiration beaded.

In the British papers that had come on board there was the news of the Russians' latest success in space. They had turned a rocket into the first artificial planet. It was launched 'in the direction of the moon', and was now circling the sun. Within a month or so he would be decoding its progress on instruments. Among the progresses of other things. And there would come a time soon when rocket weaponry could be called down precisely upon any terrestrial target. Possibly from space. Possibly by him. *Black Knight* and *Skylark* had both been tested at Woomera – a modest but slightly triumphal note in the paper.

Robert found himself imagining how the Air Force must have come in on just such a morning, and filled this very place, in a few moments, with explosions. A column of water, a column of fire, deafening reports, splintering, screams. The neck of the Canal had been completely blocked with the burnt-out steel of ships – such as this one. It was frighteningly recent.

24

'What *are* you wearing?' Finlay Coote stood before me at the head of the outdoor stairway down to the foredeck. I had on a Hawaiian shirt. On a lurid pink background there were tropical beach and margin-of-the-jungle scenes in vibrant greens, blues, greys and floral reds. It had a silky wetness about it as though recently painted. It had been presented to me in our terraced house near Woolwich. I could never have worn it there. But in the ambiguous cool heat of the Canal zone that morning, Erica had thrust it towards me and I had complied. Moreover, I had teamed it with my blood-red swimming shorts, around which I had fastened the snake-clip belt from school. On my cropped and Brylcreemed head was the tasselled fez, the result of a bargain struck with a bum-boatman; on my feet, grey socks and cut-work sandals. I held a small horsewhip I had bought from the Arab. A man had said some of the whips contained hidden swords – you would find out when you snatched at the handle. They were thin, deadly things, like a scorpion.

'Is that your mum's blouse?'

'Mr Chaunteyman gave it to me. In the Coral islands the men all wear them.'

'You're mad. You look a real dill. Where's your father? Is he dead?'

I had met her yesterday, through Penny. Today her hair was freed from its braids and held back with an Alice band. She wore a pale mauve top and immaculate white shorts. Her thin legs made her just taller than me.

'No. Mr Chaunteyman's taking us. He's my dad's commanding officer. They're Navy friends. Only he's from America with the real cowboys and Indians, actually. You have to go where the service says. United States Navy. So he's taking us and my mother says it's right for us to go.'

The salt sands of Egypt lay all about, guarded by towel-headed sentries. We could just see one now, standing not fifty yards away on the bank. The Canal fitted so tightly around us that it was itself invisible from our vantage. We were a dream of a ship slipping through land. Every now and then, beside us, there came into view a parked jeep, or the odd military house. And, far beyond the concrete strip of road which accompanied us, across empty and intervening miles the colour of mud, it seemed there were always two dhows minutely rigged, sailing the shimmer of the desert.

'It's idiotic. You just look mad,' Finlay said again.

'I don't.'

'You do.'

'All right. I don't care. I like it.' She hurt me, but I brushed it off. 'I'm going down to look at the Canal. Are you coming? We might see some pyramids.' I showed her my whip.

She said, 'All right. Have you seen Penny this morning?'

Yesterday, as the ship closed with the coast of Egypt we both became Penny's friends. I recognised Penny: the distraught woman who came out of that bathroom during the storm. She began to take us under her wing. Today at breakfast I had been enraptured again with her long legs, her pretty skirt, her waist, her soft bosom and lovely face, kind, and momentarily frightened by my appearance – until she relaxed it into a smile.

Yesterday, after we saw the squid, she played some card-games with us in the main lounge, took us up to the boat deck to try deck tennis, and, between the lifeboats, talked to us about the sea. Then she hurried off through the port doorway, when a man, and after him a woman, came into view at the far end from behind the protection of the smokestack's central housing. Finlay and I had bathed in her attention.

'Yes. I've already seen her.'

We stood, hanging over the starboard rail as near the bow as passengers were allowed. We could watch the cut of the dirty green water, and the trouble of its wake from the tanker ahead of us in the slow queue. On the planking just at our backs a few grown-ups under the foremast were haggling with the Arab.

Finlay spoke again. 'What toys have you got?'

'On board? Couple of guns. This.' I held out the whip again. 'What you?'

'My jigsaws, Andrea my doll, colouring book, cards, writing-paper, my nurse's outfit, my three small koala bears that fit together . . . er, board-games compendium, French knitting. That's all I was allowed. Mummy said there wasn't room for much else and it's only for five weeks. Oh, and gummed coloured-paper shapes and some Japanese paper flowers that you put in water and they open. We got them in Singapore on the way out. But I'm not going to do them till we get back to Melbourne and I can put them on the window-sill in my bedroom. Oh, and my ballerina musical box. And my doll's clothes and hairdressing things. And I've got just four of my best story-books.'

I thought of my diminutive blue suitcase. 'D'you want to see my magic things?'

'Where are they?'

'In our cabin.'

'Is your mummy there?'

'No.'

'All right.'

The cylinder of brilliant sunlight from the porthole created a special, glowing bar above my suitcase's battered blue. Finlay peered in. There was a packet of itching powder; lemon juice for spy writing; the rubber toad; a bandaged-finger illusion stained red as if it still leaked; a nail-through-the-finger trick that might have caused it; two false beards with elastic; scarlet plastic starlet lips I held in my teeth; trick cards; swap cards of aeroplanes.

There was also a shoebox, and to my consternation Finlay opened it. Inside that were graver things: part of an amplifier on a bit of grey chassis; a sealed-up metal box; a soldering iron that would not work; the Holy Bible I had at school; my sheath knives, three daggers and one with a handle made out of a deer's foot; a compass my grandad gave me; a *Letts Schoolboy's Diary* with secret diagrams; my shrunken head; a flattened sheet of Plasticine that had gone dull-coloured and not like girls' skin at all; and the embarrassing picture from Erica's *Woman* magazine.

Her first choice was the folded picture – homing in before I could hide it: the illustration of two lovers embracing.

'What's this?'

'Nothing.'

'It's romantic.' The woman wore a ball gown, the man a dark suit. She clasped the picture to her front and looked at me strangely.

I said, 'It's stupid.' But I watched for the moment when Finlay, holding it by its edges, would bring the picture sufficiently away from herself. Then I snatched it back.

'Oh, Plasticine!' she said, swooping again. 'Let's make people. A family of animals. Let's make a farm.'

'No!' I put my hand over it. 'All these things I'm getting rid of. They're not toys, you know. They're not girls' stuff. They're magic. They tell you things. I've said, haven't I? I had a special jar of stuff. I left it by a doorway in Port Said. I'm getting rid of it all, now Mr Chaunteyman's come.'

'I'll help you. Let me help you.' She grabbed the toad.

'No!' I put the lid down on her arm. 'You're only supposed to look.' But she proved too resilient and yanked the toad out. She sat there on her heels, holding it up to her nose.

'It smells like rubber chocolate.' She smiled to herself. 'Ugh.' Then: 'You hurt my arm, dill.'

'Mr Chaunteyman brought it from Disneyland.'

'Oh! *Bambi. Lady and the Tramp.* Can you go to the films and get things? Can he do that?' Her face was earnest, spellbound. 'Could he get me something? A dog?'

'No, stupid.'

'Don't call me stupid. Don't you dare call me stupid. You're just a Pommy. I won't bother bloody playing with you.'

A girl had sworn. I had never heard that.

'You think just anyone can get things out of films.'

'No! I didn't say I believed that. I didn't. Disneyland. Get a bag, Pommy!' She held my eye. 'Anyway. I'll hide the toad. Let me hide the toad. I'll hide it in your bed. I'd like to see you get into bed and think there's a horrible slimy toad crawled into the bottom of your sheets; and when your foot touches it . . . Aaaah!' She mimicked me screaming. We both smiled, she with a certain seriousness, as if she relished my falling into her trap.

I thought of her snooty, beautiful Australian mother. And then of my own, with her bright red lips, her wired bras, and her American admirer.

'Give it back. It's mine.'

'No!' She hid it behind her so that I was forced to wrestle for it. 'Don't you touch me!' I had been up close against her for a moment, and now had let myself down. I came within an ace of hurting her. She smelt of soap and clothes, and, very slightly, of food.

'Mad boy! You look really stupid. You look like a bloody squid. Is this your bed?' Our steward had been in and the bunks were tidy. Everything was neat and in its place.

'No. It's my mother's.'

'Let's hide it in here. She'll think a toad's come out of her in the night.' We both laughed at the idea. 'Out of her . . . thing.' She looked down for an instant. Then we were convulsed with giggles.

'No. It's got to be wrapped up. Put in something.' An idea struck me. 'Why don't we,' I snatched the toad suddenly from her, 'play a joke on Penny. I know where her cabin is. This deck, same as ours. Why don't we put it in her bed? In brown paper.'

'Why in brown paper? You're mad. Your dad's dead, isn't he?'

'No. He's alive. He's in England.'

'Why isn't he here? Why does your mother sit with Mr Chauntey-Fauntey-what's-his-dill-name? He goes arm in arm with her. I've seen them.'

'He loves her. He's looking after her. He's taking us both away. My dad's too . . . important to come. He's working for the government.'

'Bull. I thought you said he was in the Navy.'

And so I have opened the suitcase at last. Just a collection of trifles.

Who then would be perverse enough to imagine that in the hold, under that well-known Merchant Navy label *Agricultural Machinery*, the *Armorica* bore a consignment of weapons-grade hatred; bound down and sealed in the assurance that no common tempest nor disturbance of the voyage could disturb its security?

25

'My little children, of whom I travail in birth again until Christ be formed in you, I desire to be present with you now, and to change my voice; for I stand in doubt of you. Tell me, ye that desire to be under the law, do ye not hear the law? For it is written that Abraham had two sons, the one by a handmaid, the other by a free woman. But he who was of the bondwoman was born after the flesh; but he of the free woman was by promise. Which things are an allegory; for these are the two covenants; the one from the mount Sinai, which gendereth to bondage, which is Agar. For this Agar is mount Sinai in Arabia, and answereth to Jerusalem which now is, and is in bondage with her children. But Jerusalem which is above is free, which is the mother of us all. For it is written, Rejoice thou barren that bearest not; break forth and cry, thou that travailest not: for the desolate hath many more children than she which hath an husband. Now we, brethren, as Isaac was, are the children of promise.

'We are the children of promise. You children, are the children of promise. I especially wanted to bring you this extract from today's lesson. Who knows what a promise is?'

'What's he saying?' I nudged Finlay.

'Don't you know what a promise is?' She wore the sneer of sanctity.

'Of course I do.' The scripture sounded as intimidating as such things always did. I had only gone to the Sunday school because of Finlay. And it was only because I wanted to sound her out that I had nudged her.

She melted a little. 'He's going to be a missionary.'

'That man?'

'His name's Mr Tingay. My daddy said. He's going to bring Christ's word to the Abos.' She held her piety a moment more.

'Mr Tingay?'

'Tingay.' She spelled it out in a whisper. Then her face slipped and she started giggling. 'Mr Thingy.' I giggled too. Everyone looked round.

Mr Tingay glared at us from behind his wire glasses, and from amidst the extravagance of his beard. 'What is it you find so amusing, those two children?'

'Nothing. Nothing, sir.' We stifled ourselves.

'Jerusalem that is above.' Mr Tingay pointed to the roof of

the dance space. The glass door-panels all down the sides had been removed at last, giving the illusion of a tent or pavilion. On either side stretched away the bright yellow–brown of the sands. 'Jerusalem that is above is heaven. It's where you will go if you are good. It's where I'm going, I hope. And it's where all your mothers and fathers are going, and all your brothers and sisters, and all the people on the ship, the captain and his crew. And all the people of this world who are in Christ Jesus.' He intoned the phrase backwards with a clerical tang.

'Yes, in him we may all go to heaven above. To Jerusalem that is above. All the people here on this ship today may choose salvation. We are born of a Christian country and a Christian Commonwealth. We have the chance to be good, and follow the teachings of the word. Jesus.' He nodded his head slightly. 'Avoiding sin. Sin is in us all. Sin is in me, in you, in our parents. And there is no help in us.' And then his voice changed to his other mode, to engage us. 'Who thinks they're good?'

A forest of hands went up. Then wavered, and fell back in case there was a catch.

'Yes,' he said enigmatically. 'And who thinks their mummy and daddy are good?'

The hands shot up confidently this time.

'Of course they are. And who thinks I'm good?'

There was an overwhelming show.

'I try my very hardest,' he acknowledged modestly. 'But beware of pride. In even the best of us there is sin. As in Adam and Eve, our first parents. Just when we think everything is safest, the Devil tries to tempt us.' He jumped the words out at us, and as a group we recoiled, visibly. 'I want to urge you all to put sin behind you. Put the Devil away. Say no to him, if you can, while you are so young. Because the only people who aren't allowed in are sinners. No sinners can go. God says to sinners: I'm sorry. You've had your chance to be good. And you wouldn't. You wouldn't be good. You wouldn't keep to the law. So you can't come in.'

Several children fidgeted nervously.

'Do you see?' He reached for his biblical singsong once more. 'Sin is not just keeping the law as the Pharisees do. God's law. If we sin, children, we stop Christ being formed inside us. Christ wants to be formed in us, in our hearts. If we sin we say to him:

No, you can't come in. That hurts Christ very much. He wants to come inside us. We must all try our hardest not to sin. And we must say sorry. If we do sin the only thing to do is say sorry, and really mean it.' And then again with his teacher bleat: 'Now, who knows what things are sins?'

While the others were obliging, I thought of the plan of the toad. I had the creature in my pocket. I went over in my mind the route to Penny's cabin, and imagined how it might look inside. Finlay had taken a brown paper bag from the shop. I looked at her hands, pressed demurely together in her lap. I supposed she was praying.

'Yes. The dead shall all be raised.' The Reverend Mr Tingay, broad in the beam and sports-jacketed, had moved on. 'In Jerusalem that is above all our family will be with us, our loved ones from generation unto generation. Their bones shall be joined up again and they shall be clothed anew in shining flesh. Ezekiel in his sands tells us this. From the Old Testament to the New, you see?'

His words made me think of Erica's ageing family of great-aunts and decaying widows in their darkened South London terraces. She was a permed and painted oddity in their midst; a lighted insect sipping mildew in a Dutch still life – I in her strange shadow.

'The dead shall be raised.'

Then we had to do colouring. The wood of the dance-floor decking came through into my picture of Jerusalem above.

The Torboys children erupted from Sunday school with plans for a game of Dragnet. It was a game of spies, factions, rivalry; in practice it was an enormous hide-and-seek, taking full advantage of the ship, with so many ladders, levels, nooks and crannies. In the Red Sea days that followed it would become our staple entertainment, I remember, binding us children together, Peter, Warren, Frances, Martin, those I had only really met for the first time that morning. We would soar into flights and escapades along three open decks at once, dodging bewildered cotton and silk, buzzing regimental blazers, infuriating walrus-faced old money. I recall Dragnet in the Red Sea as a Jerusalem I began to have faith in.

But that first Sunday Finlay and I were still cautious. The Torboys children were newcomers and untried; the scope of their game appeared grandiose. We had only just found each other, and besides had our own plans. At the start therefore we exchanged a look, which related to the toad.

Then we set off together as agents on the run. We had five minutes by the main lounge clock to make good our escape. To hide in one's own cabin was against the rules. To hide in someone else's was unthinkable. But how should we know whether Penny would be in hers?

The matter was solved by our flight through the Verandah bar. When we came out we saw Penny standing with the woman in the sari. They were surveying Egypt together.

'Quick! Which way is it?' Finlay whispered.

I led her down the aft stairs to where, on the same level as ours, I had seen Penny's cabin, back in the time of the storm.

Once Finlay shut the door behind us, I felt the interior of Penny's privacy close about me. It was a very precise strangeness, that experience of her folded things, the arrangements of what she put in her hair, on her face, in her mouth, the framed black-and-white photograph of two little boys in school uniform, a small leather camel. There was a distinct womanly smell, a powdery, perfumy, woollen flavour; on the floor her casual shoes, on the chair back the starched petticoat of an evening dress and some strewn stockings; her long filmy nightdress thrown on the lower bunk.

'Well? You've got the toad.'

'We shouldn't do it.'

'Are you scared? All right. Give it to me.' She drew herself up and held out her hand.

'I'm not scared.' I took the bagged toad from my blood-red swimming shorts, and wrapped the paper more tightly about it.

Baked yellow mud, silica-bright and glazing in the midwinter sun, was ring-framed in the porthole of Penny's cabin; guarded by soldiers – as if anyone should want it. I stuffed the toad mummy between the sheets of the lower bunk, made good, and turned to Finlay as if to agree on immediate escape. She made me stop and listen at the door for the sounds of pursuit.

'Why don't we stay here? They'll never find us.'

If I recall the smells and flavours of the room, and see now the speckle of face-powder spilled on a photo frame's corner, how is it I am at such a loss for what occurred between us in those next few moments. *Did* something occur? I have the sense of disgracing myself, of taking some foolish advantage of her willingness to delay. 'If you show me yours'? I am ashamed. I cannot be sure what I did. Nor how she reacted. I do remember that, overwhelmed by something, I grabbed for the door handle and ran out, straight into the religious-bearded and sports-jacketed bulk of Mr Tingay.

'Look to it there, young shaver!' he said, like a character in a schoolhouse yarn, and gripped me by the shoulder. 'Watch where you're going,' he added, as Finlay came flying out after me. 'Mind you behave yourselves, you two.' He bruised on past us in the narrow corridor, then turned. 'Did you enjoy your Sunday school?'

'Oh, yes, sir. Thank you very much, sir.'

'Aye aye, sir.'

Finlay giggled. Then it was all right between us after all.

He paused a moment before turning to go. 'Good. Good. Carry on, then.'

As he turned the bend of the corridor by the bathroom, I said in a loud whisper, 'Maybe the Abos will cook him and eat him.'

But she lifted her nose preciously. 'He's doing good work.' Then changed again; I was beginning to know her fickleness. 'He'd feed a good few of the bastards.'

26

It is a matter of a hundred miles or so from Port Said to Suez. Not all of that held the *Armorica* in so strict an embrace as the word 'Canal' might imply. There comes the Great Bitter Lake, and then the Little Bitter Lake, where the water, opened out, eats back into the land. They are hardly oases, and the convoy of which we were a member plodded resolutely across them until the banks drew in again for the final run of the cut. It was not so much hot as drily unforgiving. Our throats were like sandpaper.

But at last the *Armorica*, having paused briefly at Bûr Taufiq to make contact with the shore authorities, burst in the Sunday night from her confinement, and entered the Gulf of Suez, duct of the Red Sea. And by chilly dawn she was quite back in her element, making her accustomed twenty-one knots. The Red Sea itself, almost a lake, forms part perhaps of a continuing Canal, which only reluctantly yields up its passagers through the rocky teeth of Aden, over a thousand miles to the south.

Robert's agitation did not decrease, it merely became more diffuse. He found no opportunity to prosecute his interests with Penny, nor was he entirely certain he wished to. Perversely, after the intense awareness that had occurred between them at Port Said, he set about forbidding himself her sight. He stalked the lonelier spaces of the vessel like an outcast.

There had been a housey-housey session during the last sunlit crawl through the flat land; Robert did not attend. He was absent from dinner, too, and asked for something to be brought to his cabin. All that evening he had studied in the Festival-of-Britain-style library, with its bright distracting patterns, its modern armchairs and coffee-tables. He made notes unremittingly. The air was full of cigar smoke from a four at bridge. It hung in wreaths.

Later, despairing, he had taken down the heaviest tome on the glazed shelves and put himself to reading it – for the duration of the voyage, if necessary. So, at eleven, carrying his Gibbon's *Decline and Fall* like a millstone under his arm, he had returned to his cabin and been unfairly abrupt with Joe. Pent in the upper bunk he was acutely conscious of his cabin-mate's laboured breathing.

At midnight through the frame of the bed he felt the exact surge of the engines picking up again to full ahead, and was reminded by the renewed rattle of the door catch of that nervous first night out of England in the Channel. How far away the small damp country felt – as recalled through the windscreen perhaps of a cramped black car, grumbling, wipers sporadically on, a cocoon of dank leather. Those number-coded arterial roads he would never see again, advertisement hoardings, urban peeling-under-cloud sunsets reduced to postcard size. He allowed the impressions to follow one another. Nothing more than fragments of imagery leaving town: concrete street lights, a woman whose bicycle had a stretched, tie-on skirt shield, depressing semi-detached houses keeping pace with the road in a double ribbon, glimpses sideways through drizzled dusk into electric-lit rooms, roadhouses, poor cafés set back, a framed miniature waitress in her cap and apron. Going north. Going nowhere; to the industrial outlands if you drove far enough. He shook off the dust of all that.

He wondered whether it was hot or cool in the cabin, whether he should reach up and adjust the little air-conditioning nozzle overhead. No. He pulled the covers around him – and then threw them off. He could have anything he wanted.

How he loathed England's already potent nostalgia for rationing and the Blitz. It was the Blitz that had broken open the East End; everyone pretended to be a damned Londoner now. Except the actual Cockneys who came flooding out, uncomfortable, into the green fields. A whippet-skinny woman in a turban for her curlers, standing at a prefab's door. Harlow, Stevenage, in ready-to-stain cement. The tawdry, sugary popular songs. The trash and stuffiness of television. Bicycle chains, flick-knives. How glad he was to be away.

As dawn broke in the Red Sea the Lascars put out reclining chairs on the promenade deck. Exhausted at ten thirty-three in the morning, according to his faithful oblong watch, Robert flung himself on to one of them. He judged the sun half warm enough at last to still his relentless pacings. To himself he denied it was a strategy of thrusting himself in her way without the responsibility of speaking, or even looking.

In the afternoon there would be frog racing, that ludicrous petty gambling set-up where you worked a board, painted into the likeness of a compressed frog, along the dance floor by means of a rope. He opened his telemetry manual, smashed it down on the planking beside him as incomprehensible, and took up the Gibbon:

> *These voluntary exiles were engaged, for the most part, in the occupations of commerce, agriculture, and the farm of the revenue. But after the legions were rendered permanent by the emperors, the provinces were peopled by a race of soldiers; and the veterans, whether they received the reward of their service in land or in money, usually settled with their families in*

111

the country where they had honourably spent their youth.
Throughout the empire, but more particularly in the western
parts, the most fertile districts, and the most convenient situa-
tions, were reserved for the establishment of colonies; some of
which were of a civil, and others of a military nature. In their
manners and internal policy the colonies formed a perfect
representation of their great parent; and as they were soon
endeared to the natives by the ties of friendship and alliance,
they effectually diffused a reverence for the Roman name, and
a desire, which was seldom disappointed, of sharing, in due
time, its honours and advantages.

Midwinter in London is quite different from midwinter off
Alexandria. Midwinter nudging through upper Egypt is warm,
dry, not unpleasant – temperate you might say. What Robert
neglected was that the *Armorica* had been forging southward
all night at full speed. Midwinter off Mecca was tropical.

Robert's dream was like a Bible story with water-colour
illustrations – like those in the school Bible he had when he was
a boarder, a little boy away from home. He had become very
pious then, and taken to poring over the pictures for comfort.
A man in a blanket sat at the roadside, with his wares laid out
for sale. Robert was choosing a weapon. A woman's husband
was forcing him into a duel. Behind the Arab some Israelites,
or were they Ishmaelites, pulled at the arm of a shaduf, bringing
up water from a well.

Penny Kendrick was walking alone, along the bank of the
Suez Canal. There was a pyramid close by; and a palm tree. In
her arms she held a baby, swaddled, or mummified. She was
looking for her husband. She poked about in the reeds and
bulrushes every now and then. He was down there somewhere.
Under the water, possibly dead. Her dress was of a filmy white
gauze, pleated, gathered to her shape.

Robert was very close to her in the dream. He was almost
under her beautiful white garment. He could smell her skin.
He was intimate with her, yet he could see her at the same time.
He could almost feel lovemaking, yes, he was sure of it, they
were entwined. She was very beautiful to him, very desirable.
The angled light of the stars was woven around her.

There was a terrible shudder in the water, hardly a yard from their feet. A huge crocodile, suddenly emergent, struck. He did not see the jaws, he saw the dark plates and ridges along its back snaking and lashing the water; then came the frenzy of its roll, the yellow–green underbelly, glistening and delicately put together, glimpsed in an unforgettable flash of movement.

The sky was black with a kind of unholy rain. The rain was metal. It was on fire. It was glistening, oily, like tar.

Robert was lead-lined in a coffin, among the various grave goods, the extraordinary pictures on the wall, the inscrutable hieroglyphics. He could feel how hot it was, burning, scarring, like the skin of a crocodile. His body was wide open, yet he felt nothing. There were men and women who leaned over him. They would make him pure in spirit. They held instruments, a curved knife, a hook, a soldering iron, and peered inside the cavity below his ribcage. They would take out the last of his body, his brain, his mind. Preserve him against pain and decay.

They looked scornfully at his liver. They painted the walls with his pulped innards, and kept back some of the scrapings in a dish, for him to eat. Like food in a hospital kidney dish, in a sauce. Somewhere, far away, there was an explosion, bright as the sun. Mary Garnery, someone he had spoken to over coffee, came in and placed herself in profile. A voice said, 'She has been put in an intolerable position.'

27

Situated on D deck, off the foyer that led to the dining-room, were the two shops, the counter that gave access to the purser in his office, and the hairdressing salon – where Cheryl had her appointment. Lucas left them there after breakfast. Penny and Cheryl drifted about among the clothes for a while, pulling out a few of the scarves, discussing a bag or two, very expensive, kid, crocodile, finest calf and so on, until, with these informalities complete, it seemed reasonable to go and sit down together in the hairdresser's.

'Of course in Africa we were spared all that. I'm a sun lover. I bloom in it. Lucas had this farm in Rhodesia. Imagine, just nineteen and he comes into his own farm. His father spent all those years building it up, out of virgin bush really, you know; and he thought he'd be stuck there for life – until he met me. It was what he'd been raised to. I was up seeing some boyfriend or other. Actually we met at the VJ night dance. Couldn't take our eyes off each other. Or our hands. Talk about virgin bush – my dear! Oops. Don't mind me, I'm always outrageous. I can't help it, darling. That's how I am.'

Penny smiled and nodded. Cheryl was so easy about every-thing. Her little laughs and looks were like racy punctuation.

'But for all I was crazy about him, Penny, I wasn't going to stay being little boss country wife. There are more things in this world than watching your black boys bringing in tobacco, for goodness' sake. And he was just itching to be off, himself. I could see that all right. I knew it – he just hadn't told himself how bored all those acres made him until I came along.'

The hairdresser was finishing up with his client. 'He'll be ready for you in just a moment, madam,' said the girl. 'Can I get you tea?'

Cheryl nodded. 'Thanks. We sold up, Lucas and me. Headed south. Penny, we really hit town. Haven't stopped since. Just not the same town, my dear. Of course, you have to find the right crowd. Otherwise it can all seem frightfully stuffy, can't it? We didn't stay long in the Cape. Lucas met a man in a hotel and got offered something in the Gold Coast, would you believe? What we're supposed to refer to now as Ghana, isn't it? I can't get used to all that, Penny, can you? White man's grave. And white woman's, darling. If they hate us so much, all right. We'll pull out and see where that leaves them. We've tried to do our bit, God knows. Let them get on with it. Let them eat each other. That's what I say. Rather us than the Germans. Or the Portuguese. My dear, they don't know how lucky they are. But they won't be told. You can't tell them anything any more. Let them find out for themselves, then.'

She picked up a magazine, and then put it down again. 'I kept thinking, would I be the only girl? For miles? All very well. But we were young. We didn't care. Off we went. You know me, game for anything, go anywhere. Turned out it wasn't much after all. But that didn't matter. Ran into some Americans. Now they were really nice boys. And it wasn't the money – we had enough of that. You can live so cheaply in Africa, darling.'

Cheryl made a musical, joking sigh, and rolled her eyes. She glanced briefly at the two other customers waiting.

Penny wondered at the freedom: to find adventure so natural, so effortless. To play life, take such distances in one's stride. It made her feel parochial. 'Why were there Americans in the Gold Coast?'

'Because they were looking for oil, darling. Everyone's looking for oil. And that put Lucas into the way of following a hunch. Lucas always has such a nose for business. He can smell out a deal. Some you win, some you lose. We don't mind. Hopped into Nigeria. Hopped into shipping. Shipping what? Never mind. Shipping anything. Don't ask me how he does it. Hopped across to Kenya, never mind Mau Mau either. Everyone panicking and losing their nerve. They never frightened me. Fell in with a really good crowd in Nairobi. Those were good times, Penny. And if they don't like us, let them get on with it. That's what I say. Like children, isn't it? You do everything for them. Don't know if I like the look of Alphonso much. Maybe I'll just get a shampoo and set after all. I mean, would you let a man with sideboards like that near you with the scissors?'

Penny laughed. 'Have you ever been to Australia?'

'Passed it, darling. Never actually stopped. Somewhere on the right, I believe. Passed it on the way to Hong Kong. Five years in the beautiful East. Now there's the life.'

'I'm not sure what to expect. You make it sound so easy.'

'What's his name . . . Hugh, didn't you say? Pity you couldn't travel together. We go everywhere in harness. Lucas says he doesn't want to let me out of his sight. Can't think why, darling, can you?' And Cheryl drew wide her bright red lips and made a knowing chuckle in her throat. 'He likes watching me, you see. Now young Bobby likes watching you.'

'Oh, ridiculous!' Penny could not but laugh in turn. 'You're extraordinary.'

'Oh, I know that, Penny, dearest. I know that all right. I know when to get in, and when to get out. The Houdini thing. Escapology, do they call it? That's the name of my game. A great crowd pleaser. Take my advice.'

Penny determined to take up her journal once more. Everything was all right after all – positively forging ahead. She chose the

115

open-air route back to her cabin, breathing the good cheer of bright skies. The sea was a dusty blue. Robert Kettle had disappeared, and she could address the aberration of her last entry with spirit, with equanimity. She did not, after all, *have* to show the diary to Hugh. She did not have to be *available*, in every way, just because he was her husband. Perhaps she just needed privacy.

She unlocked her cabin, walked firmly in, and, standing beside the lower bunk, took firm grasp of the bedding. Cheryl was outrageous. She lived in a made-up world. She ought to have been in one of those silent films that ran too fast. But you couldn't help liking her. Poor thing. Marriage was something quite different now, since the war. It had to be. Surely Cheryl and Lucas were dilettantes, too hectic and frothy, like children still. She and Hugh were soul mates, of course. People always said as much. Or they could perhaps become so, in the new world. Now Mary Garnery, on the other hand, knew exactly . . .

Just as she was about to brace her back into the weight of the mattress, however, she noticed the bump which raised the blanket at the unused bed's centre. It was a small bump. She backed away for a moment. She regarded it with distrust. Her mind flicked the pages of an extreme tropical bestiary. Who knew what might have come on board?

She caught up last night's high-heeled shoe. Very gingerly she advanced to the bed again, and poked at the bump. Lightly. Cautiously. There was no movement. No. It was all right, perhaps. There was no horrible, smothered awakening. She tapped the place with more assertion. 'Well?' she said, out loud. The bump did not stir. 'Perhaps just somebody's sock, or a pair of knickers.' It was about the size. Too large for a stocking; too small for any other garment. Yet I would have noticed, she said to herself. Is the steward getting slack, or odd, stuffing my things in here? In the very centre?

She allowed her guard to relax a degree or two and waited, listening, watching. No. It showed no signs of life at all. So she stepped to the bed once more, seized the sheet's turnover in both her hands and, ready on tiptoe to make emergency exit, flung the covers back.

It was nothing. It was a brown paper bag, twisted and creased as if with much use. She picked up the shoe and hit it again with the heel. The paper tore. The colour of a bruise was inside. She picked up the other shoe and, leaning over boldly, employed both heels to rip at the hole.

What she found made her feel sick. It was a vile rubbery shape with hands and feet, knobbled over with warts, spines. She continued to stare, uncomprehending, until she remembered everything, and the tears welled up and she was given over at last convulsively to sobbing.

She had lost the baby and there had been no one to tell, and it was as if it had never happened. Only a couple of months or so old anyway – kept that a secret. A surprise for Hugh when she got out there. A surprise for herself. She had put it out of her mind. They had not wanted any more children. They had decided. She had hardly acknowledged she was pregnant – all that excitement, the packing up, leaving, the anxiety. So much to attend to. Parting from the boys. Dealing with Mother.

And then that moment in the storm, when something shifted inside and it was lost. It was lost. And she just carried on. As if nothing had happened. As if it was all over and forgotten there and then and someone else had had the pain – all that awfulness in the toilet. Clearing up the spots on the floor afterwards, leaving no trace. Someone else.

But it was her. She didn't forget. She knew all along. It was hers.

Someone knocked and came in, his hands full of cleaning implements. 'I'm sorry, madam. I thought the cabin was empty.' The steward's eyes flicked from her distraught expression to the toad on the opened bed.

Penny hid her face in her hands. Then she hurried past him through the door and fled along the corridor.

So far we were the only people on board ship who knew someone had been killed. Finlay stood on one side of him and I on the other, holding my Winchester repeater popgun loosely on my finger by the trigger guard. It almost smoked.

He was stripped to the waist. He lay collapsed across one of the special deck-chair loungers, flung right back, so that his head cricked over its end rail. His face was in stark shadow from the overhang of the deck above, but below his neck, across the skin of his throat, his arms and his stomach, under the wisps that grew there, shone out a bright, unbasted pink. One of his arms hung down touching the deck at the wrist's bend. The other lay across his chest, as if clamping the huge book to it. But I could see no sign of a wound.

'Is this him?' Finlay said.

I nodded. As soon as it happened I had run back to fetch her.

'Well?' she said, trying to sound unimpressed. But her looks gave her away.

I scanned up and down the walkway. There was only the departing back of one of those old men in blue shorts and socks, staggering on round the deck. What Mr Chaunteyman referred to sneeringly as the last constitutionals, I did not know why. And beyond him, some people were scattered, sitting out, sunbathing with drinks, or reading, absorbed in themselves. In the other direction one of the Lascars was painting the metalwork white.

'Do you think we should do something?' I said, weakly. Only I knew the truth.

'You're sure he's dead? Are you sure?' Finlay held away, with gathering horror.

I held away too. I looked down and all along the smouldering body. There was no sign of movement. It seemed quite defunct. Then the book and the hand that rested on it slipped down and hit the chair frame with a soft thump. A real dead man's jolt. That and the sheer oddness of the vast stripe across his surface fused my guilt.

'Yes.' I stared at the deck, thin greyish planks with the tarry black between them.

'We've got to tell someone, I suppose.'

'Yes. I suppose we have.' Then I noticed the cherry stone I had fired. I had been stalking imaginary cowboys, seen some, blasted; reloaded, seen more and fired my popgun indiscriminately round a bulkhead frame. The cherry stone lay on the deck, not far from my sandalled foot.

You could get the cherries out of empty glasses. I had a supply in my pocket. But I was not dimly credulous. Even to my child's grasp it seemed extremely far-fetched that a person might be wiped out by something so puny. Yet here lay the slain proof. I struggled to make sense of it all. I had heard at school of the fragile pressure points in the bones of the skull. If you pressed on your temples you could kill yourself. Or that place just under the ear – true. Supposing, by the most hideous kind of accident, I had got one of his pressure points. It could happen. It would be the worst kind of luck but it could happen. I trod cautiously beside the stone, stooped to retrieve it, and then slipped it into my pocket.

'Don't be stupid,' she was saying. 'We've got to tell someone. We've got to hurry, Pom. In films they always scream and go running and shrieking. Why do you keep wearing that dill hat?'

I put my hand up to touch the fez.

She seemed to be on the brink of tears. 'Why don't you do something? You're so useless.'

Once more I looked ahead and astern. The grown-ups in the distance were calm and preoccupied.

'*You* do something. Why should I do everything?'

'Why should *I*? Why should *I*? You found him.' Her face changed. 'What do you think he died of? Do you think it's a murder?' She inched closer. 'Wait. Look. I know who it is. He came ashore with us at Port Said.'

But now I had pocketed the stone and no one could pin anything on me. 'What's his name, then, if you know him so well?'

'I don't know his name. Why should I know his name? I bet he died of some disease. My mummy said. Port Said. That stinky place. I bet he died of the poo of Port Said.'

'That's a rhyme. Maybe his poo was poisoned.' And I ventured on, looking for the giggle of her acceptance. 'Maybe they stuffed poison up his . . .'

But she stamped her foot. 'Don't be disgusting. You're just a dirty Pommy bastard and I'm telling.' And she was about to rage more and hold my preoccupations over me, when I saw behind her a shape that looked familiar coming along the deck in our direction.

'There's Penny.'

Finlay turned and ran to her, and was almost instantly at her side, explaining everything, tugging her hand, pointing back at where I stood next to the dead man. 'And that's just how we found him,' she said as they came up, pointing again. 'It's terrible, isn't it? It's that Port Said man. They put them overboard, don't they? Wrapped in a flag.'

119

Penny looked, and then drew in her breath as her body seemed to jump. She made a small noise. I could see her eyes looked different – swollen and strange, her face, even with the fierce sun behind it, puffy, darkened here and there with blotches.

At that moment Robert awoke, blinked and groaned as he tried to sit up.

28

Penny burst out laughing, full of relief. He was ridiculous. She wanted to embrace him. But his surface screamed: *No!* The skin is so excellent an organ, so responsive, tough, and yet fragile; so beautiful. She wanted on the instant to tend to him with cold creams and healing unguents, soothe him with her touch.

'Now, Penny, which is the most emotional of the animals?' Michael Canning had teased her last night in the lounge. The others had joined in, suggesting various behaviours: screeches, grunts, tail-waggings, chest-beatings, crocodile tears. They had made quite a party of it – but the riddle was insoluble. 'Everyone give up?'

When, with his schoolboy grin of triumph, Michael Canning offered his bizarre answer, Penny had gone straight off to the library in disbelief, to look it up. She sifted through navigational memoirs and natural histories until she found it. It is the octopus; which, frustrated of a voice by water and heritage, wears its feelings on its eight sleeves and flushes the bulb of its head with chromatic waves. The octopus is the most candid of creatures.

Now Robert, similarly naked, wore his feelings on his skin. Cut off at the neck by the shadow of the overhanging deck, his body flagged up his heart. There is no simple code-book. It was after all an enormous self-induced blush to be in her presence; yet it forbade her to respond. With his bluish-white stripe across the lobster pink he was all valentine. But Penny was reminded of the boy, Pom or whatever his name was, with his predilection for blood, making those gruesome enquiries of her about punishment. Did he *ask* his mother to dress him like that? Odd child, but boys will be boys. It struck her suddenly that Robert had been chastised. One might almost say his skin showed the first flogging of the voyage.

At the frog racing, Penny could not stop thinking about Robert's body. She lost eight shillings. How he lay there sprawled out. For a terrible moment she had thought he really was dead. Then the poor man moved and, in waking up, made that heart-rending groan. She was mortified now by the laugh that escaped her. She realised as soon as it happened he was in a bad way after all. People had begun to cluster round. Someone got hold of the quartermaster from the dance space. He had come, clutching one of the frog ropes.

Robert brushed the attention away. 'No. It's nothing. I'm quite all right. Just a touch of the sun. Nothing to make a fuss about. Please.' He made to walk. Then collapsed.

They took him to the sickbay. There was a stupid distraction, a shriek, when that wretched boy managed to hit Finlay Coote in the teeth with a cherry stone. Why must he act up now, the child. The kind who would try deliberately to lose at board-games.

She went back to her cabin. In her mind she did soothe the burns, tracing the shape of his arms, smoothing his breast. It was as if the shape of him glowed inside her own, or that she was gone out of herself like one of the saints obsessed with wounds. Not that she worshipped him. Nothing abasing or ridiculous like that. More that she knew she was fascinated in a manner not experienced before. She longed to see him; simply to see again what had disclosed itself to her: his body, from the waist up, clear, strong yet very delicate and damaged. It was strangely marked.

She wondered if she might be allowed to take him something – some fruit, perhaps. Or flowers. Or perhaps something less intimate – for she would not want to be giving the wrong signals. She should not need particularly to visit him at all. He was nothing to her. So what if his body had taken up residence in hers – well, that was a private thing of her own. What was the phrase? A sexual fantasy, no doubt. Apparently they were considered normal. Of course she would not go. How violently her emotions were playing tricks on her. Why, only this morning she was weeping over the miscarriage. It was intolerable. Quite intolerable. Vulgar, even. Like Brighton beach, even. And she knew, as everyone did, exactly what Brighton stood for.

Yet she had a certain proprietary right to visit him – as the person who found him. Not counting the children who thought he was dead. And what a shock that had been: the thought, just for a moment, that he was . . . It would not leave her alone. Why should she not visit him? He would be covered up. It would be the decent thing to do. She did know him – after a fashion. He was ill. She had discovered him.

What more natural thing in the world than that she should call in at the sickbay, one of the cabins on C deck – she had happened to find out exactly where – to visit a friend who had been silly enough to get himself roasted in the Red Sea. They might laugh about it. A lucky escape, maybe. From something worse – if she had not happened to be passing, and woken him. He might be grateful. He damned well ought to be. She ought to give him the chance to say so, ought she not?

Cheryl had said . . . But Cheryl was Cheryl . . . Yet he *had* been avoiding her. She was sure of it. What was he expecting, then? An *affaire*? Surely not. The impudence. But he had made no overtures of that kind. There had only been the message of his eyes. About which in her heart of hearts she understood all too well? To be absolutely honest? And now the meaning of his beautiful, painful skin?

Then she had better keep well away; or she would be getting her fingers burnt. And that would not do. Surely that would not do at all. So she made the best of the remainder of the day and turned in early.

But in her bunk-bed in the dark she continued to feel him lying there almost next to her, and could find no balm. He burnt her on the edge of sleep, where images chased one another off the rim of the world. The toad no longer troubled her. She could not be frightened by it and did not care. The phrase 'free woman' swelled in her mind – from the lesson at the service yesterday. St Paul. She had not noticed it especially then, whereas now it filled her head. Her thoughts sailed ahead of her, into the tropic zones, beyond Sinbad, beyond the Spice

Islands, through the Strait of Malacca and out into the Pacific. She saw the delicate charts of Cook, the log-books and sketches of Bligh. She had found them in the library. Now the whole blue binding of the book of the sea, wearing red as its signature, was quite indelible.

There was a knock at her door. Cheryl came in. 'Penny? You all right, darling? Thought there might be something the matter. Just wondered if there was anything I could do?'

'Oh, God. Cheryl, it's you. No. Quite all right, thank you. Yes. Just thought I'd turn in early for once. Catch up a bit on my beauty sleep.'

Cheryl hesitated just inside the doorway. The light from the corridor outside made a faint sheen about her hair. 'You sure? Can I get the steward to bring you a glass of chocolate or something?'

Penny shook her head.

'You didn't look too good. I was watching you at dinner, you know. You really ought to be eating better, dear. Enjoy yourself, darling. That's what we're here for.'

'I'm fine, Cheryl. Really I am. Tummy ache. Headache. You know.'

'Of course, darling. See you tomorrow. Sorry to wake you.'

'I wasn't asleep. Really.'

'I'll let you alone, then. If you're sure. Remember, if there's anything on your mind . . . anything at all.' The light was behind her but Penny thought she appeared to wink.

'Thanks, Cheryl. I do appreciate it.' Penny yawned. Cheryl closed the door behind her.

Mr Chaunteyman had no such scruples, apparently, and called on the still slightly delirious Robert in his sickbay the next morning.

29

He blew in like the simoom, the bad wind.

'A word in your ear, old chap.'

Robert registered an American, speaking the phrases of an

Englishman. He wondered whether he was properly awake, and looked around the room to check. Then he recognised the tall, dark-haired, slightly balding visitor as someone else who had once bought him a drink in the Verandah – an obvious alcoholic. He had made that judgement on the spot. Very likely an ex-serviceman, killing memories. Not an uncommon thing, if you knew how to look for it. Robert had lived with the problem all his life, and could tell the signs. It was a family secret. He hated it. The father was fine – could go on for years, provided nothing real was allowed to touch him. If it did the balloon would go up. But in general the drinking could be managed, kept dark. Robert's was a close family; in which everyone did their bit.

For it never actually showed up in the music-hall sense – these types did not slur their speech, nor fall down. Their noses were rarely pickled; they did not sing. They were ostensibly quite ordinary chaps. Gentlemen. It was just that certain conjuring tricks involving alcohol happened around them. And only if you looked very carefully would you catch the exact quantities being put away. That was the constant thing. He was quite sure he was right.

'We met at lunch last week. Dave Chaunteyman. Remember? Heard you'd got a touch of the sun. Pretty bad luck, eh?'

He extended his hand; a good-looking man, well built. His looks gave him a stylish, indeed, slightly English flavour. And, with that thin moustache, he could 'old boy' Robert, who was a decade his junior, as if he had picked it up through long association. Which Robert was sure he had not, for the rest of his speech was more or less thoroughly transatlantic – though he had 'manner'. Chaunteyman was possibly, he thought, the son of some well-connected Yankee family.

But behind his suave veneer and air of command the man was plainly desperate for company – that too had been obvious to Robert in the Verandah bar. Half an hour then and he had felt compelled to escape. This time Chaunteyman's need was as unsubtle as the flavour of his breath. Clearly he had started early. Robert felt uneasy; and escape was impossible.

'Hurt much?'

'I was a complete idiot.' He spoke lightly. 'Absolute bloody fool. I thoroughly deserve all I got, I expect.'

'C'mon. Might happen to anyone. Guessed you could use a

little company. Adversity makes us all the better shipmates.' He grinned. 'I took a liking to you, Bob, the moment I set eyes on you.' And then he paused. From his left pocket he produced a bottle.

Robert sighed at the remorseless inevitability. Something like this would have had to happen. He had known it, of course, deep down.

'Guessed you might need a little cheering up. If that nurse doesn't show her nose.' Before Robert could reply he had located a pair of tumblers and was placing them on the locker top. He pulled up the metal-framed chair.

'Kind of you, Chaunteyman. I'm afraid I feel ill.'

'Sorry to hear that.'

'I won't, if you don't mind.'

'Ah. If you're sure, then? Hey, call me Dave. I can't convince you, then? Tried and trusted cure?' Chaunteyman hesitated. 'You don't mind if I . . . ?'

'Please. Go ahead. Dave.'

The bottle shook very slightly. 'I get frustrated, cooped up with you passengers. No offence, but it's foreign to my nature. I'm used to sailing the god-damn things.'

'Oh, yes. You said.'

'Sure did. US Navy. And proud of that I can tell you. Where would you guys be now if it wasn't for us?'

The excuse was lame. The bottle rang warning bells. Something had driven this man to blow his cover.

'I guessed we should try to get to know each other better. Since we're destined to become partners, it seems. And I thought all along we were just rivals.'

Robert started. The skin across the top of his chest roared against the sheet. He groaned, and lay back.

'That's right, old chap. Take it easy. You'll be fine soon enough. You're an invalid, remember? Take it real easy, why don't you?'

'How could I forget.' The front of his body throbbed where the burn was. And he was nauseous. 'I may have to . . . Is there a bowl?'

'Sure. Sure. It's here. I'll hand it to you. Just say the word. Shall I call for a steward?'

'Partners?'

'Hey. Well, yes. In a manner of speaking, old boy. We're in the

125

same ship. Bound for the same port of call. If you remember.'

'Adelaide?'

'Why yes, Adelaide. And thereafter you for Woomera, me for Pine Gap. We're both going to be watching the fireworks, isn't that so. There may be a trade-off. You understand me? If I'm impressed I'll make a favourable report.'

Robert just stopped himself from reacting. 'Oh, really? I can't recall . . .'

'Sure. I told you, I'm headed that way myself. Your government and mine, there's a joint agenda. A special relationship, don't they say? For a while I'll be around in Salisbury.' He slightly mispronounced. 'We have a client company or two. I mean the Pentagon. That's who my employer is, Bob. I make no secret of it. You'll have worked out as much in any case. I'll need to touch base. Then up to the desert. Uncle Sam has quite an interest there . . .' Chaunteyman showed his teeth. 'Australia. Hey.'

Confused, Robert's eye avoided his companion's. The jacket was a discreet check, but the tie was brighter than an Englishman's. 'I didn't know you . . .'

'Hey. We spoke about it.'

'I must have got hold of the wrong end of the stick.'

'That's OK. Maybe we'll run into each other.'

'In Australia?'

'Surely. Thought I'd look in. See how you were.'

'It's very kind of you.' Robert settled back. He felt his eyes heavy. There was a pause in the conversation. Then he enquired again, pondering, 'Rivals?'

His look must have given him away. Chaunteyman chuckled. 'He thinks I'm going to steal his girl. You folks are paranoid. We're the good guys, remember? But with you it's always: Go home, Yanks. Overpaid, oversexed and all of that. Give it a break. Relax. Relax especially about women.'

'I'll try.'

'Women. I've had it up to here with women. Don't get in where you can't get out. Didn't your old man ever teach you that? My dad, Commodore Chaunteyman . . . But hey, the military on this boat. Phwee! Top heavy. Enough brass to capsize us, one way and another. Isn't that so? Now don't play the innocent. I'm Navy. I said, didn't I? US Navy and mighty proud

126

of it. Don't you ever forget that. What outfit were you in?' He took another large swig, and refilled his glass.

'Me? National service. Barracks. Square bashing. Spud bashing. And how to steal cars, I'm afraid. Sorry.'

'Is that so?' Robert felt himself being studied intently. 'Well now, Mr Kettle, that does surprise me. Are the British losing their grip?'

'Eh?'

He drank. 'I just want a little god-damn respect around here. Is that understood?'

'Of course.'

'That's OK, then.' Chaunteyman held out his hand. Robert shook it. 'Now don't you get me talking about women, Bob.' Still clutching Robert's hand, Chaunteyman leaned forward, conspiratorially. 'Hey, women are the bane of my life. They won't leave a man alone. They just won't let us get on with our jobs – or our lives, Bob. Isn't that so?'

'Yeah.'

'You'll be OK with old Dave.' He squeezed the hand. 'I'll show you a thing or two. You're missing your girl? You're young. There's a woman on this boat, Bob. I don't mind saying you can bet she's crazy about me. I'm talking tail, Bob. English tail. At least she talks English. English woman very good jig-a-jig. Hey? Joke. Now, I've had my share of women. But I have commitments. I have my job. Hey, someone else's girl, Bob.' He finally let go his grip and poured himself another large one. 'Have you ever had a Hawaiian?'

Robert shook his head.

'The Japs are good, the Filipinas are great, but the Hawaiians . . . ! The Hawaiians are prodigious. Hey, but there's the kid. Not mine, I hasten to add. But there's the kid. OK? You and me are men of the world, Bob. You're young. You've got a way to go. You can have any girl you want. I have commitments. I have my job. Women. I make her feel like a tart, she says. Tart? I say. What's that Britisher for? We have an altercation, Robert, old chap. A mighty big altercation. Jesus. I am so bored on this trip. So damn bored, Bob. Thought you wouldn't mind if I dropped in for a chat. You don't mind, do you?'

Robert shook his head.

'Look, Bob. I've been a fool. You know me. I see it, I buy it.

I've got it, I spend it. I'm a generous old . . . crawfish. People come and people go. I like to make a woman smile. A sucker for a pretty face.' He looked abstractedly at his glass. 'Guess I get myself in over-deep.'

Robert lifted his sheets away from his chest. He eased the fabric of his pyjama jacket; it did nothing for the feverishness. When he looked back the man was holding a gun. It was a dark blue-metal revolver, just like the films. Like a toy. But not. Incredible – just like that. Chaunteyman had put aside his glass and was playing the tooled grip from hand to hand, looking down, apparently unaware of anything out of place. The weight of it thumped back and forth in his palms – pure Hollywood. If the thing had not been so incongruous, so stark in those cared-for fingers, Robert would have laughed. In fact it was a complete anaesthetic: he froze.

'Guess I get myself in so, so, damn – bloody – over-deep.' The American looked up and chuckled. 'Can't seem to get anything to go right. D'you know. Happens every time. Too soft-hearted. I get taken advantage of, Bob. Taken advantage of.' He parked the gun in the one hand to free the other for the glass again. 'Happens every time. And again. A kind of a repeater, you know.' He chuckled again. 'I'm not really the settling-down kind.'

There was a long pause.

'The way I feel this morning, Bob, I wouldn't care if I never saw another woman. Found the one beside the Thames. Trapped in a . . . What d'you call 'em? Trapped in a terrace and just too terribly sexually grateful at being swept away, Bob. And the other one loose on a liner.' He smiled sadly. 'Crazy about me. God-damn them all to hell. That's what I say.'

There was another silence. The objects in the sickbay, curtains, chair, pile of blankets, took on a disturbed extra clarity.

'D'you know I sometimes think, Bob, I sometimes think I wouldn't care if I never saw another damned thing.' Chaunteyman gestured with the gun towards his own head, meeting Robert's eye once more.

'Life's certainly a problem.' Robert's mouth smiled back. 'I know just how you feel.'

'Do you, Bob? Do you?'

Slowly the gun came down. Chaunteyman cradled it in his

lap. 'We're on the same side, Bob. No question of that. Just a little friendly rivalry. Don't worry about that girl of yours. She's a great girl. We're both on the side of democracy. Hey? Freedom and democracy. Isn't that right?'

Robert's pain had roared back with a vengeance. His arm felt as though someone were striking a match on it. 'Could you pass me that water?'

'Making the world a safer place. Making the world . . . a safer . . . place. I guess there never has been a time before when the notion of war was on the point of going right into retreat. Deep down the Russkies know that. Your government knows it. Even the French know it. I served in the Korean, too. Those days we still had to fight to show the Commies who was boss. They still thought it was worth a shot. But now . . . Making the world . . . hey . . . a safer place.' Chaunteyman held his gaze again. Although his head made faint dodging and weaving movements.

'I guess I shall wind up in the Pacific this time. You know I'm an authorised observer. A buyer.' He bared his teeth. 'Look, I realise you're not feeling the best at the moment, Bob. So I thought maybe you could use a visit. Thought maybe you'd like to join me in a drink. No? You don't mind if I do, though? How is your skin, now?' The gun jabbed loosely in the air. 'Let me take a look. I'd like to see the damage, shipmate, if you've no objection.'

Robert drew down the sheet and undid his jacket buttons. Chaunteyman stared, put the gun on the bed and then placed his hand into the space marked by the book. Robert flinched and gasped.

For several seconds neither man spoke. The hand on his chest felt as if it might leave another imprint. Then it was removed.

'Well. We've come through.' Chaunteyman's eyes were glazed.

'Come through?'

'The Canal zone. Of course all that's blown over now. There was no question . . . Still, I felt a touch of unease. They didn't much like the look of us, did they?'

'Hardly surprising.'

'World War Three. You British took us to the brink, eh? Trigger happy. Jumpy, eh? Who are the cowboys now, Bob? You know the Reds are pledged to world domination. I guess you Brits would know all about that. What is it with you guys? What is this need for power? You always have to have what you haven't got. You want to control everything and everyone. You want to swagger about still as if you did.'

Close to panic, Robert heard breath bubble in his chest. Upon which he could still feel the ghost of the hand.

'Yes. You can laugh, Bob. You can laugh all right. You want to bring us all down with you. If you have to go down. Which you do, Bob, you do. You want to go down fighting. You want to bring the rest of us down with you. God-damn bastards.'

'I'm sorry?'

'Oh come on, Kettle. There are top brass on this cruise. Now just what's going on? Don't act the innocent with me.'

'Here?'

'Here on this damned ice bucket of a liner. I can tell because I'm involved, dammit. It's my business to know these things, you sons of bitches. I have some mighty influential connections. What's the little cookie you fags have? There's something right here in the *Armorica*. I'm dead on target, Bob, aren't I just? Something cute. A piece of ass.' He banged on the bedclothes with the gun handle.

'Look. I don't know what you mean.'

'I don't know what you mean.' Chaunteyman mimicked Robert's accent. 'Stuck-up, taffy-nosed pinks. And we'll have to come bail you out again. Now look Kettle, I need you to give me . . . I'm telling you, for Christ's sake . . . You'd sure as hell better cut me in . . . ' He stopped, aware of the door opening behind him.

Robert looked over Chaunteyman's shoulder. The nurse was showing in Mary Garnery.

Chaunteyman stood up and, knocking over his glass in the process, shoved his gun away into one distended pocket, and his bottle into the other. 'You fucking British make me sick.' He pushed his checked shoulders roughly between the two women, and disappeared from the sickbay, leaving Robert completely stunned.

30

'I'm sorry. I thought you might like these.' Mary Garnery held
out some crystallised ginger. Her skeletal wrist appeared briefly
from a white cuff, before she could hide it again in a casual,
almost defiant pose. 'That's almost all there was that was any
good. I seem to be intruding.'

'God,' Robert said, taking a long, painful breath. 'He . . . I
don't know. I thought he was going to . . . Christ! He had a . . .'

The nurse picked up the pieces of glass and placed the chair
back under the dispensing desk. 'Dear me,' she remarked as
she took herself off.

Mary said, 'I'll come back. I've obviously caught you at an
inconvenient moment.' She deposited her gift and left too.
Robert's 'No. Please don't mind . . .' followed her out of the
cabin.

He was stranded here like . . . like a piece of raw flesh.
Cooking, almost. Slowly cooking in his own . . . presump-
tuousness. Its turning of him was so unbearably slow. Eventually,
he would be done.

There came another knock at the door. Appropriately named,
Mrs Burns in a floral frock with white belt, white gloves and
white shoes wondered whether she could come in. Her husband
crept in after her. They were the mouselike middle-aged couple
who dined at Robert's table.

'We hoped you wouldn't mind if we just . . .' She advanced
timidly to the region of the bed. 'We thought you might like
these. Oh dear.' She saw Mary's cellophane bag of crystallised
ginger resting already on the locker top where she was about to
place her own gift of the same.

Robert recalled, then, having seen the packets placed
prominently in the shop. 'Extremely kind of you. Thank you so
much.' He smiled. Pain ignited suddenly across his chest, like
the petrol douse under a flicked cigarette, and the smile turned
into a grimace.

Mrs Burns was concerned, drawing breath in between her
pressed lips. 'There. It's bad, isn't it. Dear me. Well . . . I'm sorry
you've already . . . we thought.'

'Oh, yes. Somebody just came in. Don't worry. I'm terribly
partial to the stuff.'

'Only we noticed you weren't at dinner,' Mr Burns chipped in. 'We heard . . .'

'We made a few enquiries,' said his wife. 'We do hope you're all right.'

'Oh, I shall be all right. Such a stupid thing. I'll know better next time.' He groaned and then gave a wry laugh – which hurt again.

'It's very lucky she found you. Mrs Kendrick, that is. Or who knows . . .'

'Take the skin off a man's back,' said the mild Mr Burns, suddenly and with punitive relish.

'It's the front actually.'

'Jolly good.'

Mrs Burns creased her face into a wince. 'Oh dear, yes. It would be. Is it awfully painful?'

'It's not too bad if I don't move.'

'Ah. Well, we just popped in.' She glanced at her husband. 'Perhaps we'd better be . . .'

Robert seized the moment. 'Have you seen her this morning?'

'Who?'

'Mrs Kendrick. I'd like to say thank you – and all that.'

'Oh no. We haven't seen her at all. Now you get plenty of rest, Mr Kettle.' She was taking charge like a nurse. 'We all want to have you back with us fit and well. All right? We don't like to think of you . . .'

'Soon have you back on your feet, I expect. Now you just take it easy, there's a good chap. Grin and bear it.'

They edged themselves out of the cabin. Mr Burns put his finger mysteriously against his nose; his wife gave Robert a little fluttery wave.

Paul Finch-Clark called. He pulled back the metal chair and hung himself over it the wrong way round, like a poet. His blond hair flopped in his eyes. His knees in his old navy cords thrust out round the canvas in the chair back. They discussed for some time the shades and degrees of sunburn. Robert felt it strange that someone else he hardly knew should take an interest. If a set had formed, then he was on its fringe – while Penny was close to its centre. When he eventually managed to steer the conversation around to her, he found his visitor evasive.

'It was dance night last night. I didn't see her. She's a dashed

132

nice woman, Penny. I don't mind saying so. I was looking forward to asking her. One gets attached to people, doesn't one, on this sort of jaunt. In the nicest possible way, of course. Wonderful girl. Pity we all have to lose touch at the other end, Kettle. It's a good crowd, don't you think?'

'You haven't seen her this morning at all?'

'No. To tell the truth I have an idea she's been a bit cut up about something lately.'

'Cut up?'

'Missing hubby, I expect. Don't you? And the boys back in England. It can't be easy for her, can it, the whole family split up. Women miss those sorts of things more than men. As far as I can see. Don't you think? Bless 'em. I know Dilys gets fretful if I'm away just for a day or so.' He dashed his hair back. 'She likes to know I'm around. Not up to no good.' He chuckled. 'As long as I'm not under her feet, of course. Women hate that.'

When he had gone, Robert pondered the implications. He came to no firm conclusion. He felt jangled and could not think clearly at all.

By late morning much of the feverishness had subsided. He worked out the only bearable resting position: lowering the sheets to the limit of decency, abandoning all coverings whatsoever on his affected parts, and spreading his arms wide. That way what cooler air there was – the cabin was heating up – could circulate upon his tender surface.

In the corridor outside, there came frequently the sound of running feet. At first he was puzzled. Then he remembered it was the children. They had got up some enormous spy game of late and were forever dashing here and there in gangs, pulling people out of hidey-holes, or dodging behind pillars.

He wondered how far gone Chaunteyman actually was. With his hints and insinuations. Was he just about to disappear over into the DTs, or had he actually had a painful row with one of his 'women' that made his early-morning performance seem so extreme? Could he really be some sort of military agent for the Americans? He had, after all, managed to find out a good deal about a fellow-traveller's plans. And had taken Robert for something he was not. Perhaps he believed his own fantasies.

And had any of Chaunteyman's remarks applied to Penny? With the anguish of a lover Robert would have it so: she was in danger, Chaunteyman was a seducer who thought he detected an easy conquest. Worse, her appetites were uncontrollable. She had delighted in leading Robert on while being all the time 'crazy about' this ageing playboy; by whom she was cheaply aroused and reduced to 'English tail'. Which, if that were the case, was all she was damned well good for.

Such tormented imaginings. They hurt him like his own skin. But every so often they would cool and return him to reason: that Chaunteyman's chaos was of his own creation, that Penny was Penny and separate from it; and that he, too, was his own distinct self.

In the aftermath of these saner moments he became able to prop the *Decline and Fall* against his knees and browse half-heartedly on Gibbon's rolling periods. And when he felt he had done enough with one pair of pages, he would swing up a naked scarlet arm, taking great care not to bend it, and gingerly perform the page turn – although Penny's image was still imprinted there.

Thus he occupied his time, with occasional testy interruptions from the nurse.

It was shortly before lunch that the Madeleys appeared. Mrs Madeley gave a gasp when she saw him, but whether it was at his nakedness, his affliction, or the extraordinary book-marked stripe of white in the centre of him she did not make clear.

They brought grapes – from the chef. Robert was compelled to pull up his bedclothes. She turned the metal chair round again and sat, pleated and pink, while Douglas stood, his bare knees close to his wife's careful folds. They were full of sympathy and retrospective advice. Their children, the daughter now grown up and married, the son killed in the war, had always burned terribly at Sidmouth, where they had been accustomed to go each year. There had been no telling them, they would never listen to sensible advice, playing in the sun.

Robert commiserated.

'Of course, before the war we had better summers,' Stella Madeley was saying. 'As a rule I think we did, although you can never be sure if the mind isn't playing you false, can you? I always think of that as the golden time, Mr Kettle. Since then there has been so much . . .' She drew off. 'I do feel though that the present decade really has been appalling for its weather, don't you? But then you're quite young. Nothing to compare. Childhood is always sunny. But such disastrous Augusts. And one can't forget Lynton, Lynmouth, just washed away. Heavens. North Devon, we used to tour . . . Didn't we, Douglas? So delightful. Since the war all our efforts just seem to have been, how should one put it, rained off. Of course they say it's the bomb . . . One never knows . . .'

Stella Madeley glanced up at her husband. Robert sensed that Douglas had been deputed to say something. He was looking away. His mouth twitched slightly. His dangling hand fiddled with the seam of his navy-blue shorts. Cued by the silence, he launched in.

'Look here, old chap. Don't mind saying we're a shade worried about Mrs Kendrick. Stella found her in her cabin this morning. Shaken up, you know. Not quite the thing. Being a bit emotional. Naturally we're concerned. Very nice sort of woman – as you realise.' He paused. 'Feeling a bit vulnerable I imagine, with no husband on board to look after her. Hugh's already in Australia. I expect she's told you. We wondered, Stella and I . . .' he placed a hand on his wife's shoulder before continuing, '. . . we wondered whether you might be able to throw any light on it.' He hurried on. 'Whether you might have noticed anything. She wouldn't confide in Stella. Said there was nothing the matter at all. Brushed the thing aside, you know. But we want to look after the poor girl. Feel she's rather our responsibility, do you see? Several days now. Missing meals. Whether you'd . . . Whether you'd any idea what the trouble might be . . . any light to throw on the . . .'

'No.' Robert shifted in the bed and indulged in some genuine grimacing – and some gratuitous. Anything to cover what his true face might give away. Though of course there was nothing for it to betray. He had done nothing 'wrong' at all. And yet he shifted nervously; and all his wretched skin flared again. 'No. I've no idea. I hardly know . . . I wonder what made you imagine . . . ? I understand it was Mrs Kendrick who found me yesterday. I've been hoping she might call in. So I could thank her. But as for anything else . . . ? No. I'm sorry. No idea. I had no idea.'

'Of course. Of course. Felt we had to ask, you understand.

Feel responsible. Well. Just have to hope she comes round soon. Shakes it off. I'm sure we all want what's best for her, don't we. I'm sure we'll all do our best. Just thought I'd mention it, old chap.'

'Of course. Of course,' Robert echoed, heartily sick by now of 'old chap', 'old man'. So that was it. This message at least had got through. He was being warned off.

> *The Armorican provinces of Gaul and the greatest part of Spain were thrown into a state of disorderly independence by the confederations of the Bagaudae, and the Imperial ministers pursued with proscriptive laws and ineffectual arms the rebels whom they had made. If all the barbarian conquerors had been annihilated in the same hour, their total destruction would not have restored the empire of the West: and, if Rome still survived, she survived the loss of freedom, of virtue, and of honour.*

'Cut up?' The words came back. Penny was 'cut up?' A horrible image. It occurred to him to wonder where the war had gone off to after VJ. Where was all that horror and carnage, that unbelievable Roman spectacle of an affair . . . Where on earth was it lurking? And now these 'friends' she had acquired, who were so worried that she was 'cut up', were using his imprisonment to tell him how to behave. How dare they. Why, it seemed the only person on board who did not have some interest in his conduct was Joe. He could really have done with talking to Joe.

Cheryl sat herself amply on his bed. It strained the covers over his navel. 'Help yourself,' he said, meaning the crystallised ginger.

'So, Bobby. What *have* you been up to now?'

'Sunburn. But I think it's high time I got up.'

'Did I say something wrong?'

'Sorry. I don't mean you. I will not be stuck here to be . . . to be . . . to be at everyone's convenience. I must get out of this room.' He was furious, and resolved.

'Oh! Well. If you say so, darling.' She stood up and turned her back.

Robert thrust himself into his trousers. 'I most definitely do, Cheryl. Most definitely I do.'

31

The *Armorica* sailed between the rocky bite of Yemen and Djibouti to dock at Aden in the sunset of the next evening. She had curled and twisted around the unfriendly-looking jags, to waters progressively calmer, stiller, darker. The breakwaters, long low arms, one with a small house on the end, marked the edge of a continent. Egypt had been a glimpse. But with that Africa was over, hardly seen, hardly touched. The dark continent, with its uranium and its manpower, an immense weight back there under the sun's disc, back beyond those coastal rocks.

Robert gazed astern, at the streaked water. He watched the accompanying pair of tugs begin to scurry up alongside. A covered launch plied across the confusion of their wakes, not far away; and in the clear there was an open boat, dhow-rigged. Two crying seabirds swooped, but apart from a few mid-sized vessels they had passed at anchor, fixed now in the glare behind like floating impurities in a melt of gold, the whole gulf was empty. It held an eerie beauty. Robert felt it. The sun visibly, almost audibly, dropped; the ship slid under him. Half-way already. From here it were as well to go on towards the East as ever dream of going back.

The bows were nudging towards a wall of rock. Lit up eerily white on the first promontory, Government House loomed over a small destroyer moored up under the bluff. Its arches and palm trees echoed Port Said. Those hills behind looked grim and resistant, like a collection of Alp summits, sliced off. No plant could grow upon them. The terrain was extreme. There were white blocks on the foot slopes, slabs and terraces pierced with windows. That was the town.

Half anxious, half excited, he was determined this time not to submit to its otherness – and be forced to retreat as in Port Said. And he could move himself about now, with care. Under the light shirt and linen jacket, his body was anointed with a lotion for the pain. He slipped below to see to his passport, change some money.

When he emerged again, it was quite dark. Aden was a loose cluster of lights and their watery reflections. The breeze smelt mustily of rock and powder. As for the *Armorica*, she was still moving almost imperceptibly. At last he felt her screws go into the gentlest of reverses. There was a splash as the anchors went down. The thirty thousand tons of steel came to rest: the weight ran through his body like a tremor, a flicker, followed by the tenderest of slingings away, and the firmer jolt as the hawsers caught the strain again, swinging her a degree or two further round towards the jutting land.

'Don't whatever you do buy cameras.' Douglas Madeley stood by his shoulder. 'Even if the brand is reputable, the lenses are invariably cracked. They get them by some back door or other, hoping to palm them off on the unsuspecting traveller. Only a trained eye can tell. Sure you won't come along with us? Might be safer, you know.'

They had only the evening. The captain was still trying desperately to make up time. Their schedule was all blown to pieces.

'I rather fancy trying my luck on my own. You don't mind, do you? I'm still feeling a little groggy. A little down. Not up to company much.'

'We don't mind. Anything, of course. Entirely up to you. Just take care, though, won't you. Don't let them put anything over on you. And take it easy. Are you sure you're really ready to be up and about?'

'I'll manage, thanks.'

'Have you got one of these?' He held out the leaflet of advice produced by the shipping company.

'Oh, yes.' Robert patted his jacket pocket – and then wished he had not. He winced and bit his lip. Thankfully the running out of the gangway stairs – from the doorway that opened out of C deck – prevented Douglas going through the leaflet with him. And in any case, after his stream of visitors, Robert hated all this concern. And so, at odds with the cruel sun, he would thrust himself, for the moment at least, into the night.

The situation recently has been extremely unstable. Thanks, however, to an agreement signed by HMG only a matter of five days ago, we have a right to expect some easing of political tension. Passengers are nevertheless reminded that they go ashore at their own risk. While every effort has been made to secure the co-operation and goodwill of the port authorities,

138

the Company cannot be held responsible for any unforeseen
difficulties arising as a result of shore visiting.

We recommend that you keep together in groups and treat
the blandishments of street vendors or touts, as always, with
the utmost caution. It would be wise also to avoid remarks
which might cause controversy or offend local opinion.

Forgetting her meal, Penny sat at the dressing-table in her cabin
with her wrap round her. Four cigarette stubs were in her
ashtray. She poised the Parker Fifty-one – Hugh's early
Christmas gift – over the note pad. The gold of its nib glinted
in the flare from the light bulb over the mirror. With her free
hand she curled up the pages slightly, rereading the letter:

My dearest,
Tonight we are in Aden. I intend to go ashore, but probably
only briefly. To be perfectly honest I can't imagine much profit,
except of course the reassurance of solid earth underfoot. We
have to go at night, and be in by such and such a time. It all
seems so rushed, such a problem. The place is 'delicate', 'touchy'.
Not entirely safe, then. Phrases are bandied about: political
situation, British Army; and people speak of Sheikh this, King
that. I don't know. But then again it would be so very foolish
to miss an opportunity of seeing the world, now that I have the
chance. Such a chance. I should be grateful, I know, darling.
Most people would give their right arm, and I don't mean this
to sound ungenerous.

I confess I've been having a bad patch. There are several
nice couples, though, who've taken me under their wing. You
remember when I wrote from Port Said I described the Cootes,
Russell and Clodagh. There are also the Madeleys, and the
Finch-Clarks – and Cheryl Torboys and her family, of course;
and all in all quite a good 'gang' of pleasant folk with whom I
generally find myself going about. So that is all right, isn't it?
Do I lack for company? You can rest assured. Tonight we shall
make up some sort of shore party, I don't doubt. I shall join
them when I've finished writing to you.

There is the special smell of the ship in my cabin here. I love
it. It's dark outside, my curtains are drawn. The vibration that
always runs through the walls and the floor is still going,

faintly, even though we're at rest. The flavours of the wood, the
spiciness, the delicate saltiness of everything – it all seems to
come out at these times. The ship's side is just here, I can touch
the metal; it runs right down between me and the water.
Well, I say I have grown to love it. It is my own place. For the
duration, of course.

As for the bad patch, it is nothing, dear. Mostly homesick-
ness, I'm sure. Wherever my home is! Just been a little off colour
perhaps the last day or so but that is no more than a passing
headachy affair – you know how I get. And trivial really.
You may be certain I shall be myself again tomorrow. So I am
being self-indulgent, and would not be writing gloomily like
this were it not that we have to catch the post wherever the
ship stops. If only I could be allowed to write to you tomorrow,
out on the high seas again, with a clear head and true heart, I
should not be burdening you with my troublesome little affairs
or grievances. But that is not permitted. How could it be? So
I am petulant now. I'm so sorry.

All is not helped by a general sense of strain about the boat,
almost like an impatience, a rush against the clock. That is the
fault of the wretched storm. We were set back days, as I told
you, and the captain seems to be an absolute slave to schedule.
One would have thought that in voyaging to the other side of
the world a day or so was neither here nor there. But apparent-
ly not. How many thousands of miles is it? Everything would
be quite different if we had to make Cape Horn in time for the
best of the roaring forties, or whatever, as they had to in sail.
You could be set back months, couldn't you? But these days
when we are not really at the mercy of wind and tide any
more you'd think they might let us get our breath back. I don't
know; it's just a sense, a kind of tension about everything.

I suppose I must have been brought up with accounts of a
more leisurely era, when life was more settled everywhere.
Are we lucky, or unlucky? Looking back, the Canal feels rather
'skin of our teeth'. This is nonsensical; yet it was really quite
threatening. Going through what amounts to a Russian sphere
of influence. Feeling hated.

She was dissatisfied. Certain words had crept in which might
give the wrong impression. The part about tomorrow bringing

a true heart. That odd sentence in which she referred to her little affairs and grievances. In writing it she had not noticed. Now they shouted at her from the page; the more she queried, the more she could not tell whether her whole tone was simply normal, or pregnant somehow with Robert Kettle's burnt limbs. Glaring even. Loving the ship. Not knowing where home was. And all that talk of a bad patch. Why did she have to tell him that? She would be all right by tomorrow – she had said so already. Why could she not just write him a cheerful letter, then, with nothing worrisome in it? Why could she not simply *deal* with her feelings? She had always done so before.

She should redraft. That would be better, less disturbing for him. She would have to redraft. Glancing at her watch, she took a new piece of Company notepaper:

Dear Hugh,
There have been no more storms, you'll be pleased to know.
This evening finds me in good spirits, on the point of going
ashore. In fact, I must be brief. They're waiting. So do excuse,
darling, this rushed letter. We are in Aden, and set sail again
in the morning in order to make up lost time. Every day brings
me nearer to you, which is an advantage . . .

She stamped her foot under the dressing table and swore silently. '. . . which is an advantage'! What a thing to say! Even Hugh could not fail to miss the lack of passionate feeling. And if, under pressure of the post, she sent just a quick letter, what in any case would that mean? That the whole length of the Red Sea she had not thought about him sufficiently to manage a few pages of tenderness and affection?

She ripped the paper, screwed up the pieces and threw them towards the curtained porthole. Then she glanced again at her watch. She had missed the high tea laid on instead of dinner for those who wanted to make the most of Aden. Now she was supposed to be meeting Russell and Clodagh, and the Madeleys. Like last time. They would all keep together, which would be perfectly all right. But the letter had to be done tonight. Why could she not achieve so simple a thing?

With the prickle of tears beginning in her eyes, she tried again. This time the words came out in a flood, which she found she no longer had the will to censor or resist:

141

I am in the middle of nowhere. Everything I ever knew has been left far behind. I long for news of the boys. Why should I worry over them so? You will think it foolish of me, I know. To tell the truth I have not been well; nothing serious, I'm sure. Homesickness? Presumably. Separation from the children – and from you, no doubt. Of course. You must remember I am not used to being on my own. So these are just my wilder thoughts thrown down. Think nothing of them – I do not want you to turn into a worrier too. I suppose, Hugh, it just helps to spell it out on paper. It actually feels disloyal to be as agitated as I am. But it is nothing. Everything is all right. Will be all right when we meet and I am . . .

She had been intending to write '. . . in your arms again'. But could not. Simply could not. It was infuriating. And the watch said twenty-to-eight. They would give her up; she was not even dressed. She would have to find a postcard in the town somehow, and just send her love. Then write at length from Colombo to explain. Explain what? Oh, it was too maddening.

She had her spotted frock ready laid out. Underclothes. Stockings? Perhaps. Covering one's legs – a seam up the back to assure the locals of a degree of formality? The elasticated roll-on. One dirty, the other nowhere to be found. Laundry not back? Nothing would go right!

She reached the door to the gangway having run across the ship's waist and down the ladders. But her party had gone. She asked the officer. He had no idea when. She felt half finished. Her make-up was skimped. The officer, in his neatly pressed shorts and starched white shirt, looked at her steadily. Her stomach felt obscene, as though her horrid stretch marks might be visible beneath the frock. He was very sorry, madam, but he didn't know her people by name. Several groups of passengers had recently gone ashore. There was a launch waiting just now, as it happened.

'Thanks. Thank you very much.' She hurried down the long flight of metal steps into the Arabian night. She would catch them up. There were a few places left. She stepped into the crowded and jittery little boat, with its two lamps and wooden seats. They could not have gone far.

32

Afterwards, her remembrances of Steamer Point would not keep still. They were full of stars and the tungsten filaments of naked bulbs. And of how she met Robert in a cramped dusty street that ran up towards a great clock tower. Of how they stood and talked by the people's beds – low wooden frames with woven string to lie on – placed outside in the hot, peppery darkness with the crowds and the bustle of the ship's community all spilled out. How it looked as though the whole town had always been full of chattering and bargains, in a language that rose and fell, half song, half nasal shout, to the humming of generators; full of brightly dressed travellers like paper flowers.

And they were invited by voices, importuned, or beckoned with thin, desperate fingers. 'No. No, thank you,' she had said. There were disputes like dreams. Smoke rose from lighted bins down back alleys and mingled with the drain fug that pervaded everywhere like the cooking of sour herbs.

It had been difficult, she thought now in her cabin bunk, saying clearly at once both no and yes. But at the time absolutely certain, moving along a certain line: no to things she did not want and yes to what she did oh most definitely want just at that moment – to walk in company with Robert Kettle under the stars and electric light.

You would not think of venturing off the main street. Yet despite the swirls of children who ran in and out of the shadows calling, begging, selling, ready to pick your pocket, no doubt; despite the hooded and armed desperadoes no doubt behind them, waiting with curled knives and moustaches, she did not feel threatened. She felt there was a safe route. She had said so to Robert Kettle. They had laughed about it, about the lack of menace.

With people from the ship all around them, they had pressed on up. They saw soldiers roistering, almost in slow motion, around a grey Indian-looking building. The cries of basket-makers, leathermen, tinsmiths, camera-vendors grew fainter. How slowly they went, looking into this doorway, noticing there a roof made out of overlapped carpets, commenting on that dangerous-looking web of power cables. How jealously they husbanded their time. She could remember every word he had said – how he had talked about his work, about his growing up, about the voyage – and almost none of her own, though she had chattered away too. She was sure of it. Had she said too much? He had been concerned that she missed Peter and Christopher.

The beggars were hideous. No one had ever begged from her. Nothing so stark, she thought. A light hung from a pole. From under its yellow blaze a man with no legs had lurched forward at them. He held twisted pieces of wood, like miniature crutches, polished shining grey by his grip. With these he kept up, calling in English for money, running alongside on his sticks and embryonic feet. And next there were outstretched hands holding cups, from the figures squatting by the walls, so that you must pick your way between, saying, 'I'm sorry. No. No, thank you.'

In the small flattened square before the clock tower at the top they drew breath. Robert had pointed out Mr Chaunteyman amid the knots of other passengers straying up thus far. 'Do you know him? He came into the sickbay this morning and lost his temper at me. I've no idea why. And that fellow with him is called Barnwell. Doesn't he look grotesque in his suit and trilby hat?'

'They've got Pom with them.'

'Pom?'

'The boy who found you in the sun. He was convinced you were dead. He wanted there to be a burial at sea. He was quite fed up with you for your poor old signs of life. I only know him as Pom. That's what little Finlay Coote calls him. Oh, and that's his mother, I believe.'

The blonde woman had come up to join Chaunteyman. Then, failing to secure his attention, she drifted slightly away, taking the boy with her by the hand.

Robert asked, 'Do they make a family, then? Chaunteyman and his woman?'

'I suppose so. They're difficult to make out.' The boy had pulled the woman to follow him until they had their backs to a white building. The mother seemed reluctant to be removed from the two men, but submitted. Penny had watched the paper bag twitch for a moment beside the red shorts, then slip out of the boy's hand against the wall and fall to the ground.

'Come on.' She had taken Robert Kettle's hand. It was on an impulse. And just at that moment it had seemed what one did and what one must do. She pulled him through the crowd until they stood a few yards up from the boy and the mother. 'We must wait here a moment.' She looked up into Robert's smiling, surprised face and kept his hand, just a moment longer than was needed. It was a firm, safe hand. She found she had always wanted to hold it just so. Then she let it go.

Like everyone else they stood looking down at the little harbour where the *Armorica*'s floodlights blazed, and the town rose up in layers to their feet. The faint outlines of hills and rocks stood out all around.

'It's beautiful, isn't it, in such a strange way? It's like the fairground you could never have invented.' He had made no reply. Only smiled into her eyes.

Then Chaunteyman and Barnwell moved off. The boy and his mother followed. Penny had darted forward and pounced on the paper bag just beating two Arab boys who appeared from nowhere in their striped and ragged night-shirts. They cried out in disappointment.

'Wait a moment and you shall have it,' she said. 'Just wait, all right.' They hung back muttering. 'I only want to look,' she told them.

The paper bag contained a pair of plastic Jayne Mansfield lips and a piece of Plasticine. 'What do you make of these, Robert? May I call you Robert?' She turned the items over in the glow of one of the light bulbs.

'The kid's little treasures, I suppose. Probably be lost without them.'

'But I watched him drop the bag. He did the whole thing – deliberately. It was a manoeuvre.' They laughed at the word.

'I don't know, then.'

'Treasures!'

One of the Arab boys spoke. She did not understand.

'Here then.' She let the items fall back into the bag and handed it over.

On the way down they had found the Madeleys and the Cootes in the middle of the small, makeshift market next to a pyjama-clad coppersmith. There was still quite a press here, people flickering like the flames and moths of a softening camp-fire. Douglas was bargaining for a coffee-pot. A man with an old First War rifle was trying to move his bed. The animation of voices hung like a sweated flavour.

'Oh, Penny. You're here!' Stella clutched Penny's arm a moment. 'We gave you up. Thought you must have decided to stay in your cabin . . . And Mr Kettle.'

'I was late. Trying to write a . . .' She glanced round. She had forgotten all about the letter. And now she was supposed to be finding a postcard. It had quite gone from her mind. 'Do you know where I . . .' It struck her that it was the least likely place for postcards she had ever come to. As if you might expect to find a stick of Aden rock, or trips round the pitch-dark bay.

'The shops are owned by Jews, and Indians,' Russell explained under his breath, catching her gaze. 'Shops are foreign to the Arab temperament.'

'You didn't come out on your own?' Stella studied her reproachfully.

'Yes. Why not?'

'All right then. But not a penny piece more.' Douglas handed over his coins and received his pot. He nodded to Robert.

'Luckily I ran into Robert,' Penny added. 'It was quite all right.'

'You took a risk,' Stella scolded.

'Surely not.'

'My dear. The notice. Didn't you read it?'

'What notice?'

'She's not been quite herself these last few days, have you, Penny,' Douglas said pointedly to Robert.

'I'm perfectly all right.' Penny laughed. 'Perfectly.'

'Well, we'd all better stay together now, at any rate, I think,' Stella said.

Penny glanced at Robert, then replied, 'Of course. If you like.'

'Of course,' Robert added. 'Good idea.'

'It's best to keep together, Penny.' Clodagh Coote linked arms with her. 'What do you think of the place?'

Penny surveyed once more the extraordinary scene. There were even some donkeys. And camels, surely, packed in over there amongst the people. She made out their silhouettes as the acrid, heated presence came to her nostrils. 'It's wonderful.'

'But doesn't it smell absolutely frightful?'

'What do you think of this, Kettle?' Douglas held out his purchase. The brass fittings glinted with points of light.

'Pretty hideous,' said Robert.

Everyone had laughed nervously. Except Penny, who laughed with sudden happiness, and thought of his burnt naked limbs; and, in one way or another, she had made up her mind to forget about the postcard.

<h1 style="text-align:center">33</h1>

Now it was her duty to say no. It was what was expected of her. She had the strength of will, too, if it was truly right. There was no sleep for her. The night had turned torment. After such happiness she felt prickly; a quiet fury. The hours fretted away. We should be gone from Aden by dawn, and she would pursue the course laid down for her. If it was truly right. Her thoughts plagued her – like toads – because she could not work them out.

Much as she liked Cheryl and the way she could live two lives at once – for she was sure Cheryl . . . Yes, of course she knew Cheryl was not just saucy insinuation and would have no hesitation in flirting, in entering a liaison even, entering it physically if she wished to . . . Yes, she was sure enough now that Cheryl *would* take the necessary steps to gratify her inclinations, no matter for society or gossip. No matter for marriage vows and God and all that. Just so long as she could be reasonably certain of getting away with it. Good luck to her, then.

Cheryl would regard it as her right, her *freedom*, darling. Why, it could well be Cheryl was already 'romantically involved' this trip. There had been an extra edge to her suggestive comments of late, since the tail end of the Red Sea.

Penny thought so. Now for her, too, the matter of Robert Kettle was suddenly a real choice. Between real yes and real no. And it was horrifying. Her feelings were aroused. Her flesh had known before she did. All the others had seen it coming.

Their anxiety had grown as they sensed her body beginning to assert itself. They could have had no idea, of course, how her womb had thrown its helpless little passenger overboard. But while she was drenched and grief-stricken with that, they had caught the meaning intuitively. They had all gone on to a state of alert.

And so had she. Eventually, she dozed with exhaustion. But sleep was fraught and shallow, and only held her fitfully. The preoccupation circled, around and again. It would not stop. Eventually she thrashed the bedclothes from her bunk and sat up. Then she descended her ladder and flung off her nightdress. She stood naked in the dark. She scratched at her skin with the nails she had not filed for several days. Robert. Robert. She was pincered between two moral schemes, the one full of courtly sacrifice, her mother's, with its iron will, school discipline and the greater good; the other represented by a woman such as Cheryl. The conflict was hateful.

Probing with her hands stretched out in front of her, she established the three or four feet of space between sink and bunk, door and dressing-table, and paced as best she could. How she would have loved tea and daylight and counsel – but none was available. The electric light in her cabin would merely mock her before the mirror. In this dark, in this cramped space she must create some resolution for herself. She must.

Renunciation was her duty. But that simply would not square with what could only be described as the wonderful purity of it all. It was like a call. Yet as far as she could see, the only passage to her feelings for Robert was a sort of grand harlotry. She was being tested, then? Surely Cheryl had been placed in her way as a snare and a delusion. By day Cheryl loved to talk, loved to burst out, almost, with innuendo – her body strained at her clothes. By night, if her chatter were to be believed, she luxuriated. Penny had the odd sense, however, that Cheryl's men were inconsequential, and she wrapped herself somehow in her own rich and freckled skin – to hide, in a way, behind that. There was something unreal about it. In any of Cheryl's intrigues or *affaires*, Penny suspected, it was always Lucas she thought of deep down.

Did she feel that of Hugh? As she turned, her foot stubbed against the bunk support. She cursed.

Cheryl 'loved' Lucas. Each intoxication would come to an end. Theirs was a tropical species of love, strange, strongly female, casual. It flourished in the heat. But then again, Penny realised, it was perhaps to be found everywhere in England too, if under glass and protected from draughts. She had lived so strait-laced a life at home, so sequestered, that she had misread her own class. For surely this voyage must show her what Cheryl kept saying: that in all probability the Torboys situation was in no way unique – just explicit; and there were already a number of sexual intrigues in progress, out of the starboard glare.

Blinkered fool. In books, where morality mattered, she could see through people so easily. Here, in real life, it did not matter. Because nobody actually minded. If the old dowager voyagers, as Paul Finch-Clark called them, tut-tutted at Cheryl Torboys and gave looks, it was only because they were jealous. And because their rheumy, domed and sun-freckled old men followed Cheryl's passing with their eyes, as though she were some seagoing Marilyn Monroe. And her own passing, come to that. Probably with their tongues as well. Nobody cared. The truth was disturbing. Most of all, nobody would have dreamed of taking Cheryl under their wing. So why, then, was such especial chaperonage being extended to herself? For it definitely was. They must think there was something very serious about her. If so, what?

Penny sat down in the chair in front of her invisible mirror. She knew the answer well enough. Why not admit it? Let the word into her head. It was desire. On the instant, her brain felt effervescent, transplanted. Her thought raced white-hot. Desire was neither inclination nor instinct, but something much more dangerous. She was beginning to understand that – and its implications. The journey: it had shaken her up, like the genie in a bottle. She was primed to explode. She laughed out loud. A starburst was happening.

She opened her door and immediately shrank back. Subdued lights were on in the corridor. Then she grew bold. Let them see. She was being challenged in her sex. Subjects never spoken of had been raised. For Robert she felt desire, not instinct. There was a difference, and the others knew it, deep down. Nothing more threatening to those self-appointed guardians could occur than that her whole person should make a choice of Robert

Kettle. It was her they would be defending themselves against, sharpening up the daggers. Her intelligence had fallen in love – the brand on her imagination of his sunburnt body. It scared them stiff. How they were lining up against her, against the pair of them – even though they had committed no . . . Why, they had not even kissed.

Robert was going out to do the same work as Hugh. He was in the same trade of weapons and missiles and the like. Her heart sank and went dark, momentarily. There was some conspiracy. Hugh had gone out in September. He had said he was going via the Pacific. A stopover. A few tests. Some sequence of events, letters, news reports and former vague uneasinesses clicked together in her mind. The name of Christmas Island against the crackle and fireworks of happiness.

But she was in love. And if from Robert somehow had come that joy, then it could not be that he was the same as those frightened people. How defiant she felt. So far Robert and she had merely touched hands. She resisted the impulse to stride out. Instead she closed the door.

The boys. What could she do? She could not undermine them. Once more her spirit sank. She gripped the wash-basin before the porthole, then, straightening up, yanked her curtains roughly apart. There was the beginning of dawn. She turned. Even now the items of her cabin were becoming visible. In a moment or two it would be day. With the boys she had a duty as a woman beyond anything laid on a man. She could never leave the boys. She was tied utterly by her love for them. And by that everyone had a hold over her.

Except that having left them . . . She had left them in fact. It had given her this platform, this space in which to fall . . . this region of illumination. Having left them to think and gather herself as it were, why, what were they to be called to if not a new life, a new world, a new way of being. She seemed to see the whole position from high up, very detached and clear, a floodlit, now dawn-lit vision of her place in things.

But she was building castles in the air. It was all in her mind. She knew nothing, not even that he felt anything for her in the way she was beginning to feel for him. Not for certain. Not quite. Through her cabin floor she felt the engines start into life. It would not do.

'In this great ship, my dear little children,' said Mr Tingay, 'it would be all too easy for me to occupy you with the easiest things. The great Bible story of Noah, for example, is the story of a ship. That's something we all learn at Nanny's knee. Yet there are many folk who have never heard even this charming and instructive tale. In the lovely words of the hymn we have just sung:

> 'The Bible they have never read
> They know not that the Saviour said
> Suffer little children to come unto me.

'And indeed, in my mission to the original peoples of Australia, I shall, sadly, children, be starting "from scratch". These are folk who have never seen the sea, who couldn't imagine what the great flood might be like. Yet the signs of God's work are there, even in the baking centre of Australia. Would you believe it, there are sea shells in the very floor of the desert. So it must have been some time after our great lesson in the dawning of time that these poor Aboriginal people chose to live in the waterless wastes of an unvisited continent. Yes, these odd, furthest-flung children of Ham actually preferred living in the hottest, harshest place on earth. God has painted them black for it, but they have so far missed out on his message. I shall have a hard job getting them to think about Noah's Ark, shan't I?'

There were polite titters as on the previous Sunday. Sitting on my own at the back of the dance space, I tried to catch Finlay's eye, but she would not look at me.

'But you, young as you are, are already capable of so much more. You are privileged. You are intelligent. Think of your scripture classes at your prep schools, or wherever it is you went. How lucky you are to have met Jesus in the Bible, in your churches. Met him in person. You are children of the promise. We had that last week. Do you remember?'

Heads nodded, some possibly with boredom.

'There was another ark, children. Wasn't there. Oh yes. We know there was another ark. Hands up who knows what the other ark was?'

Several desultory hands went up. Unfortunately, I put up

mine too. 'The *Ark Royal*, sir. It's an aircraft carrier.' I had seen it at Chatham with my father.

There was a burst of laughter as the gathering came to life. Finlay turned round and led the scorn, and the faces.

'Don't be facetious, that boy. Or I'll report you,' said Mr Tingay.

'The Ark of the Covenant, sir.' It was one of the anonymous little English girls.

'Of course it is,' said Mr Tingay, and went on to detail the sacred container that caused the walls of Jericho to collapse. I listened, humiliated in front of the ship's company of children.

We all waited for Dragnet. I found myself wondering about the conversation I had overheard between Messrs Chaunteyman and Barnwell, under the clock tower back in Aden.

'I can assure you, Mr Chaunteyman, nothing is being hidden from you; there are no secrets, there is no conspiracy.'

Mr Chaunteyman had started to get angry. He shook Mr Barnwell's shoulder. 'Hey, now. What do you guys think you're playing at. You've got no damned authority over my comings and goings, mister. Dave Chaunteyman sails where he pleases.'

'I can't abide an officer who won't hold his liquor, Mr Chaunteyman,' Mr Barnwell had said coldly. 'No doubt you'll soon be finding Reds under all our beds, but they'll be entirely of your own troubled fantasy, sir. Now please get a grip on yourself, before you embarrass your ... good lady here.' He indicated my mother, and Chaunteyman seemed to subside, abashed. That was the moment when the illusion I had of him first began to crumble. I could not believe what I had heard.

Through a long lens I see myself again in that moment. I have had my week of Dragnet and the Red Sea; now something has changed. Two more items from my suitcase have been dropped into the world. Maybe if I empty any more I shall go critical, targeted to destroy the wrong parents. I am turning myself into a man of war again. The hatred in my body is like a hot iron. I am gradually making room for it – like a heavy-duty soldering iron left switched on against a lead box. The silver melt runs off in a little pool, dripping and hardening on the deck below. How hatred itches to get at the intricacies of things. It works them loose. It finds out the weak points.

152

34

The Arabian Sea lay under an intense blue-white dome, its taste was warm, its own colour the blue of jewel stones.

If I was unsure of Finlay, what matter. Rejection I had dealt with before. Dragnet ran its course and I stayed apart, uninvited.

At last there were flying fish. They were revealed by Rosalind Finch-Clark – and her mother. Dilys Finch-Clark I had imagined to be a very private and retiring woman. So far she had proved elusive, seen only in glimpses, usually through the doorways of small interior spaces. Perhaps she liked creating an aura around herself. She was unsuccessful. I never heard anyone express romantic curiosity concerning her at all. Even her husband Paul seemed to show no interest in her.

Now she was made flesh I could see she was completely ordinary – of ordinary size, colouring, features and dress. And she happened to be occupying the place on the foredeck rail nearest the bow – a place I liked to regard as mine. Barnwell's aircrew had commandeered the other side, and were throwing things into the sea. Rosalind leaned out next to her mother with her feet on the first wire. 'Look. There's one.' She pointed.

Her mother studied the bow wave. I stood up next to Rosalind and followed the line of her finger. A small streak of silver leaped and skidded in the wave's glitter, keeping pace with the white cut of the ship's stem. Then another. Then a rush of five or six at once. They were easy to see once you believed in them. All exuberance, they appeared to love racing us. We watched for ten minutes or so. Dilys wondered whether it could be the same twenty or so fish who kept swimming so fast as to escape the surface; or whether they were replaced by new relays.

'Look! You can see their wings,' Rosalind said.

I studied them. I could just detect the exotic wings, frilled out beside them, on which they would glide. There they leaped again, skimming like chromium-plated cigars, like surface-skimming missiles. The timelessness of the sea and the flying fish held me then, as it does now. Sometimes a fish skims ahead, and I am pulled along. It is a happiness. And yet the story must be told.

Rosalind was aware of my presence without taking her eyes

off the skimmers. When she had looked enough, she told her mother she would go down to the hold to see their cat. Dilys suggested she invite me. Dutifully, Rosalind enquired did I want to go with her?

We collected Finlay and a boy called Peter from where the ping-pong was set up. Finlay looked at me but made no objection. So I tagged along. Then Rosalind took us on a route through ante-rooms and passages I had never seen, down to the storage realm – before the hold proper – of miscellaneous pets and odd accoutrements. It was through a strong door which gave on to a short flight of metal stairs. In my imagination I cannot find it again with any precision, though I know it was somewhere in the very rearmost part of our first class region. I cannot be sure quite by what password or key we penetrated that lowered environment of the pets.

'Only people with an animal are allowed down here.' Rosalind, of course, would come down frequently to look at her huge cat.

To begin with, the region beyond the door was utterly different in character to the finished and panelled appearance of the passenger accommodation. There was a strong smell, as you would expect. A dog began barking as soon as we entered. Then another took up the sound, and then two more. Rosalind threw the handle of a large metal switch. Pools of low-wattage electric light illuminated the between-deck space. Its headroom was reduced. There was barking all around and it stank. Its floor was of untreated planking, upon which our feet sounded with a booming echo amid the din of the dogs.

'Shut up, Pokey. Doc! Stop it this minute!' Rosalind located the excited ones and settled them down.

Electric bulbs were fixed here and there to girders or stanchions. Where their lightwash reached, boxes and crates of all sizes could be seen. Rosalind pointed out where in this village of packing so-and-so's tortoise lay labelled, or whose guinea pig or pedigree rabbit was usually to be found asleep around which corner.

'A steward comes in to look after them. That's his job,' she explained. 'They mostly sleep.'

We felt clearly the ship's recovered movement beneath our feet; I imagined the pets had learned to be both bored and soothed by it. And to have given up because of the dark. Perhaps they were drugged. But now there came sounds of scuffling and stirring from all quarters. They hoped we would feed them, or reassure them. Rosalind appeared to know all their names. She took Finlay in tow. We boys followed on. Interspersed among the cages and sealed crates were other inexplicable pieces of hardware: a vintage motor bike, a squat palm tree, a small fleet of prams and parked pushchairs. Some of the crates were standing open as if their contents were presently in use.

In the unusual light the ship's skin was also visible, showing its flanges and bolts; while above our heads a great number of pipes ran off into the darkness; some as thin as the conduit for wire, others as fat as drainpipes.

The dogs took up barking again. Rosalind shouted at them. We followed her, impressed, as she led the winding way along a particular 'lane' to the Finch-Clark pet crate. Someone in the crew had attached a notice to it: 'Danger. Man-eating Cat'. We gathered round in the dim light and peered inside. 'Titus' was indeed prodigious. He was the size of a respectable dog.

'It's a hormonal abnormality,' Rosalind pronounced. 'It started when he was fixed.'

'Fixed?' Finlay enquired. A dog barked again. Another. The community of the semi darkness all became excited at once.

'Now then, Sukey! Just you stop it! She's the ringleader. I'll come in a minute.' They seemed grudgingly to respond to her, settling down. 'You know. Fixed. So they can't have kittens.'

'Oh, that.'

'So they can't . . . you know. Do it.'

'So he won't want to.'

'Having his balls cut off,' said Peter. We nudged each other as boys.

'Having his bits all off. He won't try anything then,' Finlay said firmly.

'What. Willy and all?' Peter sniggered.

'Don't be disgusting, Peter,' Rosalind intoned loftily, before shouting at the dogs again.

And Finlay sided with her. 'Yes, Pom,' she said, looking scornfully at me. 'Don't be disgusting, Pom.'

We all poked at the extraordinary creature, which seemed docile enough, then explored further the resigned and morose animal world that lay about us. Rosalind was in her element. Perhaps she spent much of her time here. Perhaps, I pondered morosely to myself, they had kept her mother here until today.

'This one died.' She indicated an empty cage, and assumed a tragic tone. 'He was so lovely, Ben.'

'What was he?' Finlay asked.

'The loveliest golden retriever. He was so silky. But he was so old, too. He died in the storm.'

'There's a free cage, then?' Finlay said.

'Yes.' Rosalind affected a kind of sob.

'Pom could go in it. There's a cage here for you, Pom.' Finlay turned to me.

The others all laughed.

'He's so disgusting. He needs to be in a cage. Don't you, Pom? Disgusting!'

I was shocked. The other three children seemed united in their laughter. It seemed they knew exactly what Finlay was laughing at. They had grouped themselves together, subtly, insidiously – leaving me quite out, quite stranded.

I tried to make light of it. 'Yes. I'll go in the cage. It's a cage for a wild Pom.' I made a step forward.

But they laughed with genuine derision, taking their cue from Finlay's piping Australian accent. 'Yeah. Wild Pom! Wild Pom! Wild Pom!'

'Shut up!' I heard myself call out. 'Bloody shut up!'

'Oh, it swears does it? Bloody Pom! Shut up, Bloody Pom!'

They all laughed again.

'He'd just fit in nicely.'

'Then he'd be fattened up and eaten.'

'In his red shorts!'

'And his stupid shirt!'

'And his disgusting fez!'

'He's a Commie!'

It was no more than that. As if in complete accord, they moved away together, back towards the door, making the message complete, and leaving me alone in the middle of that maze. I had fooled myself for a brief interlude that they were my friends again.

Rosalind paused by one cage that stood upon another.

156

'This is Rocky, the McAlisters' mynah bird.' She flicked its wire mesh.

'Doo wah wah. Doo wah wah,' the bird sang. 'Last tra-a-ain to San Fernando.'

They all laughed. I tried to laugh too from where I stood, but they ignored me.

'You'll wonder where the yellow went when you brush your teeth with Pepsodent.'

'Dirty Commie. Dirty Commie,' Finlay crooned to it. The others were delighted.

'Don't step on. Don't step on . . . my blue suede shoes,' the bird replied.

And then they departed, leaving me for the moment paralysed, watching them climb the metal stair – 'the ladder' as my father would call it. So the habitual naval word comes to mind now watching them again in my mind's eye, seeing the slot of light from the open door.

'Turn the light out after you, will you?' Rosalind's face appeared in the slot. 'When you decide to come out. And make sure the big door's shut.' The slot disappeared.

35

They did not lock me in. Fighting my tears, I made towards the stair. I heard the mynah bird, Rocky, flutter cramped wings inside his cage, and whistle the beginning of a hymn. 'Lead us heavenly father, lead us. This is the BBC Light Programme.' He subsided, and then shook up his feathers one last time to get off a parting scold, 'Washed in the blood of the Lamb!' like some Baptist great-aunt.

I thought of the sea, through the moving floor. We were just under the water-line now, perhaps. Beyond the metal skin, there would be flying fish lagging back, making ready to accelerate the length of the hull and fling themselves off the bow wave. There would be sharks also keeping pace, maybe, hoping for kitchen waste. There would be barracudas, sea snakes. And, I let myself imagine, further off, sea horses, starfish, Portuguese men-of-war, nautilus conches.

The dogs barked again. I would not give Finlay the satisfaction of meeting me soon about the ship, knowing I had crawled after her out of my humiliation. I stopped and began to cry. Then looked about me. Nor would I pay her the homage of tears.

I should become hard at last, after my father's wishes, become a man as brazen as my tradition demanded. The barefoot sailors on the gun deck, tested, grogged, unmoved by heat, cold or the lash, stood to the cannons ready to do their duty. They could lose life or limb. They were willing slaves, duty-at-noon. Proud of it. Iron hard on the inside. Steel-proof on the outside. Proud of the way they could bear it.

It is the facility of children to sneak into places they are not supposed to go, to solve puzzles, to open those seals and stoppers designed to flummox adults. The fiercer the child, I believe, the more against the odds, the more slippery and impossible its achievement. But at first I employed my energies merely destructively. There was, for no good reason that I could see, a radiogram, standing beyond the cages, wedged in between cabin trunks. I opened it, took out the twenty or so heavy discs from their slot inside and stamped somebody's precious old gramophone collection into the decking. 'Oh, it was the storm, the storm,' I said to myself, by way of explanation. 'Oh, dear. Oh, what a pity.'

I sat on the vintage motor bike for some minutes and, unable longer to stifle the tears, wept again.

The next remembrance I have, however, is in a different space altogether. I have come down another ladder; we are surely well underwater now. There is the vibration noise of the ship, much louder. We must be near the drive-shaft housing for one of the screws. Yes, near to me somewhere I fancy I can hear the blades taking endless hold of the water, forcing it away from us, driving us on. Here, it is much darker, and more cramped. In my imagination I have to stoop, but this cannot be right – for I am a child. Yet there is a sensation that I have gone far deeper still into the nautical past. Though this is a colour I put on it. And maybe from just such associations I insert the obstinate hang of tar to the stink of paint, sea-rot, old oil. For stink it does. How hot it is, too, and heavy the air.

There is a very faint light – perhaps through some door I

have got undone, from the other place, but perhaps not – to which my eyes are becoming accustomed. It is an empty space, set aside in a low region of the hold; I sense by the floor's motion I am nearer the stern of the ship.

But I am not here on my own. I said it was empty. Not a human presence; no indeed. But there is something. Some very sentient life is here, a hidden creature which I loathe and detest; and yet I feel at home with it. I have been drawn here. I have come to pet it; to feed it.

But this is all far too unlikely; and my memory is playing me false, surely.

There is a very long flat shape – I can just make it out. Most probably large crates. Something very stale and ancient like strong sunken piss. It has about it the feeling of sea deeper than light has reached; of water far below the play of currents, which has remained for millennia over the same bedded mud and ash. It has the quality of being very occupied.

But this is my fantasy, surely.

I edge close up to it. It could, of course, be a set of long, low trailers, maybe, boxed up, bright as newly painted Dinky toys; some consignment of tyres, rubbery-smelling; of medical supplies; of bricks. It could be munitions – steel-blue, a little well greased gunrunning; which might explain its requiring such isolation down here. It could of course be anything.

It is speaking to me. I know its old heart. I recognise how huge and terrifying it longs to become here, right up near the surface where the pressure is so much less. It is cramped. Has always been. Longs to spread out its great nose-wrinkling shape, to lie massively upon the world finding easement at last. It whispers to me to let it out, let it out. That it would mean no harm.

Faint light clings along what seem to be wires growing and seeping out of the crate. They are black lines, phosphorescent, as if they have broken the tropical sea by night and are still wrapped in a mantle of curious plankton. They stretch up and out like the elongations of wings. They are extravagant. They clutch to the smallest cracks in the decking, the bolt ends in the interior skin of the hull, the rust-fretted girders in the low ceiling, the pipes. Look how they cling to that conduit there over by the side. And one of the ducts they have netted around so thickly it appears to be a lifetime's sea-web of a great crab spider. There are lines, cages and traps, like so much flotsam of a whole wrecked trawler. As if the presence in the crate had hooked its existence to this one support and would cling to it come hell or high water. It wants me to let it out.

I cannot. I have a knot in my tongue and we are back in the house at Woolwich. But it is not old picture-books and kid's stuff. Someone is speaking to me very quietly, persuasively.

'This is the old way, boy. This is the Navy way. Bite on this. Chew on the pain. Hot as you can bear it.'

I will not remember.

'Not a word to your mother. Bright little chap like you. Keep you safe from sharks and shipwreck. Make you a man.'

This is one of my bad dreams. I will not remember . . .

'Just you and me, Ralphie. Don't tell a soul. You'll drop the both of us in jug.'

Anything to take my mind away. I think of the South China Sea, the typhoons, seaspouts, the swordfish and narwhal. Old family stories . . .

'You and me. It's in the blood.'

I think of the two great Capes, of Horn and Good Hope. Of the shoals and schools and angelfish. I think of Penny and coral.

'Dirty little whore.'

I think of the squid and the great whale locked together. I think of the one line of the Bible I know by heart: *I am that leviathan whom thou hast made to take his pastime therein* . . .

So we are here at last. And I must remember, whether I like it or not. Everything is hard and clear: the bookcase–escritoire, the two bronzes on the mantelshelf, the useless piano, *The Fighting Temeraire*, the jar that says White Petroleum Jelly, and, from my point of view now at this minute, here on my elbows with my bare backside pointing up at the picture rail, my father unrolling the flex on his soldering iron.

PART THREE

Foam

36

I KNEW THIS airport before the office I work in was even dreamed of. My father brought us out once by train, and bus – for the day. Erica and me. To watch the planes. It was a great excursion, across the whole of London stretched east to west. A clutter of buildings stood here by the roadside, and, where a loose stick fence enclosed the gravelled observation plot, we ate our sandwiches and waited. On the green an occasional aircraft taxied. They were so unwieldy, they bumped along the Tarmac – I had not imagined. The largest had three fins. Its propellers whined in dark circles. Half-way across the field it sat up, then climbed slowly into the air above the houses. He held my hand.

There is a cigarette and a cup of coffee ready. I have worked my night-shift. Now the computer glare softens as grey seeps through the venetian blind. Over Terminal One a rim of winter light shows. The only movement is the main control tower's scanning dish. They are bringing in the planes to the runway just behind the buildings. The jets hunker down and then drop out of view.

The dawn itself is astonishing. The sky has a herring-bone, of which the eastern quarter is gold. But there are carmines and greens high above on the cloud wisps, as if down from a blue plumage is caught falling. And the reach is a vast arch; where the string of planes, three, four of them, queue gold-silhouetted, landing lights on.

The sun is erupting like an angel. From his outstretched arms hang seabird's quills. His sword is fire.

My department has run satisfactorily for another night. There will be a couple of shivering dark-skinned men waiting for me in the interview rooms before I finish. They will be detained at Her Majesty's pleasure – until turned away. I see at the gates a vast stream of desperate people edging towards my desk. They are the measure of my life, my patriotic duty.

I am at a turning point. Plain family stuff: my father's heart attack, his funeral; all those lovers on the high seas. That was what I could offer you at the start. And surely even now this appalling flash upon the inward eye – that moment in the 'best' room – is some trick of the bereaved mind. It throws me into uncertainty, where there is no comfortable chart room for the spinning of yarns, and where the one other tale of myself I could recount – of the Falklands War and the bold dash of my shipmates – is swamped. I cannot tell you the lengths to which I would go to cancel out that image: me and the voice of my father.

Everything is tainted by it. Everything that was fought for. The service I had been led to think was in some way pure – and I did think some part of me had a veteran's pride, though who knew why we were down there in the South Atlantic; and who had been supplying them with arms all that time? The fleet stole into the Sound under cover of night, miraculously undiscovered. Beneath the stars the great white ship lay in San Carlos water like a ghost in the moonlight. The men she carried waited to be disembarked; waited also for whatever air attack the enemy would throw at us. As attack they must. She was so defenceless, like a huge white target, but for the cover it was our duty to provide.

Because on the shores of Falkland Sound none of the Army's anti-aircraft weaponry had yet been deployed. Protection would be a matter of the outdated missiles we carried and a sharp-shooting effort from machine-guns and small arms on deck. Quite the old story.

The attack came as soon as it was light. Oddly, unexpectedly, it was in the shape of a single fighter on routine patrol, who, no doubt astonished at the flotilla that lay beneath him, attacked and ran. He got in some rocket hits before skimming off over the mountains towards Port Stanley with everything we had loosed after him. The Argentinians had seemed lulled, drowsed, unaware for so long – now they would know exactly what was down here at the entrance of the bay. And would deduce that it was this morning they must throw their entire force at us from the air if they were to have any hope of winning. Since *Belgrano* had locked up their navy this was the moment of their only remaining chance. It was therefore kill now or be killed.

Yes, I was there. This memory is still like the hull of some fellow passager, glimpsed now, and then lost, and then briefly visible again in the foul wind-blown fogs so dreaded by mariners. But I mislead you: the day of the battle itself was clear, cold and bright – hard as an etching plate; it is just the recollection of it that falters.

And from that first attack there is on the one hand the sense of eternal waiting, of elevated vigilance; the stomach tense, the routines gone through a thousand times – the pure abandonment, if you like, of concentration. The worst will never happen but must always be anticipated. It is tangible, it is real. This is no exercise. Death is almost certain and we know its shape and size; we know its engine speeds and its precise capabilities. We have learned its firepower; yet it never comes.

When it is upon us, all hell is, proverbially speaking, let loose. I can tell you, father, grandfather, this too lasts for ever, even though technically it is over in a matter of seconds. The Daggers, Pucaras, Skyhawks are always up there, incoming, attacking, and the rockets are going up in a rush right next to me, always.

I know nothing more with clarity. The rest is the nightmare, and has that quality. I have on my flash-suit, and am choking. There is total darkness except, in the next instant, the torch of two of my shipmates on fire. I have no idea how I got out of *Ambleside*.

Every time now, what remains is simply the endurance of heat, and my father's voice saying again and again, 'Tell me. Tell me, then. Only tell me when you can't bear it no longer, and then you'll be nicely warmed up. Won't you, boy?' And I have to judge the moment when it is manly and acceptable to cry out. I always cheat. I have to judge the moment that he won't guess. I always have to be on my guard and alert – so preoccupied, so attuned to the nature of his threat – to determine when the heat reaches the acceptable degree and he will turn it off and begin. Which was the same thing on the destroyer, about cheating and not cheating, and overcoming my fear finally so that when it was burning with the bomb, missile, torpedo, what have you shoved right inside it, it was the same thing, the same dilemma . . . and in my cheating I consented all the more to the contract, and bound myself to him for ever. The binding is the forgetting – which is also feeding.

There. I have said it, untied the knot.

But it is too shameful to be true. Just my imagination – I have made it all up. How I should like to be transported out on the instant, away from all I have got myself into, away from Carla. Who keeps herself to herself, who has rearranged her shifts so as not to coincide with mine. I long to be out of it. But I am cast adrift by my own telling, amid wind and weather with this creature of the deep. I must dive where it dives, and you with me. Nothing is as it was: the world is changed, and I see it from this moment through watered eyes.

37

The next morning Penny thought she would drown with feeling. The surface of the sea was lit up with desire. She hung out to watch the bow wave like the children. She understood foam, mingling flame and ocean, which had always stood for love. She grasped, by the bold weakness in her stomach and the tremblings of her legs, how such a seemingly evanescent assembly of droplets – which, transparently, was all it was – could support the whole weight of the *Armorica*.

Where the ship drove, the water clung and gave itself up to lightness. But beneath that embrace's white there were angles from which the ocean was always an unfathomable green, and yet others from which it stretched away hard, dazzlingly opaque as polished blue stone, black, white, grey, yellow, aquamarine – of course. At once transparent and dazzlingly opaque. How utterly beautiful were the water's brilliant scales, its strings and loops and spangles, how generous the sea was with its skin.

She turned, expecting to see Robert standing behind her, or just descending the stair from the promenade deck. She expected to see him everywhere. The ship's white steel was like a photographic paper on which he was bound any minute to develop. Her blood had turned to transient foam. The surfaces of the ship were clear and sharp in the tropic brightness and desire clung about the shine of things – handles, white-painted steelwork, the furniture, the mirrors, rails. Desire slipped and slid on polished tops. Everything was real, and unquestionable, and at the same time awash, aflame.

She wandered through the observation lounge, then out and all round the promenade deck among the navy-blue-shorted old men doing their laps. If her route was identical to theirs, her perception could not have been more dissimilar. Why, the sturdy vessel carrying us all was transparent with Robert Kettle. It multiplied him. It bubbled with him. How should they have any idea of that?

This delight it was her duty to renounce.

She went in. 'I think I need to talk to someone,' she said to Mary Garnery over the iced-tea table. 'Do you mind?'

Mary shrugged. 'Why should I mind?'

'I don't know. You look . . . You're sure you don't mind?'

'It's about Robert Kettle, I suppose.'

'You know?'

'Not so hard to fathom, shouldn't you say?'

'But . . . What should I do, then?'

'What do you want to do?'

Mary's directness took her back. Penny had hoped to think of her as becoming a special friend. She hesitated. 'Wanting's not the point, is it?'

'You've got him, Penny. What are you going to do with him?'

'I'm married.'

'So you have two men, now.'

They sat down on the same settee in the main lounge. Penny stood her glass on the teak table in front of them. She had two men, now. She made clear sense of the other woman's new manner towards her.

'I know what you're thinking,' Mary said. 'He and I happened to dance together. Shouldn't we? It was nothing.'

'Nothing? I'm so sorry. You always look so calm. So untouched.' Penny faltered.

'What are men to me,' she stretched each arm, one at a time, pulling back the beige linen of her jacket to reveal mere covered bones, 'when the metaphorical chips are down?' Then she made Penny a wry smile with pressed lips.

'I didn't think . . .' Penny hung her head, like a child suddenly.

'Just because I . . . Never mind that. Tell me about it, then, if you want.'

'No. I shouldn't have spoken.' Penny took her glass and made to get up.

But Mary laid a hand on her wrist. The iced tea spilled over. It just missed the printed pleats of her skirt.

'Oh . . .'

Mary found a paper napkin in her bag. She mopped the base of the glass. 'Do stay. I didn't intend to be offhand. Why don't you tell me. Yes. Tell me everything.' Her style was disconcerting. 'I should so love to hear.'

And then Penny, confused, felt she had to comply. 'Yes. You're absolutely right. I have my husband. And now there's this. I don't know what to do.'

'Forget about him. That's what they say in the films.' Mary mimicked the actressy voice, and laughed. 'You must forget him, dear.'

It was a very unnerving laugh. 'How can I? There are two weeks more. Two and a half. We shall be in each other's company. We've tried avoiding each other, though we didn't know it. But now it's a firm thing. It's here. On board. I can't deny it.'

'A firm thing, is it?' Mary's smile was sardonic, the lips pressed tight again. 'Then you'd better use my cabin. There's a good double bed. In which I am like a mere reed.'

'How dare you.'

'Oh come, now,' Mary said. 'You expect me to be pleased?'

'I thought I might talk about it with you. As a friend.'

'What is there to talk about? Talk it over with your priest. That's what we were brought up to do.' Now Mary went through the gathering up of her bag. The conversation was being closed.

'But I don't know what to think about it. Heavens, I hardly know what to wear any more.' Penny looked at her newly varnished nails. How foolish they looked.

'Married woman or painted lady. *Which twin has the Toni?*'

Mary did not wear lipstick. Her features were hollowed and striking. Her nails were natural. She stood up in her cream slacks and her expensive blouse under the beige jacket thrown casually on as if an afterthought. She was assured. Despite the calculated hostility, Penny still felt she wanted to ease Mary of her sardonic mask, loosen the pull of the brown hair scraped back under its band.

'Mary, I wish you might have . . .' She looked again at her nails. 'I thought you would . . .'

'Let me know what you decide,' Mary said. 'About clothes, for example. And whether you intend to include the spectacles. They are so original.' She walked out toward the port deck.

Damn you too, Penny muttered to herself. She was duly rattled; her oceanic sense of a few minutes before had become an anchor sinking inside her. She took herself off, back to the starboard side. I am all froth and folly, she thought. Love has made me ridiculous. My judgement is addled.

But she was not long in the sea's face again, sunned and breeze-whispered, before the enchantment returned. Its folds were oriental, sensuous as silk.

She consulted the Reverend Mr Tingay. She and Hugh had always been church-goers.

She told him she was troubled about a friend. Mr Tingay appeared buoyed up, with his broad expanse of clerical black under his tropical linen jacket, his broad beard afloat on that, the straining waistline, the great thighs inflating the tops of his black trousers. He balanced on short goat legs. He wore sandals in which he pumped his socks slightly, lifting one after the other, as if just treading the water out of them. She could feel him oozing sea lust; keen to engage her on the troubles of her, *ahem*, friend.

'Marriage, my dear Mrs Kendrick, you may tell your friend, was ordained for mutual society. You will remember the words of the ceremony, I expect. When there is some separation, regrettable, unavoidable – as in a long, *ahem*, sea voyage – we must not be surprised if the *ah* temporarily sought gift of continence proves somewhat of a struggle. The man . . . The man you say is in Australia?'

Penny nodded. 'In Adelaide I believe. Or was it Melbourne.'

'The man will have his work. He can distract his impulses, throw his whole attention into his . . . Do you know what nature of work . . . ?'

'She didn't specify.'

'Never mind. While on the other hand you . . . While she . . . While we . . . are here with nothing to engage in but idleness after all, with no means of *channelling* our energies, do you see? The whole function of marriage, no matter for the particular faith, is *channelling*. You find it the world over. Anthropologically . . .'

'You would not believe,' she said to Cheryl, 'the things men say when they think they have some sort of opportunity. And he's a reverend.'

'Of course I'd believe it, darling. The people who wouldn't believe it are other men.'

'Then it would be pointless, I suppose, to make a complaint to somebody.'

'Completely. He's already tried it with me. And Joan Tanner. He's completely desperate, but more or less harmless. I should have warned you. But then you've been so preoccupied . . .'

'Harmless! That includes touching, I suppose.'

She did not want to confide in Cheryl. She longed to share the decision with Robert. She felt her body becoming once again delicious and uncomfortable. All around her the loveless stalked, damaging her sensibility. The younger marrieds, trivial, pretentious; the dowager voyagers, prosaic duennas; Mary's face, sneering almost, in its mask of sacrifice; the Church, satyric. Now her own English clothes, suddenly quite, quite wrong. Everyone knew.

Penny Kendrick had become a subject of gossip and a laughing stock.

38

Penny imagined the talking-to she would get from Mrs Madeley, the look of blank incomprehension from Dilys Finch-Clark, the stunned joint coldness from Clodagh and Russell Coote, the wounded features of the Piyadasas. Michael Canning, the colonial civil servant with the glint in his eye, would shake his head, having seen it all before. The Tropics, the Tropics.

If she were to act, she would lose everything: husband, children, place, home. It would be catastrophic. How would she survive? Where should she go? She would be damned. The family would be blown apart.

Then, horror of horrors, she nearly bumped into Robert and his cabin-mate Mr Dearborn as they came out of the Verandah.

Robert said, 'Good morning.'

Joe raised his straw hat.

She was completely caught out, and swayed off balance, her heart thumping. Joe helped her off the rail. 'The ship,' she said. 'The movement. Thank you.' She moved on quickly before them, and hid just inside the dance space, whose glass side-screens were now permanently removed and made fast in a stack to the rear wall. In full view of those inside, she waited for Robert and Joe to come past. From her bag she extracted lighter and cigarette case and pretended to be struggling with them away from the breeze. By chance Joe stopped to light his pipe, flashing at the lever with his thumb, she could hear the click. Robert's back was three feet away from her. With her own pressed to the wall next to the fold of the screens, she looked around at the assortment of people, the ping-pong players, the children, the coffee drinkers. She held her own cigarette very still, smiling, folding the skirts of her dress unconsciously around her legs with her free hand like a six-year-old.

'Because they lock them all up.' Joe too drew on his smoke at last. 'Didn't you know that? They lock 'em all away.' The two men moved on along the deck. Robert slipped his own silver lighter into his pocket. She watched him; but she had not heard his voice.

Then it was over. Russell and Clodagh and some other couple, Perry, was that their name, were coming towards her – nice, vacant, unknown people. She must chatter her way through another afternoon.

Much later she was free again. It may have been the same day. The sun was well past its height. The worst thing was that she had never felt like this about Hugh. There! A terrible admission! She recalled the change in Hugh's eyes whenever he began to . . . She had never liked that. She shut the thought of it away.

'Penny!'

She turned. It was the boy Pom again. He seemed to want to latch on to her at the most inconvenient times. He reminded her of Christopher in some ways. And in others he made her shudder.

'Yes, Pom. What can I do for you?'

'I saw something.'

'Oh. What's that. Have you all found another squid? More sharks?' She could not resist the scornful edge to her voice.

'Worse than that.'

'Oh. Worse than that? What could it be, I wonder?'

'It's something I can't tell about. Not to an ordinary woman. But then a man . . . I thought you'd be the only one . . . No. It's a sea monster. From space. It's from another planet. You'd most likely be frightened.' He turned nonchalantly, knowing even. 'It has seven eyes and nine arms. Horns. No. It's a cyclops. With a conger eel for a body.' He laughed. But she had to admit he looked shaken, and pale beneath his freckled tan.

She laughed too. 'Oh, is that all?' Unkind. 'Look, Pom. I'd like to talk to you, but I'm not feeling too well. Would you mind? I'm sorry.'

He looked aggrieved. 'I should tell Mr Chaunteyman. He'd know about it. I try to talk to him. I tried before. But I thought only you—'

'I'll talk to you later, but just now I have . . . a headache. Do you see? I'll talk to you about it later. Promise.'

'All right.' He faded off.

She made her way back round to where they set out the trays of gherkins and olives with the jugs of iced tea. She poured the tea and immediately dropped it; then stood quite motionless while one of the stewards cleared up the mess.

So she waited in one of the wide spaces where the side-screens had been, looking out over the horizontal pattern of exquisite blue fracture lines the ocean had become, heated and glazed. How terrible she felt. He might stroll by again as he had done before. She was ready for him now. She thought what if these, her travelling companions, were the last people on earth? And none of them knew. Her heart leaped suddenly: then she would be free to love Robert Kettle. That was a terrible wish. How had such a thought entered her head? Mrs Piyadasa came with a fold of unnaturally-coloured postcards showing views of Ceylon.

'I thought you might like to look at these.'

'We should have another chat.' Cheryl made her sit down at the open tables behind the Verandah bar. 'You are a little struggle.' But she said that to her stomach, as she eased herself into the cane chair. 'Come on, Penny.'

Penny allowed herself to be persuaded, though refused a cocktail.

Cheryl began. 'The great thing about being betwixt and between like this – you know, neither one place nor the other . . .'

The noise from the swimming-pool was irritating. The children splashed and shrieked. A few of Barnwell's aircrew were there. She could perhaps gather up her courage and tell Cheryl after all.

'The great thing is that no one is watching. Not really. A few stuffy old pussies, in the main lounge, but who cares about them.' She made a gesture with her left hand. 'And no one from home.' She placed her pussyfoot cocktail glass on the cane table. 'I'm not sure you've twigged. Off the leash.'

Penny sighed.

'Have you been to bed with him, then, Penny? Is that why you're looking such a . . . Was he unreasonable? Has he behaved badly?'

Penny felt her mouth fall open. 'Heavens. No. Nothing like that.'

'It's not what I thought then. Apologies, darling. It's that I thought I had to . . . do something. I couldn't go on letting you . . . No offence.'

Penny shook her head.

'Then have you seen the doc? Is it something physically wrong? Do you think you rather ought to? I'm sorry. I didn't mean to blurt out. You know me. That's my way. No offence, Penny, darling.'

'None taken. But you were right. It is him. And no. Of course I haven't been to bed with him. And I don't intend to, thank you very much.'

And she left.

173

39

Finally: 'Penny, dear. Do you think we could have a word?' It was Mrs Madeley.

'Stella. I'm so sorry. I didn't see you.'

'I've been wondering whether I shouldn't warn you, dear.'

'Warn me?'

'I've plucked up the courage at last.'

'Warn me?'

'About that young man Mr Kettle.'

'What?'

'There has been some talk, dear. People have noticed – I don't know whether you'd be aware of it yourself – but some people . . . They're quite convinced he's rather, you know, smitten. I wouldn't mention it, dear, but I rather had the impression you weren't quite aware how far he . . . Do tell me if it's none of my business.' She poised herself on one mule sandal in an attempt at archness.

Penny regained her composure. 'I'm sure I'm quite all right, thank you, Stella. I appreciate your concern. But I can assure you there's nothing at all to worry about. Nothing to worry about at all.'

'If I could make a suggestion about dress, dear. It could be that—'

Penny cut her short. 'I really think there's no need, Stella. I don't actually care two hoots about clothes. But I thought just for once I'd dress to please myself. I've probably got it quite wrong, but do you know it really doesn't trouble me. It is a kind of holiday, really, isn't it? And one can wear what one likes. Until dinner. It really doesn't trouble me one bit. And I'm sure it doesn't trouble Mr Kettle at all. In the slightest. I'm just sorry it troubles you.'

'Oh no, dear. I was just worried for you.'

'There's absolutely no need.' She smiled and pressed on forward. She took the pince-nez from her bag. Holding it defiantly on her nose, she leaned over to watch the flying fish. How thrilling they were.

As she passed the purser's desk, it never occurred to her that there might be incoming mail for her. To her shame there was a letter from Hugh. She opened it with a curious mixture of feelings: anger, anxiety, even a twinge of hope.

The letter was extraordinary because of its omissions. He hardly mentioned her. Or the boys. It was full of his doings and descriptions – subject to official secrecy restrictions. It contained lists, a small map, and what virtually amounted to instructions for her life in Adelaide. He had settled in. He was obviously in his element, had bought a new car. He was exploring and had met some people. Very well, it was newsy, affectionate even; it carried on from when they had last breakfasted together. And that was it. Their separation had failed to register with him. It was not, though it ended with the word, a love letter, but he was 'looking forward very much to her arrival'.

There had been three earlier letters from him, before she set sail on the *Armorica*. None of those had struck her like this one. Not that they had been much different. But there had been so many details to organise. She had not noticed. Hugh had never been much of a letter writer; and before this they had not needed to correspond for years, obviously – they had never been apart. She knew he was no Shakespeare. But . . . It struck her that before she would not have expected anything better.

That was true, yes. She read the letter again. That would account for some of the feelings it had provoked. There was something else though, something between the lines . . .

She happened also to notice a pile of mail waiting for Colombo. On the top was a letter addressed to Mr Hugh Kendrick. Betwixt and between, she thought, scornfully. No one watching you. Is that it, Cheryl? Someone has decided it is necessary to write to my husband. The sight of that other letter galvanised her. She stole it. On her way out, she contrived to throw it over the side, unopened.

But back in her cabin, she made herself be scrupulously fair. She tried to give Hugh the benefit of the doubt. He had fought a war for her. She felt guilty. Although a man may not be able to articulate his feelings, he may still have them. He may still be a very fine soul of a person. One looked for decency. Nothing grand, it could show up in small ways. Just to be decent in a bad world is heroic in its way, never mind war or blazes of glory. To be gentle. If she could still find in her husband that small heroism she required, she would do her duty.

She read his letter once more. Her mind blanked. The time was hastening by. Outside, through the porthole, the Indian Ocean dreamed on, its days summers, its nights trances. Her powers were stolen under a spell. She placed her hand on the steel rim of the window and felt the drive of the engines.

Hugh was a good-enough husband. He went about his business. She brought up the children. They talked. But not about his job, of course. Most of his work was covered by secrecy laws. That was understood between them.

Then the Test Ban Moratorium had come, which in her usual way she had not trusted enough to pay much attention to, on the wireless, or in the papers. Just before Hugh went out? Or was it after? No, she had not been concentrating. Always followed blindly, some distance behind; she would never let all that enter her head.

His work caused him no problems.

The thing in his nature she had never spelled out to herself came as the shock. He was happy enough with the weaponry; in his element. Maybe he was more excited by the weapons than by her. That was vile, yet such a liberation. It fell like a stroke, God given, almost.

And it was true. So true. And that was why she could do it. She could act unilaterally. Upon the instant. With no more dithering, no more uncertainty. He was without love. Hugh. Of course! He did not know the meaning of the word. And she – incredible to relate – had never noticed.

There would be time enough to work that puzzle out. For the present, she would be direct. She would approach Robert Kettle and ask him to behave heroically with her instead.

She changed her clothes. She was satisfied. For surely the problem of the children would become clear. She did not, could not love Hugh.

It was only then – when all that was settled in her mind, the fine words and intellectuality of her self-descriptions had evaporated, and she was cleaning the silly varnish off her nails – that she finally realised. The real truth of the matter was how routinely Hugh would hit her. And how hard. And she cried for the sorrow of it – and also for the gladness that now she might perhaps begin her life again.

40

So it came about on the boat deck as I described at the outset. The sun that evening – some evening or other between Aden and Colombo – dropped without ceremony into the Indian Ocean just to the left of the ship's wake, scorching it for a moment or two with orange flares. And, on cue, there rose a warm, slightly scented breeze from the sea. There the lovers' agreement was reached, as you have heard.

Mr Chaunteyman was in our cabin, and Erica was dressing for dinner, that very evening of Robert and Penny's tryst. He had his hands on her shoulders while she brushed her blonde hair, teasing the waves of her perm.

'There's an awful thing in the hold. I spoke to it. It fell from outer space, into the sea. Finlay Coote shut me in the pets. I went down and then it was all dark, all different. I promised not to tell. But I'm willing to break that once. I thought you'd know what to do. It's sub-thermal-kryptonial.' I made an irritating buzzing noise like my imagination of a Geiger counter – until they told me to shut up. 'It gives off lines around the pipes.'

'You brought him too many of those comics, Dave,' said Erica.

'Don't go on at me. It's not my fault.'

'I'm not going on at you. I didn't mean it like that. Honest, Dave. Now don't get in one of your moodies with me, love.'

'Yeah.' He turned to me. 'So there's a space monster in the hold. How many tentacles has it got?'

'It doesn't have tentacles. It's made of metal. Brass, I think. Something like that. Only all gone black. It has lines. The lines are creeping up the pipes, going everywhere.'

Erica craned her neck round. 'Has something scared you? Has someone been saying things—?'

'No. I'm not scared of it. We have a deal.' I used an American phrase. 'But everyone else ought to be mighty scared. It could go off.'

I saw Erica exchange glances with Mr Chaunteyman in the mirror. 'It could go off, could it?' she said. 'Very fishy. We don't want that. Phew.' She shifted herself back and forth in his hands.

In the reflection I noticed his fingers pointed down the front of her shoulder-straps, lying over the bare flesh below her throat.

'Dead whale. My, oh my,' said Mr Chaunteyman. 'It could go off in a big way. I'll say, honey. Thar she blows!'

Erica giggled.

'I thought I could tell you. Just you. Dad's not on the ship, is he?'

Another glance passed between them in the glass, anxious this time.

'OK. No. That's good, Ralph. That's good.' He gave me some coins from his trouser pocket. 'Why don't you go get yourself a drink of fizz. Give us twenty minutes before we have to go to dinner, hey? Then you can stay up. Find your little friends again. Meet us in the lounge when we have coffee. Hey?'

'I thought I ought to warn you. I'm taking a risk, telling anyone.'

'Sure. Sure. You did the right thing. Now give us a little time on our own, can you?'

'See what ideas you've given the boy, Dave.'

Robert made his way through the main lounge, where Penny was sitting in the light-cone of a standard lamp, and then outside a few yards along the promenade deck. At dinner he had been most acutely, most joyfully aware of her. He had no recollection of the meal.

A dinner-suited night figure now, he peered back through the window to see her put down her brandy glass, wrap her cream stole about her shoulders and excuse herself from her party, the Cootes, the Cannings, and the Australian Freemason, Masters. She was leaving them as she had said she would. Robert turned away.

She had requested him to knock at her cabin, after the meal and the coffee.

He had no practice at all.

His feet absorbed the very gentle rise and fall; his cheek was touched by the mild winter monsoon, the eastbound sailor's friend. How one became at home; he was completely accustomed now to the sea. He strolled down beside the rail.

The night had set in to amaze. On the horizon there was a falling moon. The *Armorica* was drenched in a soft silveriness;

the nightbreath of India pressed upon its mirror, the ocean.

He brushed his lips with his wrist. They had kissed.

His footsteps drifted him yards aft towards the rear staircase; beyond the dance space even. He had simply not registered how, inside, the smug little band was knocking out a quickstep. He had not noticed the sounds, though the strains were quite loud; nor noticed through the screens the couples swaying.

His body shook with pent-up nervousness. Here at the rail, he saw how the Arabian swell of the last few days had fallen back; the wave tops were as if beaten faintly with strings of pearl. He breathed in the warm air. Right beside the hull, the water sweeping along had a milky transparency; there might have been the subtlest of lights from below as well as above.

When he finally allowed himself to look up and recall that starlit understanding with Penny by the boats an hour or two ago, he was awestruck once more. The sky was a tree and the stars nothing but hand-high fruits of burning metal. By them, dull, blighted, horn-rimmed and cabbage-smelling England was annulled: its rain, its milk bars, its sinister gangs of Teds on street corners . . . and he remembered as a child tracing the picture of an enchantment with his finger, until he was certain he would step inside the book of it – as surely now he had. It was a fact. Nothing was trivial.

He turned and stepped so much the closer to the aft stairs. A few couples he did not know were standing out. The odd smoker. The voices of Barry and Queenie Parsons carried from somewhere. He saw Joe's back on the other side of a stanchion, and crept past in the shadows lest he should have to account for himself.

It was just as he had made the full length of the first class deck, that the boy Pom – the one Penny had pointed out in Aden – appeared from the darkness by the turn into the pool area.

'How's the sunburn?' A breathy, almost hissing voice.

'Much better now, thank you.' The familiarity took him aback; the boy might have been waiting for him. But his manner was not rude.

'I saw you come down the deck.'

'Oh yes?'

'You're going to see Penny.' It was a statement; there was only the merest interrogatory note.

'Yes.' Caught by the truth, he blurted it out.

'Then I shan't go myself. Only . . .'

'Only what?'

'Do you believe in God?'

'No, I don't actually. Sorry, but there it is. Hope I haven't disillusioned you.'

'It's all right. My family doesn't either. Makes you feel a bit left out, though, doesn't it. D'you ever worry about the hydrogen bomb?'

'What's the use of worrying?'

'Space. That's what I'm interested in. Ray guns that paralyse you. And gadgets. I've got a book of gadgets. D'you think there's life on Mars, or anything? Have you ever seen a flying saucer?'

'No. I haven't actually. But who knows?'

'I've got a book. It says it's impossible to get people off the earth. It would be like being crushed by a steam hammer. But the Russians got a dog up there, didn't they? Do you think sharks are following us?'

'They may be, I suppose. Look, old chap . . .'

'It said on the news they were going to stop letting off all the H-bombs all the time.'

'There's supposed to be a complete ban in the pipeline.'

'In the pipeline?'

'Coming along soon. Look, I'm actually . . .'

'There's strontium-90 in the milk. I know what that is. My dad told me. It's fall-out. It's the same thing as when you're in the shoe shop and you put your feet under that big thing with the binoculars and you can see all the bones in your toes. They look all green inside the shoes, don't they?'

'Yes.'

'Only there's something down there. In the hold, sort of. It's not that I'm frightened for myself. But I'm not to tell. It told me not to speak of it. Couple of days ago. I think.'

He was like a little talking shadow, with his solemn tones. The starlight made that ridiculous shirt he wore glow grey.

'It wants me to let it out. To let it off. It might go off any time. So I thought to tell Mr Chaunteyman. Only they were busy. I was nearly going to tell Penny. Now I've told you and I

180

shouldn't have said anything. But I had to tell someone.'

'You're a bit bothered aren't you, old chap?'

'No.'

'Are you sure?'

'It's just that it might go off. In the hold. Can a person turn into metal? A stowaway? I don't mind for myself, but someone ought to be told. For the ship. It might . . . I might . . . It's the ship I'm worried about. Tell Penny. She'll know what to do.'

Some of it sounded like a rehearsed speech, as if he had manipulated the conversation round to his subject. Penny was right – Pom was odd.

'All right. Then I'll notify the authorities. Is that sufficient?'

'I suppose it would be. Yes, I suppose that would be . . . all right. It wouldn't be me told them. Thanks. I thought you were dead.' The boy grinned suddenly. The starlight caught his teeth. 'Sorry.'

And as Pom slipped past him and vanished along the decking, Robert found himself facing the aft door which would take him back into the ship's interior, and, if he chose, down the staircase to Penny's cabin.

He could not go. The boy's appearance like that was disconcerting. His fear hung in the balance with desire. Just a kid. Children these days had never known a world before the wretched bomb. All that and space rockets had got right inside their minds. Television was presumably to blame. From the experiences of his own generation they were completely cut off. They must live in a dream world. They would question nothing either, poor little wretches. The children were always inventing.

He would go now to Penny; he must. She was expecting him.

He plunged inside to the lit stairhead and, with her door number drumming in his head, made his way down by the mahogany panelling, like a diver seeking a pearl.

41

They stood like two mannequins, as though the cabin walls were shop glass and they were on show to the night outside. Penny moved to draw the curtain across the porthole, then laughed.

'As if the dolphins would jump up and see us.'

'I don't think anyone . . . I checked to see the corridor was empty.'

'Well, good. But what does it matter? It's nobody's business but our own.'

'I'm glad. I was worried for you.' Robert shifted his feet awkwardly.

'How so?'

'In case you . . . In case people . . .'

'It doesn't matter. I'm prepared for that. Do you know somebody has already written to my husband? I saw the letter on the purser's counter.'

'Have they really? And there's no one who'd have ordinary cause?'

She shook her head.

'How people like to interfere. Have you an idea who?'

'No idea at all. I don't care; not if you don't. I threw it out. But I shall have to tell my husband sooner or later. You do understand that, don't you? You do understand what it is we're doing?'

'Yes. I think so. I believe I do.'

'And are you scared?'

'Terrified.'

'That's a good sign, isn't it? So am I. Scared . . . but, strangely, not the least embarrassed.'

'But you have so much to lose.' Robert looked around and fixed on the dressing-table for a moment. 'Whereas I . . .'

'Maybe Hugh could get you sacked. Have you thought of that?'

He had not.

'You want us to go on?' She held his gaze, quite level and determined.

'I do. I want that. I want us to go on.' The words came out of their own accord, before he could deliberate. He was pleased; he knew it was himself that spoke.

There was a pause.

'Perhaps you should sit down. We can't simply leap into bed together.'

He sat in the wicker chair, flooded with relief, and a little disappointment.

She went on. 'Just like that. After all, we hardly know each other. I should get you a drink. Will you take coffee? Or tea? Oh, but then the steward . . . I could go out and get you something?'

'No,' he said. 'It doesn't matter. It's all right.'

She smiled and perched on the edge of the lower bunk. He noticed what she was wearing at last: a very dark purple frock, wired and fitted above a full skirt. She had put a loose white cardigan over it. Its folded edge brushed at the artificial posy stitched to a corner of her neckline. There was a string of deep green stones against the skin of her breast.

'To tell you the truth, I feel out of my depth. I haven't even called you by your name.'

'Call me Penny. Do please call me Penny.' She kicked off her high evening shoes and pulled her feet up on to the mattress; side on to him, hugging her knees, she laid her head down on them so as to fit neatly in the bunk space. The skirt hung behind her arm and over the bedside like a drape.

'Penny,' he said in a whisper. He felt his heart turn over. 'But you know I've never been married . . . or anything.'

'I'm sure I've been married enough for at least two of us.'

'But . . . I'm younger than you.'

'So what if you are. Do you think it matters to me precisely how many times we have gone around the sun since you were born? Oh, but you're an astronomer. It will matter terribly to you. I'd forgotten.'

'It doesn't matter in the slightest to me.'

'You promise?'

'Of course.'

'Then we'll say no more about that! Robert Kettle! Well.' She stood up and came the one step towards him, to the centre of the cabin. 'And how is your sunburn?'

He started. 'The boy, Pom, or whatever his name is. He spoke to me. Just as I was plucking up courage to come down and knock at your door.'

'Ha! And what did the ubiquitous Pom want, to be keeping you from your destiny?' She fixed his eye again with hers.

Robert felt it was a test, wrapped up in joking, in dramatics – of his commitment. 'He knew I was coming to see you.'

'Did he? Wretched little monkey.'

'He wanted me to tell you about something. Some nonsense. I've forgotten already. No: he said there was something in the hold. I said I'd inform the authorities. That appeared to satisfy him. He went off along the deck. He gives me the shivers, to be honest.'

'Oh, Pom's all right. He noticed you were burning.' Penny dropped her gaze, picked up a hairbrush from the dressing-table and, bending her knees, touched at her hair very briefly in the mirror.

'Is it obvious?'

She turned back, laughing. 'In the sun that day. He was the one who realised.'

'I should be grateful then. But . . .'

'Perhaps he's looking after us.'

'He was worried about the ship. He's strange. Penny, I . . .' There was something he wished he could say, though he did not know what it was, and the words would not form. Instead some sour tone came out: 'Wretched kid should have been in bed. Little toad.'

'Don't.'

'What?'

'Sorry. It's nothing. Foolish of me. The mention of a toad. It brought something back. But I'll tell you another time. It's all right. It's all right, honestly. Darling.'

'I'm sorry.'

'It's nothing. It's nothing, Robert.' She leaned forward and placed her hand on his shoulder. 'Your skin. I couldn't forget it.'

And he caught her hand, passionately, yet his voice still came out wrongly – prosaic. 'It's been peeling. I'm a mess. Though it's stopped hurting. Almost.'

'It will be all right. You'll see. And you understand, don't you, Robert Kettle, that from now on I shall be the judge of whether you're a mess? You do realise this, don't you?'

Robert nodded. He felt his face cover over with a wide, unstoppable and childlike smile.

'Then we must say no more at all, I think, until you've held me in your arms. There aren't prying eyes in here.'

He stood to embrace her for the second time in his life. Her back, her sides in the dark purple dress, felt softer than they had under the stars on the boat deck, as if, on stockinged feet in the privacy she had thrown about them at last, she could let her body speak plainly. From the pressure of her mouth on his, he read what he wanted.

<h1 style="text-align:center">42</h1>

'There. The Southern Cross. Crux, we call it.' From the black horizon the cross had risen. It lay slightly on its side, wearing its bright interior star like a beauty spot.

'How lovely,' she said. 'How unimaginably lovely it is.'

They had come back to the boat deck. It was long past midnight. Not a soul was astir; there was no sound more than the murmur of the engines and of the sea against the side. Off to the right, beyond the equally deserted steerage, the wake stretched behind them in a double line of muted white; mixing, and then tapering off into an exquisitely extended dark curve that ended at the sky. Everything was quite clear and absolutely visible. There was light of a different kind; light, you would say, with the lightest of touches.

'It is so new.' Penny gazed upwards. 'They've become, well, intimate, the stars. But these, the ones I could never have seen back in England. So familiar.' She turned to him. 'And still so new.'

He smiled. 'How must sailors have felt when they first came here? On the brim of the southern seas. Where are your bearings if the stars change? Everything is different.'

'Everything is quite different.' She smoothed her fingers over the side of his neck, tracing the turn of the chin down and then back, where he shaved. A minute regrowth of bristles was detectable even from four hours ago. 'I'm just learning you. Can you imagine that?' She pressed upwards to kiss the place, grazing her lips on him, back and forth.

And in return he pressed her tightly against him, and, boldly, opened the zip of her dress to feel the route down her spine where her body narrowed and then filled out again to her hips.

'Do all lovers feel like this?' she whispered.

'Of course they don't,' he said. 'There are no lovers but us.'

The confident words surprised him. Perhaps they came a touch too sharply.

But she did not mind. 'Oh yes. Of course. None in the world. I was quite forgetting. I still had the foolish impression, darling, that under the decks there were a thousand real people all asleep. But they're not real at all, are they. I was forgetting.'

They explored again the little wave motion they had discovered, where their bodies fitted all along. The arousal bathed them in a sudden heat that sprang up like the flavours in the breeze.

'And can you seriously believe Stella Madeley is real?' Robert said, gently now, after a moment.

'I thought she would cling on to the bitter end. I thought they were never going to let us be. As if the world depended on it.'

'As if it's their business. Nobody real would mind. Surely.'

She laughed. That was it, absolutely. Nobody real would mind. She pictured Stella Madeley – a perpetual head prefect, her grey hair still trapped in some undefinable school 'shape'. No, neither she nor her fussy, diffident Group Captain of a husband could ever be real. This was real.

She looked up again. A meteor shower speared out of the zenith.

'I love your neck,' Robert said. 'Your shoulders.'

'You may have them, then.'

They laughed again together, at their childlike lovers' discourse, laughing in the same murmur as their speech.

'I shall. I want nothing more – except the rest of you.' Again the roughness of tone. It was as though his body spoke for him, while his head hardly coped.

'You shall. For Stella Madeley and all those other frightened souls are absolutely not real.' And as she felt herself melt together again with him the thought struck her: then neither was Hugh.

A sharp, painful incident came to mind. Hugh had tried to get her to discuss which of the rooms they should set aside as the 'fall-out room' – that Civil Defence leaflet. She had been panicked, and made a stupid scene. Irrational. While he and the boys had played hiding under a table in the spare room, she had just cried. He accused her of mental cowardice. She had felt stupid all the time, living with a clever man like Hugh.

But she was not stupid, and had never considered herself so until marriage. This thought was like the lifting of a great weight. She had permission to be happy, and it was all right.

'This is a most absorbing topic you've raised. Darling. Robert. But I should really rather replace it with kissing. How naked my back feels.'

And so the subject of Stella and all the rest of them was put aside. And they gave themselves over to exploration.

There is a difference between exploration and any other kind of seagoing enterprise. Exploration is the making of charts with the finest of lines. It is never the whole picture – it leaves gaps, intriguing, full of delight. There is fear and danger: it coasts what is perpetually strange. Map-making demands all hands; all intelligence. It is a matter for the most absolute concentration – steering is paramount. It is the act of meeting, of love. I believe so.

'No,' Penny said. 'I have to tell you. I . . . It was during the storm. I lost . . . You see, I was going to have a child. Another baby. I must tell you. I was pregnant. I . . . Do you know, in some extraordinary way I hardly knew. Can you believe that? Something going on inside and you can't bring yourself to face it. So you don't. Face it, I mean. I knew somewhere. Do you understand? But at the same time I didn't know. My body knew, but my brain didn't. Wouldn't. Robert. Have I spoiled everything? Do you hate me?'

'Why should I hate anything about you? I love you.'

'I don't know. It's so vile and messy. And another man's child. I'm ashamed. You must think of me now with all that mess. I was upset. I was so upset. And do you know part of the thing I was upset about was that I was glad. It's awful. I must be horrible.'

'Penny.'

'I'm not a terrible woman, am I?'

'No. No, you're not. Of course not, Penny. Of course not. It's all right.' And he wondered where his assurance came from. It was the naturalness between them, he thought.

'Does it make any difference?' she said. 'Men are . . . Sometimes . . . Men don't like . . . Does it make any difference? I feel . . . You see I can't . . .' There were tears in her eyes. 'I'm not a terrible woman, just for loving you? You see, it still hurts.'

'Of course.'

'Only a bit, now. It will be all right. It doesn't make any difference, does it?'

'How could it? How could it, darling?'

She clung to him.

I have entered responsibility, he thought. Everything I have done and been before, that was irresponsibility. He saw her for the first time clearly as a woman. The things which had troubled him so greatly – her marriage, her children, age – they fell away and no longer made him anxious. Her life was her life. Her lips were delicious; because of what she said. How beautiful were her breasts, her belly – not because they were breasts, but because they were hers; not as a belly, but because he could trace with his fingers the stretch marks left by her children. And below that there was still the pain of the creature her body had given up in the storm.

'I understand,' he whispered. 'I understand.'

The Southern Cross had mounted up. They lay under one of the boats on a combination of her stole and his jacket. 'It's the smallest constellation of them all,' he said. 'It used to be just visible from the Med – in the time of the Greeks and so on.'

'Do they move, then? They told us stars were fixed.'

'There's a wobble. It's called the precession.'

'How extraordinary.'

'There, do you see? That patch of brilliants. It's the Jewel Box. And the other famous thing, that dark area. That's the Coal Sack. The Cross is actually almost absorbed by a larger, the Centaur. But right along,' and he drew a great arc with his hand, 'there's the design of a ship splashed across the Milky Way. That group there is Carina; that's the keel.'

He led her sight along his finger, and drew it to the right. 'And Vela, the sails. And there is Puppis, the poop deck right in the stern. So that makes the Crux rather like a flag, doesn't it. The ensign.'

'We shall make love, Robert.'

'What?'

'You may think it's obvious. But I want to say it out loud. In case you're in any doubt.'

'When I . . . Before I came down to your cabin. I nearly couldn't come. My feet wouldn't move. It's not . . . Don't think there was for a moment any doubt about my feelings. It's just that . . . Well, I was so scared. I felt as though I should need to be something of a Casanova. D'you see? The skilled . . . American hotel films, that sort of thing. I mean in order to . . . And I'm not, you see. The fact is . . .' He turned to look into her eyes. 'The fact is I've never exactly been in the situation – of going into a lady's . . . of being exactly in that situation. I've never done anything of the kind at all.'

'Oh, bless you.' She threw her arms around him. 'It's absolutely all right. I said I believe I've had quite enough for both of us. I knew what you meant. It doesn't matter. Don't worry for a moment, my dearest. We shall be wonderful.' There was a pause while she thought. 'So that's why you've spent your life gazing at the stars.'

Infinitely relieved, he looked at her.

'To avoid looking for me. But I have found you. It will be all right. I promise you. I say we shall be wonderful.' She allowed another few moments to pass. 'We were both frightened, weren't we?'

He nodded.

'And of course,' she continued, 'what else should we expect? But there is a blissful thing, darling, I think. That if it's all right between us, and we aren't afraid of each other; then when it gets rough . . . When it gets rough, I say, up ahead . . . Well then there's no need for us to be afraid of anything they throw at us, is there?'

'No,' he said. 'No need at all.'

'Good. We shall get through, darling. We shall.'

43

As the *Armorica* approached Ceylon, Robert and Penny became set apart from the circle of shipboard society, like a gemstone raised proud of its ring. More absorbed in one another with each passing minute, they hardly noticed Russell and Clodagh's calculated snub when the shore plans for Colombo were discussed at the observation lounge bar. And, discovering that to spend the rest of the morning strolling back and forth along the shady port side of the promenade deck talking softly in murmurs and smiles was the occupation that came most naturally in the world, they were oblivious to the Madeleys' pointed removal of their deck-chairs to some other station.

When they were apart, as they must be at meals, they were each dreamlike and rapt, seeking every few moments to find the other's eyes across the dining-room; so that the studied coolness of their dining companions was entirely lost on them. Dilys Finch-Clark's 'It's the openness that I mind, actually' was a wasted barb. Cheryl's 'You've really gone and done it now, Bobby' from behind his chair, elicited only another warm grin from Robert. He mistook the acid in her voice. Mary Garnery's brusque cut of his greeting as she passed he put down to a slight deafness. He ate with relish, the sooner to be with Penny again. In the afternoon of the last day before Colombo they sat out in full view on the Verandah sun trap and paid not the slightest heed to the looks offered nor the shoulders turned. Jokes were even made in their hearing, about somehow 'going native', of all things.

Curiously, the one couple who did not shun them were the Piyadasas. But that was because of their own slightly precarious social position, despite their perfect English. Or was it that they could still not quite bring themselves to imagine the English behaving other than perfectly? For if she was anything, Robert reasoned, the *Armorica* was a floating showcase of all that. He did puzzle himself over the apparently naïve friendship the couple continued to offer. At university he had had a friend from Pakistan, and remained confused about the precise nature of that relationship.

'Darling. They're just nice people who don't leap to conclusions. Perhaps they're the only nice people on board.'

'Ah. You remember I promised to show you around when we got to Ceylon,' Mrs Piyadasa said to Penny. 'We'll soon be home. You must both come. Maybe we could even go to Kandy. We'll see to everything.'

One must steer very discreetly. Why, he almost wanted to apologise – apologise at the very least, though the matter of imperial occupation was far too large for that. As large as a subcontinent. But these were Penny's friends. Robert cautiously allowed himself to be liked by them.

'When I first came to England I was amazed to see poor people.' Mrs Piyadasa had laughed. 'I thought only we had them. Now of course I am used to it.'

They were watching a school of about five whales keeping pace, fifty yards off the starboard quarter. 'There. Did you see that one breathe?' Robert pointed. 'And what exactly is Kandy?' he asked, when they had all admired the plume of a genuine spout.

'Kandy is the old city in the hills. It is right in the centre of the island.'

'I see.'

Penny said, 'It reminds me of that song Christopher always likes when it comes on *Uncle Mac*. Every Saturday morning,' she explained. 'So many children write in. They usually have it sometime during the programme. Christopher learnt it off by heart.' She sang, in a low, self-conscious tone:

> *The buzzin' of the bees*
> *in the cigarette trees,*
> *the soda-water fountains;*
> *The lemonade springs*
> *and the bluebird sings*
> *in the big rock-candy mountain.*

Everyone laughed. 'Bravo,' said Mr Piyadasa; then added, 'Not quite all that. But it's well worth a visit. Sculptures, dancing. There's a wonderful lake, and of course the temple of the Buddha's tooth. It's our greatest relic, if you like.'

'Oh, and elephants!' his wife exclaimed. 'Elephants galore! You'll just love it. It's all very beautiful. But in one day I shall see my children. How sad I feel for you, Penny, that you're still parted from your boys. Mother always longs to have her sons by her, doesn't she?'

'Yes indeed,' Penny said, thoughtfully.

Robert was checked. Hearing her sing he found himself not so enchanted as he should have been, for it located her firmly with her husband and the boys. It recalled nothing so much as BBC family life, as issued to a generation by the wireless, in its stifling values, its children's hour, its housewives' choice, its Uncle Mac with his bears at perennial sinister picnic in the woods. They had no real plans. Everything was in cursed abeyance, until Australia; and they would have to live with that.

Penny began to stroll aft with Mrs Piyadasa, leaving Robert to cherish the prospect of Kandy. They might find themselves alone there. He imagined a jewelled Eastern garden, set high, surrounded by rich jungle. Where, even if the child-flavour of sugar–sweet came to it from her lips, there would be an immediacy of life, and of love. There would be nothing petty, because what they felt for each other made even the simplest things profound.

He wanted to speak to her again, immediately. He wanted to reassure her about the children, and to tell her how their mention had made him feel. It would all work out. At least the visit would give them time. They would have to have time, in order to consolidate; in order to be ready, yes, for what the other end had to throw at them. In paradise, then, they could not actually afford dalliance but would have to do some hard talking. He girded up his mental loins.

The other person who did not shun them was Joe.

'You got home late enough last night, Bob.'

'Well, yes. I had some things to attend to, Joe.' Robert ferreted in his half of the cupboard.

'Studying I expect, was it, Bob?'

'Something like that, yes.'

'Very fine woman, that Mrs Kendrick, don't you think, Bob?'

'What? Yes. I suppose she is.'

'Not going to get much chess in from now on are we, Bob?'

'No. Perhaps not.'

'Shame, that. But aren't you going to bring her back to meet the folks? Maybe she plays. Couldn't be much worse than you, could she now, Bob?'

'All right, Joe. You win.' He stopped what he was doing.

'Well, I might hang around in the bars too much, old mate, but I'm not blind and stupid to boot.'

Robert turned. His straight face split and he laughed.

'Only I want you to know, Bob, that if there's anything I can do . . . You know what I mean; it's not going to be easy, now is it?'

'No.' His face clouded again. 'No, it isn't. Not when we get there.'

'It isn't so much plain sailing just now, is it? Either?'

'Oh, the wagging tongues? We don't mind about them. Why should we?'

'Caused a bit of a stir, somehow, Bob. Joker came up to me with a drink in his hand. Never noticed him, hardly, all voyage. Wanted to bone on about the deeds of my cabin-mate. Lot of people doing the same, it seems.'

'Nothing better to occupy them?'

'True enough, Bob. The curse of idleness – drink and gossip. A lot of harmless fun at somebody else's expense. Irresistible to most. But then you'd think – a lot of ladies and gentlemen thrown together, holiday atmosphere perhaps, some of them off the leash, in a manner of speaking. Throwing away the old life, and putting on the new. Dancing, and whatever not. It's a cocktail, isn't it, Bob? Sea passages like this are known for it, aren't they? Anybody could tell you that. And I daresay, by this far out, you two aren't the only ones – by a long way, Bob. Yet I can tell you, it's caused quite a stir, you and Mrs Kendrick. Can't quite work out exactly why.'

'Because we won't skulk around. Because we mean it.'

'Because you're both somehow defiant about it. Did you know that? Yes, that's the word. Defiant. It's only happened a day or so and yet everyone's suddenly buzzing. Like you've both been electrified.'

'Surely not.'

'Take my word for it.'

'None of their business.'

'Agreed. But as I was going to say, Bob, if you need . . . If you get into a tight spot and need a hand, you can rely on me. I like you, Bob; and I like the look of her. And I like the way you're not dishonest and creeping about. Some things are just OK, no matter what the rules are. You both look as though it suits you, you both look right, somehow. That's what I feel in my bones, Bob. Sounds stupid, doesn't it. Sounds a bit crook. But from what I see it can't be much of a bad thing.'

Robert gripped his hand. 'I'm really grateful, Joe. Believe me. Really grateful.'

Joe returned the handshake. 'Still, I'll miss the chess. Oh, one thing.'

'Yes?'

'It's long gone half-way. You don't mind if I take the top bunk from here on, do you?'

'Utterly not. Think of the deal as done, Joe. Take it with my best wishes.'

'Thanks a lot, mate. And if you're going to be coming in late, you won't have to climb on my head, will you?'

'Yes. Or rather no. Sorry about that, Joe.'

'All right.'

44

I watched their progress. They were the lovers now. They were being swept away by the woman in the sari and her husband. They had eclipsed Chaunteyman.

I considered what I knew of the East.

He's a Hindoo hoodoo how-do you-do man. So sang George Formby often enough on *Midday Music-hall* – an idiot with a banjo, who had been given the brief of interpreting these matters. Erica's father admired him. But in our house my own grandfather was regarded as the true oriental authority, because he had spent so much time there in a battleship. He had brought back the curiosities on display in the front parlour. He knew India was bursting at the seams with beggars and princes; one China baby was born every minute. I used to look at our clock. And at the map. Where would they go: Malaya, Burma, Siam? Women were thrown on fires, infants eaten, girls had their feet bound, and boys climbed snakes to disappear. If East met West we should be overwhelmed by conjuring tricks.

Oh Mr Woo, what should I do? I've got those kind of Limehouse Chinese laundry blues.

Earlier in my life the wireless had often said the situation in Indo-China was worsening. My grandfather explained, 'It's China in India'. Our miniature carved ivories proved his point. They were complex and strange – all that displaced flesh: wrists, ear lobes, a long-fingered hand. There was an elephant head with an array of arms; a willowy, soft-faced woman with a long beard. There was an intricate parasoled moon-maiden; a monkey; someone with an enormous tongue; and a tree with girls, rocks and a crocodile. There was a pot-bellied bald man in jade-like stone, and a little bronze dancer in a ring of flames. The top of our folding Benares table was hammered with divinities afloat above the Taj Mahal. And there was that boat-shaped relic made from a large bamboo tube.

I've got a bimbo down on a bamboo isle.

On waking suddenly from his nap my grandfather, who kept old Navy pronunciations for things, might quote from an obscene poem he called the 'Ganges Layment', and then deny it. His life had been spotless. He had visited, of course, the *Maylays*, could describe from first hand the pigtails on Chinese pirates, turbanned boatmen in the dawn at Calcutta, and the astonishing foods of curried dog, horse, hundred-year-old egg, sweet-and-sour pig, bird's nest soup. He told of a British cruiser up a Boxer river with a snake aboard. The snake had its neck shattered in a shower of mess plates, and its skin made into a walking-stick.

Grandad was our natural arbiter on anything far-flung, anything unimaginable. He knew how to handle it. He could even speak Indian, *pani, jaldi*; and pretended to some Mandarin. So no unnecessary mention was made in our house of the parts of London where it was suddenly becoming common to see brown people, or black. Because of Grandad's heart. Except for once – where this subject caused the only row in which I ever saw *my* father's smouldering hatred for his own. Grandad had no interest in Jamaicans, as designed for slavery by whatever god made that puddle, the Atlantic. They were a flash in the pan. But he declared the Indian in general more work-shy and less trustworthy than the Chinaman. The Chinese were better organised and could only be crossed at the sailor's peril, whereas an Indian would steal a man's anything and everything. 'You watch your pockets on them bloody buses, sonny,' he instructed me. 'Should never have let 'em in. They'll see me under, you mark my words. Old England's done for, you wait and see.'

My father burst out in a rage. 'What d'you think we were bloody fighting for, you fucking senseless old bigot! Talking to him like that.'

I was very frightened, and felt myself lifting up in a panic like an angel near the picture rail, looking down on the browns and greens of the room, the exposed floorboards round the edge of the rug, the drab walls, the dark skirtings, the cramp of the men and their furniture. But it was over as soon as it started, and I began immediately to doubt I had actually heard it. Yet there remained an atmosphere stretched to bursting; the fire flickered in the hearth and the work-light bulb blazed flatly. It was only resolved by Erica returning home with various items of new clothing for us and a box of sweets; she had been taken out in Mr Chaunteyman's huge car to shop in Oxford Street. She calmed Grandad down and got his tablets, and then mollified everyone with crystallised ginger.

There were the bad words Erica's aunts would say openly about the blacks in the South London streets. I looked to my father for guidance. He became inscrutable again. At other times – say while he was absorbed in some electrical repair – he would sing a line of an obscure ditty in a wry, whining voice: *Ship me somewheres east of Suez, where the best is like the worst*. Or the line of a rhyme: *There's a green-eyed yellow idol to the north of Kathmandu*. He would snigger to himself, like a shameful boy. 'You and me, Ralphie.' In my grandad's company he never again exploded, but would jolly him along, or play the sap.

In my comics everyone except the English stayed where they had been put. My story-books threw no more light on race, or guilt. Mr X fought the wily orientals in Kowloon; Kim was nursed in the wisdom of Tibet. There was a secret poison from the dark jungles of Burma in *The Sign of Four*; Mowgli was loved by Indian wolves. I preferred Rikki-tikki-tavi who could kill snakes, or the djinns stroking their beards. No one was ever homeless or thought of migration.

On the ship, Robert and Penny's love reminded me of the tune Erica sang along to in the cramped little dark green kitchen among the pots:

Take my hand, I'm a stranger in paradise,
all lost in a wonderland . . . with an angel like you.
I saw your face and I ascended,
out of the commonplace, into the rare.
Somewhere in space I hang suspended,
until I know there's a chance that you care,
won't you answer the fervent prayer,
of a stranger in paradise . . .

She said it was *Kismet*. Her face had that rapt look of certain women and girls. But now I mistrusted Chaunteyman and with him even rapture itself. The lover, Robert: had he told the authorities as he promised? Had he told Penny there was danger? They had made no contact with me since taking up with that sari woman. I had not much time.

45

The morning we anchored at Colombo, I noticed one other realignment as a result of the Kettle–Kendrick entente. Cheryl Torboys appeared to declare herself Erica's bosom friend. And then we discovered Mr Chaunteyman was suddenly, like them, going to get off at Singapore, the next port of call after this.

I was touched on Erica's behalf. Mr Chaunteyman had always felt free to put himself about, I could see that. No doubt he already was 'buddy' enough with Lucas and Co., as he was with so many people in the bars, but without feeling the need to include his 'fiancée' and her son. I was never precisely aware of his movements. I had put myself about too; but by this stage in the voyage, and after being left in the hold, I was on the fringes of things. Such had been Erica's position all along. I see now it must have been obvious – from her dress style and slightly gauche manners, and most of all from her accent – that she was out of the wrong drawer. Cheryl's patronage came then as a bolt from the blue, and Erica was flustered and rather thrilled. Overnight she was entering *High Society*, her favourite film.

Ceylon embraced us, a waving harbour of brightness. While port formalities were being completed, Mr Tingay cornered me near the foredeck and asked whether I was troubled about anything, anything at all. He had been watching me, he said. I was on my own a good deal. I looked low. He had the care of souls. Did I feel the need of someone to confide in? In view of my mother's, *ah* . . . ? If so, I should think of him as of a father.

I regarded him suspiciously for a moment, and then in a new light. That I might have misjudged, and made foolish mockery of him. A listening ear was being offered in my time of need. I told him that something down there might go off.

'Ah!' he said, starting back. 'Yes, but so young. You're surely not . . . Can it be possible? My dear little boy.' He told me that sin was transmitted through the female and I should say my prayers. Did I say my prayers every night like a good boy? I nodded. He would pray for my mother, he said.

Mr Chaunteyman had broken the news to Erica and me before breakfast; there may have been a telegram for him. He called at our cabin.

'You won't mind, sugar, if we make a slight change of plan?' Yes, he held a piece of paper in his hand. 'Something's come up. I need to do the last leg by plane. Uncle Sam wants me to spend a week or so in Changi, courtesy of your RAF. What you people call *hush hush*. They'll pay for everything *pro tem*. And the Pentagon will pick up the tab.' He smiled his all-American smile, bright as chromium, yet he looked nervous. 'It's only a little bit of business for me. You wouldn't mind that, honey, would you?'

Erica acquiesced without a murmur. 'Whatever you want. Whatever you have to do. I know you'll look after us, Dave.'

'Sure, Erica. Sure I will. You'll be given the best. I'll see to it.' And he tossed me half a crown to make myself scarce for twenty minutes.

Changi spelt horrors to me. I had read my father's paperback about Japanese tortures, or rather glanced at it, put it down in a sweat, and then, agonised, continued. And he would be leaving the *Armorica* to go precisely to Changi? To hell more readily, surely. How could anyone bear it? I may have been ostracised, but at least on the ship I was safe. For that reason I loved it – and almost began to whisper my thoughts in prayer, to God, or the Leviathan. I did not want Erica hurt; I did not want torture mentioned. I smelt a rat. Did Mr Tingay know what I knew?

Perhaps, underneath everything, he had been trying to tell me he understood.

So Cheryl Torboys took up with us and I found myself chatting now and then with her sons, though their names still escape me. Cheryl dominated Erica. She needed someone on whom to vent her spleen about Robert and Penny. I remember how we all got into the launch to go ashore at Colombo. The water in the harbour was milky-green and spangled in the sun. It was more than spangled, far more. The light was intense, coming from all directions. Each wavelet, or the smallest reflective angles of ships, or buildings, or cars, or windows in the near distance, might have had flares, glass, diamonds, perpetual flash bulbs. The launch had a canopy supported on iron struts. Of the true East it was my very first.

Cheryl made sure our little party occupied the space in the stern because she had seen Robert, Penny and the Piyadasas in the bow. She spoke loudly of how sad it was that we seemed to be in such a rush once again. All because of that dreadful storm she still kept hearing so much about. What a pity folk who'd got excursions worked out to here and there in the middle of the island – that native place called Kandy, for example – should have to give them up. I tried to catch Penny's eye and wave. Erica discouraged me.

'Will you tell him, Dave?'

'Look, son. Your mother and I think there are certain people you'd better steer clear of from now on. Some ladies and gentlemen are not so nice to know. Right now you're too young to understand; but just take it from me you're better off with your own kind. Say, did I ever teach you "The Ballad of Davy Crockett"?'

'That old hat?' I said, rudely. The adults stared. I looked back to the hull of the *Armorica*. My time was running out. They were cutting me off from Penny, but she only had eyes for Robert. Clutching my blue suitcase I turned sulkily forward again to stare right through the lovers at the other end of the canopied launch to Colombo. I could make no ballad of my own, and Finlay would have nothing to do with me.

46

When Robert whispered, 'We've made it, Penny. We've done it,' she was thrilled that she knew him well enough to understand. Though it was said lightly, almost as a joke, his response to the Piyadasas' house was significant, and gave her hope. For the extraordinary place was so different from anything she had known or conceived of as a home, that she too saw how it proved the legends and the pictures of another world.

There were still new worlds then. Through a doorway not far from the harbour Robert and Penny were shown into one.

There was something Venetian about it – Colombo sits on water – and the house was austere from the outside as a small fort among small waterside forts, with passages and all the business of bright streets. But if a vague notion of Venice was the only visual reference through which Penny could describe the exterior to herself, once inside she was left to flounder with churches and the past and some general evocation of India that spilled over from schoolroom Kipling.

The house was made of marble that swam in a pale light like a glimpse into an opened coconut. The light came through arched windows and, sinking down, like a cool whiteness, it spilled from level to level, and swirled between the pillars that led away, presumably, into some other quarters beyond; only to be refreshed once more from above. Heavens, she could not tell if it was a small room or a cathedral, whether it was the living area for an established royal family or only an entrance hall.

There were carpets laid upon the stone, and people were sitting on them. Steps led down to make a garden floor by the open doors. Tables were set around the sides, with upright chairs, like those a hotel might provide near the foyer. The Piyadasas floated through the space in a mystery of greeting, from whose language she was withdrawn, so that she had the idea they moved in an aquarium like brilliant fish. Why, she had never had the faintest inkling, from their quiet demeanour on board ship, their polite engagement when spoken to, that in their own place they were merchant princes, who lived in such simple magnificence. The house was full: family, servants; trestles supporting plates of food and drink; patterns and plants. She had the feeling of having entered a painting.

Robert and she should sit on chairs.

'Now these are my sons.' Mrs Piyadasa introduced them, and her shy daughter.

Despite her best endeavours Penny found disconcerting the way the well-spoken boys loomed over her, tall, very dark, and somehow incomprehensible. She had thought she bore no prejudice. Now she perceived through her discomfiture that prejudice was written into everything she had grown up with. All that fell away as softly and simply as the light drifting down from above. She knew in just one more subtle mode that she was right to pledge her future to her feelings for Robert. That if she felt uncomfortable here when her inherited notions of race and home were so delicately yet decisively challenged, it only made sense of the doubts that still haunted her hours away from him. Prejudice was in her bones. It was deep down. She was ashamed and wanted it there no longer. Simply by falling in love Robert and she had scratched the surface of everything.

And when the pieces of spiced food had gone round on a metal platter, and they had drunk the chilled coconut milk which the oldest of the servants brought, and when they had made polite conversation with the whole family, stretched their legs and taken tea in the garden so leaf-sworded and fragrant with many kinds of strange blooms, together with the brilliant, nectar-sucking bird, and the strutting peacock, then they must make haste to one of the cars, for their time was short and there was so much to see.

Mrs Piyadasa was to be their guide, and one of her sons, since her husband had immediate business to attend to. Penny sat with Robert in the leather back of the upright, black, old-fashioned limousine, while mother and son sat opposite, as in a railway carriage, in order to call instructions to their driver through the glass. She felt established. It was curious and delicious, but she felt all the time now with Robert as though she had always known him, and that this was their true life; while her other existence back in Essex, and the Australia waiting for her, with Hugh, were phantasms.

But it would be very foolish, she thought to herself, to imagine that these people were the answer to everything. It was tempting for the one day. She had to keep reminding herself that they would have their difficulties and desperations, too, and that this sheer torrent of outdoor light, this wonderful heat, this endlessly mobile scene of brightly-clothed people in their sarongs or reddas, the rickshaws, the bullock carts, the cars, the bicycles, pedestrians, fruit-sellers, cloth-carriers, snake-charmers and businessmen was probably not part of some permanent stream of happiness. No, it probably was not, though she had difficulty believing it. For everything here made sense, and sprang home to her like an old friend. She knew absolutely where she was. This, she told herself, is an illusion. How I love him, sitting beside me with his fine limbs and gentleness, his decency. That is not an illusion at all.

47

Robert, sitting next to her with the old leather hood of the car framing softly over them – no matter how the car jolted at pot-holes or shuddered over rails – felt an arousal not threatening, not squalid, not prurient, but embracing like a flame. It was nothing he had known. Deprived of intimate speech – by the decorum required in front of their hostess – they might communicate feeling only through glances and the stealthiest touch. But it was not that; it was not that the delight fed on restriction – for they had broken the last barrier of speech the previous night, and he would have told her every nuance of impulse had they been alone.

All the while the city reeled and unreeled around them. Mrs Piyadasa explained what mangosteens were; and which merchant lived in that great house; or which coppersmith, from whom she bought all her kitchen requirements, in that diminutive booth. She spoke lightly of how the Indians had come first of all, and then the Portuguese, the Dutch, burning and torturing, unfortunately – the ones for God, the others for cinnamon. And here were the buildings of such-and-such descent and here were those of another, though this was not the ancient capital.

And there was the house of her best friend from school; and

202

there was her husband's warehouse. And from just here they could see both lighthouses at the harbour entrance. And then last of all the British came. Did they see the clock tower while driving past the street's end? And over there stood one of the few Muslim temples; until one drove through the Pettah where the Tamil people lived, who might be either Hindu or Muslim, of course. Sorry for the rails again.

Over here a sweet stall, would they like sweets? How difficult it was these days to keep reliable workers; but the world market in tea was holding up well, she thought, smiling at her son, and would do as long as there were English people to drink it, smiling at them. Such, there, was the national dress, but very few of the men still wore it, only the women, really. What would they say to the zoo, the beach as well, perhaps, to kill two birds with one stone? Ah, here was her son's school; he must return to his studies now that his mum and dad had returned safe from the sea.

At Dehiwala they left the car, and strolled among the creatures, the palm trees, the unstoppable vegetation, which twisted up over everything, then cascaded down a precipice to the lake in great lavender drifts. A gang of long-legged storks was working the shallows, strutting in the green reflection; close at hand a tiny hen ran over lily-pads. And as they moved in the perfume of frangipani by the lawns and between the quiescent beasts in their cages – languid tigers or apes preoccupied amid the straggle of bougainvillea that quite covered them over with a froth of purple flowers – Robert longed to catch her, delay her in a stolen embrace.

Still, again, he found himself flaming patiently, deliciously, without question. They climbed back up. The paths were narrow; creepers and bladed bushes thrust at them from either side. Mrs Piyadasa led the way, and Penny followed, a step in front of him. A pair of Buddhist priests in their pleated saffron, holding their umbrellas up against the dappled sun, passed by them on the slow earthen steps while butterflies large as birds, black and velvety-winged, flapped across their route.

When they returned to the car, they drove past the great former Residency at Mount Lavinia and on to the beach where there was the same jungle stretching right to the edge, almost.

203

They could believe the butterflies had followed them – great butterflies fluttering to the sound of surf. There were swimmers where a notch in the coastline made the hint of a bay, and one enormous palm drooped low over the sand towards the jut of a ridge: rock or coral he could not tell. Mrs Piyadasa found a table among the lilies at the edge of a shaded clearing where you could watch the waves, and ordered the white-suited waiter to bring them some tea.

'As if we haven't seen enough ocean to be going on with,' she said, and laughed.

'Poor Pom would have worried something might eat him,' Penny responded, eyeing the white holiday-makers breasting the surf. 'Sharks and crocodiles are his particular *bêtes noires* at the moment. And if you leave the water alone, there are still snakes, he says, that might drop on you from the trees. Now Finlay and the others appear to have dropped *him*.'

'Can't say I'm all that surprised,' Robert said. He found himself having suddenly to picture the boy. It threw him off his absorption in her.

'You won't see him any more, anyway, Mrs Piyadasa,' Penny said.

'The boy Ralph? No. The one my husband lent his field-glasses to. How he loved to look at the waves during the storm.'

Mrs Piyadasa told them about Kandy. 'Ah, you would have seen the Buddha's tooth.'

'The Buddha's tooth?'

'You can see his tooth?' said Robert.

'Ah, well. You can see the casket in which its casket is hidden inside another casket. Or so we're told.' She laughed again.

'Did the Buddha come to Ceylon?' Penny asked.

'Well, yes. We like to think he did. And when the moon becomes full – you will have gone, I'm afraid – there is a great celebration of his visit. In eight days' time. But the tooth was taken from the actual flames of his cremation, and smuggled here from India.'

'How astonishing.' They saw another monk leave the thick margin of vegetation and begin to walk across the beach. 'But must a true Buddhist really give up everything and renounce the world?'

While Penny engaged their hostess about religion, Robert

felt jealous again and left out, as if a snake's hood collapsed on the instant and the gaze that had held them fascinated with what was dangerous, yes, but wonderful and worth everything, turned merely to slink off back to the jungle.

'I thought the Buddha was a kind of god,' she was saying. 'I thought you . . . forgive me. I thought people worshipped him.'

'Oh no. He was a man. A prince. He was married, and then renounced the world. He fasted until all his bones showed through and then he returned to teach. He enjoyed eating again. Then he died. That's how the tooth became available.'

At least there wasn't God in it, Robert thought, angrily. He hated the thought of the tooth: how would anyone know it was there? He wished she would just laugh at it and turn back to him. Mrs Piyadasa was being polite. He looked intently at Penny, seeking to recover his feeling, wondering what had happened and what on earth they were going to do when they got to Australia. How on earth would they survive the landing? Hugh, and so on? Where would they live, supposing they did just declare independence, as it were? He felt himself smile sardonically at the joke. But surely it would be an impossibility after all?

'He was born a Hindu then?'

'In India. But far away, in the North. Ceylon was supposed to be the kingdom of enchanters and all manner of wicked spirits.'

What were they after all but a pair of momentary sightseers? Here they touched so lightly, once more knowing nothing about the place they were passing through. The English again floating by, holding, bleeding dry, but never encountering. Surely always the worst kind of tourists. The greatest empire the world has ever known. He looked around at the extraordinary, exotic scene in which he sat. It was incomprehensible. He was adrift and almost held on to his chair.

'The king of Lanka abducted Sita away in his flying chariot, you see. And afterwards when Ram had crossed Adam's Bridge with an army of monkeys to rescue her . . .'

It could not have happened without overwhelming violence. Where, he asked himself, did you see the scars? How did one ask a polite hostess about that?

And Penny looked such a stranger, incomprehensible female

flesh by the sea, in her trim blouse and printed cotton skirt sitting there with her cup of tea chatting about who knew what. She wore a blue belt. He felt the weight of that great book across his chest, and remembered the Roman examples, the strange atmosphere of his schoolroom Latin.

'But the Buddha renounced his renunciation, in a way?'

'In a way he did. One tries not to do cruel or hurtful things, to others, or to oneself I suppose. You are right. I suppose that is a way of putting it, yes. So as not to be reborn too often . . .'

He had turned to the schoolroom science that had determined his career. He had been at home nowhere, like the English; now he would somehow drag Penny too into perpetual homelessness. He felt the weight of the invisible stars, his work.

'And though she was restored to her true husband's love, Sita knew she had been dishonoured, and could do nothing but give herself to the flames.'

48

But it passed. Seated once more in the car, he knew the mood had passed and that he loved her – and that they must and would go on.

'I'm sorry,' he said. 'Haven't said much. I was thinking. I hope I wasn't rude. It's all right now.'

Back on board the *Armorica* they made their consummation. They went to her cabin, turned the key in the lock, and there they were: the moment had come. They say the drowning man sees his life flash in front of him; Robert spun and whirred and found himself conscious as never before. She was naked in front of him.

'It's all right, darling,' she said. 'It's all right.'

The curious thing was that she actually seemed to be pleased with him. How beautiful she was. How delicate, gentle and vulnerable. How disgusting intimacy might be.

'You do understand it's you I want, Robert. You do understand that, don't you?'

He nodded blindly.

'It's not just any man, Robert, but you. Precisely and exclusively you.'

'I'm sorry, it's . . .'

'And that means whatever you do or are, or will be.'

Lovemaking was a thing entirely unexpected and on its own terms. No one could have anticipated that. He discovered the saltiness of her skin, her sweat, the odours of her body, her intimate irregularities, her moles, an abrasion, a cut, the individuality of every strand of hair. He found his own strength against hers. She pulled him to her and filled his ear, until his brain felt like a tactile cavern of happiness, with the splashings of her voice and tongue. She embraced him with her legs, strained him to her with her arms, breathed him with her lungs. It was a contract. She nodded and kissed him back, again and again.

So the world flooded over them, until they lay panting in the lower bunk, sprawled one over the other, tangled in an exchange of limbs. It was as she had said it would be, wonderful; and yet, strangely, nothing out of the ordinary − because they were lovers, and that was what they did.

Australia, of course, was altered for ever; it was not what it had been. Who could consign himself now to the desert? Who could imagine, now, that endless futility of brandishing and spear-throwing, that exhaustion of the heart to which he had committed himself? Lying in Penny's arms he remembered Ceylon. His mind was like the flapping of a butterfly's wing, lovely and erratic. He remembered the colours, the profusion, all now past. He remembered the parting from Mrs Piyadasa at the edge of the harbour; and, curiously, the boy Ralph, who shared the same return launch. His thoughts came back to Penny. But when they had finished their kisses, and he was drifting to sleep in her arms, the thing he had unconsciously noticed nudged into his head. 'Poor kid. He must have lost his little suitcase, forgotten it somewhere. He came back without it. You know Chaunteyman's getting off next stop. That's one thing I shan't be sorry about.'

'Is he really, darling,' Penny murmured.

49

The open-air swimming-pool was filled with sea water. It looked like a normal pool but tasted quite different. To port and starboard its sides had blue tiles. Fore and aft there were close-set bars running vertically the whole depth. The water was in a cage. The sea was taken up through one end; and slowly given back by the other – but the apertures in the grilles were too narrow and the regions beyond too dark to see how the whole system worked.

I used to worry, especially as I lay in bed, that we would hoover up a shark one day. The idea tempted me to prayer and I thought of the Leviathan. I needed to reassure myself whenever I swam that the bars were solid and in place after the night, and that the pool contained no camouflaged man-eater waiting on the bottom particularly for me.

Since Aden the place had become a social focus, of course, and began to occupy a great part of each day's agenda, particularly for the families with children. The week before Colombo had taken on a bright, half-dressed seaside quality. But after the resumption of our passage eastward the first excitements of exchanging English winter for Equatorial summer began to wear off; and for the children swimming fell away as the prime activity. Not all of them really liked the taste, or the way the water would sting the eyes and blister the very fair skins with salt. And always for parents and children alike there was the danger, day after day under this high un-accustomed sun, of bad burns cruelly delayed until the pleasure was over and the damage done. The pool was deceptive, leaving its marks.

Sometimes too the water-level would be sunken well away from the rail, for reasons I could never explain; and since there was no shallow end, then only good swimmers could hope to do anything more than cling to the ladders, or drift helplessly in water-wings and rubber lifebelts. But I could swim like a fish, and took more and more to the pool as I was included less with the others. I stayed in beyond the children's official times and swam with the adults. Mr Chaunteyman bought me a face mask so that I could save my eyes and peer into the secret places of the grilles.

Barnwell's aircrew continued to enjoy the pool, and liked to swim in a group. Just after the children's time, while afternoon tea was being served, they would roister out of the Verandah bar and take the pool over, diving and shouting. They were given a wide berth, and there were comments about the apes of Gibraltar. But I held my course, and they did not bother me, with their guffaws and horseplay; nor I them – it was only the fez and so on that had set them off before. For my part, I believed they frightened the shark. They ignored me. And when all five got out at once, as if by some signal to go off to sunbathe, the pool area was left sometimes quite empty, and I would be free to survey my kingdom.

It was water from nowhere, water that for all I knew had never touched a human being before. An immense outside was sucked in and contained in our small pond, permitting us to occupy it for only the briefest while.

So when not troubled about the shark, I amused myself with various speculations: that while swimming forward, I might actually be swimming faster than the ship. Or that we were not moving at all, but the earth was rotating under us and sluicing a continuous wave up through the dark body of the hull for me to ride its crest. Or that the people who stood around the pool were somehow looking out to sea when they watched me. Sometimes I was a ship within a ship, and the Leviathan lay concentrated inside me. Sometimes I was Jonah, or Geppetto, or the sailor in the *Just So* story who had forced a grating into the *Armorica*'s throat.

I thought to myself how all water was joined up. We were far, far from the murky green stuff I had bathed in at Brighton, or the toxic tide which slunk past Woolwich, yet there was a fluid chain. Out here the only thing which might have contact with my home was the sea, caged but not caged.

I considered the shape of those scoops in the ship's belly by which the sea must be caught; and how the great ducts might rear up so high through its body. What were they made of and how were they shaped so as to form into the cave behind the gratings? If I inadvertently drank, did I take up plankton? Phosphorescence? Would I die horribly of dehydration? What did my shipmates add to the sea before sending it back? I queried, too, whether the water we had sported in went straight down to the smaller pool used by the ten-pound emigrants behind the drop of the steel wall, almost out of earshot, almost out of mind.

At other, more sensuous times, I simply allowed myself to float, and have the wavelets of my own making lap back over my chest from their reflection against the sides. Or I would lie face down for as long as I could hold my breath and wonder how it would feel to have been born a pearl fisher, to spend a life of bursting lungs amid the rocks and rays and giant clams. I would dive to the bottom of the pool and come up holding an imaginary shell, which would contain the longed-for pearl. I should perhaps give it to Penny. Or to Robert to give to Penny.

And whenever I looked down again it would strike me how clear the Indian Ocean was within these tiles, while all round the ship it lapped so thick a blue. I could make no sense of that. The water held me for mockery; then when I came up it laughed and sparkled. I made it my friend and wore it next to my skin like a dolphin.

A day or so out of Colombo, a new buzz started to replace the indignation at Robert and Penny's brazen love. I did not encounter it myself until the Sunday morning. By then its alarm had widened out, and built up – into something quite substantial enough to place alongside and even overtake a sexual scandal now several days old.

My memory, fishing for meaning, locates its source in the pool, or near it, where a couple of Barnwell's aircrew, maybe, loosened by drink one afternoon, perhaps, gave the game away: should I say set a live shark among us, wriggling, slashing, showing its rows of teeth and growing by the minute. The talk ran from bar to lounge, from deck to deck, from cabin to cabin quicker than flames, almost more immediate than a tannoy announcement.

We were carrying the bomb.

It was not just a sensationalist rumour – as put like that it must sound. For who would believe such a story? What sense would it make? So bald, so ready-made a fantasy, so simplistic an extravagance could amount to no more than the foolish imaginings of children, from whom it would inevitably have come. And who would have listened to children in those days? That nonsense of the squid!

No, it came quite otherwise than that. It came in such a detailed and comprehensive form, and fitted in so well with certain undeniable features of the voyage, that it was either a brilliantly insane forgery or the absolute truth. No child could have dreamed it up. Why, it promised to ruin our whole enterprise. Of course it had versions, some conflicting, some silly. If you will, like the varieties of shark: nurse, tiger, hammerhead, whale, carpet, wobbegong and the rest of their kin. They are all still identifiably shark. I heard all the rumours. I did not understand them – children's minds do not jump to adult conclusions. I summarise:

That we were helping to run a massive stockpile into Malaya, contrary to explicit parliamentary assurances to the Tunku. That moreover, despite the new Testing Moratorium, there were assemblies and materials to be slipped into Australia for continuing experiments at Maralinga, this time without the knowledge of the Canberra Assembly. That the *Armorica* was therefore being used to get round the official diplomatic position and killing two fabulous birds with one stone.

Everyone was preoccupied at the evening dance. The following day's housey-housey was abandoned. For report furnished detail: even such precise code-names as Rats, Kittens, Vixens and the like; or the fact that if you stored a nuclear device disassembled of its trigger then it did not count as what it was, and that was how Parliament . . .

But even if all this were very well, none of our business and what you never know can never hurt you, yet the rumours said that there had actually been some sort of accident during the storm. That a sealed container had broken loose somewhere in the bowels of the ship, got up speed and ruptured a duct or pipe. That sea water was extremely corrosive. That a small leakage of one – or a considerable flood of the other – had occurred which, because of its extremely sensitive nature, had only just been able to be repaired.

This accounted for the presence of Barnwell's aircrew, who had come on board at Gib to make good the damage; and it also explained the ship's unseemly haste. Yet even there it did not end. There was worse to come: the suspicion of contamina-

211

tion. Which had been covered up – naturally. Whoever would dare admit to it? Ha ha! – and people did emit grim chuckles at first. But, to compound the whole intricate and lunatic suggestion, Mr Barnwell, who it turned out had been the link, the person responsible, the voyage-long minder as it were, had said that persons affected by contamination were to be covertly monitored in Australia, since this was exactly the kind of data which no one could legitimately get, and if there were to be a nuclear war, the more we knew, the more effectively . . . You could at first not help laughing.

The voyage was transformed. The legend rose *fully-formed*, yes, out of the pool – by some indiscretion, some overhearing, some camaraderie – who knows how exactly. Suffice to say it rose, without warning. And even as it thrashed and snapped it remained, contrary to the regular habit of rumours, curiously intact and self-consistent – for we had plenty of leisure for examining the detail, for going on to cross-check with what so-and-so had heard, for arguing and talking it through. And further, as time went on it somehow refused to drop away; rather hung on grimly.

Which was the more surprising, since it could not possibly be true. It was a damned lie. For who could imagine the government allowing such a deception in the first place? Who could ever believe that those entrusted with the duty of care, the maintenance of standards, the upholding of decency, the pilotage and welfare of the future, would ever contrive to do such a thing against their own, and against their allies?

So the whole company of the ship in the first class section – which is to say the vast majority of the vessel's population – were thrown into surges of alternating belief and incredulity. For two days they endured in a torment. Denial – the refusal to submit to inconvenient nonsense – was plagued by anxiety over what might be safe to eat, to drink, even to touch. Acceptance was mocked by the general reluctance actually to broach the matter with the authorities, as if that would be the ultimate breach of decency, even though if the rumour were true there was clearly not a second to lose. Children's lives were at risk. Everyone's life was at risk.

And yet no one was doing anything. Surely they secretly prayed for some counter-story to begin: that it was all a hoax, that some Lascar had gone mad and floated the whole tale for a grudge against the English, that it was actually a parlour game – like a murder mystery – arranged by the quartermaster as part of the entertainment. That like that *War of the Worlds* broadcast by Orson Welles before the war, it was just something that had gone wrong at the outset and got horribly out of hand. That the wretched thing would lie still and die.

50

A thousand miles out from the Bay of Bengal, the sea lay mysteriously flat and oily, heaving fractionally in places like glass made flexible. Only where the *Armorica* was sluicing her way through did it assume its normal character of wave with spray thrown off; though the water itself lacked clarity, as if an invisible weed grew below. On deck there was always a breeze, of course, because of our movement; but no natural wind lay beyond us.

In addition it had become very hot; the air seemed to have been baking for days above the stale surface. Such oppressive conditions filled the ship with a stifling tension, though I steeled myself to that and sat apart in the improvised classroom, the better to apprehend any secret codes or messages contained in Mr Tingay's lesson.

The Sunday school had been moved to the little ones' play room. Mr Tingay's general text related as usual to how lucky we were. He told us the story of Abraham and Isaac. I did not know it – or had never attended when they had us read it in the religious instruction class at Bostall Lane. I was struck, and moved, by the hint of bleating that entered his voice as he read the passage:

> '*And Abraham said, My son, God will provide himself a lamb for a burnt offering: so they went both of them together. And they came to the place which God had told him of; and Abraham built an altar there, and laid the wood in order, and bound Isaac his son, and laid him upon the altar upon the wood. And Abraham stretched forth his hand, and took the knife to slay his son.*

'You see,' said Mr Tingay, 'Abraham desperately loved his son, but he also loved God.'

Mr Tingay continued with a discourse on the promised land, which I now saw formed some kind of overarching theme to his lessons. God's chosen were always on the run, leaving something unspeakable behind, some Moloch or other. God's chosen wore the mark of their bargain with him, a mark in the soul as well as upon the body. Some hint of recognition flickered in me, of the mark that left no mark, no scar. By whom had I been chosen? I was thrown into agitation. Mr Tingay knew.

None of the other children seemed surprised or upset by his words. Mr Tingay was considerably exercised about the world-wide proliferation of Molochs and Baals and used the terms to tell us something about himself and his mission to the heathen. I pictured the Molochs as huge sea creatures, although some were probably wild animals from the desert. The Baals were enormous poisonous lizards.

This, however, was to be almost our last meeting, he said, and we had come to know each other quite well already. He wanted to describe to us the challenge and importance of his work. For there were still those benighted black heathens aplenty who were doomed to abominations of their own kind, and it was his calling to venture into the interior and rescue them from their falsehoods.

While we, his little children of the promise again, would be safe eating the milk and honey of our new life in what he referred to now as White Australia. Because the sacrifice of Jesus, as opposed to the failure to sacrifice Isaac, which was all part of it, had made us Christians. It was all very confusing.

'Now which of you children knows what a sacrifice is?' I watched the others search their heads for an answer. Mitchell Coote knew. 'It's when you have to give something up to God, sir.'

'It's when you have to give something up to God. That's right, that boy. And God so loved the world He gave up His son. So that everyone, not just the Israelites, could enter the Kingdom. And soon we all are going to make our own kind of entry, aren't we? We're all going to make a new life for ourselves; which puts us in the same boat,' he chuckled, 'in one sense at least, with those first wandering fathers in the Bible. We too are on an adventure.'

214

'But we live in Melbourne, sir, me and my sister,' Mitchell said, ingenuously. 'We're just going home. Does that mean we're Philistines?'

'No. Of course not. *Ahem.* Very good. Very good. Some of you are not quite English. I was forgetting myself. Well, no matter how you came to be in Australia, that doesn't make you Philistines, who were the people of the sea and worshipped Dagon, you remember, and not the true Jehovah.'

I looked at him sharply, muddled. And then Finlay asked whether the Abos were black Philistines who had human sacrifices and were cannibals, and I hated her for the fact that I was excluded now from everything, and I tried to grow self-righteous in Mr Tingay's defence. I did my best.

Until, by some stretch of meandering and theological argument even more obscure and above our heads than all before, he told us the story of Samson. From that point, try as I might, I found myself completely bamboozled and frustrated. All I could make out was that in the promised land the father was uncertain whether to stab the child, set him alight, or do it to a ram; but the blind hero would, in the brilliance of rage, find a way to pull the whole of creation down upon himself, killing everyone in the process. Poor Jesus was unfortunately sacrificed in there somewhere. And this was love.

By the time it came for me to draw my picture I was very angry: I could not tell whether I was doing seagoing Philistines, or leviathanic Israelites, or white-marked Christians and thus-chosen-to-pass-through-the-fire-to-Moloch. I chose to represent the strong man on Brighton pier tearing it down from underneath. His false wife was there. Of course it exploded in a huge column of flame which obliterated much of the drawing.

If I had a last hope it was to be reinstated in the game of Dragnet afterwards; but Finlay said that were I to be allowed she would not take part, nor would Mitchell. She gave her older brother a compelling look. The Torboys children had no hesitation in sacrificing me instantly. Finlay pushed me and said, 'Shit to buggery,' at a moment when the others were just out of earshot. I was as hurt as I was meant to be.

Thus it was that I rose to the promenade deck to pay attention to what the adults were doing, and sidled into the back of the dance space where it seemed a special meeting had been in progress since the ending of the various church services. Adults were packed in; some of them were standing. There was a raised dais at the far end, where a table had been set up. A panel of very important people, glittering with rank and including the captain, were sitting at it. A hot debate was going on. And as much as the instruction according to Tingay was incomprehensible, and infuriating, so this made sudden, absolute sense. For at last I put two and two together and realised it was on the subject of the Leviathan. Robert had come good and told.

51

A man was on his feet speaking. In a little while I recognised him as Mr Barnwell. I had never seen him so. His uniform had tabs and rings and gold. He had his peaked cap on. The voice was disconcerting, tight and clipped.

'I repeat, even if there were any such devices on board, and I do not for a moment admit it – but even if there were, you should all realise that there could be absolutely no danger from any such thing in transit.'

'So there are more than one?' Someone in the assembly was pressing home an attack.

'This is a strategic matter, and as that is the case I may remind you that I am not required to divulge anything further. These are subjects, as I have already said, of national significance. Since this . . . er . . . unfortunate rumour got about, I have, of course, been in touch with my superiors. Her Majesty's Government have given me certain discretion as to disclosing information,' he looked down at a note he was holding in his hand, 'so that the minds of passengers may be set at rest. What I am at liberty to say is that HMG routinely makes use of all normal forms of cargo shipment for various purposes in the same manner as any large concern. No . . . er . . . *sensitive* material, however, would be dispatched by any transport other than military. Of course, for non-sensitive consignments expediency might require at some time or other . . .' He coughed. 'We are all bound by the laws of supply and demand.

Where there arises an urgent need to supply...'

Several people tried to speak at once. A woman's voice came out above them. 'What I don't understand is why? This is a passenger ship. There are children aboard.'

Mr Barnwell sighed visibly and showed his teeth. 'I have assured you and I can assure you that there is absolutely no danger to personnel from anything aboard this ship.'

'And how do we know that?' A man at the front stood up angrily. 'How do we know that? Why should we trust your damned word for it? Do you think any of us would have taken passage on this ship if we'd had the remotest idea?' He was supported by a host of others. 'How do you think it's going to feel ... I don't know, just sitting down to breakfast with our families now that this has come out? Worrying that just underneath us there's ... It's intolerable! Surely something must be done immediately. To reassure us.' The man looked round, as if for suggestions.

'Let us meet this thing head on, sir,' said Mr Barnwell. 'Let us imagine for a moment that this preposterous rumour were true, and that by some extraordinary chance HMG had found it necessary to include in the routine provisioning of one of our main bases, some consideration of capital ... armour. Yes. Let us look this slanderous rumour full in the eye and face it down. Supposing it *were* true. Would there be the slightest risk? Would anyone have behaved irresponsibly, after all? There can be no danger, sir, if a device is not armed. Why, the same holds for any weapon. And this is not a case, even, where there could be any instability in the materials. We are not talking, ladies and gentlemen, about anything at risk from vibration or percussion. No unexploded bomb in the cellar.

'To be frank, I don't know exactly what any possible military shipment on this vessel might contain. But I tell you again, if by some ludicrous stretch of the imagination we allow ourselves for a moment to assume the worst, out of the question though it be ... why, you could have the latest American ICBM lying in your garden and your children could hold a tea party on it without the least danger. That is the kind of risk for which you seem to wish me to get the whole ship's company in a pother – what with all this talk about winching people into the hold. And besides all that, haven't I assured you categorically that this rumour about H-bombs is in itself no more than a fabrication? A complete and malicious pack of lies, dreamed up by someone with nothing better to do.'

The meeting had grown quiet, sullen. It was the same mood as came over the whole school whenever the headmaster harangued us in the hall about street behaviour, or not wearing caps on buses. We wondered how he could touch us out there beyond his jurisdiction, and how he had the right, and yet he managed to make us all feel guilty.

'Ladies and gentlemen, our captain has your interests at heart. He would never dream of letting anything come on board which could pose the minutest threat to his passengers. It is unthinkable; trust my word in this. Unless you want me to be over-literal, and talk of all that is absolutely *necessary*. Think of a can of fuel, if you like – think of all the fuel oil in the *Armorica*'s tanks, which is slopping about down there in enormous quantities. Does anyone turn a hair at that?

'Do you see? When any of us drives a car, do we imagine for a moment that the highly inflammable liquid without which we could not move an inch is going to explode under us? Of course we don't. And yet it's quite capable of doing so. There is a risk. And there is a risk on *Armorica*. Of course there is. If you don't accept that we carry our own fuel then you had better get off at once.' He chuckled. 'There could be a problem. The kitchens might catch fire. Someone might smoke in bed. But nuclear? Nuclear?' He elevated the word as if it were the keynote to an enormous joke. 'Ladies and gentlemen, an accident of the kind some of you seem to be envisaging is simply not possible. Ships like this carry all sorts of things. Always have done. You do not ask to see an entire inventory of the hold. No passenger would.'

Mr Barnwell's tone had grown more emollient. He seemed to feel he was winning. There was a moment's silence when he finished speaking; as if the propositions he had put were indeed reasonable, and it would be impolite to speak further to an officer in such a uniform.

But then again came the woman's voice from somewhere in the middle, as if she had not heard him at all: 'Will you tell us why, though? I don't understand the need. There are children.' And a stout man from the back called out, 'What's all this about going behind the backs of the Malayans. Are we supposed to be smugglers or something of that kind?' The body of passengers drew renewed heart. They murmured. I murmured myself, but for a different reason, for I thought the Leviathan might be provoked, hearing all these voices raised, and become angry in its turn.

More people stood up and indicated a wish to speak. The figures at the table peered intently in the stout man's direction. One of them made a note. Mr Barnwell sighed again, glanced at the captain, who nodded, and then looked briefly down once more at his piece of paper. 'Very well. I will exceed my brief. The only condition is that you will each be required to sign a document of confidentiality upon leaving this ship. This is regrettable, and may appear something of an imposition, I grant, but it will ask no more than all ordinary citizens were asked during the war. Careless talk, I'm sure I have no need to remind any of you, costs lives. Disclosure will be treasonable. That is no more than any serving member,' he eyed certain areas in the audience, 'of Her Majesty's Forces is required to undertake; nor, for example, those of you – and I know there are some present – who work in the weapons industry.'

He looked up. It was oppressively hot. Only the slightest fraction of our breeze was managing to find its way in, despite the open sides. He waited. Nobody moved, or spoke. 'I take it there are no objectors, conscientious or otherwise?' He waited again. 'Very well. There is a strategic imperative to secure our interest in South-East Asia. This much is common knowledge. We need a full capability in the Far East and must make use of our possessions. The ability to supply this *full* capability is a comparatively recent achievement and there is no time to be lost.

'Unfortunately, there are local misapprehensions as to the need for security. At least in public. *Tacitly*, a spade is generally acknowledged to be a spade. *Tacitly*, there is not much of a question about it.' He allowed himself another faint chuckle. 'If I were to say it suits the parties involved to move with a certain amount of stealth over this very sensitive issue, you would understand me, no doubt. If I were to say that we fear our local air bases might have become a little leaky, you would understand me too, I think. A sudden flurry of cargo flights in a highly populated location would be difficult to disguise, I'm sure you'd agree. All sorts of people might get all sorts of wrong ideas. Public unrest.

'If I were to say that any quantity of large and small tubes, casings, or other metal objects of industrial nature – I merely quote the actual bill of lading, which is as far as you would expect me to go in all fairness – are better transported by sea; if I were to say that the Navy had no vessels available at the short notice required for this particular shipment, and you were in HMG's position, you would naturally, ladies and gentlemen, look for other routes. Wouldn't you? In the national interest. It has always been so. Happens all the time. But there would be no reason to alarm people, would there? Especially as there could be no possible danger. It's virtually a matter of routine, I assure you. Nothing out of the ordinary at all. Happens all the time.'

52

A silence followed. There was grudging assent; as if a mischievous storm had somehow been brewed in a teacup. Perhaps they had over-reacted. After all, there was a cold war on. He had involved them. The government and the military had to do what was necessary. And if there actually were no danger, now that the truth had been told . . .

It was Robert who rose from where he was sitting next to Penny. 'There was also talk of something having gone amiss.'

'Amiss?' said Mr Barnwell. 'I don't think so. Amiss? Is anyone else aware . . . ?' He looked at his uniformed companions behind the table and then around at the assembled company. 'No. I don't think so. Nothing I've come across. And it's been my responsibility to get the whole thing through as smoothly as possible. I'm the man at the helm of all this, after all, and nothing has come to my notice. There are always rumours upon rumours . . .' He dared to let a full smile out at his audience. 'That's why we felt it necessary to convene this little meeting. After all. So that by presenting the truth, fairly and squarely, we can both allay any fears, and scotch into the bargain the more excessive fabrications that tend to accumulate in matters of this kind before they can get a grip, in a manner of speaking, on the minds of decent ordinary people. Two birds with one stone, if you like.'

There was a hint of amusement from his audience. Whether Mr Barnwell knew that a question hung over Robert; whether he had had time, in his tireless supervision of our harmless cargo, to lend an ear to the only other all-absorbing topic before the nuclear story broke; or whether his reply was just a lucky shot, he succeeded in tapping into something. The audience, deprived of its prey by glozing and inconclusive rhetoric, was ready to channel its anger elsewhere. There were murmurings now against Robert.

But Robert pressed on: 'A possibility of contamination. That was the information which came to my ears. I heard that in the storm there was an accident, a slip-up; and as a result, a threat occurred to one of the water supplies.'

'This is plain nonsense.' Mr Barnwell took a drink from the glass of water in front of him. Whether he intended it, or whether, perhaps, his mouth was dry with the touchiness of his position, it worked as convincing theatre. Hostile eyes continued to be directed at Robert. One or two remarks were passed: 'Pipe down, can't you?'

'I can give a categorical assurance that none of you assembled here, not your children, nor anyone else present, can possibly in any way have run the risk of contamination. Categorical.'

'Excuse me, Mr Barnwell. May we know how it's possible for you to give such an assurance?'

'You're doubting my word, sir? Not sure I like the sound of that. The word of a British officer.'

'Which word do you mean, exactly, sir?' Robert said. 'The word by which you assured us it was unthinkable that capital armaments *were* being carried, or the one where you indicated that those we did indeed carry were harmless? I merely ask for information – for the sake of accuracy. This is, after all, a crucial point of fact. A matter of life and death, even. Who knows? So little is certain about the effects . . . If perhaps it was the less accurate word of the two which was given over the contamination question, and not the reliable one, then surely that is important.'

221

If embarrassment had a sound of its own it would have filled the dance space. As it was, there was nothing to be heard except the background of the bow wave, regular, distant; and the faint stagnant sigh of air against the superstructure. But the atmosphere bristled, and the assembly held its collective breath. Everyone looked at Robert. It had become an act of mutiny.

Barnwell had struck a chord. It reminded them of the war. By his gesture of military candour he had assumed the mantle, almost of commanding officer. In the first class ballroom of a British liner, a man who was obviously an important military spokesman, possibly governmental, too senior even to bother to disclose his rank, and in the presence of the ship's officers to boot . . . suddenly such a man was in his element, and everyone knew where he stood. This swing to Barnwell was a legacy of wartime. And all this time, the very soldiery who had once returned, demobbed, vote-happy, were fenced off astern behind steel doors.

I listened, hardly comprehending. Mr Barnwell's face was white, presumably with fury.

'How dare you.' He enunciated slowly, tightly, while appearing to survey the faces before him. The other officers at the table stared stiffly out in front of them, eyes focused on the rear wall, except for the captain who turned his pencil over and over in his hands. 'Why, I could have you . . .' Mr Barnwell's gaze came to rest on Robert's own as his speech failed him.

'Yes?' said Robert.

The two men stood, some ten yards apart, locked in their inspection of each other's resolve. But it was Barnwell who broke. 'I see no further purpose to this.' He gathered up his papers. 'I declare the meeting closed. I've given all the information I'm required to. I did not come here to be . . .' And by his agitation he intimated to his fellow officers that they should wind up and follow him, almost challenging them not to. They did so, and the meeting broke up.

What followed was inconclusive, of course. There were independent disputes and hot debate. One or two people who formerly had cold-shouldered Robert came up to shake his hand. But the majority did not. Thus was the *Armorica* transformed into an unhappy ship.

I did not like the conflict. It reminded me of my attempt at a Turk's head. With the rope's end stuck up in front of me all unlayed like a sulky Medusa, and my father getting crosser and crosser. 'No. Under that one. Under! Of course you can. I could at your age. I told you. There! Under!' I had burst into tears. The knot was an impossibility.

I moved away from the sounds of disagreement, of which there were by now plenty; the distinct air of menace rose from several quarters. It was at this point I felt I heard the voice of that thing in the hold, whispering to me to let it out. I slipped away from the meeting, and ran as far aft as the pool, where the promenade deck ended in its high steel barrier over the drop to the tourist class. Then I drew back and went to the stairs I had seen Robert on the point of going down that night, and had dared to tell him about the great presence.

I could not make sense of the meeting. Had Robert told the authorities after all? If so, what were they all really talking about, and would anything now actually be done? For they had been very cross with him. Mr Barnwell seemed to be implying that there was no possibility of risk. That was good. That was all I could have asked, really. Mr Chaunteyman was going to Changi.

I found the way down to the heavy door to the pets' hold. But it was locked. And in any case I had no clear recollection of exactly how it was that I had once moved from that space into the region where the Leviathan was contained. Yet I was so near I could hear the creature right inside my head. I could not but think of the soldering iron, heavy-duty with the rounded end, torpedo-shaped. Love, suggested Mr Tingay, was not clear-cut. What a fool I had been, then, with my cut-out picture from a women's magazine. Love, suggested Mr Tingay, was a matter of bargains and pulls, splits and disintegrations. Then escape was a fantasy.

When I came back on deck the sky had grown dark with a great heap of cloud, as if from nowhere. The molten blue-white that had stared down at us so oppressively for the two or three days of our passage from Colombo had been exchanged for a bruise. I had never seen such a sky, not then; like lead, like solder sweating over a silver pool; and yet it was of many other colours also, of rust in places, and indigo, and yellow, yes, like the trouble of a bruise on pale, overprotected skin.

And even the ship had no breath, though there was the smell of cooking – or maybe rotting, some tinge of dung or decay; perhaps the carcass of a whale lay over the horizon on a beach of the Nicobar Islands, being rendered down. That distinct and horrible smell returns to me. So I slip with the *Armorica* past the Sumatran coast and into the Strait of Malacca, where the water is a vile dead colour and the wrong odours drift out to meet us, hang in our nostrils, and are sucked slowly up into the wrong sky.

Then the rain began. I had not seen rain to speak of since we left England. Even the storm was for the most part a dry blow, bearing only that fine sharp mixture of sleet and spray. Now there was simply an emptying, as of a vast punctured container dragged overhead. I saw it coming. The rain crept across the polished sea, made it one angry fizzle, and then engulfed us with a deliberate and leisurely bite.

In the drench I was instantly soaked through. It was made of enormous warm globes, full of weight. They exploded around my feet and flooded my sandals. The deck streamed and steamed. All the painted steel tops of the superstructure beside the pool appeared to give off a fine spray. It sprang out in every direction as if piped with sprinklers.

I went inside and found a place from which to watch. We sailed for two hours through curtain after curtain of the densest rain I had ever seen.

PART FOUR

Trench

53

'AH, THERE YOU are, Bob, old mate. A rare visitor to these shores. A welcome one, though, I hasten to add. It was your move, by the way. I think you'll be surprised by the little teaser I've had the leisure to line up for you.'

Robert laughed. 'And g'day to you too, Joe. Did you go ashore last night, after all?'

'Course I did, Bob.' He indicated two large brown paper packages.

'What are they? What did you buy?'

'What do you think?'

'How the hell should I know, Joe? Something for Mrs Dearborn?'

'Yes, for sure.' Joe tapped another bundle lying on what should have been Robert's bed. 'Kimono for the missus. The full works. Top-quality stuff. But these . . .' He indicated once more the first two items. 'Open them.'

Robert did as he was asked. One of the packages revealed a new twin-lens reflex camera, similar to the one he had already used to take Robert's picture.

'But you got a camera on the way out.'

'Can't have too much of a good thing, Bob.' Joe chuckled. 'Go on.'

Robert unwrapped an ornate box, quite large, made of a japanned hardwood cunningly inlaid with mother-of-pearl. It opened to become a superb chess set with the stark ivory and ebony pieces mounted on platforms of the same hardwood. It was a medieval Japanese army. 'This is astonishing.'

'Quite smart, isn't it?'

Robert was stumped. He peered closely at Joe's face, in which there lingered, he thought, an oddly mischievous light. 'How many of these have you got?'

'Altogether? Could be fifteen. Could be a couple of dozen. Two more this trip. Under the bunks. D'you want to see?'

Robert held up his hand. 'You could show me later. In fact, I'd be very interested to see. But we're planning to go ashore, Mrs Kendrick . . . Penny and I. I just came to find my . . .'

'I'm going myself. Show you around, if you like.' He stopped, embarrassed. 'Except you two probably don't need some gooseberry tagging along.'

Robert, too, stopped for a moment. Then: 'But of course. We'd be delighted. And I'm sure that would go for . . . That is, if you're sure you want to be seen abroad with the likes of us.'

'Really admired what you said at the meeting, mate. Wanted to speak myself but couldn't get the words when it came to . . . came to the crunch, if you know what I mean.'

'Of course.'

'No bastard there supporting. No bastard with the guts to stand up and say: Yes that's right. Self included, I'm afraid.'

'It doesn't matter. I suppose they'll unload it while we're here, anyway. I suppose that'll be that.'

'Not all of it. You heard what the bloke said. There's still the bloody Kittens and Vixens and God knows what.'

'Well. We're going ashore quite soon. Shall we meet you . . .' Robert looked at his watch.

'No worries. I'll just get into my Fletcher Joneses and find my jacket. I'll come right along with you.'

'As long as we don't have to go looking for any more chess sets.'

Joe made a wry cackle. Robert turned discreetly away for him to finish dressing. When he turned back he found he had misjudged the timing and his cabin-mate was still in the act of changing his shirt. The older man hurried to arrange the gape of his cuff. But it was too late.

'Christ! What have you done to your arm?'

'It's nothing.'

'It's certainly not nothing. Let me have a look. Have you seen the nurse? How the hell did you do that?'

The horrible, angry-looking thing that snaked down Joe's arm ended in the blueish twist Robert had thought was a tattoo. And indeed, if you had not seen the rest of the wound with its pepper of stains and leaky lacerations, you might still have mistaken the twist for something artful and contrived. But the arm was mangled.

'Just something I got in the war.'

'But it's been bleeding.'

Joe met his gaze with a hostile glare. 'No, it hasn't.'

'But, Joe. You should get some treatment for that. I saw. It's been . . . It's dried on your arm. Look!' He moved to hold the other man's wrist and show him the damage.

Joe snatched back his arm. 'I'm telling you, it's all right!' His voice took on the crushed Australian vowels. The two men eyed each other, stonily. Robert held his ground.

'All right. It was the Japs.'

'What?'

'I've got a few more to match.' He shrugged.

'You opened it yourself.' It was an intrusion. Robert regretted the words the moment he said them.

Joe shrugged again. 'Singapore. Can't keep away from the fucking place. Each trip I tell myself I'll stick this one out in the cabin. But once we've tied up I'm off and away come rain or shine.' He laughed and gestured helplessly at the packages. 'Once I'm there I just hang around in the city. End up buying these. Chess. And the cameras. Can't get over the cameras the Japs turn out. Best fucking cameras in the world all of a sudden. Out of nothing. Out of nothing. Makers of knick-knacks for Christmas crackers and paper flowers – for the foreseeable future. So we were given to believe. Isn't that so, Bob?'

Robert watched his companion bite his lip.

'D'you want to tell me? Joe?'

'Give us a hand, mate. We'd better be getting along.'

54

The Chinese driver stopped and leaned round. 'Boat Quay.' He pointed through his open window to the street name, written in English on a low wall beside the prospect of the river. The crowds of people swirled around them making a pattering sound with their sandals. The day was hot, humid. Creamy sun poured out of the sky, picking up the colours of the river, the soft, thin clothes of the Chinese, and the grand, white buildings on the opposite bank.

They got out. 'Lion dance,' Joe said contemptuously. He was referring to the entertainment which had been planned to greet the ship the previous afternoon. A Chinese activity of some kind was to have occurred on the dockside, but had been defeated by a torrential downpour, as had most people's will to go ashore too soon.

They strolled a short distance. 'Got my stuff from a joker ready with his own car,' Joe remarked after some time. 'Whisked me off in the dark; in front of the noses of his mates. Took me to his shop. Nothing more than a big shed, really. But you name it, he had it.' His efforts at conversation lapsed into a moroseness at odds with the bright daylight. Despairing of him, Penny linked arms with Robert. The day wore on. They made constant efforts to engage him. Joe, however, merely tagged along, punctuating their chatter enigmatically. He would respond neither to direct question nor to gentle hint.

It was not until the afternoon, when they had eaten the *Armorica*'s packed lunch – Joe's own idea, for parcel-wrapped reasons of his own – that he stopped them meaningfully before a shop-window. Its owner, by the characters on the blazon outside, was plainly Japanese. Words began, slowly, to spill out of Joe.

'OK.' he nodded at the shop sign. 'You want to know? This is what I don't get.'

The owner, visible behind the array of bowls and kitchen equipment stacked on the other side of the window, peered out at them.

'What I don't get, Penny, mate . . . and Bob, is how these fellers are allowed to be here, untouched. You see?' Without looking in he gestured through the shop-window. 'And how we three English faces can walk about here and never a word said, apart from: Yes sir, no sir, and: Can I get you cup of tea, sir, while you make up your mind which dirt-cheap optical you want to buy most. See.' He glanced sideways at last. 'My knees are knocking at the sight of that bloke.' Robert peered at the owner, who peered back and smiled.

'The violation of a city. See? After that, how can life go on? See? These streets were full of bodies.' He gazed around blankly. 'People's heads were hung from lampposts. People's heads. And other bits and pieces. Can you imagine that? There'd been bombing all the time before. See?' He indicated with his arm as if the disaster he conjured were still present. 'The Japanese Empire, eh? Imagine sitting here waiting for that to arrive. Ruthless as Romans, eh? Bob? Romans, eh? And just as efficient.'

'Joe,' Penny said gently. 'Were you here?'

'No, love. Not me. It's just common knowledge. Me, I ended up in Rangoon. Rangoon gaol. No, it was that bloke at the meeting, Bob. That Barnwell, talking about strategic importance. All that bull he was giving us. Strategic importance. I should say so.'

'Joe,' Penny said again. 'Was it someone close to you?'

'What I can't get, you see, is these. These blessed things.' He indicated the new camera slung in its brown leather case from his neck. 'It keeps coming back to these unbelievable things. Jokers on bicycles. Jokers out of the Middle Ages. Jokers who think a beautiful city is a kind of . . .' He looked up at Penny and smiled helplessly, glazed. 'These are the best cameras in the world, you see. Not just cheap rubbish. No. Cheap best. What only the Germans used to be good enough, clean enough, up to date enough to do. Out of nothing. How's that done?'

'Who was it, Joe, if it wasn't you?'

Joe's lip quivered. His eyes filled. 'You see, Ted married this Chinese girl. Really nice sheila, she was. OK, Bob? Sheilas? Name of Poppy – I don't know what her Chinese name was, but Ted called her Poppy. She liked that.'

'Who's Ted?'

'Brother. Ted was my brother, Penny.' Joe buried his face in his hands. His shoulders shook. The shopkeeper peered out now from close behind the glass in his door.

'What happened to them?'

'How should I know?'

Penny held Joe by the shoulder and looked at Robert. 'Do you come here looking for them?'

Joe nodded. 'Suppose I do. Yeah. You might say that, I suppose.

Stupid, isn't it? Don't know where to start. Don't know where to bloody start.' He raised his face. 'Sorry. You know what they did? When they'd stopped showing off about capturing the city. And we all know what that means. Well, when they got tired of that they separated out everyone that was left: Whites, civilian and military, Chinese, male and female, Malays, Indians. Took the Whites off one way, and the Chinese off another. And so on. And so on. More English than the English in a way.' He laughed. 'How about that?'

Groups of people flip-flopped by, taking no notice, the women in pyjamas or cheongsams, the men in trousers and shirts. A group of peasants in straw coolie hats carrying poles across their shoulders made their way along the pavement opposite.

'You know I come here . . . Look around you. Would you ever guess this was the greatest British defeat in history? You folks know that, don't you? Do you? Gets forgotten. I go back to the old country. Who won the war, they say? Look at the Germans. Might be doing all right. Who won the war, after all, they say, all aggrieved. You were on the winning side, I say, but the British Empire lost the war. The Empire was smashed to pieces. See these folk here.' He gestured at the street. 'They took the brunt of it, didn't they? I want to go up to them and shake them. Why are you so nice to us? Why do you still speak to us? Good camera. Good transistor. You must hate us all, surely.'

Robert stood awkwardly.

'You shouldn't blame yourself,' Penny said, still hugging Joe's shoulders.

'I should have been the dead one,' Joe said. 'By rights. If I couldn't be of any use I should have been dead. What was I doing instead? Playing chess. Playing bloody chess, chess, chess in Rangoon gaol.' He looked meaningfully at Robert.

'Is that where you got your arm?' Robert asked.

'What arm?'

'Arm?' Penny looked up at him sharply.

Joe gripped his shirt-sleeve and winced as he did so. 'Look. I'm sorry about this, you two. Sorry. Unforgivable. Something triggered it off. That meeting. That bastard. Tone of voice. Reminded me of a Nip I once knew.' He looked back at the shop door where the owner's face was accompanied, now, by the faces of his family. 'You don't want to see this, Penny. Believe me. I go for it sometimes. Pick at it. Open it up. Can't help it. Bob here happened to catch some nasty little habit not normally on public display. But you don't want to see it. Of course Ted and Poppy couldn't get to Australia. They wouldn't let her in, would they. So when the crunch came they were stuck in Singapore, even though they had nothing to do with the military. And there was I, Australian bloody Imperial Force, and couldn't do a thing about it.'

'How did you get to be in Rangoon?' Penny asked.

'Long story. They got me in forty-four. We were joined up with some British unit. Stupid mistake, getting caught. And for some reason I ended up there. Not sure why, to be honest with you, Penny. No doubt they had reasons of their own.'

'What happened to you in the prison at Rangoon?'

'Ah, nothing much, to tell the truth. Not enough to eat. We used to spend our time playing chess. Nothing much else.'

Later, in Fort Canning park, when Joe had regained something of his old composure, he said, 'You know, I was so glad when they dropped that bomb. You'll hear lots of folk say as much, won't you. I hated the lot of them. I wanted them all to roast in hell. I really did. But when I think of that meeting the other day. And your Prime Minister says to ours, "Mind if we let off a few of ours in your back garden, Bob?" And Menzies says, "My pleasure, Harold. Help yourself." And I find myself thinking: Wait a minute, exactly for whose benefit is this being done? As the child country might ask the parent. And the answer comes: "Trust me, mate. Affairs of state. Security reasons. We're the ones doing God's bidding, after all".

'And I remember, you know, Penny, they weren't going to waste any ships defending Aussie, if it came to it. They weren't, after all. They'd have let us go down; you know that, don't you? And you know something else? When a nice little radioactive cloud comes drifting over my house one day, I'm going to say: It's all right, I'm a Commonwealth citizen. They're only doing it to look after me.'

That night, Penny lay again in Robert's arms in the cramped

confines of the lower bunk in her cabin. She dreamed of Hugh. It was quite definitely Adelaide, although in truth she knew nothing of the geography of that place, beyond the little maps he had sent her. She looked around in terror, and noticed the low, gentle buildings of the city, the wide streets, the subtropical greenery fanning and fringing up here and there under the fair blue of the sky. No one else was troubled. No one else seemed to realise the threat from Hugh.

Men in suits with open necks and trilby hats leaned on rails under the sunshades that ran above the pavement on one side of the road. There were cars of an unusual design, and different markings on the tarmac; and none of the crush of London. She felt it could never rain. She began to walk. The air was warm and sharp, flavoured with cigarette smoke.

Oh, yes, they had landed. She found herself running. She ran and ran until it was night and she was somewhere in the suburbs which looked like a broad open place with low houses and hardly any pavements. And then she was in a strange house with no stairs and Hugh was slapping her back and forth across the face while Joe was forced to watch. He slapped her hard on the cheek, until it bruised. He was furious with her. She could feel the stinging throb of it in the bone. Her ear rang with the buffeting. Someone was calling out Robert's name. And then he bundled her into another room where there was a bed. There he raped her, and Robert was nowhere to be found.

She woke, and Robert was there, in the dark, next to her. Burying her sweat-laden brow in the nape of his sleeping neck, she pulled in great lungfuls of air from the warmth between their bodies. It was the smell of his skin that was such a comfort, quite different from any flavour of Hugh.

But the dream. It was so shocking, Hugh behaving like that. It was not the Hugh she knew, the man she had lived with all these years. She felt so guilty, betraying him like this, the father of her children. He was not so bad a man. It was the war that had made him difficult. Things had happened he had not told her about. He was not an easy man, not a happy man. Now she was doing this to him.

Robert stirred in his sleep, turned over in the cramped cot and threw his arm around her. Very quietly in the dark she traced with her hand where the sunburn had been along the surface of his arm. To her mind's eye it still glowed. She had begun by thinking that sex was for him, Robert, a gift, a pledge. She had looked forward to it, yes, but really it was *for his sake*. Whereas it had turned out, to her extraordinary surprise, to be like nothing she could ever have imagined: it was absolutely *for her*. It was delicious, intimate, loving. It was something that rested like a pearl at the centre of everything.

Then at last the dream fell into its rightful and shocking place. Part of her had always hated sex, intensely; but she had always explained that away: No, it's just his way, he loves you really; he can't help it after what he's been through, it's really your duty, Penny, as his wife . . .

Robert had shown her something different. There was a world of relationship in which cruelty had no place. It was true. Lying here, they were the living proof. She had never known. How stupid and naïve it sounded. But genuinely, absolutely genuinely, she had never known. Or simply never allowed herself to know. Why, that realisation changed everything. At last she permitted herself to see her husband for the man he was.

Frightened and exuberant, she clasped her lover in her arms.

<h2 style="text-align:center">55</h2>

A fisherman stands in a bamboo boat, rowing forwards with crossed oars. Like an image on rice-paper, his little craft slips on the lake between two generous brush strokes of separated land, wet, leaking in. He leaves a scatter of ripples which never quite catches him up. I am looking out from the *Armorica*'s starboard beam. We are moored at the wharf in Singapore, and today's afternoon rain has just cleared.

The evening is warm, perfumed, and streaked with yellow light. We are at the Equator, among the Spice Islands. But these are my last moments on the ship whose lovely lines, romance and stability problems have preoccupied me day by day, hour by hour for the weeks of my voyage. I am saying goodbye to her.

So delicious is the picture that I have to pull myself up – to remind myself that I have left out the fear. I did not stand at the rail in equanimity. My gut churned inside. Everything was unravelling, slipping away. We had been disastrously ashore. In minutes we should be off to Changi. Because, after all her impassioned scenes, Erica had finally made him agree to take us with him. And therefore I was helpless. For nothing had been done, and still that whispering voice at the back of my mind squeaked faintly on and on, shriller now, like Silver's twisted parrot, getting louder. I was frightened for Finlay, she had made me very wretched. I was frightened for the ship. And I was furious with Erica.

'They wouldn't let me in on my own. With the boy. What does that make me look like? Eh, Dave? What does that make me? I had to push my way in.'

She had taken me by the hand and shoved past the uniformed attendant. So we had found the lovers dancing cheek to cheek in the faded splendour of the Raffles Hotel. Caught behind the fan palms at afternoon tea.

'Honey, it was just one dance.'

'Dance, my eye. Tip of the iceberg, more like.'

'Honey, it's all OK.'

'Oh, that's what it is, is it?' Icy with rage she had marched him out until we found ourselves in the crowded Chinese streets. Cheryl was left to settle the bill. Then Erica started in earnest.

'Making me wait. Telling me you had to see a contact. You and your contacts. Me and Ralph've been walking round this God-forsaken place since ten o'clock this morning. Contact!' She was working herself up. The crowds gave us a wide berth. Chaunteyman was frightened; yes, I could tell by his eyes, he was frightened. He looked like a schoolboy up before the beak.

'Hey, honey, it's nothing. It doesn't mean anything. She's just a friend.'

'Oh, it's called friendship now, is it? All this time I've been thinking she was *my* friend. You take me for such a fool, don't you? Just because you've been to these places and done things. Just because you can pull strings. Or your old man can, to pull his spoilt little boy out of all the holes he digs himself. Don't imagine I don't know, Dave Chaunteyman. You think I'm stupid, don't you. You think I'm rubbish. Well, you're not pulling my strings no more, Mr Lieutenant-Commander or whatever it's supposed to be. Business. You call that business? I call it funny

236

business. You think I'm just some tart you can pick up and put down whenever you like. You didn't have no business here in the first place.'

'Erica, I swear. I have to see people. Government people.'

'How much of *her* have you seen? That's what I'd like to know. How much has *she* had on display these last couple of weeks? I want to be told, Dave. I mean it. You tell me just what's been going on.'

'Honey, the kid. Can't all this wait?'

'How can it wait? How can it wait when the blimmin' ship sails tomorrow. How can it wait? Dave! Look at me! Look at me, why don't you!'

Passers-by stared.

'If you'd just let me speak—'

'Now I know why you've been so off with me recently, don't I. Well, if you think you can just pack me back on that boat while you hang around here trying to have it off with that fancified slut you've got another think coming.'

I tried to detach myself from them. It was going to be a long one. She had momentarily desisted but I knew it. We walked on in silence. I hardly noticed the streets, their doorways and traffic, nor the people parting to gaze at us wherever Erica stopped to begin again. She would reach a new pitch of feeling and then suddenly refuse to budge. And he would look around helplessly and try to take her arm. I had seen it all before. The row reminded me only of Woolwich – another man, another river. We moved on. And on.

It was late in the day. 'Come on, honey. We need to be getting back.'

'You two go on. I'm not going anywhere.'

'How can we, then?'

'Go on. You don't care about me. I'll find my own way, thank you very much. You don't want me spoiling things for you. Too common, isn't it. Too common for the likes of you. But not vulgar enough, eh? Eh, Dave Chaunteyman?'

'Erica, come on. How many more times do I have to tell you it was nothing. A crazy moment. We just forgot ourselves a little.'

We were not far from the waterfront now. A cooking stall made out of a bicycle had live crabs from the afternoon's catch hanging from its hood. Girls stood around on the slight slope. Over the tops of the darkening greenery Mr Chaunteyman noticed a British destroyer, fiddling about close to one of the offshore islands.

'Hey there. Look at that. Sniffed up our wake out of Trincomalee, I shouldn't wonder.' He pointed, then recollected himself. 'C'mon, son. We'd better be finding our way home. You can see why it is guys take to the water, can't you?' He began moving me along again.

'I mean it, Dave.' I knew Erica was standing stock-still, behind us. I could feel the distance stretching as we walked. It was a battle of wills. Eventually I looked back. To my relief she had started to follow, but slowly, fifty paces behind, keeping us in sight. We stopped. He tapped his foot. She stopped too. We continued. And again she followed. We stopped. The same thing. Three more times. Eventually, by the bridge, we waited it out. But she waited too. After five full minutes he broke and went back, towing me by the wrist. 'OK. What do I have to do?'

'I'm not getting back on that ship.' She was twisting the handles of her bag in front of her. The string was visible through the breaks in the imitation leather.

'What?'

'You're not getting me back on that ship. I mean it. Not if you're staying here.'

'But, honey.'

'I know what you're like. You're a liar, Dave. That's what you are. You're a liar. Business. You haven't got no business here.'

'Erica, I—'

'You're not government. You're not big time. You're nothing. All right, you've got the money, so you say. Dealer! You're just a sort of playboy. That's what they call it, isn't it? You live in a dream world. A boy's world.'

'Honey, listen. I do have this deal to close. It's real important. For you and for me. For us.'

'Oh yes. Well, you can tell me what it is then, can't you?'

'It's classified.'

'Yeah.'

'We need the money for Australia, you and me. I promise you.'

'You've been watching too many movies, Dave. It's all gone

238

to your head. And it's went and gone to mine as well. More fool me. I don't believe you. I don't believe any of your tosh any more. About being an observer. All this Pentagon this and Uncle Sam that. If it's anything at all it's under the counter. Eh? It is, isn't it. It's a fiddle. It's something they've got on the ship along with all that caper they had the meeting about. That had you rattled, didn't it? Mucked everything up? What was you in? Something smaller. Guns, is it? Guns for the Commies?'

'You're crazy.'

'Am I? You going to tell me different then?'

'Honey, I can't tell anyone.'

'Why did you do it, Dave? Why did you bring me all this way?'

'You've got to believe me.'

'You know what Harry used to say before he met you? Never trust a Yank. That was before you bowled him over, eh? "No formalities, Harry. Call me Dave, old boy." He used to say England was just a front-line aircraft carrier as far as the Yanks was concerned. That's why they come cosying up, he used to say. Well, I got sick of Navy talk. Boat this, deck that. Like living in a blimmin' ship all the time. Like everything politics and fighting. Drove me crackers. I just wanted to be loved, didn't I?' She sniffed and rummaged for her hanky. 'But he was right. I'm your front line, aren't I, Dave? Expendable. Pity he didn't remember it himself. He'd have done anything for you, you know? In his way. And look what I've gone and done to him. Love! D'you know how you make me feel now? You make me feel used. Worn out. Just like I'm your rotten landing strip. So he was right about something, then, wasn't he?'

'C'mon, honey. Don't run a scene. People are watching.'

'Let them. I hate myself.'

'I'll make it up to you.'

'You can't. Not now. Not any more.'

'Let me try.'

'Take your hands off me. I tell you I'm not getting back on that boat!'

She won. We got back on that boat only to leave it. At the last minute the company sold the berth in our cabin and gave us a deadline to be out. So it was with a heart full of grief and agitation that I found myself staring out over the harbour, while Erica was packing up the last of our things. Finally I went below, and pretended half-heartedly to help. Before we disembarked, I made a last bid for Finlay. What did I hope to do: make up, swear friendship, exchange addresses and promise to write ever after? Or vent my revenge before disappearing without trace? Erica protested, but I roamed off, my feelings swathed about me like a magician's cloak. Finlay was nowhere to be found in her usual haunts. She must be in her cabin, then, that place I had never been invited to, never been deemed worthy of.

Perhaps they did not hear my knock; but they were surely in there, the Cootes. I could hear them. Surely they were. They must be all together playing some game – little high-pitched squeals came out through the wood, child sounds; noises of tension, panting, adult sounds. Well then, I would have my say. I threw open the door.

Neither Finlay, nor Mitchell, but a strange configuration of their parents, an eight-legged, half-naked thing, a crab, jiggling and gasping as it climbed over the edge of the bunk. Clodagh Coote's eye caught mine. I shut the door and fled.

So the Cootes were exposed by the tide. And Mr Chaunteyman's *affaire* with Cheryl Torboys was the reef upon which I foundered, cast up on that Asiatic isle.

56

Changi prison was not nearly as worrying as I had expected. Sometimes it helps to see the face of our terrors. It is only the remembering that hurts.

I remember my mother weeping at teatime in the RAF hotel, and the rain which flooded down in bucketfuls, suddenly, out of a recently brilliant sky. You could set your watch by that tropical drench every afternoon; afterwards, you could almost *see* the plants growing. Little pink lizards would scamper up to the corners of the ceiling. Looking out to sea from that sad, soft corner of Changi village, you might confuse the abating rain with the scuttling of their feet.

When it was not raining, it was always high summer. I had been used to the drab backstreets of Woolwich, with their soot and that stink from the Thames. Now I explored Singapore. I took the bus in with Mr Chaunteyman, past those grim brown walls of the prison. We could see it on our left. It was a cluster of horrible buildings squatting amid the village fields.

The bus would lurch and stagger. It was full of Chinese and Malayans. Mr Chaunteyman would invariably gasp at the fact that they really did live here, these Chinks. 'You know I can never get over it. They really do all look the same.' Then he would laugh, and eye up through the window any girls he saw walking along outside with their slit skirts showing off their thighs. 'And what a same they look! Chicks and dolls and geese better scurry.' He would whistle roguishly to himself.

One day I pressed the only item I had saved from my suitcase into Mr Chaunteyman's hand. The shrunken head. He took it with a shocked face which turned into a grin of recognition. 'Sure. You want me to have it.'

'I want you to have it,' I muttered. Once I had passed it on I began to feel at home in the city.

A Chinese painter, set the task of rendering the whole of Woolwich on a tea service, such as my grandfather's, but forbidden any dirt or grime, must have created Singapore. A thousand views of Woolwich. The dragon Woolwich. The lotus Woolwich, multi-petalled and infinitely expanded. The exotic lifts and bends of the brush, the limpid water-colour shades and hues, the flashes of intensity or transparency, all these were the port's pattern.

Filthy old Thames lighters, moored up, became bobbing tongkangs side by side on the Singapore river, their milder occupants the rough wharfsiders I had grown up with. Those grim rows of dense South London houses became bright tenements for a pyjama-clad multitude. All the surfaces were pink or blue, or pale or peeling, and from upper windows the endlessly repeated lines of washing poles sketched a street canopy of intimate laundry.

Each roof-ridge, gable, doorway and corner sprouted decoration – in concrete, wood, plaster. Or by the porcelain fixing of a telephone wire. There were great splashes of Chinese writing, red on white, white on red, red on yellow. Every

241

entrance chattered with Chinese speech. Every street was full of bicycles. It was spirited. There were so many people.

It was the busy-ness that endeared the place to me, the sense of purpose and throng – and, yes, I romanticise it. For its inhabitants had their own sufferings and dealt with them one way or another. I felt safe, contrary to my expectations, and much less conspicuous than I did in Powys Street market. Not only was my sight transformed, but the other senses as well. The tiny birds being grilled in rows on handcart kitchens by the bridge smelt strange and tempting. There were fragrant trees with hard and leathery leaves. There were rickshaws, trishaws, trams, cars, vans and carts. And everywhere, once the traffic had passed, there was the sound of rubber thong-sandals, or leather ones, clap-flapping on the ground.

On the third day Mr Chaunteyman told me that Mrs Torboys had to go to the doctor that morning, and then, realising what he had said, made me promise not to repeat anything to my mother. He took me to the Tiger Balm Gardens. Painted concrete figures of, yes, torture and fun. And in the evenings of that lyrical and fraying week, having travelled back on the bus, I would hang about the muddy alleys of Changi village itself, looking for trinkets in the Chinese shop next to the thatched longhouse – where some Malayan families lived on stilts. Behind that there was nothing but authentic jungle. We stayed six days and then flew out by RAF Transport Comet for Adelaide, Mr Chaunteyman's business, whatever it was, no doubt complete. My account is thus wrenched high out of my control.

57

I throw up my hands at this point. So much is all I know. That's all I can tell you. As to the *Armorica*, she must have gone on, in her own way, to Australia. As I went in mine with Erica and Mr Chaunteyman – until we fetched up as I told you near a dump near a crossing, in a cheap rented cabin with splitting walls, marooned. And so my travelling companions dispersed towards their joys and tragedies half a century ago.

As for the loss of record, the missing documentation; no

doubt an administrative blunder on some register when the ship was broken up. Most likely an early computer error which became perpetuated. Very probably some day I shall come across an old book of the fifties in which she figures in all her glory. For the present she is a mystery; but a minor one. Hardly a *Marie Celeste*, since it is the ship which is missing, rather than its crew; and the only witness I can supply is myself. As reliable as you may judge. But whatever opinion you form of me, there, in a sudden flight out of Singapore Island it must end. There, in a vapour trail, I must wash my hands of it.

Why then does my recollection of Adelaide flash and streak? That prim, sun-drenched city is established in my mind's eye – focused, clear as a consequence. Yet, like the picture on an old television set, it gives way now and then. Its bright parks and suburbs are troubled with sheets of flood and inexplicable rain. Its seaside bask is shot through with cold and despair.

Of course there was occasionally rain, sometimes torrential. It could feel cooler, and sharper. But my sense is not of that. It is as though one image is at the mercy of another; inside the water an invisible fire lies. This is not bushfire, that common hazard of the tinder dry, but of something else, smouldering deep down. It is electrical, hydroptic. I cannot tell you about Adelaide without the thought of something terrible happening out at sea. I have four memories.

In the first, I am at a beach. Glenelg, or is it Largs? Men stand outside the hotel bar in their relentless formality of suits and trilby hats, holding empty glasses; across the wide empty road, they lean in ones and twos on the barrier which fences off the beach. The Gulf of St Vincent lies silky green and languid under the glare. Past the curl of desultory wavelets breaking on to the sand, past the paddlers and the few bathers, the pointless wooden pier stretches out towards the horizon, only stopping short at a little makeshift stand with a bleached roof. The children see dolphins and come haring back along the planks to press the shark alarm. Then, to the sound of hooter-whoops, a mother picks up her toddler and strolls out of the sea. It is roasting weather, yet I am shivering desperately, unable to get warm.

In the second, someone drives us across the level plain from the port to the township. We have been on a day-trip to see the yachts. The stink of the canning factory hangs in the air. But looking back through the rear window, instead of those two rust-streaked tower vats raised up out of the flat brown there is the nose of a ship. It stands up vertical, in silhouette, like the towers themselves – and all the ground is awash, as though tiny Dry Creek had burst its banks.

Then, the opening day of the new term, my new school. The headmaster lifts his brown hat to dust his brow. He has fierce tufts of greying hair. There are about a hundred children in the centre of the compound. The headmaster has a cane under his arm.

On the one side stands the cement-white school block, two storeys high. On the other, the concrete shed for lunches. Cement dust is everywhere; it has whitened the hard, bare ground so much that the morning sun glares up into our faces and we screw up our eyes. Builders' rubble lies in heaps; their machinery is dotted about near the perimeter wire. Beyond that a few huge gum-trees stretch up out of the clay. At least they cannot be new. For everywhere here, whether inside the school compound or beyond, looks to my eye half-finished; because there is no tarmac, nor concrete paving-stones, nor green grass. It is as though they have put down odd buildings and forgotten to build streets.

'I want all the Catholics over here.' The headmaster marches to a region over by the shed. A gaggle of children follow him. 'Presbyterians?' He paces to the front of the new block. Then nearer the wire. 'All Anglicans over here.' Another clump of young bodies – those who know what Anglican means – surges towards him. But he is off again, trouser cuffs flapping round his ankles. He calls the Methodists to the cement-mixer, the Lutherans to the workmen's shelter, the Baptists and Anabaptists to the pile of breeze-blocks, and the Unitarians to where the bicycles have all been lain down, like a desiccated herd of cattle.

When I am the only one left, nearly crying in the middle, he waves me towards the Anglicans, and I am saved. I see just outside the perimeter a different tree, alive with blossom. On every blossom hangs a milkweed butterfly, feeding, flickering. I am on the *Armorica* again. My bone-dry clothes are soaked with downpour; the tree has burst into flames. Each butterfly is an explosion. We are wrecked and there will be no help for us – for all the water in the ocean.

Last of all, Erica and I are on the veranda of the crack-walled house. When the north wind blows in the afternoon it feels as though an oven door has opened behind the thin strip of houses on the other side of the road. Now there is a red tinge to the clouds.

'You see that? Here we go again, Ralphie. Let's get the windows shut.'

Then quite high up the sky streaks with rouge. Before too long there is a dark, red-coloured shadow, looming from the northern sweep over the low roofs opposite. It spreads out. Soon its wings stretch as far as the crossing one way, and right behind the hills the other.

The first fingers of grit come at us, thrusting through the bungalows. They whip our faces and we are driven inside. From the window we watch the full storm build. By a quirk of the air currents there is a succession of dust-devils like pillars of fire, up the dirt road from the crossing. That is the advance guard, stalking sideways. Then the main force hits us full on and we are no longer in any doubt about its intentions. Blasting and stinging at the glazing and brickwork it is like a red mist that has gone out of its mind. It is Australia on the move, all furnaced up, lifted from the rocket-range deserts beyond the black stump and brought down by the baking wind.

Afterwards there is a mess, and we have to clear away, brush off, shovel out, while the wind is set to broil on for another three or four days. Yet I see myself bailing out water instead of sand in the downpour, and the red cloud is a drift of ship smoke on the horizon.

This is a madness of picture postcards. I have become distracted. I believed I had told you everything: of my home in Woolwich, my career. I outlined my service in the Falklands, to make sense of things. I have given you my childhood's voyage, over half the world. I have confessed to the burnt-out Holden. I have said much, much more than I knew at the start – of love, and my father, and the best room. I told you as clearly as I could how we jumped ship at Singapore.

Then why will the story not arrive at its destination: aboard the Comet next to Erica, clutching my Reader's Digest

Condensed Book from the hotel? However hard I try, I cannot make that plane go south – from Changi to Darwin, and then on to Adelaide's Edinburgh Airport. The direction is all wrong – a mental compass is awry; and I cannot place Mr Chaunteyman with us at all.

There is a faintness and nausea. I have the sensation once more of hanging, without a body, without a history, above the whole thing – high up with the great seabird, adrift on the upper currents, the albatross, the booby, the frigate bird, or even the legendary roc. It is a terrifying drop. I am returned willy-nilly to our dalliance at Singapore, the row, Chaunteyman's silver-screen looks, and the mention of Lucas's new venture. I have deliberately muddled the sequence in my mind. It did not happen as I have described at all.

I see now that I have constructed my whole life precisely in order to avoid seeing. Yes, there were the rows, but Erica did not prevail. Yes, I gave Mr Chaunteyman the shrunken head. But it was at our parting, to protect him from a Changi I had not yet visited; did not visit, in fact, for more than a year. Yes, Erica wept in the hotel there, but not on *this* trip. That was on our return to England, and my memory has tricked me, matched one set of weepings to another.

I have done it before – left out a whole ship. I told you that tale at the start about my battle stress, little thinking that was the regular way of things. Let me make this quite clear. Come alongside me, I have it now. I went *out* through Singapore on the *Armorica*; I *flew home* through Singapore more than a year later. In my premature account of Changi I have confused the two, laying the one direction on top of the other and marrying the events – shaving off loose ends, as we story-tellers will without knowing it. We fool ourselves as well.

Memory can do just that. Does it all the time. I have not wilfully deceived you. Memory hides whole coastlines, tampers with truth. It spares us pain. It takes away the hurts that cannot make sense, that go against everything we know to be right and regular. Memory is the doctor. But under its drug there is no real home-coming, no prospect of release, no hope that in spite of everything Carla . . .

I did not leave the ship at Singapore.

58

In fact we must sweat our way through the islands. The sky is an upturned drum with its sodden skin sagging upon us. It bellies over our foremast, touched with an unpleasant green as the sun tries to finger through. Perspiration runs from every pore, and we have hardly the energy to move. There is a hint of mould: it settles on rope ends, makes straw hats limp. Tobacco smoke leaves a stale, whiffy flavour in the main lounge and in the bars; and every carpet begins softly giving back its accumulated spills. Many people keep to their cabins.

It was in the Java Sea, the Sea of Whispers, that I detected the plan against Robert.

'You don't need to tell me. Give them an inch and they'll take a mile.' The two old men passed me, struggling on, identically dressed. 'Damned poor show. Probably Communist inspired. Chinks.' Their dark blue shirts were plastered to their backs.

'Damned poor. Reds. Know what I'd do?'

'I jolly well know what I'd do.'

A moment later, I nearly bumped into Mr Barnwell, no longer in uniform.

'Sorry, sir.'

He scarcely gave me a second glance, but strode on down the port strip of the promenade deck, towards the aft stairs. I followed. Another man, whom I did not know, emerged to greet him from the region of the pool. They stopped and spoke together. I made out some of the words: 'Once we're in open sea . . . In the nature of the job . . . Thoroughly deserves everything he gets. It's a thorough nuisance, but I was speaking to Jeremy, and he said the idea was perfectly feasible, and probably the best thing in the long run . . . Take care of the practicalities.'

'All right. We'll see what we can come up with.'

'To encourage the others, principally. It's a worry, otherwise.'

'There's a serious risk then?'

'Hardly. I wouldn't go quite that far. Just needs to be fixed.' They passed out of sight.

Erica was listless in her bunk, and nagged at me.

'They're out to punish him,' I said.

'Shut up. I'm the one who's being punished. And what's more he knows it. He wants me to be like this. They're all so . . . perverse.'

'What?'

'Perverse. It's a word. You don't know it. Why not go and find someone to play with.'

'There isn't anyone.'

'Of course there is. Why must you be so difficult, Ralphie? Can't you see I'm upset. Go and play ping-pong, for heaven's sake. Find that girl, what's-her-name. Only leave me in peace, can't you. Moping around, in here. Fidgeting. And for Christ's sake stop that tapping.'

'I'm not.'

'Of course you are.'

Finlay and a knot of other children were in the dance space. They had colonised the ping-pong table for some other game. But it was nothing much. 'You go there and I'll go here. No, not there. There! I'm not playing, then.' 'Can't we play Dragnet?' 'That's old hat. Anyway, it's too hot.' Apparently there was no consensus without the Torboys children.

I pressed on past the looks, taking the stairs up to the observation lounge. Finlay's parents were there with their son Mitchell, who seemed suddenly grown-up in long trousers. Russell and Clodagh sat at coffee in the recliner chairs; their legs were up on the padded stools. I stood behind them for a moment, looking out. A coastline was in view to starboard. I fancied I could quite discern the great fat leaves of palms, see huts on stilts and the native boatmen putting out in their praus to attack us with spears and krises, spitting betel until we would buy their sweet-sour pigs, gutta-percha, cloves and bird's nests. But of course I could not. The coast was little more than a dark green line of jags that sloped down in a wedge to the steamy pond we were caught in.

On the foredeck the Leviathan seemed to speak very distinctly. It was horrible. We were heating up. I must find Robert. Feeling sick, I searched the length of the ship.

A group of ladies and gentlemen stood on the pool concourse behind the Verandah bar, where the cane tables were set out. One woman said to another that she thought Saturday would be best. 'Otherwise before we know it we'll be docking in Fremantle. It would make an example of him.'

248

'You know, I shan't mind when it's over and done with. This is all so oppressive. Don't you think so? I never imagined I'd say that, but actually, yes, I shall be quite glad. He has it coming. Then we can get back to normal. Pick up the pieces, if you know what I mean. My husband hasn't been himself at all. He positively hates it.'

'Excuse me. Have you seen Mr Kettle?'

'Mr who?'

'Mr Kettle.'

'You know, Olive, the one who . . .'

'Oh, him. No. Sorry. I expect he's . . .' They laughed.

A man in a blazer was smoking a cigar. 'Mind where you're going, young shaver. You'll have yourself over the side if you're not careful.'

I did another circuit of the ship, combed it from stem to stern and from top to bottom. But Robert was not to be found. In fact it was strangely empty – compared with the normal hustle and bustle. The heat. I stole past Penny's cabin. The quartermaster and the steward who acted as his assistant in the entertainments were facing each other at the end of the corridor. There was some disagreement. The one had hold of the other's wrist.

'I saw you.'

'You bloody didn't.'

'Quiet.'

'You never told me. That's what sticks in my throat.'

'Quiet. Not long now, anyway. Not long now and it'll all be over.'

'What about the blood?'

'There'll be no blood.' Their heads both turned in my direction, then the pair of them seemed to melt away around the end of the panelling. I checked they had gone and then went back to Penny's door. There was no sound; but this time I dared not go in. Besides, if Barnwell and the captain were holding him somewhere it was hardly likely to be here. From another direction altogether came the plaintive call. Perhaps that was Robert crying and not the Leviathan at all. I tried to locate the sound more precisely, and to follow it. It led down and down – only to leave me pressed against the mahogany partition at the aft end of D deck, where, yes, it was a fraction louder. But my sweat made me clammy.

I ran back up the succession of stairs to the concourse.

'I thought it was quite disgraceful. I've an idea to ask for our money back.'

'The crew are in on it, of course. Regard it as their perks. Get a kick out of it. Have you seen the way that tall chap looks at one? You simply can't be too careful.'

'Human nature. To want to watch, I mean.'

'Did you manage to get up the others? A rubber or two would help get us through, at least for the time being. Till the fun starts.'

'I don't think so, Roger. Can't get the sullen beggars rounded up. Skulking.'

'Bad show. We'd have thrashed 'em.'

'Nonsense, old boy. They'd have murdered us. Positively.'

'You're a fool to yourself, dear. I never leave anything about in my cabin. Items walk.'

'Oh, I know. You can't trust any of them an inch. Damn good hiding would do the trick.'

'Monica! Monica! Over here.'

'Strike now, would be my advice.'

'Lance the boil, I suppose you mean?'

'Why not?'

'While the iron, so to speak . . .'

'I'll have another, if you don't mind.'

'Wretched tub. Any news?'

'All be ruined for the sake of a measly two bob.'

'Ha'p'orth o'tar, and all that.'

'Not actually dangerous, is it?'

'No, no. Keeps them on their toes.'

So draining was the atmosphere that the voices became mere listless gasps, rising above each conversation as a vapour which immediately dispersed. The effect was dull, mesmeric.

'Wotcher, cock.' It was one of Barnwell's aircrew, at his own table. 'Have a drink.'

'No, thank you. I'm looking for someone.'

'Aw, go on. Don't you know it's rude to refuse.'

'All right then. Just water, please.'

He snapped his fingers at a passing steward and added a Scotch for himself. Then he turned back to me. 'You're Johnny, int'ya?'

'No.'

'Don't tell me. Let me guess. Archibald? Monty? Arbuthnot?'

'No.'

'Claude. That'd be it?'

'Ralph.'

'Oh, you mean Rafe. You don't talk much like a nob, though.'

'Have you seen Mr Kettle?'

'Mr who? Don't know no one of that name. I could've sworn you were a Johnny, though.' He laughed. 'That woman gettin' off at Singapore because her hubby was goin' into rubber. I nearly died. Got a girlfriend, have you?'

'No.' The drinks arrived.

'Take it neat, do ya?' He swigged off his own glass in one.

'What?'

'All right this side of the wall, mate. Wouldn't touch it back there, though.' He gestured aft to the tourist class beyond the divide.

'Pardon?'

'Water. Wouldn't touch it, mate. Not down there with the riff-raff.' He laid his finger along the side of his nose. 'Never know what's got in it. Poor buggers. I tell you one thing, I'm bloody glad I never went swimming in their little pool. All right for some, eh? *It's the rich what gets the pleasure.* Meantime I'm sticking to booze. Can't be too careful, can you. You sure you ain't got a girlfriend?'

'Excuse me.' I drank up and left

For I had seen Robert, up on the boat deck. Leaning over. I was certain it was him, silhouetted against the bright patch in the sky. I stood back to see.

He spoke: 'Be careful, all of you. Because I've managed to get into the hold. All of you! Look what's going on! Why don't you all listen? There's a fault. The ship's going to get hotter and hotter until it melts with us all in it. The rails are going to start to glow red in the intense heat, the planks of the deck beneath your feet are going to smoke and start to char black, even as you're standing on them. The ship's plates and the ventilator tubes and the funnel and everything. They will all start to glow red and no one will be able to bear it. The ship itself will start to melt from the top down, right to the water-line. And the sea turn molten red, like burning oil, like the sunset poured out upon the waters.'

But the sounds of his words were turned into whispers, and no one could hear him. Leastways, nobody listened. Except me. 'Look!' I said. 'Wait!' Then his figure disappeared and I supposed they had caught up with him again and taken him back to the bridge.

Mitchell came past me. 'How you going, Pom?'

'All right.'

'All right, yourself.'

And it was *then* I went down to Finlay's cabin and saw her parents on the bed like a crab.

There were announcements on the tannoy but I could hardly catch the words. The ship itself seemed to whisper. It was warning us. Something was not quite right. They had got Robert Kettle. And something down there was heating up. Was it the engine-room? The bearing? Might it be one of the circuits – an electrical fault? He had tried to warn them. But they would not listen. They refused to listen.

No, surely, I was deluding myself. It was nothing. Only the movement through the waves, the steelwork. The captain would know, if there was anything. If there was anything, anything at all, he would make it all right. That was his job. I must go up to the bridge then.

Unless the captain himself . . . Suddenly I heard the ship's radio. 'Let me out! Help! Let me out! Please! No!' It was coming from the bridge itself. There was some amplifier connected to the Leviathan. Why was nobody taking any notice?

'Listen!' I shouted. 'Why don't you listen?' But there was no one left I could trust. It was a paralysis, an awful, bright, mask-like sinking feeling, among the grins and grimaces – as though I were in the wrong ship at the wrong time.

Erica was sent for. She put me to bed. The ship's doctor gave me a drink and made me take some tablets. But later, in the night, I could not sleep at all because I was listening for the punishment they were giving Robert Kettle, close by our cabin. 'Seize him up to that grating will you, Jeremy.' So near the passengers.

They were far gone. They did not care. They were past caring. Whether it would be the whistle and dull crash of the cat, until he screamed out. 'No. Better shackle his hands behind him.

Make him fast to that stanchion.' The choking cough of the gag. 'I've just the thing for Johnnies like him, gentlemen.' Then the hustle as they swung him outboard followed by the faint splash into the sea, a rope around his ankle, to drag behind us in the wake where the hammerhead sharks who had been following us all the way were closing in, jaws agape. 'No. Pull him up, now, Jeremy. I've a better idea . . .'

There came a point when I could bear it no longer. I stole down as we children had done to the pets, and I remembered how the ones I thought were my friends had humiliated me, and left me alone, and how I had found myself in the presence of that mightiest of sea creatures; and I remembered how to do what was instructed. I followed the procedure, and, for want of the more technical phrase, unscrewed the stopper of his bottle.

59

Perhaps the creature made straight for the Pacific, to disport himself there awhile, in that watery waste half the size of the planet.

The true Ocean that floods the earth, the Pacific, lay almost unknown for millennia. All routes to it from the little peasant monarchies of Europe were legendary, mysterious and fraught with danger. The westward passage, by the southern tip of the Americas, was the Horn. That, as everyone knows, is a monster whose teeth are giant waves, whose beats lurk for the lee shore and whose refrigerant breath loads spars, masts and rigging top heavy with ice, bursts sails, breaks hearts.

When the Horn proves too terrible, as it did famously for Bligh, there is nothing for it but to run eastward past the Cape of Good Hope. A ship under sail can hammer round the globe in the Forties, if she has good food and good faith. This is the navigator's route, an emptiness with nothing in your way. Sooner or later, coming clear south of Tasmania and then New Zealand, she may turn up into the vast blue yonder. For what? Breadfruit? A cheaper pap for slaves? And in all that time before the wind, Fletcher Christian's imagination has been turned gnawingly inward: between the Devil and Antarctica. It is a recipe for cooking up an event. No Transit of Venus here. No spirit of exploration.

The other gateway into the Pacific is through the Orient. In the *Armorica*, we had only just entered that region, docking at Singapore, before we nudged out again. Those who before steam or battleships went on up into the South China Sea found every assumption challenged. They were captivated, enchanted, intrigued, appalled. They fell in love and died of fever. If they came away it was bragging or blinded. The Pacific would not receive them, it fought them all the way with hostile winds and currents. They found themselves put about where the desperate whalers roamed, at the mercy of pirates and cannibals, in an emptiness dotted with coral as the heaven is with stars.

That is a dangerous gate. A string of islands stretches down across the Equator in a graceful curve: the East Indies. By the reef-littered Torres Strait, the cordon is made fast to a boulder, once thought part of a nameless land mass, *Terra Australis Incognita*.

Australia promises comfort. The *Armorica*'s official route was to skirt around the west of it, as if to reassure ourselves that we had after all made it British. Perth, Adelaide, Melbourne, Sydney. Only then need we concede to the Pacific at journey's end. The big regular thousand-mile swell is manageable there. We give it a swimsuit and pretend it is less like death.

Yes. Once across the last leap and through the convergence zone, where the monsoons debate with the trades, once safely past the old atomic test-site of Monte Bello Island, and in the imagined lee of Australia's North West Cape – there promises comfort.

So from the Sea of Whispers we struck due south at last. By breakfast we were threading the Sunda Strait close between Java and Sumatra. By mid-morning we had started across that corner of the Indian Ocean which contains its deepest pit, the Java Trench; and which fades into the comparatively shallow, shark-infested, crab-infested Timor Sea. Everything felt different: fresh, warm, and if anything, quite English.

My own troubles were forgotten. Standing in the bright sun, I reminded myself idly that there would come a time when Mr Chaunteyman would fly over us, as Achilles must pass the tortoise. I recalled our Singapore moment during the row, when we stopped beside the bicycle crab-stall and looked out to sea at the destroyer. I did not quite understand the dancers I had seen, Mr Chaunteyman and Mrs Torboys at the big hotel. They were the image of that picture I had cut out and kept with me, and then dumped in Colombo. I knew it was a version of love: I knew that was what had made Erica so angry that she was moved to speak of my father. Yet I did not fully grasp that it was fatal to our project; or that the embrace was anything other than what he kept protesting – nothing. She was surely being difficult. Love.

And then there were the Cootes.

I wrenched my mind away. I amused myself with comic speculation. Chaunteyman was a spy. He was using Cheryl to spy on Lucas. He was a rubber spy with my shrunken head in his pocket. He would come over our funnel sometime or other while we were still at sea, like a breath, like the spirit of rubber solution when you mend a puncture; his pockets would be stuffed full of rubber money.

I looked up. There were long cat-tails of cloud. High winds up there – my dad had taught me. But down here all serenity. And even had we been able to glimpse over the horizon, we should still have been unable to foresee such a thing as a succession of tropical squalls. Not yet. Nor should we have had the faintest idea of a building sea, funnelling through on a gathering blow from the north-east, unfiltered by any such breakwater as the East Indies might make. A touch unusual for the time of year.

We hurried on. We made haste without seeming to. For there was only this one stretch. In a manner of speaking, home from home lay just across the bay. We had made up our schedule, so now there was no actual rush, nothing of that sort. There was in no sense of the word a chase. We wore our future like our pennants, with a confident air, a jauntiness. And as for the unpleasantness over the cargo, well, that was over and done with. The greater part of the embarrassment had been unloaded, after all. The part that mattered, surely. Yesterday everyone had just been under the weather. Tropical fatigue. Mr Barnwell had given the impression that after Singapore there would remain of that consignment only odds and ends – the very unimportant bits and pieces to be ferried on to Maralinga. Kittens, Vixens and the like.

Below us, under our keel, was a seabed ridge named Christmas Rise. Nothing to do with Christmas Island where, before the Test Moratorium, the British government had just managed to cram in the world's largest thermonuclear explosion ever seen through pressed fingers. That Christmas was out in the Pacific. This was a different Christmas, just on the edge of the Java Trench, whose depths, by the way, had we tried to plumb them, would have required a piano wire five miles long.

And below us in the hold was merely a little local electrical difficulty, possibly an awkwardness in the main power circuits.

60

The first explosion occurred at about four in the afternoon. Its dull crump had a deep metallic note which rang the *Armorica* from stem to stern; with the result that no one knew precisely where the disturbance had come from. Some hurried forward, while others began to assemble aft near the swimming-pool area, enquiring of each other what might have happened.

After a few minutes a certain unreality developed. For nothing appeared to have altered. The ship remained on course, ploughing dutifully ahead. The wind, which had been freshening all day and was now a stiff nor'easterly, continued to work at the swell. But all ahead was blue, the water foamy, colouring up underneath to a blue–black. And behind, the wake was regular and intact. No freak rock had been struck; no radarless rust-bucket had lain breached across our bows. On the port quarter horizon, back in the direction of the Spice Islands, a line of clouds appeared to bubble slightly here and there into brightly lit heads, like the gentle distance in a Constable painting. Perhaps there had been some mistake.

Then the people at the rear concourse heard screaming. Three children came struggling out of the rear staircase, burnt and incoherent. At the same time the ship herself began to screech as the fire hooters were triggered. The rushing air became full of noise.

It happened to be Robert Kettle who grasped what it was the children were trying to indicate. He dived down the stairs against the flow of passengers rushing up. By the time he returned carrying the girl, Finlay Coote, the deck was crammed with folk in all conditions, flushed from their cabins, bars and saloons, some angry, some bored or sceptical; some wearing life-jackets, some immaculately turned out in their best casual clothes, as if at the sound of the alarms they had spent precious minutes going below to make their toilette. And some were obviously panicked, rushing about half dressed.

He was himself begrimed and flame-marked, his black curly hair singed away; but the girl was the centre of attention. She was conscious, though only just. From head to foot she was a hideous black scorch. Her play clothes were shredded, still hot, and burnt to her body. Every now and then she opened her mouth as if to cry out in pain, but no sound emerged above the din of voices and the constant squawking of the hooter. Some announcement was being made over the tannoy, but it was impossible to make it out.

Between them, Robert Kettle and Mary Garnery got the girl through the press of people and into the swimming-pool, holding her level, and splashing the cold salt water over her. Queenie Parsons clung on to her husband. He shrugged her off, trying to force his way along the run of the pool seating.

A woman beside Penny began screaming too. Penny grabbed her, and held her shoulders still.

'What's happened? What's going to become of us? I knew something terrible would go wrong. What is it? I must know.'

'Clearly, there's been an accident,' Penny replied. 'Clearly, something's on fire and somebody's hurt.'

The woman shook herself free and opened her mouth again.

'Look here. You can't do that,' a man was saying to Robert. 'Where's the medical officer here?' Then he was lost in the general confusion. The screams were taken up at the far side of the pool. They gave way to an exchange of shouts and threats lifted above the general clamour. From down behind our aft wall, too, there were calls coming up from the tourists. 'What's up? What's going on?' Then the knowledge that the engines had

257

stopped – learned eerily through the soles of the feet – brought everyone to a sudden silence.

Abruptly the hooter stopped, too. A moment of uncanny quiet followed, filled only with the sea sounds and the wind in the wires. On the boat deck above us a white-uniformed figure stood holding a loud hailer, like an angel with a trumpet. His voice rang out, electric, artificial. He called for calm.

'I'm grateful for your prompt attendance, ladies and gentlemen. There seems to have been a problem below decks. We are in the process of investigating. Specially trained units of the crew are at this moment combing the ship systematically, ready to identify and deal with any difficulties they should find, and to make sure all personnel are accounted for.'

The *Armorica* had slewed round. The low sun bucked behind the officer with the dead rise and fall of the swell.

'As you will know from your own cabins the ship is fully fitted with a fire-sprinkler system which is designed to isolate and contain any excessive heat source as it occurs – until the crew can bring full-scale fire-fighting equipment to bear. I can assure you the whole business is in safe hands, and would ask you to rest assured that everything that should be done is being done.'

A chair was brought for the old dowager lady who had passed Penny in the dining-room at the start of the Atlantic storm.

'Could someone bring me a rug?'

'But any fire at sea, ladies and gentlemen, is a matter of the utmost seriousness. You will be inconvenienced until the accident has been dealt with, and I would remind you that this is for your own safety. Officers and members of the crew will soon be moving among you to answer any questions you might have, and to attend to your needs. In the mean time I would ask you to remain completely calm, and to organise yourselves as best you can to cope with present difficulties and conditions.'

As soon as he finished speaking it became generally known on the concourse that the *Armorica* was not alone on the sea. Not far away to windward there was a small smoke plume, and under it, plainly visible in the illumination of the fast-westering sun, lay the low grey shape of a destroyer. But above that, and still miles off though plainly arriving with equally unsuspected and far more dramatic haste, the mass of cloud filled now a great part of the sky. It boiled white and cream, in magnificent shapes and domes, some of which were just beginning to slip over sideways at the top of their reach. And at their far bases the band of blue-grey; that too was expanding almost by the minute, into a heavy leaden bag heaving at its own weight. The wind at sea level had dropped to nothing. So we passed the next subdued hour, feeling the sky change on us.

61

On the lull the sun set. Against the interior glow from the Verandah bar the crew could be seen moving through the crowded deck space. They brought reassurance, sustenance, handed out blankets, hot drinks. The floodlights came on, and then failed. The lights inside failed. Then the storm wind proper sprang up in the starless dark – and the first of the rain squalls, a merciless deluge hurled nearly sideways.

The second and third explosions occurred. As if by cruel orchestration, they were intermixed with the start of the thunder bursts. The play of lightning revealed snapshots of endurance: two families huddled under one blanket, an old woman trying to stand, a father and child. In the pool seats where there were no tarpaulins, no bits of cover nor makeshift protection, a whole section of the crowd was shiveringly exposed – oddly cowed and quiet.

There was, of course, not the remotest danger of anything 'nuclear' taking place – Mr Barnwell had been explicit about that. His speech, as anyone could have recalled, was categorical. Nothing of that sort had ever been, at the wildest degree of human error even, on the cards. And this was quite true. To liberate the energy of pure matter takes a precise configuration of shock waves. There is a rigmarole of tampers and seals. Even in the simpler weapons metallic casings must be machined absolutely, the chemical high explosives precisely configured – tolerances are minute. Electronic detonation is synchronised to the microsecond. And the big thermonuclear devices require their own atomic trigger. Each system must be delicately assembled, armed – or it is of no account. Remember my grandmother with her fingers in those cartridges. She was quite safe.

What remained on board the *Armorica* was non-fissile, idle in itself. There was no question of chain reaction, that technical phrase which had slipped luridly into common speech. And among these experimental bits and pieces the only one which could in any real way be described as controversial, if it existed on board at all, was an expensive plum-coloured metal. Plutonium uningested is relatively harmless. Pyrotechnically speaking, its curiosity value lies in its rate of neutron emission. If it was going anywhere it was only for the sake of tests: about handling, toxicity, flammability, contaminative permanence – that sort of thing. Everything would be under control. As a substance it was here to stay, it was the future, a positive boon, both militarily and, much more importantly, in the civil sphere – where it was produced in power stations.

That was why it was *en route* to Australia. Safety testing. If indeed it was. Whatever, it could not, of itself, get out of hand. At normal temperatures and pressures it was as reluctant to burn as any ordinary metal. Chemically, that required activation – by duller substances which, as to the *Armorica*, no necessity had been found even of mentioning. The complexities of that side-issue simply had not come up. And why should they? Experimental protocols were exceedingly technical, after all. Specialist stuff. And the risks, such as they were, had been very fully assessed prior to outset. Any ill-informed, open-toed flapping about nuclear matters was, in a word, laughable.

Something deep down in the lower reaches of the hold, however, was showing a very great propensity to burn, explode, and otherwise get out of control in an entirely conventional way. The explosions were not 'earth-shattering', nor did they appear to endanger the structure of the ship; and there were no more than five in all. Beside the insistent thunderclaps hammering the eardrums on into the night, they were a nothing.

But they were enough. By ten o'clock it was clear, and announced as soon as conditions permitted, that the *Armorica* was uncontrollably alight deep down below the shop on D deck; and that a plan for controlled evacuation was to be put into effect. The destroyer hung off, flashing and signalling.

The rain came in bands, each lasting about half an hour. In

between, the blow maintained its force. It was during one of the so-called dry spells, when the pitch-black wind chilled through our soaked clothes and our meagre protection, that the word went round there had been casualties. Many casualties. Most were due to asphyxiation by smoke of people trapped in cabins in the after part of D, C and even B decks, when the flames had first caught hold of a crew-only stair route and a flue, and had blocked escape from two directions. These parts of the fire had subsequently been doused – before the new explosions.

But the damage had been done. The bodies had been found, and were being brought out, along with the injured, even as the renewal of the fires below had forced the working parties to retreat again upwards, as high as B deck in some places. Of the tourist class there was little information, beyond the fact that their steel bulkhead had so far protected them from the tragedies afflicting our side. They too were all crowded up on their highest decks, and we could sometimes hear them, down behind the amphitheatre wall, coping much as we were.

The news of the deaths was horrifying. It turned a managed, and almost manageable calamity into a living nightmare. Paul Finch-Clark recognised the quartermaster as the beam of a gesturing torch flashed momentarily across his features.

'What ships are in the area? Do we know what ships are in the area?'

'There's the destroyer, sir. She's going to start taking people off via the boats. The boats are the next thing, sir.'

'Nothing else in the vicinity? This is a regular shipping lane, isn't it? You've put out a general distress call, of course. There must be something else that could help.'

'The Navy is going to look after us, sir, as far as I'm aware.' The quartermaster compressed his lips in the mockery of a grin. 'That's all I know. The boats, sir. We're going to begin moving people up to the boats any minute. If you wouldn't mind, sir. As far as I've been instructed everything's been taken care of.'

'And anything else, I said? Have any other ships answered the Mayday? Please could we be kept informed? What are Darwin saying? Jakarta? My daughter has had a terrible shock. We feel so isolated.' He spoke almost as if at a large railway station where the train had been cancelled. The scale of the situation lacked appropriate words. It was ridiculous.

The quartermaster compressed his lips again. 'I'm instructed to make it clear to you, sir, that everything is being done to ensure as safe and orderly an evacuation as possible. As to distress calls,' he fixed Paul Finch-Clark's eye with an intense and troubled gaze, 'I'm afraid we have no information. Beyond the fact that there's an Australian Navy ship, I believe, will be able to make it up here by morning. And a frigate coming up from Fremantle.'

With that he moved off.

The rain came pelting across at us once more, driving into the eyes. It was debatable which was worse: the cloudbursts, or the terrible wind-chilled parch of each interim.

Fire-fighting was taking place, however, somewhere deep in the lower regions of the ship. The problem had been localised and contained, if not yet neutralised. The fuel tanks were at present in no danger. Command, it appeared, felt there was time to use the boats, in each of which there was a supply of oars, to convoy the ship's company across to the safety of the destroyer. That vessel's now blazing lights showed her to be riding about four hundred yards off the *Armorica*'s starboard beam; and also showed in graphic detail the increasing fury of the waves.

But the operation to evacuate the ship proceeded with neither speed nor facility. Everything was against it. Because each boat had at least to be partially crewed; which reduced its capacity. Moreover, its complement had to include some men, rather than the priority groups of women and children and casualties, in order to make up the power necessary to negotiate such a sea.

Nevertheless it was begun, and proceeded with. The chosen boats were lowered away, one by one. We watched them inching across the gap – like waterlogged moths caught white by the arc-light beams. Two rapid inflatables which the destroyer sent out hovered around the action, detectable sometimes by their buzzing engines, as insects of another dark. Soon the whole stretch of sea dividing the two ships became a painful toing and froing, as the little craft persisted doggedly at their task. It was a grim operation.

And, to be fair, it was certainly a situation foreign to any concept the captain had of seamanship and proper practice. That it was forced upon him by other considerations must go without saying. Considerations which can only be conjectured at. Considerations where, several ranks above him, an overruling priority to limit leakage of information was at war with duty, principle and honour. Taken out of the captain's hands, the thing had become political, in the worst sense of the word. It bore all the hallmarks of a panic – an agonised, long-winded, drawn-out loss of grip.

Whether command lay with Barnwell, or by tortuous radio link higher still, must remain uncertain. Truly, the more the project surrendered to its shameful premise, the more the net of disaster drew tight around it. It began as folly and turned into gross irresponsibility. Any seaman will tell you what happens when crucial decisions are taken out of a competent master's hands.

Of the lifeboats themselves, only four were aft of the dividing bulkhead between the two classes of traveller. They were held in reserve. Only twelve of the eighteen in all lining both sides of the boat deck were lowered – to avoid cluttering the seas with more flailing traffic than the situation could bear. For reasons of discipline and good order, the command was given that the fire doors in the dividing bulkhead should temporarily remain completely sealed, until such time as the flotilla of boats was ready to begin evacuating the tourists. Nor could the cries and disturbances behind the steel barrier be attended to, in any case, above the din now made by the tropical storm.

62

Perhaps we were supposed to draw comfort – that there was no thought as yet of 'Abandon ship'; no 'Every man for himself'. Perhaps there was an underlying strategy: to lighten the eventual loading of the boats. If the worst came to the worst. As we sat in that frightful sluice we had present evils enough to cope with. We had already calculated a hundred times the number of survivors a single destroyer could possibly cram on board; but there was an unspoken collusion among us never to voice the answer. Somehow we would not bring ourselves openly to admit that for many of our own contingent, let alone our emigrants, 'evacuation' would be a euphemism for something else. But then surely the lights of a tanker would appear on the horizon, a cargo vessel threading through from Japan or the Philippines, a Dutchman, a South American. They would all have been alerted by now. They would all be racing in our direction.

All night the boats kept at it. The exercise took on a significance of its own, almost as if its delicacies and manoeuvrings in the dark threw a charmed circle that fended off the world beyond. How many brave acts were performed, how many feats of endurance by both crews, and by the shivering passengers, it was impossible to know.

Nor was there opportunity to gauge accurately what point the process had reached. That there was a widespread, silent valour of waiting goes without saying, for the crush of ship's people filled the boat deck and the promenade deck. We knew we lay on the wooden lid of a furnace. By an occasional throw of the destroyer's floodlights we could not but be aware of the unnatural blur of smoke surrounding the mouths of the aft ventilator-shafts. We could even smell it when the slew of the ship brought the wind across our stern.

Caught between the choreography of the boats and a slow fire, the *Armorica* put a brave face on it. A paralysing pincer grip tightened infinitesimally, of the two converging pressures – God forbid they came together – the point at which the destroyer said: No more, and the sudden storm flash by which we should notice steam in the rain sluice. And as the night wore on, the void of this horror dramatised itself in glimpsed spaces on deck – caused by the creeping exodus of first class passengers. What those aft of us felt – the emigrants locked in their own cage – we had no way of telling. Occasionally someone addressed them by megaphone. There arose sporadic hymn singing. But by and large they were quiet, as were we.

Finlay was stretched on the deck under a makeshift shelter, a broken cane table with a blanket over it. So the burns were to some extent protected. Her head rested on Robert's thin pullover – he stood guard. She was alive, and kept whimpering and trying to turn herself on to her damaged skin. Mary

264

Garnery knelt beside her. The parents still had not been located.

Penny clutched at the lapels of her linen jacket and tried to imagine being warm. The material was soaked through, of course. She picked her way past where the Finch-Clarks were sitting on the deck sharing a raincoat, and craned out over the rail. Peering forward, she could see the fragile structure of the passenger ladder, the same one they had used in Aden and Colombo, strung close against the side. It was focused in the destroyer's light. All night it had hung from A deck, and the people had been dark insects creeping down into boats that threatened to crush them against the hull.

'I'll go and look again.' The wind in the wetness turned the stitching of her clothes to thread ice. Ignoring the cold as best she could, Penny made her way across the uncertain teak, waiting for the lightning flashes before picking a route among the remaining huddled shelterers. She had already tried three times but had got no further than the entrance to the Verandah bar, because the press at the stairway down to the boats had completely blocked the route forward on both the port and starboard gangways. But now she found it easy enough to slip through and along the deck – as far ahead as the side doors to the dance space. She noticed that the queues had turned and now stretched along the promenade deck itself, facing forward instead of clogging towards the concourse 'It's all right.' She elbowed her way grimly along. 'I'm not pushing in. I'm on business. Somebody's child.'

At the rail amidships an officer was talking to a group of engineers. One of the lifeboats was being brought to, somewhere down there. But she guessed they must be trying to rig the passenger ladder one deck higher. A confusion of ropes and wires lay on the decking. Perhaps all the stairways had become impossible and even A deck was alight below them. She imagined going over the top from this height. The drop down to the boats would be unnerving, a descent right past the fire. The sailors gave a heave and made something fast. There were shouts. She envied the men their activity. It was, she thought for a second, what sailors did in films.

A huge electrical streak parted the sky behind the destroyer. And as if the storm read her mind the scene was offered in a photographic instant: the foreground desperate faces bleached white against black; the distance waves, with the other vessel tossed in stark silhouette. Then thunder went off for a shell burst. A hit, she said to herself. A very palpable hit. But she knew she loved him. They were being forged in the fire.

Inside the lightless dance space the quiet was eerie. The *Armorica* was creaking again, softly to itself. Penny struggled to keep her balance. She was reminded of the Atlantic storm, so long ago. Like a lifetime.

Men's voices boomed suddenly from the darkness, where the doors gave access to the stairways. There was another tangle of torch beams – she assumed they were a relay of fire-fighters coming up. Then a hand grabbed her arm. 'No passengers. Haven't you been listening? You can't come in here.' A light flashed in her face.

'I've got to find some people. Can you help?'

'Sorry. You can't come in here.'

She thought she recognised the purser's voice. 'It's Mrs Kendrick. I'm here about the Cootes' daughter. We've got her. She's been badly burnt. We're not sure. We're trying to find the parents before she . . .' The torch beam dropped. Her eyes adjusted a little. She could pick out the purser's shape. He let go her arm and played his torch across the floor by way of answer.

Revealed were the dead. She realised that at once. The dance space was being used for the casualties. They had brought them up and laid them here. It was an obvious, sensible thing to do. Nevertheless she was horrified. The torch showed up her shipmates, half-known faces she recognised in the sweep of its passing. They had teeth and hair. They wore clothes she was familiar with. They moved, some of them, with the pitch of the ship. But they were all dead.

'See what I mean, ma'am. No passengers, please. It's for the best, I'm afraid. You'd better leave this to us.'

She swallowed. 'Russell and Clodagh Coote?'

'Couldn't say, ma'am. As you can see there's quite a few of them.' He flashed his torch back on her and then showed her the door. 'You'd really better go.'

'All right.'

The sluice of rain hit her like something thrown. The force of the wind pinned her momentarily to the superstructure. But it was better on deck, better than that shifting morgue, though she found she was shivering uncontrollably. She hit her arms with her fists. 'Come on!' The queue was moving. People were hoisting themselves gingerly over the rail. She pushed aft against the flow.

Robert embraced her when she got back to him. But she shook her head. 'They would have come looking for her. They wouldn't have gone off in the boats without her. If they were alive they'd have come by now. Wouldn't they? Mitchell would have come.'

'You think they were among the people who were trapped?'

'I saw them. In the dance space.'

'Russell and Clodagh?'

'No. Just . . . rows of them. Bodies. Rows of them.' The tears sprang up against the rain. She buried her face in his soaked shirt. 'Robert, this is terrible. I mean really terrible. And the worst thing is that it feels like our fault.'

63

Mary Garnery had not moved from her kneeling position beside Finlay. Now she looked up. 'I've been meaning to say,' she fixed her attention on Robert, 'I admired what you did.'

Penny stared back at her, still in Robert's arms. She could not tell what the other woman had in mind. Was it his saving of Finlay? Penny pictured again the sight of her lover emerging with the injured girl, hours ago. Now his black curls had been plastered down by the rains. Or was it how he spoke out at the meeting? She recalled Mr Barnwell's face, and smiled despite everything. Or was it perhaps, after all, that Mary admired what they had done together, becoming lovers, and had spoken to reassure her. Penny doubted it. She felt guilty and frightened. She felt Mary wished only to have dealings with Robert. What was the matter with her, this difficult, emaciated woman who took nothing, and would give nothing away?

Mary broke her gaze and looked down at Finlay again. But she said something else. 'You must both come and visit me –

when all this is over. Come to Sydney, will you? Both of you?'

Penny said, 'Thank you, Mary. We will.' It was suddenly as though a weight had been lifted from her shoulders.

'If she doesn't get some sort of treatment . . .' Mary's voice faltered away, and then became firm again and matter of fact. 'Still, shouldn't be long now.'

It was three o'clock by Robert's spattered watch when the quartermaster mustered them, with the megaphone, to join the queues. The destroyer had left for Darwin half an hour ago.

At the head of the ladders, by torchlight, the officer said, 'You may be on the water for some time.' He wore an oilskin against the rain. His eyes were strangely visible, in the hood made of his sou'wester brim.

'Yes?' said Robert, bracing himself on the rail.

'We're waiting for the Australian Navy. Another little destroyer. And there's a frigate coming up by all accounts. They shouldn't be too long. The order's been given.' The wind whipped the words away. 'Better to get you all away from this bloody death-trap as soon as possible. Every boat's been given the instruction to pull for it. The able-bodied among you should see to that straight away, as soon as your boat's full.'

'But what about all the other people?' Penny indicated the stern of the ship. 'They've been waiting as long as us. More cramped. More dangerous. What's the situation? What are the casualty figures?'

The officer's sigh was audible above the weather. The torch's beam flashed on to Finlay. 'The captain is with them now. We've done all we can, ma'am, for the time being. He'll give them the solemn assurance of what we know to be the case: that another ship will be here within the hour. The fire hasn't gone through to them, you see. And probably won't. Actually they're safest where they are for the minute. But it's a terrible situation, I know. The worst decisions have to be made. Now if you'll get into the boat please, and we'll have your little girl dropped down to you in a sling. Badly hurt, is she?'

Penny and Robert climbed down into the pitching boat, which jostled dangerously alongside the *Armorica*'s hull, one in a line of three. It was nearly full with people they knew only by sight – faces and families with whom they had shared the voyage but loosely. They took their place near the bow, and then looked up, waiting for Finlay.

'Ready!' Penny shouted, as they swung on the wave. The rain, which had eased for a minute or so, grew worse again. Spray from above and below dashed off the white metal into her face.

But Mary called down, 'I'm not coming!'

'What? Why? Mary, please hurry!'

'I can't. I'm not coming.' Mary thrust her head out defiantly over the rail. The torchlight silhouetted her hair, loose and soaked and haphazard about her unguessable features like black seaweed. The shoulders of her ruined jacket made a stark, obstinate outline. 'I'm going to stay! I'm insisting on staying. Someone has to! There's no sign of trouble yet. I can stand it much hotter than this.'

'Mary! What d'you mean? Do hurry! Please!'

But Mary's figure disappeared from its station and Penny was thrown back against the gunwale of the lifeboat, as the ship, lying awkwardly right across the sea, found herself rolled in an ungainly wallow between ridges. The boat smacked hard into the side, and, in desperation, the two men holding her on her lines cast off. She drifted free, leaving Penny's cry unanswered. 'Mary! What about Finlay?'

In pitch dark for another two hours before daybreak, the company of the lifeboat endured, stunned, waterlogged, saying little. Robert and Penny clung together. Presumably so did their neighbours, for the little craft so leaped and skidded that it was a matter of holding on for dear life. There was an attempt at the oars, an attempt to understand the shelter that could, theoretically, be rigged. Neither was very successful. One of the ship's officers slumped in an oilskin cape next to Robert. He was exhausted and had difficulty breathing.

The rain stopped. The thunder went away. Someone near the stern was overcome with persistent tears. The officer woke with a shudder and passed his waterproof along to her. He was dressed in his tropical whites, very faintly visible. 'Bloody smoke,' he coughed to Robert. 'I shall have to bloody give it up.'

Gradually their contact with the *Armorica* was lost. The

pinprick glows and needle streaks of her torches became harder and harder to locate. Then, much later it seemed, in the far distance there was a glow of flame-coloured brightness against the black. It was hard to say how long it lasted. Time stretched and contracted under those circumstances, even as the water heaved and raced, twisted, or collapsed suddenly into a dizzying slide. There was a moment when it looked as though the sea all around the distant *Armorica* was on fire. The officer was watching intently. 'Wish I had my binoculars.'

Robert watched too. He wondered precisely what nautical ghoulishness it was made the other man so keen to see the tragedy magnified.

'Bastard. I never thought the bastard would do it. If that doesn't beat bloody everything.'

'What do you mean?' Robert asked.

'If you've seen it before you know what to look for. Mum's the word; but oh, Christ, this is a bloody bad day and no mistake.'

'I don't understand.'

'No. You wouldn't. You don't know what we know, do you. And best you don't, old son.'

'Why?'

'Military matters. Nothing I can say. The daylight's coming, you see. She'd be visible for miles.' Then he muttered something under his breath which sounded distinctly like the word 'torpedo'.

Robert heard himself gasp.

'I didn't say anything. Is that understood?' The officer shifted his position and turned away.

But Robert could not help staring at the *Armorica* from the top of the next wave. And although there could be no hint of phosphorescence in that great churn of a swell which the storm had whipped up, it was almost as though he could see the path of the thing, still there, straight as an arrow towards the now leaping streaks of flame.

Then dawn came, like a light bulb again, and everything was changed. A boat and its collection of people was delivered suddenly out of the dark. On the horizon rose a great plume of black smoke. It appeared to coil and snake into a vast column, widening as it climbed. And then, within twenty minutes as they

270

watched, there was no more sign of it, and the traces of its cloud lifted upwards and faded out.

64

My lifeboat is much nearer. Smoke billowing, the body of the thing lifts momentarily, as though a whale has mistakenly tried to surface under her keel. We hold our breath, and curiously, there is no sound other than the wind. Then we are in a trough. The roiling column of black flattens and streaks to the south-west. When she comes into view again, the burning *Armorica* sits back in the water, not well.

Now every time a sea lifts us up, while the sky lightens and lightens, we watch the poor creature sit lower and lower in the water. But it is not until about twenty minutes later that there comes the frightful tip-up of her bows against the horizon, by which the fire's tumult is suddenly extinguished. The sea boils. I watch the twist that reveals all the cloud-wreathed red paint under her water-line. She gathers pace, gathers, and slips away. There is almost a hole in the burning slick. Then nothing. It is unbelievable. It is too much to take in. We have and have not seen.

Hours have passed, perhaps; or perhaps only minutes. One other lifeboat is visible far away in the rain, which has started again. Next to it, there is a small black square standing up, like a matchbox flipped endways and carried along the wave crests. I know it is a sub. I have seen them at Chatham. When the sea permits, I can just make out the dark line of its topsides. Now a man in a life-jacket stands right next to us in a buzzing noise. He hails us from an inflatable. He is looking for Mr Barnwell, the senior officer. And the captain. We do not have them. We have no officers in our boat. Help is on its way, he tells us.

No one speaks of what has happened. The talk is of muddling through. A couple near the stern have taken charge. They have found a bar of chocolate in somebody's handbag and are busy dividing it into twenty-seven equal pieces. We are all for rationing. There is no attempt to make sense of what we have seen: the dawn, the clearing skies, the sub. No one wants to put two and two together. Not for a moment.

A man has a watch that still works. There is a desultory singsong every ninety minutes: hymns and camp-fire songs, even Vera Lynn.

'Not long to go now, everybody. We have to remember that. Just keep saying to yourselves: Not long now. All right? All agreed?' It reminds me of school assembly.

'That chappie in the rubber boat's been gone at least three hours. Can't be long now. Could be worse. That lady, there. Your turn, dear.'

The lady cries for a moment.

'Now, now!' The man from the stern jollies her.

She steadies herself. She recites a poem she has by heart. It is a jig-jogging, classroom thing. We all applaud. Her chin trembles. We all feel better and I wonder what piece I shall do myself when the hands tick round. 'The Lion and Albert'? We do not know each other's names.

'Do you think the sub . . . ?'

'Lucky they happened to be passing, eh? Pay us a visit, so to speak. Lets you know you're not alone.'

This close the waves loom right over us, like glass slopes, up which the boat slips sickeningly sideways at the last minute. Some crests break over the gunwales. They have a taste and a weight. There is a slopping surge running back and forth about our feet. We chart the progress of the next rain. Then it pelts on us and the men take awkward turns with the baler.

I wake and look at my knuckles. They are split open and bleeding slightly. Erica's are similar. It is the cold, and the salt. Waking is vile; for the wind blows again and yet more rain sluices down. Nothing is dry inside the boat. A man in the boat keeps shaking me, saying to Erica, 'You let 'em drop off like that and they get to like it. Seen it happen. That was in the Atlantic. Quicker in the cold seas. Still. You be careful, sonny.'

I smile foolishly at him. The impression he has ruined for me is that Erica plays a gramophone in the middle of the lifeboat, that the swimming-pool of the *Armorica* is contained right within the gunwales of our wretched tub, and that we are all getting ready to dance and take dips. I hate him for returning me to my flimsy, soaking clothes. Then my eyes open and there are the same speechless faces, the same heave of the lifeboat, the chasing clouds, the intolerable cold. I renew my grip on the rope and start to shiver.

'That's a good sign,' the man says.

'Yes,' Erica replies.

I am very hungry.

Erica moves to touch me. 'Cuddle up, Ralph.' I shrink away. I cannot bear her near me. A military aircraft with two propellers slung under each wing scratches about in the cloud base, turning once, and turning again.

The second day of rain gave way to a profound calm. It was not my hallucination that in the afternoon we sighted two of the other lifeboats, far away. We waved, they waved back. On the horizon there were smudges of smoke, but they did not alter course. I did imagine one was the *Armorica* still burning. Then I remembered.

As for the third day, a tropical sun came out and dried us up. And shortly after that there was the smudge that turned into the frigate.

65

Hatred did for the *Armorica*, we can be sure of that. Hatred is an oddity. That it exists is undeniable. Perhaps it is scattered through the universe, between the stars.

A floating city, Penny thought, before she boarded at Tilbury. There are some shipwrecks that are part of our folklore. There is no need to spell out their names; we are all brought up on them. They are famous because they staged themselves. They lead us to believe such losses always happen in the glare of publicity. The *Armorica* was not so big, nor so close to home. As an officer I am ashamed, and as a man.

It was given out that there had been a fire and a certain loss of life, and that the wounded vessel had been towed up to Jakarta. That is what we survivors were told, and what the Press were told. Let me remind you that there was at that time no satellite communication, no front-line journalism, no instantaneous world-wide news network such as we have today. Australia was the other side of the globe. The long-range jet had only just been invented. Portable videotaping equipment had not.

And in so vast and rudimentary a territory as Australia then was, the news of the sinking could fragment itself, one account appearing in this state newspaper one week, but denied the next week in that. A shape here, an outline there. Popping on to the ABC's radio news as a lead for two evenings but disappearing for ever after. The pattern is not an unknown one, even now. But in any case, stories had to work hard to escape that continent in those days. Witness the test fall-out details, which were not welcome in England. Neither were those of radiation research, nor of the human guinea-pigs. So far out of sight, so far out of mind, as far as the old country was concerned.

Reuters would have it world-wide, of course, though in the UK there might well be phone calls to certain newspaper proprietors about the national interest and military secrets. There might even be D-notices. The odd snippet of Australian footage might trickle home to London eventually, in a newsreel of survivors; shown in this Movietone cinema or that, but referred to only once or twice, perhaps, on the Home Service, or nudged out of television space altogether by some larger, more pressing domestic crisis. To be picked up later. Or not.

Questions might even have been asked in the House. But answers can knock some matters stone dead. There were no pictures of the sinking ship, therefore no loss. A crime at sea is the most perfect, for the victim buries herself. Everything depends on the witnesses. Albatross-eyed, but lacking the missing evidence, I am making sense of what must have been.

You will still not believe me. There are times when I do not believe it myself, dare not. It would be told, though, this tale. I am detained by it. A thousand families at either end touched in some way and no furore? No marches, petitions, protests? A whole ship? No screaming headlines? Exposures, investigative documentaries, royal commissions, private prosecutions?

No, none of that. Ships go down all the time and we hear nothing. Passenger ships, too. And many far worse things go unseen. But that is not the point. It never matters really how many separate people know, are desolated, have their lives broken. So long as they are kept in isolation. So public life, too, loses its memory; I too signed the promise after we were picked up.

After the adventure of rescue came their delivery to Adelaide, almost as if nothing had happened, almost by sleight of hand.

'We *have* done it, darling. We've made it,' Robert said.

'We can still hope,' Penny replied. 'But doesn't there now come the difficult part?' She smiled ruefully. 'There's nothing for it. You'll have to leave it to me, Robert, I'm afraid. He's got to be told. It's got to be made clear.'

They put out their cigarettes, embraced, smiled, and parted at the roadside in Port Adelaide. She clung to the memory of his words. 'Love is an island that really exists. No matter what. You've taught me that. That's where we shall live.' He had held the little brass box she had given him in his hand.

In the first week she wrote to him every day. Sometimes twice a day. Then she tried telling Hugh. It was as though he took no notice of what she said but claimed her there and then, brutally, like a possession. And after that Penny could not write any more. Every time she picked up the pen the words 'my dearest' seemed to sink out of reach, as crumbs beside a lifeboat. The very paper felt soiled.

So also did the dashing blooms in their garden. They should have been beautiful. The orange tree in the centre with its little green fruits struck her as a worthless nonsense; the two fig trees had some sort of leaf blight. Once, after the boys had arrived, she binged on the half-ripe fruit and made herself ill. The violence of it gave her a grim satisfaction.

She could not approach Robert in her mind, could not make sense of what had preceded this endless summer which now seemed to be appointed for her; these flat, verandaed houses, all like her own, in their spacious plots; that insistent bird with a voice like a rusty gate; the tiny red-back spider that could kill; the regular invitations to meat-feasts outdoors at night with Hugh's fellow researchers. The *Armorica* and its catastrophe became a dream. Something so great, so incongruous against this basking suburbanism could not really have happened, surely. Now no one ever said anything on the wireless; there were no more press reports. The Finch-Clarks made the effort to write occasionally, but, being dutiful citizens, they never mentioned the ship.

She held on to small things. The memory of Robert's hand on her shoulder in the boat in the rain. They were sharing rations. How personal the sea was, even here, green-black, half transparent for the first inch of its down-drop – and then quite lightless when the grains of biscuit sank. How close the crazed surface of it had come. One might almost catch hold of it at last.

She grew listless and withdrew behind a brave face. Hugh hardly noticed. The boys took up at new boarding-schools. She got her driving licence – a few questions on a piece of paper at the police station – and was free to drink tea with other women whenever Hugh had a lift in to work.

And each letter from Robert, ever more anxious, bewildered, desperate than the one before, which she retrieved various mid-mornings from the letter-box on the garden gatepost, made her less able to answer.

Once or twice she did manage a reply. But she could not say what she meant. Only what she hoped for. The passage of time slipped into a long flicker of anxiety and despair. Every minute seemed to ache past, and yet the months evaporated, like spills on the cement floor of her washroom, disappearing while she watched.

66

In the December, on a day when the north wind off the central scorch was making breathing itself almost intolerable, two security policemen called on Robert. One picked up the empty bottle of Scotch, the other made himself comfortable in the only armchair.

'Like a drink, do you, Kettle?'

'Now and then.'

'Cigarette?' The man who was sitting down pushed a packet of Stuyvesants towards him. 'My name's Wheatfield, by the way.'

'Thanks. What can I do for you?'

'I'll get straight to the point. It's come to the director's notice you've still got a loose mouth.'

'What?'

'Don't let's beat about the bush, Bob. We both know what I mean. Shipping yarns. Salt water. Okay, you like a drink – now and then. What bloke doesn't? Only in your case it leads to . . . flights of the imagination.'

Robert heard himself give a single laugh. It had a bitter edge.

Wheatfield permitted himself a chuckle, too. 'Yeah. Who doesn't like a few beers with his mates? But it's come to the director's attention that despite the personal chat he had with you a couple of months ago, there's still something of a problem. And of course the base out here is a relatively small community, where it's pretty bloody important to maintain morale, don't you agree, Bob? Now, Sergeant Petter and I . . .' He glanced sideways. The man who had remained standing was holding the whisky bottle by its neck above the unwashed breakfast things on the table. He left his inspection of its label to look coldly at Robert.

'Sergeant Petter and I have an unpleasant duty, I'm afraid, Bob. It concerns the matter of nationality, rights of residence and so on. You do realise that this is an important strategic project up here. A significant front line, if we're to be strictly honest. Even if it doesn't look much.' He grinned and spread his palms as if to apologise for the ramshackle network of concrete prefabs and army huts which formed the community outside.

'Has there been a complaint against my work? Do you mind if I ask who you're actually representing?' Robert said quietly. He turned from one man to the other, raising his eyebrows.

By way of reply Sergeant Petter opened his grip and allowed the whisky bottle to drop. It shattered in the plate below it. The breakfast table became a waste of glass and white shards. 'Sorry.' The sergeant spoke without expression.

'To put it bluntly, Bob,' his colleague smiled, 'your stay in this country is conditional on security. Watertight security. To the director it's a moral issue. One bad apple and the rot starts.

You get what I'm driving at. One communist influence—'

'Communist?'

'Booze and sedition.' He drew leisurely on the cigarette. 'It's not just that you're in the habit of shooting your mouth off when you go on these . . . benders of yours, it's what you've been letting yourself come out with. Now, if it was up to me, I'd be inclined to give you the benefit of the doubt. It's a strain up here, after all. Problems with the girlfriend. That kind of thing. We all have 'em. Even Sergeant Petter has 'em.' He paused. Robert felt a bead of icy sweat trickle down from his armpit inside his shirt. 'They don't like it, do they, Neil?' Robert dared not catch Neil's eye. 'The sheilas. It's hard on a woman. They're apt to consider their options, you know. It's a fact. It's got to be faced. Sometimes the tough choice gets made. I've seen blokes . . . It's a worry isn't it, Bob? Can make even the best men go a bit . . . ' He wound his finger to his forehead, and smiled.

'But of course it's not up to me. And the director has to consider his own . . . position. Basically, he's giving you a couple of months.' Wheatfield shifted in the chair, and reached down beside it to stub out the butt. 'You wouldn't consider yourself a church-going man, really, would you, Bob?'

'Not really.'

'Shame. It's a bit of a man's world up here, I realise that. Still, there are standards. There is this matter of your visits down to Adelaide. The immoral purposes.'

'My what?'

'A Mrs . . . ' He made a show of consulting his diary. 'A Mrs Kendrick, isn't it? Now what kind of woman would she be?'

'A very fine woman, actually.'

But the policemen insisted on hearing the wrong emphasis. They both laughed.

'There's a Kendrick who works down at Salisbury, isn't there, Neil? Quite a big wheel there, wouldn't he be? No connection of course, Kettle. Couldn't be, could there.'

Robert's temper flared. If only he could get any sense out of her. If only she would say.

If Wheatfield's gentle voice filled the gap that had opened, Robert did not hear. Syllables were like an intense pressure in his chest, like air bubbles. 'Thirty thousand tons,' he breathed at last. Odd, that the gasp of the metal's weight alone should somehow rise up more eloquently than the five hundred bodies it contained.

But the policeman – or whatever he was – spoke on as if everything were in its place, and so heavy a sacrifice must lie miles beneath the unscarred surface of their discussion. His parting remarks concerned Robert's passport. 'It's a precious document, you know, Mr Kettle. We'll not keep it for longer than necessary. A few solemn undertakings you signed on your arrival here. You'll have it back just as soon as we've updated our documents. Who knows, you might be needing it.'

When they had gone, and Robert had recovered from the fit of shaking which came over him, he conceded the game had been lost. Not the one he carried on with Joe – who did in fact run a long-range radio correspondence with him via the base's non-military equipment. But the larger one he had been playing with the times he lived in.

That night, his thoughts far from any radar screen, he walked to a corner of the base compound where the lights from the main block hardly carried. There was to be a launch tomorrow; some squib would squirt its way up from the desert a hundred miles west. Further away still, a team of squaddies might be rigging a scaffold tower for the next 'dust experiment'. Might – or maybe they had given up on all that now. He did not know. The outlines of the Flinders foothills were just visible, dark on dark. Beyond them the continental floor, once a seabed.

He must find her. He turned and stared up at the stars. They were peculiarly alive, yet remote. Crux hung under the Southern Pole. The Jewel Box. Reticulum, the Net. He pointed out to her Carina, Vela, Puppis. 'There! Do you see?'

The tears prickled at his eyes. 'I saw what I saw, know what I know.' But the ship was fracturing, the sections already losing themselves against a chaos of scintillation.

As for Erica and me, you know the details of our stay. We subsisted on the edge of the bush for about a year, until the draggles of commitment from Chaunteyman dried up, and a summons home was posted out.

And so we were reunited with my father. I was born in the town of Woolwich, near Greenwich itself, London's prosperous and beautiful pearl, where the whole world takes its time from a metal marker hammered into the hill. My mother told me. My dad taught me to read. I held his hand. We took the train down to the marshes on Galleons Reach. I saw a barge with brown sails from the green foot-bridge over the railway line, looking out across the allotments. The river stank in the sun, was green, too, close up; yellowish green the river from the steam ferry crossing over to Silvertown. I saw a porpoise floating dead, belly up. Silver-tarnished, and everything smoky and soot-stained before us, steaming onward with the paddle-wheels driving, and black behind us upon the rise of the southern shore we had left, far behind, back past Woolwich, as far as Greenwich where the slopes rise up to Blackheath. Dark houses. That is England. Smoking against a hot, pale sky, with low sun. That is England, a hot country of perpetual fire.

Acknowledgements

My very grateful thanks are due to Sam Boyce, without whom this novel could never have been written; Bill Hamilton, for his excellent guidance in its development; and Nicholas Pearson, who is its true midwife. I'm also much indebted to Mary Chamberlain, Peter Lamb, and my daughter Kirstie – for their help and advice.

May I further acknowledge Neil McCart's enjoyable book, No. 3 in the series 'Famous British Liners' (FAN Publications), for supplying important detail and some anecdote; and the National Maritime Museum Library in Greenwich for their general helpfulness.